THE LAST CURTAIN CALL

A HAUNTED HOME RENOVATION MYSTERY

Juliet Blackwell

D0980263

BERKLEY PRIME CRIME
New York

BERKLEY PRIME CRIME

Published by Berkley

An imprint of Penguin Random House LLC

penguinrandomhouse.com

ISBN: 9780593097939

First Edition: June 2020

Printed in the United States of America

1 3 5 7 9 10 8 6 4 2

Cover art by Brandon Dorman

To Karen Thompson:

Thank you for the friendship and the many, many hours spent on job sites, working it all out.

Chapter One

It has been my experience that when homeowners take the time and trouble to permanently seal off a room, they usually have a Very Good Reason. And typically, that means something about that room is Very Not Good.

So when my foreman, Mateo, announced that the attic of my new house had a sealed-off closet with a window, I found it hard to keep the tone of my voice casual.

"Sealed off?"

"Yeah," said Mateo. "The original blueprints indicate a good-sized closet with a little window under the eave. You can see the outline of the window from the outside if you look closely, but the whole thing seems to have been closed up at some point."

I reminded myself not to jump to conclusions. This was a marvelous old house. Dating from 1911, it featured the master woodworking and built-ins that typified the Arts and Crafts movement, combined with the original architect's artistic flair of Moroccan arches and intricately paned windows. The first time I walked in the door, I experienced a rush of déjà vu that was highly unsettling, but later, I came to understand it had been sparked by a psychic and emotional connection with my late mother and her memories of living here as a very young child. Overall, the house's vibes were good—in fact, *fantastic*. Warm, loving, embracing, just like my mother.

If some erstwhile resident had, say, set up a sacrificial altar in a sealed-off attic closet, surely I would have felt it by now, wouldn't I? After all, what good is it being a ghost-talking psychic home renovator if I can't suss out the presence of evil in my own darned house?

"Well, I guess it wasn't 'sealed off,' exactly," continued Mateo. "A big armoire was placed in front of the door."

"An armoire in front of a door could simply mean there wasn't enough wall space in the attic," I said, relieved. It wasn't as though there were cinder blocks or something permanent blocking access.

"Sure," said Mateo. "Maybe the closet was where they stored things they only needed once a year, like Christmas ornaments."

"Exactly," I said.

We looked at each other, then looked away.

My fiancé, Landon Demetrius, and I were hip deep in an extended remodel of this beautiful and rather good-sized house in Oakland, across the Bay from San Francisco. Many decades ago, my great-grandparents had owned the home for a while, and my mother had lived there for a few years when she was a child.

When Landon discovered I had a special connection to this stunning—but terribly faded—grande dame, he had purchased it for us upon our engagement in a sweeping romantic gesture. Which was swell, but . . .

My father has a saying: "There's nothing like an extended remodel to ruin a relationship."

Bill Turner is my dad and the founder of Turner Construction, and when it comes to renovating historic buildings, he's the best in the business. Since Dad (semi) retired, I'm now running Turner Construction, so it's fallen to me to moderate the frequent, and often contentious, "discussions" among our clients about everything from floor plans to choice of low-flow toilet to the precise level of sheen in the paint in the downstairs entry.

And true to Dad's adage, more than a few relationships go down in flames because the couples can't agree on how to remodel their damned house.

With the arrogance of one who hasn't experienced something firsthand, I used to believe that going through a home remodel was a relationship litmus test: If a couple couldn't handle being together without a working kitchen or a functioning bathroom, found it just too much to live surrounded by noise and dust and chaos for months or years on end, or couldn't navigate the million and one decisions that had to be made—not to mention wrestling with budget overruns and clashing tastes—then how in the world could that couple expect to face the stresses inherent in a long-term relationship?

Except now I was one half of a renovating couple's "discussion," and I was on the verge of losing it.

The crux of the problem, at least as I saw it, was that I, the professional home renovator with years of construction experience, had certain ideas about what I wanted, and what the house needed, while Landon, a math professor who had never even picked up a paintbrush, had very different and, in my view, stupid ideas.

This morning's argument circled around whether to install period wallpaper borders in the living room. Landon didn't want to use the gorgeous William Morris designs I had suggested because of the appalling history of wallpaper manufacturing in nineteenth-century England, whose use of poisonous dyes had blinded many of their workers.

"They don't blind their workers any*more*," I said through gritted teeth.

"I'll think of it every time I look at that border," responded Landon.

"I have a lot of experience in this sort of thing, you know," I said for the thousandth time.

"I understand, and I respect that immeasurably," he said in that laudable but at times annoyingly formal way of his. "But I must insist that it is I, after all, who bought the house."

"So you want to make this about money? Really?"

"Of course not. You know I don't care about that."

"Besides, I thought you bought it for *us*."

"I did, indeed. And it will be *ours* just as soon as you marry me. When will that be, did you say?"

For someone as measured and perpetually pleasant as Landon, this was a highly snide conversation. But he had a point: I hadn't exactly settled on a marriage date. Being engaged suited me quite well, but actual *marriage* still scared the hell out of me. I had tried it once and it hadn't ended well.

"The wallpaper-versus-painted-border discussion can wait a while," Mateo said in a casual but firm tone. Mateo's in-charge demeanor was at odds with his small stature; apparently he had decided to take on the role of mediator. "The plasterwork isn't even finished yet."

"But that's my point," I insisted. "We would need a different level of finish, depending on whether we're planning on paper or paint. Also, the genuine Morris paper has a long lead time—I want to get it ordered as soon as possible."

"I agree with Mateo; we should table this discussion for the moment," said Landon.

"Have you decided whether you want to repair the walls with the original lathe and plaster or with drywall?" asked Mateo.

"Plaster," I said.

"Drywall," Landon said at the same moment.

Our gazes locked, and not in a romantic way.

"Ooookaaay," said Mateo, who was not a stupid man. "Howsabout you two take some time and talk that one out? In the meantime, want to check out that attic closet situation?"

"This sounds like *your* department," said Landon to me, as he checked his watch. "And I must leave now or risk arriving late to class."

"Your class doesn't start for another hour," I pointed out.

Landon was teaching a graduate theoretical physics seminar at UC Berkeley, which was a twenty-five-minute drive from where we were in Oakland. I was an on-time kind of person, myself, but Landon was irritatingly so, blaming it on the unpredictable traffic in the Bay Area. "Better to be safe than sorry," he would say cheerfully as we sat in the car in front of a friend's house for a quarter of an hour so as not to catch our dinner host stepping out of the shower.

"Better safe than sorry," Landon said now, right on cue. He smiled and gave me a little squeeze. "This is looking great, Mel. Everything's on track, eh? We'll figure out the wallpaper thing, not to fret."

I managed a smile. *It's just a decoration,* I reminded myself.

"And good luck at your meeting later," Landon said, leaning down and kissing me good-bye. "The Crockett Theatre, yes? Let me know how it goes."

"The great old theater in San Francisco?" asked Mateo. "I stopped by there last time I was in the Mission. I always heard that place was haunted."

An uncomfortable silence descended.

My experience with ghosts tended to bring conversations to a standstill, rather like discussing a tendency toward flatulence in polite company. The meeting this afternoon was to discuss Turner Construction taking over the renovation of the old-style movie theater. The previous contractor had abruptly dropped out halfway through the project, citing an "unforeseen scheduling conflict," but I suspected something else was afoot. I was familiar with the century-old Crockett Theatre and its reputation for being haunted because not only do I run a construction company, but I'm also something of a ghost buster.

And, apparently, a glutton for punishment.

"Be that as it may," said Landon as he gave me a quick hug and took a brief moment to gaze into my eyes. "See you tonight. Promise me you'll be careful?"

I nodded and watched as Landon picked his way through a maze of two-by-fours and sawhorses and compressors, politely wishing a good day to each member of the Turner Construction work crew as he passed. Landon was tall and broad-shouldered, with slightly long brown hair and a trimmed beard. He wore his usual outfit of tan khakis, a crisp white shirt, leather boots, and his favorite old-fashioned jacket, which was long with a high collar. The first time I saw him, I could have sworn he was a Civil War–era ghost. Landon had grown up in both the US and England, spoke with a vaguely British accent, and had made a pile of money from some computer-related doodad that I still hadn't wrapped my mind around.

And he was mine. Sort of.

Remember to breathe, Mel.

"Shall we check out the attic?" asked Mateo as he started up the broad central staircase, pausing on the landing, whose massive window offered a gorgeous view of the street and the hills of Oakland.

I grabbed my toolbox and followed him. In the upstairs hallway, Mateo pulled down the little trapdoor in the ceiling, folding out the ladderlike stairs to the attic.

Something went bump overhead.

Our eyes met.

"Yeah. That happens, occasionally," said Mateo. "Don't see any sign of rats up there. Probably a squirrel on the roof, something like that."

Mateo swiftly climbed the ladder into the blackness of the attic, and switched on the light.

I took a moment to repeat the mantra my acupuncturist had given me, then started climbing, feeling pleased with myself. Not long ago, after nearly falling to my death from the very high roof of a mansion in Pacific Heights, I had developed a fear of heights—which is no small problem when one's bread and butter is the construction business. I still became dizzy if I looked down, and I avoided climbing out onto rooftops whenever possible. The acupuncture therapy was not a miracle cure—something Dr. Victor Weng reminded me of at each treatment—but I was making progress. Slowly but steadily.

Exhibit A: I could now climb a ladder to an attic without fainting—carrying my big toolbox in one hand, no less.

Baby steps.

The attic was partly finished, and the roof's gables were angled so sharply that I had to duck in some areas. Several of the reaches under the eaves had been made into storage closets, and the whole space was packed full of furniture, tchotchkes, and assorted boxes from previous residents: framed pictures, magazines, a very old radio, books, a Close-n-Play record player, a stack of old LPs.

After the most recent owners had passed away, the house had stood empty for a couple of years due to probate issues, and Landon had bought it "as is."

This was another bone of contention between us: Landon advocated tossing everything into a dumpster and "starting with a clean slate," whereas I insisted on going through it all first. Who knew what treasures might be found among the historic detritus in these boxes? A reasonable person didn't just *toss* a genuine Close-n-Play record player.

It was the classic "junk"-versus-"antiques" debate.

"Has someone been smoking up here?" I asked, catching a whiff of tobacco.

"Not on my watch." Mateo shook his head. "No smoking on the jobsite, as you know: Turner Construction rules."

"My dad, maybe?" Bill Turner was known to sneak a smoke or two, and none of the crew was willing to rat him out. He wasn't officially—or regularly—on the job anymore, but as the founder of Turner Construction, he still showed up from time to time, whenever he felt like it, and pretty much wrote his own ticket.

"Haven't seen him lately," said Mateo, sniffing exaggeratedly and tapping his nose. "Gotta say, Mel—I don't smell anything, and I've got a good sniffer. It's pretty musty up here. Maybe that's it? Anyway, here's the armoire."

The large oak wardrobe wasn't the fancy European kind that graced the pages of interior design magazines, more a large but serviceable storage unit. I peered into the small gap behind the armoire and spied the closet door.

"How did they get this armoire up that ladder in the first place?" I asked.

"Back in the day, big pieces of furniture were often made so they could be taken apart, brought up piece by piece, and reassembled," said Mateo.

"Why bother?"

"Like you said, probably needed more storage space." One side of his mouth kicked up. "Unless, of course, they were trying to keep something in that closet. Ever see *Rosemary's Baby*?"

"Very funny." I encountered enough weird stuff in my daily life; I didn't need Mateo encouraging such thoughts.

"Want to take a look inside?" Mateo asked.

"You know I do."

Mateo and I had worked together for years, and we shared a strong streak of curiosity. As a young man, he had done a short stint in prison for a nonviolent drug offense, and when he was paroled, my dad had given him a chance to prove himself on the jobsite. For the past decade, Mateo had been a loyal and reliable employee. When Turner Construction's much-cherished foreman, Raul, obtained his contractor's license and set up his own shop, Mateo took over as the boss of our crew. He had married and now was a very proud father of an adorably chubby baby. There wasn't anyone I would rather have heading up my home renovation.

Taking up positions on either side of the heavy armoire, we coordinated our movements—"One, two, three, heave!"—and together managed to shove the heavy cabinet far enough away from the wall to allow us to inspect the closet door.

"What do you think?" I asked Mateo.

He shrugged. "Nothing special about it, so far as I can see. Its twin is on the opposite side of the attic."

Across the attic a second closet door stood open, revealing nothing more sinister within than a jumble of cardboard boxes.

I flipped my toolbox open, and the clang of the metal top hitting the metal side reverberated in the confined space.

Mateo jumped. *"Ay-yay-yi . . ."*

My unflappable foreman seemed a little on edge today. Guess I wasn't the only one who read Stephen King novels late into the night. Then again, Mateo had worked with me on many projects and had seen more than his share of the unexplainable. Maybe *I* was the one making him jumpy.

He took a step back as I reached for the doorknob and gently turned it.

"Locked?" he asked.

"Sure is." The door had an original locking mechanism, the kind with the big keyhole meant for an old-fashioned skeleton key. I squatted and peeked through the keyhole, but without any light inside, it was impossible to see anything.

I smelled another strong whiff of cigarette smoke.

"Now what?" Mateo said.

"Now we get physical," I replied. I riffled through my toolbox, which had been decorated with Magic Markers years ago by my (sort-of) stepson, Caleb, back when he was a little boy who thought I was cool. The memory flooded me with warmth, and I took a moment to revel in the sensation, drawing upon that love to ground myself. Similar to what the acupuncturist had suggested, my ghost-busting mentor, Olivier Galopin, had taught me to always ground myself before encountering spirits, and though I didn't *really* expect to encounter anything more menacing than fragile old holiday ornaments—and possibly a few spiders—it was wise to be prepared.

I rummaged through my tools and found the right-sized pick and sweep to jimmy the door lock.

"Mateo?" a voice called from the hallway below. "You up there?"

Mateo couldn't hide the relief on his face. "Well, looks like I'd better get back downstairs. The cement truck should be showing up any minute."

"Coward."

He grinned. "Seriously, you want me to stay? Help you take the door off the hinges?"

"I'll be fine," I said, waving him away. "These old locks are usually easy to pick. You go deal with the cement contractor."

"Call me if you need me. Hey, maybe there's a treasure or something valuable inside. Stranger things have happened."

"You got that right," I muttered.

I watched Mateo disappear through the hole in the attic floor, wishing he weren't leaving. Who was the coward now? The thing was, not only did I smell cigarette smoke, but I heard something from within that closet.

And it probably wasn't a rat.

In the past few years, I have encountered more than a few restless spirits trapped within the bones of vintage structures, roaming the halls and corridors of old houses. Sometimes what I felt was merely the whispered remnants of those who had once dwelled within those walls, but at other times, it was much more—an active, unhappy spirit. I had long since reconciled myself to such encounters.

But they still scared the pants off me.

Too bad Landon had a class, I thought. He was always eager to back me up on this sort of thing.

I knelt in front of the door. In the public rooms downstairs, the doors were adorned with large crystal knobs, the old glass tinted purple from years of exposure to sunlight. In the rooms meant just for the family—or "the help"—the hardware was a serviceable brass, darkened with age. I'm no locksmith, but as I told Mateo, these antique mechanisms are pretty easy to open. I inserted my pick, feeling carefully for the voids in the tumbler lock, as I had learned to do as a child, at my dad's knee. I, in turn, had taught Caleb. I winced when I thought of all I had exposed that boy to over the years, since many skills used in the building trade could be applied to less respectable pursuits. Luckily, Caleb was basically a good kid, otherwise growing up in the Turner household would have prepared him well for a life of crime.

Satisfaction surged through me as the lock mechanism popped open, and I felt the bar slide back.

Now, to open the door. I grabbed my flashlight and held it at the ready.

Just as I turned the knob, I felt it. A whisper of gossamer.

This was not my imagination.

Deep breath, Mel. Ground yourself.

I pushed open the door and was enveloped in a cloud of cigarette smoke.

Uh-oh.

Not Christmas decorations, after all.

Chapter Two

The walls of the small room were lined with dresses from the 1920s: Feathers, beads, silks, and satins gleamed under the beam of my flashlight. Besides cigarette smoke, the space smelled strongly of the cedar wood with which it had been paneled.

But what demanded my attention was the woman perched on a low upholstered stool in the middle of the closet, puffing away on a long cigarette holder.

She gazed at me, eyebrows raised, an expectant but surprised look on her heavily made-up face. Her curly bleached blond hair was styled in a bob, and a glittery tiara crowned her head.

"You just gonna stand there?" she demanded after a pause.

"For the moment," I croaked.

"What on earth are you wearin'?" she asked, casting a critical gaze over my denim coveralls. "You a gold miner or somethin'?"

"No, I . . . actually, I have a dress on underneath," I said, then wondered why I was explaining my wardrobe choices to a ghost. But at the moment, I was distracted by the fact that I was able to see her so easily. In the past, most visitors from the spirit realm appeared in my peripheral vision, which was both disconcerting and tiring. "I'm Mel Turner. I'm working on the house."

"You the new housemaid, huh? Gotta tell ya, the windows in this place need washin' real bad."

"No, I'm, um . . . No."

The woman frowned, then shrugged and took a drag on her cigarette. "I'm Hildy Hildecott. You've probably heard of me."

"Um . . ."

I had been seeing ghosts long enough by now to know they are a diverse lot. Some fade in and out, some manifest as cold black miasmas and are as scary as hell, and a few were like this one, almost indistinguishable from a living, breathing person. At least they were visible to *me*; most people could not see ghosts, even if they wanted to. Had Landon been here to provide me with backup, he would have witnessed me talking to nothing but air.

I knew from experience that spirits remaining in this dimension aren't carnival sideshows. They're human souls trapped on this plane of existence or in search of . . . something. And since I was one of the few living people who could see them, I felt an obligation to help. Besides, this was my dream house, and I wasn't sure I wanted to share it with a ghost.

Renovation often stirred up spirits, disrupting as it did the bones of the place. As it were. The question was: What did this ghost want, or need, from me? Was Hildy showing herself for a reason? Why had her spirit remained in this closet? How had she died? And would she be yet another problem for Landon and me to deal with, along with dry rot and wallpaper?

Among other things, I had learned that ghosts often don't know that they are dead. That can be a tough thing to explain to someone you've just met.

"You haven't heard of me? *The Heiress*? Or *The Adventures of Lila*? How about *The Little Tramp*?" At the blank expression on my face, Hildy added: "You know, Charlie Chaplin?"

"Yes, I've heard of him, of course. But I haven't seen many of his movies."

"What, you never go to the picture show?"

"I do. But not all that often. I work a lot."

Another bone of contention with Landon: I got up at five most mornings to be on the jobsite by six thirty, so I wasn't a big one for nightlife.

Hildy gave me a disapproving look, rather reminiscent of Landon, as a matter of fact.

"You should get out more, honey. Goin' to the picture palace is like walkin' into a dream." She clasped her hands together and gave a dramatic sigh, the ash at the end of her cigarette quivering. "Ain't that expensive, neither. The cheap seats don't but cost a nickel, ya know. Even a housemaid can afford that once in a while. Anyway, shut the door, would ya? I gotta get changed for my big number."

"Hildy Hildecott, right?"

"Right. Say, why you got a boy's name? Your ma didn't like you or somethin'?

"Oh no, she liked me well enough. My name is actually Melanie, but whatever you'd like to call me is fine. Just don't call me Melly—"

"Tell ya what, Melly. Choose somethin' nice for yourself—anythin' from that rack over there. I know what it's like to be a workin' gal; ol' Hildy didn't come from money—that's fer sure! But I got lotsa clothes now, and don't wear but half of 'em. Your fella will thank you for it." She gave me an exaggerated wink.

"Oh, that's not necessary."

"Try that one there, the green," she said, gesturing to a frothy sage green concoction decorated with feathers and beads. "It has a little cut in it, but you'll hardly notice once it's mended. G'wan, don't be shy. I know how it is, to come from nothin'."

This last was said with a slight melancholic tone.

I took the dress from the rack, bid Hildy au revoir, and closed the door.

Downstairs, I found Mateo leaning over a thick set of blueprints.

"I take it you got the door open?" he said, looking at the frothy garment in my arms. "Whatcha got there?"

"No Christmas decorations after all," I said. "But some beautiful old dresses in surprisingly good shape."

"Nice. Cedar closet?"

I nodded. "I locked the door. Do me a favor and keep the guys out of the attic for now? I need to think about what to do with the clothes."

"And all the rest of that stuff up there."

"That, too."

"Sure thing. We're not scheduled to work up there until you decide about the insulation, and finalize the lighting plan for the upstairs bedrooms."

More things to go over with Landon.

"I like that dress," continued Mateo. "It looks like your style."

I smiled and held the dress up to me. It might actually fit, which was a nice surprise. I wasn't built for most genuine vintage clothing—I was what was popularly called "curvy," which meant I had a bosom and hips in ample quantities. But now that I thought about it, Hildy Hildecott wasn't exactly a stick herself.

"Thank you," I said. "I'll have to try it on later."

Here's how strange my life has become: Until Mateo commented on the dress, I wasn't entirely sure if it was real and visible to others or some kind of ghostly remnant that only I could see. But since the dress was real, everything else in that closet, except for Hildy herself, was probably also real.

But why was Hildy there in the first place? Had she died in the house and her spirit remained in this world to guard her wardrobe? And did she have the run of the place, or was she trapped within that closet?

Based on my experience with ghosts, I suspected there was more to this story.

At the moment, though, I didn't have time to pursue the history of Ms. Hildy Hildecott and her early film career. I had to fight my way through the maze of freeway traffic and across the Bay Bridge into San Francisco, where I had a meeting with the owner of a 1920s-era movie theater.

A "picture palace," as Hildy would have called it, which was rumored to be haunted.

Huh.

Interesting coincidence.

The fellow sitting on the other side of the booth in the Mission neighborhood diner-turned-hipster-locale was disconcertingly attractive. He wasn't really my type— *Landon* was my type—but there was no denying that Mr. Gregory Thibodeaux was intriguing. With golden blond hair framing a strong, handsome face, and sparkly blue eyes shining with intelligence, Thibodeaux was clad in a fine gray wool three-piece suit—not something a person saw every day here in the land of T-shirts and jeans and tech-bro fleece vests.

I, on the other hand, was clad in one of my friend Stephen's designs, a blue-and-yellow spangly getup—my coveralls were in my bag—so I suspected the other diners might have guessed we were members of an acting troupe.

"You represent whom, exactly, Mr. Thibodeaux?" I asked, and not for the first time. We had been speaking by phone and e-mail for months now, but this was our first face-to-face meeting.

"I'm here on behalf of a consortium of investors,

with varying backgrounds. They call themselves the Xerxes Group. They like to maintain their privacy, which is why they hired me to represent them."

"So you're the front man."

"Exactly."

"Just to be clear: This isn't some sort of organized-crime-related 'consortium,' is it?"

"Nothing of the sort, I assure you." He chuckled and took a sip of his coffee. Beams of sunlight cast golden highlights on his well-coiffed head.

"The thing is, Mr. Thibodeaux—"

"Gregory, please."

"Okay, Gregory . . . as I've said before, I prefer to work closely with the client. There are constant decisions to be made over the course of a renovation, from how to file the permits to what kind of toilets to use."

"I am authorized to work with you on all of that."

"Glad to hear it, but you know the old saying 'What do you get when you build a horse by a committee?'"

He cocked his head and gave me a questioning look.

"A zebra."

"I happen to like zebras," he said with a charming smile. "Very distinctive animals. The consortium donates to a wildlife sanctuary in Washington State, by the way."

"Oh, well, that's nice to hear. But my point is, I can't be negotiating every single decision with the group. We'd be working on the renovation through the end of the century."

"You won't have to. That's my job."

This whole setup made me nervous: mysterious out-of-town investors swooping in to save a neighborhood monument? This renovation would cost many millions of dollars if done properly, and though the theater had great historical and cultural value, it was unlikely to ever turn much of a profit, much less repay the investment. Why wasn't the Xerxes Group investing in computers, or the newest app, or the oil industry, or pharmaceuticals, like all the other rich people with money to burn?

"You mentioned the previous contractor walked out on the job?" I asked. "Who was it?"

He ducked his head and flashed another charming smile. "Can't tell you that, I'm afraid, Mel. Professional courtesy and all that. The point is, the initial permits are already in place, and a lot of the boring foundation work has been completed and passed inspection."

I could find the original contractor's name easily enough by checking the city permits, but I appreciated Thibodeaux's discretion. Most people who had problems with contractors, or who thought they did, were more than happy to bad-mouth them to everyone they could.

"*Why* did they walk out?" I persisted.

Don't say ghosts.

Thibodeaux hesitated a moment before saying, "I don't want to cast aspersions on anyone, and as I said, the city inspector has signed off on the foundation work. But upon reviewing the job thus far, we felt the contractor lacked sufficient . . ."—he paused as though searching for the proper adjective—". . . *finesse* to complete the job to our satisfaction."

"So the contractor didn't walk off the job so much as was fired?"

"Let's just say it was a case of irreconcilable differences, and we had an amicable parting of the ways." He smiled. "Believe me, Mel, they were well compensated and are off on new adventures. It won't be a problem."

"Do you remember the name of the building inspector?"

He shook his head. "I'm really not sure. But all of the documents are in order. All you have to do is step in and continue the job of bringing this magnificent structure back from the brink."

The table rattled, and for a moment, I thought we were experiencing one of the area's frequent small earthquakes. Then I realized the shaking was caused by my wildly jiggling leg. I willed myself to stop.

No doubt about it, this project was making me nervous.

On the other hand . . . it was my chance to renovate a historic theater. A *great* old theater. Haunted or not.

I gazed at the Crockett Theatre through the café's pristine plate-glass window. Once upon a time, its grand façade had lit up in a gaudy electric extravaganza boasting thousands of colored lights—red, orange, yellow, blue—that flashed in a sequence controlled by an ingenious device similar to a music box, and attracted admiring viewers like moths to the flame. For several decades, the huge marquee had announced the showing of movies from the earliest silent films to *My Fair Lady* to *The Shining*.

But now the only letters on the marquee spelled out CLOSED FOR RENOVATION, with the "c" hanging at a crooked angle, and the "v" missing altogether. Plywood had been nailed over the windows of the octagonal ticketing kiosk and the main entry doors, and multicolored graffiti tags bedazzled the golden bricks of the once resplendent "Moroccan Renaissance" façade.

I had been to the Crockett only once, as a child, for a double feature of *The Sound of Music* and *The Jungle Book*. It was a rainy Saturday, and my mother needed a break. My parents made their living flipping houses long before it became fashionable, and because we didn't have a lot of money, we lived in the homes during the renovations. Mom had told Dad he was on his own for the afternoon, and took my two sisters and me to the movies at the Crockett Theatre. I was too young at the time to realize how old-fashioned the films were; if my mom liked something, then that was good enough for me. Mom loved *The Sound of Music*, and the four of us hummed along with Julie Andrews in the nearly empty theater. After the movie we went out for ice cream and sang "My Favorite Things" all the way home.

I imagine the theater had been run-down even then, but to my childish eyes, its elaborately tiled and painted ceilings were magical, the golden icons enchanting. As Hildy had said, walking into that picture palace was like walking into a dream. I remembered gazing up at the massive curtain and the bas-relief lions that crept along the molding, staring at the "stars" sparkling high overhead, munching on Red Vines and popcorn and wondering if I could talk my dad into sprucing the place up a bit—even then demonstrating a propensity for lost architectural causes.

It was the one and only time I had been to the Crockett Theatre.

After a stint playing third-rate films and rereleases of old movies, the once-fine movie house had tried hosting a few Maker Faires, served a short time as an indoor flea market, and held Sunday services for a neighborhood church. But finally its doors had shut for good, decades ago.

"She's a grande old dame, isn't she?" Gregory said, breaking into my reverie. "Hard to believe there were plans to demolish her for a parking lot."

"Really? Did the consortium save it?"

"Not exactly. A Mr. Calvin Delucci inherited it from his father. He leased it out to a variety of folks over the years, always hoping to scrape together the funds to bring it back to its former glory, but he never managed. I imagine he found the scale of the project much greater than he had anticipated."

"And the Xerxes Group bought it from Mr. Delucci?"

"Actually, no. He passed away suddenly just as he was starting the work. His widow continued to lease it out for a number of years, then offered to sell it to the highest bidder. Eventually she agreed to sell it to the city,

which was about to sell the lot to a developer when a
neighborhood group stepped in to save the building from
the wrecking ball."

In the way of the Bay Area, the once-downtrodden
Mission neighborhood had undergone a revival, and
the sad old theater was now worth a fortune. Or at least
the *land* it stood on was worth a fortune.

Sharing the block with the theater were a tattoo studio, a donut shop, two mediocre *taquerías*, and a dusty-
looking jewelry store. Not long ago this neighborhood
had boasted reasonable rents and attracted a lot of
working-class families, immigrants as well as native-
born. But with tech giants like Google moving into the
area, a whole new group of young people with money
were making themselves at home and taking advantage
of the interesting, diverse neighborhood.

In between the dollar shops and discount stores,
there were now trendy cafés and bars, boutiques and
bookshops, arty installations and hopping nightclubs.

Case in point: The café where we were sitting used
to be the kind of place where you could get a weak cup
of coffee and a piece of brightly colored fruit pie from
a revolving display at any hour of the night or day. Now
it served only locally sourced food and fancy cappuc-
cinos, and the breakfast menu offered no fewer than
three vegan and gluten-free options.

Also, the prices were through the roof. This meal
was going on the mysterious consortium's bill.

"The city resisted at first, but apparently the preservationists stirred up quite the brouhaha—you may have
heard about it at the time. There were pickets and
demonstrations, and eventually the city caved and
coughed up some redevelopment money through grants
and tax credits, even billboard revenue." Gregory shook
his head. "San Franciscans. You gotta love 'em."

"And that's where the consortium comes in."

"Exactly. In conjunction with the city funds, the Xerxes Group can bring the Crockett Theatre back and still make a profit. Or at the very least, not lose *too* much money," he said with a crooked smile.

Our server brought the bill, and Gregory smoothly placed his credit card on the little tray before I could even make a polite stab at it.

"Thank you for brunch," I said.

"My pleasure." Gregory sat back and gazed at me. "Mel, the consortium members are not wild-eyed dreamers. They understand that the renovation of a run-down, neglected twenty-thousand-square-foot theater will take time and cost many millions of dollars, and they're prepared to go ahead. I assume you have studied the proposal and looked into our financials."

"Of course."

"I would expect nothing less."

Still, I hesitated. As charming as Gregory Thibodeaux was, it made me nervous not to know exactly for whom I was working. On the other hand, Stan Tomassi—Turner Construction's office manager and an old family friend who lived with my dad and me—had spent days poring over the consortium's renovation proposal and crunching the numbers and, after walking me through it all, had given it a thumbs-up.

And Turner Construction needed the work. We had ramped up our operation and hired new people to complete a couple of large-scale projects—one a castle reconstruction in Marin, the other a lighthouse remodel in Richmond—and it was time either to take on another big project or lay off a good number of the crew.

Letting people go was, hands down, my least favorite part of running a business. Worse, even, than filling out workers' comp paperwork. And that was saying a lot.

Also . . . I wasn't convinced another contractor would be up to the job. Not to brag or anything, but when it came to historical renovations in the San Francisco Bay

Area, Turner Construction had few peers. The Crockett Theatre deserved the best.

"The building dates from 1923, which was early for a movie theater—it was probably used for other kinds of entertainment before talking films, such as vaudeville acts, that sort of thing," Gregory said as he tucked his papers into a sleek briefcase.

"Do you know a lot about the early film industry?"

"I'm no expert. I just read up on things for the job. The consortium funded a smaller theater remodel in Roseburg, Oregon, a few years ago, so I did some research. Back in the day, theaters were rivaled only by churches and courthouses when it came to lavish buildings. It was an interesting era—for many people, going to the movies wasn't just a form of entertainment, or a distraction from daily life and worries. It was a window into other worlds, a way to see places and people they might otherwise only read or hear about. We're so inundated with images today that we forget how isolated people were not all that long ago."

"You sound like a history buff."

"One of the perks of this job," Gregory said with a smile. "I love old things."

"Have you ever heard of an actress named Hildy Hildecott? She was in a few early Charlie Chaplin films, I think."

"Doesn't ring a bell," he said. "But like I said, I'm no expert."

The waiter came back with Thibodeaux's credit card slip, and I noticed he added a generous tip. You have to like that in a person.

"We do have one special request," Gregory said as he tossed the pen back onto the bill tray. "It is rather . . . unorthodox."

I steeled myself: He was going to ask me to rid the theater of ghosts. Or to convince the ghosts to stick around so as to attract those who enjoyed the idea of hanging out with spirits from beyond the veil. Either way, I assumed ghosts would be involved.

"I'm not from around here," he continued. "And apparently I stick out like a sore thumb, though I can't quite put my finger on why."

Look in a mirror, pal.

"I will therefore need to rely upon your knowledge of the area and your local connections."

"To do what, exactly?" I asked, curious. Find a date? Score some pot? Fix a parking ticket?

"Get rid of the squatters."

"Squatters?" I sank back in relief. "Is that all?"

He blinked. "There are people living in the theater."

"I'm not surprised." In a place like the Bay Area, with its sky-high rents and scores of artists and others living on the edge, you can't leave a big, dry building vacant without expecting somebody to move in, whether of the four- or two-foot variety.

He looked surprised. "Well, I'm relieved you're not put off by it."

"Depending on how they've treated the place, it might actually be a good thing. Buildings don't benefit from being left vacant. But . . . isn't rehousing squatters more in the realm of . . . I don't know . . . social services?"

"There are some sticky issues of squatters' rights, not to mention the involvement of the Crockett Caretakers, the neighborhood preservation association. I don't know the local players, and I thought you might be able to help us there. Maybe find someone to come in and speak with them. I realize we are in California, and in the Bay Area, I do believe things are done in a certain way. Also, the last contractor wasn't especially diplomatic. We're still trying to negotiate on our end, but if our latest efforts fail . . ."

"Just so we're clear—Turner Construction builds things and fixes things; we're not social workers or community organizers," I said. "But if you don't make any progress, I suppose I could make a few calls, see what I can do." As if I knew anything about squatters, much less their rights. But I'd do what I could to ease things along—the last thing I wanted was a Last Stand at the Crockett Theatre.

"Perfect! You see, your reputation precedes you. The work you did on Ellis Elrich's Scottish castle in Marin? And then that lighthouse in Richmond? You are indeed a miracle worker."

"I can't promise anything," I said, wary of committing to something I couldn't deliver. "I'll see if I can find someone to talk with them, but like I said, I'm no social worker."

"But the interior work can't start in earnest until they're out—am I right?"

I nodded.

"So that's where we'll begin," Gregory said. "I'll get to work finalizing the rest of the permits, completing the applications for variances, and jumping through whatever other bureaucratic hoops the city requires, and you'll shoo those pests out of there."

"Are you speaking of humans or rats?"

"Both. Shall we do a walk-through?"

I nodded. I was itching to get inside that gorgeous theater. Ghosts and squatters and rats notwithstanding.

Chapter Three

On the street in front of the theater, I paused to take some photos of the terra-cotta work on the façade, some of which had obviously pulled away from the structure and been resecured. Unfortunately, the job hadn't been done well, and the repairs were visible to the naked eye.

At least, to *my* naked eye. I had to remind myself that not everyone looks for minute imperfections in every beautiful building they pass.

I snapped more shots of the octagonal ticket kiosk, and the golden graffiti-covered stone, as well as the original-looking fire escapes, which appeared to have been seriously compromised by nearly a century of exposure to San Francisco's famous fog. Later I would compare these to historic photos of the theater in its heyday to ensure a faithful renovation.

As we walked around the side of the building, we were approached by an elegant-looking older woman. She wore a turban and a silk scarf over her pantsuit, her bearing was upright, and though she had to be in her seventies, at least, her broad smile lit up a virtually unlined face. She reminded me of one of those models on a moisturizer commercial, telling you to be at home in your skin no matter your age.

"*Lovely* to see you, Gregory," she said.

"Coco, how are you?" Gregory beamed, and they kissed each other's cheeks in the French fashion. "Coco, may I introduce you to Mel Turner, the talented head of Turner Construction? Mel's firm is partnering with the Xerxes Group to bring this place back to life."

"Nice to meet you," I said, holding out my hand, but she moved in to give me kisses on my cheeks, as well.

"It is such a *pleasure*," she said. "I go by Coco. As in Chanel, though my actual name is Stapleton. I cannot *tell* you how happy I am that the theater is at long last being renovated. I myself am in the arts, you see—an actress and singer. I sang on that very stage when I was just a wee girl."

"It's a beautiful place," I said.

"Isn't it, though?" said Gregory.

"So you'll be doing the work on our lovely old gal?" asked Coco.

"If you're referring to the theater, yes." Were theaters referred to as "she," like boats? I wondered. I found the notion vaguely troubling. And if theaters were "she," then why not private homes? And art galleries? And sports complexes?

These were the kinds of questions that at times distracted me from the business at hand.

"I was the chairwoman for the Crockett Caretakers, the community group that convinced the city to preserve the theater. Those mindless bureaucrats wanted to tear it down and pave it over for a *parking* lot! Can you imagine? Over my dead body!" She handed me a cream-colored, engraved calling card. "*Do* let me know if I may be of assistance in any way. I have some photos of the theater, from way back when. Gregory, it has been an absolute *pleasure*. Mel, *so* lovely to meet you!"

She glided down the sidewalk and around the corner, trailing a cloud of Chanel No. 5.

"She seems nice," I said.

"She's a nut," said Gregory. "We call her group the Crockett Crackpots."

I raised an eyebrow, surprised at this expression of vehemence from the previously unflappable Thibodeaux.

He shrugged and let out a breath. "Sorry. It's just . . . these preservationists kept the place from being torn down, I'll give them that. But they've got definite opinions about how things should be done. Coco's very involved, or would like to be, even though she's not one of the ones risking their own money."

"If the Caretakers' members raised funds, and pay taxes, I suppose they feel entitled to weigh in."

"Everyone feels entitled to weigh in when it comes to a place like this."

Gregory led the way around the corner and opened a locked security gate in the temporary cyclone fence. In the alley to the rear of the building, a small portable trailer had been set up to serve as a guard's office.

"Speaking of entitled," I heard Gregory mumble under his breath as we approached.

Two men stood outside the security office, talking. One was a middle-aged, balding man in chinos and a button-up shirt who looked like he would feel at home in a downtown law office on casual Friday.

The other was tall and strong-looking, dressed in a blue-and-gold uniform with CUSTOM SECURITY COMPANY embroidered on his shirt pocket. He had salt-and-pepper hair, tattoos peeking out from under his cuffs and above his collar, and a revolver strapped to his leather belt. He had the kind of mature looks that were hard to date: He could have been anywhere from a hard-living fifty to a hale seventysomething.

I focused for a moment on his gun. I wasn't afraid of

firearms per se; as my father's daughter, I had learned to shoot at a young age. But I was very much afraid of guns in the wrong hands, and too many were the wrong hands. Many private security guards simply passed a criminal background check and underwent a brief training course before being handed the means of deadly force.

As we approached, the balding man fell silent and glared at Gregory. Then he strode past us up the alley, through the gate, and onto the street, disappearing without saying a word.

I glanced at Thibodeaux, who simply said, "Mel, this is Skeet. Don't let the uniform fool you; Skeet works directly for the consortium. Skeet, this is Mel Turner. She's heading up the renovation, so you two will be seeing a lot of each other."

"Ma'am," Skeet said with a nod.

"Nice to meet you, Skeet." We shook hands. "I'm curious, with all this security, how do the squatters get in?"

"They find a way—through emergency exits or the lavatory windows, maybe. Up the fire escape and in through the roof door, I would imagine, is a popular mode of entry. Good exercise, too. There are always ways if someone really wants to get in," Skeet said. "And there's not all that much security, actually—it's pretty much me or Thad, and sometimes Ramon. Not nearly enough men to secure a large building like this. Excuse me a moment."

He stepped into the guardhouse and jotted something in a large journal, then grabbed a ring full of keys and rejoined us. "This way, folks."

We followed Skeet to a nondescript metal door set flush with the building. Above the door, in faded paint, STAGE ENTRANCE was painted in barely legible letters.

"Skeet and the other guards are here to make sure nothing gets out of hand, but it's not their job to clear out the building," explained Gregory. "As I mentioned, it's a delicate business, evicting squatters. The last thing we want is to make enemies in the neighborhood through a show of force."

"They're an okay bunch, really," Skeet said, keys jingling as he unlocked the door. "Mostly young artists. I got no complaints about them. Every once in a while there's a little tussle or misunderstanding, but they work it out. As a matter of fact, they help keep the place up, in their own way."

"How do they do that without water and power?" I asked.

"Oh, the theater's still got power. But I control access. There's no electricity unless I turn it on," he said as he opened a large electrical panel and flipped a main breaker switch.

Skeet led the way down a narrow, dimly lit, and unadorned passageway, the pink-painted walls scuffed and dented. I imagined generations of actors hurrying along, eager to be onstage.

"That way leads backstage," said Skeet, gesturing to a branching corridor. "And over this way is the main lobby."

He opened a door, and we stepped into a marble-lined lobby the size of a cathedral.

Pillars ascended several stories to a domed ceiling. High above us, painted clouds floated on the concave surface, white against a blue sky and illuminated by hundreds of points of light from the three huge crystal chandeliers. The chandeliers appeared intact, though coated with years of accumulated grime and strewn with enough dust-furred cobwebs to delight a fan of haunted houses. The lobby walls were decorated with richly colored hand-painted murals, and up near the ceiling were richly hued borders in shades of red, green, blue, and ocher. High overhead, carved terra-cotta figures created a resemblance to an Indian temple.

It was clear why theaters such as these had been called "picture palaces." I could only imagine what it had looked like upon its grand opening, or what it must have felt like for someone who had never even experienced television to walk in and behold all of this, in the lead-up to watching beautiful people and exotic places on screen.

I snapped photos like mad and started my to-do list. At the moment, that list included just about everything, from replacing the carpet to refurbishing the sconces to checking out the state of the ventilation shafts.

Noticing my interest in the terra-cotta figures, Gregory explained, "Middle Eastern and Indian styles were popular in the twenties. They'll need a little work, as well. I don't suppose . . . ?"

"I'll find someone." I nodded, still taking it all in. The theater's abundant gold leaf and luxurious appointments, the opulent, exotic, and dizzyingly detailed frescoes, the ornate plaster moldings, and the sets of heavy velvet drapes covering niches could not disguise the overriding air of neglect and decay. The textiles were rotting, the tapestries sagged, and the spots on the ceiling were clear signs of water damage. Everywhere I looked, the once-fine finishes were marred, dinged, and faded, the murals scratched and gouged.

I sniffed. The air hinted at mildew, and there were rusty stains and something that looked like black mold in the crevices of the ornate plasterwork overhead.

Unless I missed my bet, the theater was not *too* far gone . . . but it was getting there, fast.

I wondered why the original contractor hadn't at least cleaned out the interior prior to starting work, but I supposed that if the focus was on fixing the foundation and the plumbing, the crew might have worked primarily from the outside. Scattered holes in the walls indicated the contractor had done some exploratory work, presumably to evaluate the plumbing and wiring within the walls. But I saw no signs that anything more had been done—certainly not as much as I would have expected at this point in the project.

Was that why the contractor had been fired? If so, why wouldn't Thibodeaux simply say so?

"Ah, the concession stand," I said as we neared the glass display cases, now sadly empty, which were decorated with Art Deco–style swoops and fans fashioned from metal. The elaborate Art Deco design continued onto a nearby trash bin. On the wall by the shelves that had once held candy was a large, incongruous whiteboard. I looked closer: It was a chart with a long list of chores, such as "Take Out The Trash," "Bathroom Detail," "Kitchen Kleaning Krew." At least a dozen names were scrawled on the chart. Skeet hadn't been kidding when he said the squatters were organized.

Something skittered past us; I saw it in my peripheral vision, but when I turned it was gone. Probably a rat.

Gregory looked to see what had captured my attention. "See something?"

I shook my head. "Nothing. I sure hate to see those candy shelves empty, though. The highlight of any trip to the theater, as far as I'm concerned."

Gregory chuckled. "I was always partial to Junior Mints."

"I'm more of a popcorn and Red Vines gal, but I'll trade you for some."

The large glass popcorn popper and brass cash register appeared to be vintage—and intact.

"How do you suppose all of this stuff made it through the years?" I asked. "Wasn't there an indoor flea market held here, for instance?"

"I don't suppose there's much value in an old popcorn machine that more than likely doesn't work anymore," said Skeet.

"That register could fetch a pretty penny," I said.

"Maybe. But you'd have to haul it out—those things are solid brass. They can weigh more than a hundred pounds," said Skeet. "Not impossible, but probably not worth it to a common thief."

I continued to snap photos and assess the many signs of decrepitude, such as the flourishing colony of mushrooms growing on the once-plush carpet in one corner. The musty, closed-up smell was pervasive due to a lack of ventilation. Had the theater not been so solidly built, and the original roof made of durable Spanish tiles, it would have been a ruin by now.

Still, the place was stunning. Even more so than in my memory. I felt a little-girl giddiness at being allowed to poke around all I wanted behind curtains and doors designated EMPLOYEES ONLY.

But then . . . there it was again. *Something* moving in my peripheral vision. Shadows in the corner of my eye, just on the edge of my field of vision.

I turned my head sharply, but nothing was there.

"What is it?" asked Gregory. "Did you see something?"

"Just a trick of the light, I imagine."

But then . . . I heard it. *Whispers.* A giggle at once far-off and right behind me.

"Do you hear that?" I asked the two men.

"Hear what?" Skeet asked.

Gregory shook his head.

Ghosts? Squatters? An overactive imagination?

The barely there whispering was driving me nuts. I had encountered it before, and all I have to say is that whoever devised this system of ghost-human communication had a lot to answer for.

Then I remembered that Hildy Hildecott had appeared and spoken to me as if she were a full-bodied living person. I wondered what that meant, if anything.

I took a quick moment to breathe and ground myself, touching the gold ring on the chain around my neck. My mother had given me the ring, and her mother had given it to her. It had come to serve as a talisman for me.

I should have done this before entering the Crockett Theatre. Given my sensitivity to ghosts—which appeared to be getting stronger all the time—how would I *not* attract the attention of spirits in a place such as this? As I had learned these past few years, the odds of my detecting a supernatural resident improved as a building's age increased. Landon had pointed out that it was simple math, really—the more people who dwelled within a residence, the likelier it was that a few of their spirits remained behind.

Not only was the Crockett Theatre nearly a century old, but once upon a time, it had showcased actors, imaginative and creative people who assumed and shed dozens of personas over the course of their careers. Did the years of actors inhabiting other lives, of "becoming" other people, however temporarily, leave an impression that lingered after death? Could what I was sensing be the resonance of things past, a supernatural echo rather than an actual ghost reaching out to me?

I glanced at Skeet and Gregory. They didn't seem to notice a thing.

"Theater designers used to compete to create ever-more-fantastical movie venues," said Gregory, breaking into my thoughts. "Here in the Bay Area, most theaters were Art Deco and Spanish revival. The Crockett is an example of 'Moroccan Renaissance,' though with a strong Art Deco influence in the fluid lines, such as the metalwork at the concession stand."

"It's stunning," I agreed.

"Isn't it?" said Gregory with a tone of reverence. "Back in the day, theaters really served as a center of social life. Here at the Crockett they had a restaurant, art galleries, dance floors . . ."

"Not exactly like visiting the multiplex," I said, and Skeet chuckled.

Once we left the main lobby, the original finishes were covered with a coat of faded pink paint, a bilious hue somewhere between bubble gum and Pepto-Bismol. In some areas the paint had been slapped directly on top of the wallpaper, which was now peeling away in sagging strips. I had seen this before in older buildings: In the 1950s it was a common renovation "shortcut" by those who associated the original design and decoration with their parents' generation.

"Back then, people didn't just come to watch the movie—going to the theater was an occasion, an evening out," Gregory continued. "There were entire string orchestras up onstage to entertain the audience before the show; sometimes there were ballets or vaudeville acts. And then the Mighty Wurlitzer organ, hidden beneath the floor, would take over."

"It must have required quite a crew to keep things running smoothly," I commented.

"It certainly did. The stage crew, of course, but also dozens of smartly uniformed ushers. Not only did they escort the patrons to their reserved seats—there was no such thing as general admission—but they functioned as crowd control. It required skill and diplomacy to turn the house, ushering out the previous audience and bringing in the new one in a timely manner."

"It's hard to imagine what it was like back then," Skeet said, "when people were so hungry for entertainment."

"Even during the Great Depression, when many people were struggling, they nonetheless scraped together the money to come to the picture show," said Gregory.

His words reminded me, once again, of Hildy Hildecott. What was her story?

I thought I saw someone in the corner of my eye and whirled around.

"You okay?" Gregory asked.

"Yeah, sure," I said.

"A big old place like this can get spooky," said Skeet. "I swear I've heard and seen more than a few odd things while working here . . . On the other hand, like I said, a lot of these squatters are creative types. And they're good at hiding. So it's probably just them."

As we continued our tour of the theater, I spotted signs of the squatters: half-burned candles here and there, a few faded flowers, small piles of books and personal effects jumbled in niches and corners. But there were also signs of care: A large plastic garbage pail had been placed in the middle of one corridor where water stains on the ceiling directly overhead indicated the roof was leaking. There were other indications of upkeep: The hard surfaces had been dusted and wiped clean, and the tile floors behind the concession booth had been swept.

As I had mentioned to Gregory, empty buildings still require regular care and maintenance. If people don't inhabit them, Mother Nature will.

And it would be a fantasy to live in a place like this. Certainly better than living on the streets.

Gregory led the way to the double doors to the main theater, and we walked in.

Red plush seats were ripped and dirty, the ornate wall decorations—which once upon a time had included an actual waterfall—had long since been abandoned, and the ornate ledges and carved ornaments were caked in grime. Onstage, the massive fringed and embroidered curtain was still beautiful, its golden spangles sparkling in the overhead stage lights. Unfortunately, the material had begun to shatter and split, with long tears ruining the once-fine drapery.

I could practically see this theater full of people, a smartly dressed usher standing behind the velvet curtains at the side doors, flashlight in hand, like a Hopper painting I had seen at the Museum of Modern Art.

Flanking the stage were two bejeweled statues that resembled a cross between a Buddha and a genie, with red eyes that lit up.

"Okay, now *that's* a little creepy, I'll grant you," Gregory said with a chuckle. "But they're original, so the 'golden deities' have to stay."

"I remember those guys," I said. "When I was a kid, I came here once for a double feature. I felt like they were watching us the whole time, with those red glowing eyes."

"Did they scare you?"

"Actually, I liked them." I shrugged. "I'm like that."

I gazed at the statues for another moment, daring them to move.

Once again, I thought I saw something in my peripheral vision, but when I turned to look, it was gone. Then came the whispering, and the kind of shushed murmur one might hear at a large public event—an audience shifting in their seats in anticipation, maybe?

And . . . I smelled the aroma of fresh popcorn popping.

"Ready to meet the squatters?"

Skeet's voice startled me.

"You okay?" he asked me, looking concerned.

"Yeah, sorry. We're meeting the squatters?"

He nodded. "This way."

Chapter Four

"They should be holding their meeting right about now," Skeet said as he led the way back up the aisle, toward the lobby.

"The squatters have regular meetings?" I asked.

"Oh yes," Gregory said. "As we mentioned, they're very organized."

It figures, I thought to myself. The fantasy of living in an ancient theater was all fine and good, until you realized you had to go to meetings. I would rather work a twelve-hour day on a jobsite than attend a company meeting—and Turner Construction meetings usually consisted only of me, Dad, Stan, and our current foremen. Even the promise of snacks didn't make it more tolerable.

As Stan had pointed out more than once, it was a good thing I had a knack for renovation. I was not a good fit for the corporate world.

We passed through the spectacular lobby and continued down a rather grim pink hallway to a mirrored vestibule. Handprints in bloodred paint adorned the mirrors, and a couple of the panels were shattered and cracked. Various bejeweled and beaded strings hung like decorative stalactites from the ceiling, swaying slightly in an undetectable breeze.

Skeet paused in front of a door. An Art Deco sign above it indicated: LADIES' LOUNGE.

"The squatters meet here? In the ladies' lounge?" I asked.

Skeet nodded and waved us through.

Once upon a time, ladies' lounges put the "rest" in "restrooms." They were elaborate spaces, with upholstered and tasseled chaise longue "fainting couches" as well as well-lit makeup stations in an outer room, and toilets and sinks in a separate interior room. I wondered if the plumbing still functioned. The lack of reliable bathroom facilities always gave me pause whenever I fantasized about adopting an itinerant lifestyle.

This ladies' lounge still had its chaise longues and marble counters running along the sides with mirrors overhead, but there was also an old desk in one corner, full of papers, and on one chair were a pillow and a neatly folded blanket. What looked like an old movie screen, torn on one side, covered one wall. On another, a section of the old wallpaper had peeled away, and on the bare plaster, surrounded by paisley decorations, was painted: "Affectations can be dangerous." Books were stacked along one ledge, and candles and vases of wildflowers studded all four corners. Clearly, this was someone's home, however temporary.

Several heads turned to stare as we walked in.

The woman who stood to greet us wore a long, flowing white skirt over a cream-colored leotard, and several long pale scarves were wound loosely around her neck. She looked to be in her late twenties or early thirties, and stood with erect posture, her shoulders held back in an almost military stance.

"Hello, Skeet," she said. "Who are your friends?"

"Hi, Isadora. These are the folks I told you about.

Listen up, people," said Skeet in a commanding voice. "This is Mr. Thibodeaux and Ms. Turner—"

"Mel is fine," I interrupted.

"Mel Turner," Skeet continued. "They have something important to say, so pay attention."

His announcement was greeted with rebellious hoots, though one or two of the twentysomethings snapped their fingers or fluttered their hands in some kind of signal. The standing woman, Isadora, just gave a low chuckle.

"Sir, if you two are okay here, I'm about to go off shift," Skeet said in a quiet voice to Gregory. "Thad will be coming on for the night."

"Of course, Skeet. I think we're fine," said Gregory, glancing at me.

I nodded.

"Does he need your permission?" asked one young woman.

"Yeah," chimed another. "Is he your employee or your slave?"

Skeet ignored the comments and headed out of the lounge. Gregory and I turned back to the squatters.

Isadora, apparently the group's informal leader, began a round of introductions. "I am Isadora. I'm a dancer, a creator of many things. My most fervent belief is that we must all dance as though no one is watching, whether that refers to actual dancing, or to life itself. And this is Alyx . . ."

I tried hard to attach names to faces as they introduced themselves and described their interests. Each introduction included an explanation as to which personal pronoun was appropriate: she/her, he/him, they/their.

Alyx was a young man in drag, dressed in a brocade corset, fishnet stockings, and a feather boa, and lots of makeup. Alyx preferred to be referred to as he/him and was into industrial design "but in an artistic, salvaging way." Zoey had long hair, half blond and half black, wore something akin to a dog collar and a black leather vest, and was a painter and designer. Mitch was silent and staring, projecting an air of vague malevolence, though he looked like a tortured poet. Liam was big and bearish, an older man—maybe forties?—with huge blue eyes that appeared on the verge of tears; he declined to state his favored art. Tierney was small and pretty, and dressed all in black except for her supershiny mirrorlike shoes; she was into drawing, collages, and tattoos. Mirabelle was plump, dressed in bright orange, and looked very young; she said she was still exploring her artistic side and didn't want to be defined by society's narrow-minded definitions.

A half a dozen others refused to introduce themselves, which was just as well—I wouldn't have been able to keep all their names straight anyway.

"How many are you, in total?" I asked.

"We don't believe in such tallies," said Isadora. "We don't believe in hierarchy. We're creating a new society here. As artists, our creativity comes first—whatever that happens to look like."

I nodded, wondering how to inform them that they were going to have to abandon this particular "new society."

"Creativity isn't only about painting or writing, but encompasses every aspect of our being," continued Isadora, "from how we interact with our neighbors to where we live. After all, we live in a virtual palace of creativity." She gestured around the former powder room.

I was awash in the strong sensation of women here in the lounge, rocking their babies. I could have sworn I saw a woman moving in the corner of my eye, and heard a whispered song that sounded like a lullaby. I still couldn't figure out whether what I was feeling was just the residual vibes of a historic building or something more interactive. But for now I stroked the ring at my neck and tried to ignore whatever it was, to keep my attention on the conversation.

"I'm a big fan of artists, and the artistic life," I said. "But here's the deal: Once we start this renovation in earnest, you won't want to be here. Believe me, I know. There's a reason I don't live in my own house while we're working on it."

"Lucky you, to have a house," said Mirabelle in a surprisingly husky voice.

"So very bourgeois," Mitch sneered.

"That's me, all right." I nodded. "Lucky and bourgeois. But very soon we'll have this place crisscrossed with scaffolding and extension cords, with the walls open, any inferior plumbing removed and the wiring redone, which means no water and no power. With compressors and power tools making a racket, well . . . it won't be a fit place to live, much less to create. Surely there's some happy medium between kicking you all out on the street and letting you stay here in a construction zone."

"We don't want another Ghost Ship on our hands," murmured Liam, the man with the big blue eyes.

I shuddered at the thought. The Ghost Ship fire in Oakland still haunted the Bay Area. The Ghost Ship was an old warehouse-turned-musical-venue that housed and hosted numerous artists and musicians. It was also a fire trap. In a tragic turn of events, a blaze broke out during a music event and thirty-six people, unable to escape the inferno, lost their lives. It was the worst mass-casualty fire in California since the conflagration that had devastated San Francisco following the 1906 earthquake.

Fire escapes are ugly, and safety regulations cumbersome and a pain in the neck, but they saved lives. This was the upside of code enforcement. Which reminded me: I added "fire escapes" to my to-do list. I wouldn't be surprised if some of the old rusty bolts were ready to fall out or shear off.

The squatters gazed at me, some skeptical, others outright scornful, a few slightly hopeful.

"This isn't just some regular building, you know," said Alyx. "It's special."

"I agree. Be assured that Turner Construction loves historic buildings as much as you do, and that we'll take every care to repair it and bring it back to its former glory."

"I don't just mean it's beautiful," said Alyx. "It's *special*. Things happen here, things out of the ordinary—"

"We can talk about that some other time, Alyx," said Isadora. "Right now we're discussing losing our home."

"Yeah, is there, like, a timeline?" Tierney's voice scaled up as though asking a question, even when making a statement. "Because we're, like, living here? But it's important to embrace change?"

"This is such garbage," said Mitch, swearing a blue streak and kicking a papier-mâché basketball in frustration. "I hate this kind of imposition of the establishment on the powerless. Same old story: a bunch of powerful bougie people oppressing the working class."

"Are you working?" Gregory asked.

"You're missing the point," Mitch replied, and several others nodded.

"Where are we supposed to go?" asked Zoey.

"I don't want to leave," said Tierney. "At least you have resources, Mitch. The rest of us are on our own."

This engendered a heated discussion as to who had resources and who did not, and from there branched into a philosophical debate about the historical origins of class privilege and the labor theory of value.

Good Lord, what am I getting myself into? Dealing with rusted pipes and leaking plumbing was one thing; ousting people from the only home they had, especially if they could not easily find another, was something else entirely. Luckily, I had an ace up my sleeve: my good friend Luz, a professor at the San Francisco State School of Social Work. Luz didn't actually like one-on-one social work, which was why she preferred to be an academic rather than a caseworker in the trenches. But maybe she could point me in the right direction. There must be some resources, somewhere, right? San Francisco was a wealthy city, after all, though the number of people living in their cars or on the streets was shocking and seemed to be increasing rapidly.

Leave it to me to try to solve the problem of homelessness in San Francisco.

"All good questions, though not ones we have an answer to right now," Gregory said. "Mel will give you a sense of the construction schedule, et cetera, as things are settled. In the meantime, Mel, why don't we check out some of the internal workings of the place?"

I traded cell phone numbers with several of the occupants—it always surprised me how many people had cell phones but no homes—and agreed to be in touch.

"For all the good it will do you," Tierney said, texting me her cell phone number. "Cell reception is *terrible* in the theater, and the batteries seem to drain quickly? You might want to fix that, too?"

Our meeting hadn't made much progress, but at least I had a sense of who the squatters were. They didn't appear to be menacing in any way, just a trifle deluded as to how the world worked. Like a lot of people—perhaps myself more than most.

Back out in the hallway, I took my coveralls from my backpack and pulled them on over my dress.

"Clever," said Gregory as he dusted cobwebs from his fine suit.

"Never leave home without them," I said. No steel-toed boots today, but since we weren't doing actual construction, my leather walking shoes should have sufficed.

"Did you notice the movie screen on one wall of the ladies' lounge?" he asked.

"I did see that. What's it for?"

"A series of mirrors was set up, leading from the projection room to the ladies' lounge. The mirrors reflected the film and displayed it on that screen so that women wouldn't miss the show while they were in the lounge."

"No kidding? That's convenient. But how long did women spend in there? And why?"

"You tell me," Gregory said with a laugh. "I have no firsthand knowledge of ladies' rooms. But I suspect the care and feeding of small children was a main reason, especially crying babies. Children were often dragged along to the theater with their families, back in the day."

Of course. I had heard the haunting melodies of lilting lullabies while in the ladies' lounge. Or at least, sort of heard them.

For the next couple of hours, Gregory and I inspected the theater's back areas, checking out the clockworks for the exterior marquee lights, and examining the work done by the previous contractor. I was pleased and more than a little relieved to find that the foundation work and the plumbing repairs appeared to have been properly completed. I might have replaced all of the piping rather than simply repairing the old, but that was what set Turner Construction apart from other contractors. Our standards were high.

One storage room was piled high with all kinds of items: light fixtures, corbels, old sink taps and old sinks, ancient film cameras, wallpaper samples and dried-up cans of paint, even a crucifix.

"A little bit of everything, up to and including the kitchen sink," said Gregory.

"What's with the crucifix?"

"There was a church that held services here."

"I can't believe no one has rummaged through this stuff and stolen the valuable items," I said, sifting through a cache of old movie posters and ephemera: paper rounds of box-office tickets, signs advertising giveaways and special performances.

"How do you know what's worth money and what's just junk?"

"Well, a lot of that is in the eye of the beholder," I said, thinking of the old things in our new house, hidden up in the attic with Hildy. "But that crystal chandelier in the corner? I'd bet that would sell for many hundreds of dollars. And the ones hanging in the main lobby would go for tens of thousands. Or more, at auction."

"I'm sure things have been taken, over the years," said Gregory. "But as you said, maybe the squatters have stopped them."

"I'm also surprised that the squatters haven't incorporated more of this stuff in their art—a lot of this is pretty cool. We'll put back what we can, and replace what we can't. Okay if I take this?" I asked, picking up a nickel cold-water tap. "I'll see if my guy can locate some reproductions. He may even have some refurbished originals from the same era."

"Of course," said Gregory. "Anything you'd like."

As we left the storage room and headed toward the main lobby, Gregory gestured to an alcove that had once housed a bank of telephones but was now empty. "This is where the architect was thinking of installing the elevator."

"I saw that, in the plans."

He nodded. "As you might imagine, a building such as this one is hardly ADA compliant. Because the theater is so old, we could apply for an exemption, but the consortium would rather go the extra distance so as to welcome everyone."

"I like that idea. Where would the elevator come out upstairs?"

"It will stop at the mezzanine, and again at the balcony level. I'll show you. Finding a space for it shouldn't be a problem; there used to be a bar on the mezzanine, as well as a small restaurant, and of course the seating area. Ready to climb the grand stairs?"

"Ready."

Roaring lion statuettes greeted us on each level as we mounted the sweeping staircase, whose rococo carpet had once been plush but was now worn and threadbare, and so grimy with dirt the original colorful pattern barely showed in some areas.

When we reached the mezzanine, my attention was captured by an outline of a body, the kind one might see drawn in chalk at a homicide scene. This one was made with masking tape.

"That's where the usher fell," said Alyx, startling us both.

"What usher?" I asked.

"The usher who was murdered here—back in the forties, I think," Alyx replied. "Another guy fell in love with the usher's girlfriend and killed him to get him out of the way."

"Killed him right here?" Had Alyx seen something? A ghost, perhaps? "How do you know where he fell?"

"Old crime photos."

"Oh. That makes sense then. Is this where you . . . live? And work?"

I noticed a cot in one corner covered with a sleeping bag. A makeshift table held all sorts of wires and metal pieces, gears and shafts and an impressive assortment of tools. Along one wall marched steampunk-style sculptures featuring rusty iron and an amalgamation of metal bits from screws to nuts to washers.

"Yes," Alyx said. "I like to play around with these."

Gregory seemed eager to continue our tour, but I wanted to take a moment with Alyx to try to understand what he wanted and needed. It was sort of like working with ghosts, I realized with a jolt. Everyone wants to be listened to.

"So, Alyx, are you from this area originally?"

He shook his head. "Wisconsin, if you can believe it."

"You're a long way from home."

"Yeah, but I never really fit in, I guess. One day my dad found me trying on my sister's clothes. Called me a pervert and threw me out. I hitched a ride and just kept on going and, after a few wrong turns, finally made it all the way out here."

"I'm so sorry, Alyx. Not that you're here—I mean I'm sorry about your dad. That's so painful."

"The funny thing is, I just don't buy into the binary thing, you know? Doesn't mean I'm gay or trans, not that it's anyone's business, but a lot of people don't understand that."

I nodded. Caleb had been teaching me about binary and not, trying to keep me up-to-date with things like choosing one's pronouns, for example. I didn't totally get it, but neither did I believe I had any business inquiring into anyone's sexuality or love life or style of dress. Maybe it was the result of growing up in the Bay Area— or maybe it was the influence of my family. Dad was traditional in many ways, but also raised his daughters to believe that no one should be made miserable in order to ascribe to certain arbitrary ways and social mores. As long as no harm was done to another person, what did I care who wanted to wear a feather boa? I didn't want to be judged on my own sartorial whims, after all.

"I just feel better this way, dressing like this," said Alyx. "What's wrong with that? Anyway, it works on the burlesque stage, right?"

"I'm the last person to judge someone for their wardrobe." He had seen my dress earlier, but just to make the point I unzipped my coveralls to show him the spangly dress underneath. "Believe it or not, some people don't think this is appropriate attire for construction work. And this outfit is conservative, for me."

Alyx smiled. "I like that. That's sick."

His tone suggested that last word was a good thing, so I decided to take it that way and filed "sick" away to ask Caleb about when he came home this weekend. I swear, if that boy weren't in my life, I would be hopelessly out of touch.

Thibodeaux and I said good-bye to Alyx, and continued on our tour, climbing up to the balcony, and then another small flight of steps to the projection room. Here, several painted wooden sculptures attested to the fact that this area was now home to another young artist. But a huge antique film projector still held pride of place in front of the small opening in one wall.

"From here you can see the series of mirrors set up that used to project the movie into the ladies' lounge," said Gregory.

"Talk about advanced engineering—that is really clever."

I had never had to worry about quieting a fussy baby because Caleb had come into my life as a young child, fully formed. But how nice would it be to be able to go to the movies and take your baby, knowing you didn't have to worry about upsetting the theater with baby squalls? A theater in Oakland had "Baby Brigade" nights when babies were welcome; I had seen a *Terminator* movie with the sounds of wailing occasionally drowning out the dialogue—it didn't bother me, since the film wasn't famous for its witty repartee.

"And at long last, the balcony," said Gregory as we left the projection room and headed back down to the balcony. "These were the cheap seats."

"I always liked the balcony," I said. "It felt more adventurous than down below, somehow."

Up here the chairs were plain wood, and they were in better shape than the velvet upholstery of the more expensive seats on the main level. A waist-high ledge was decorated with gold gilt, and there were dusty velvet curtains hung along the sides, but there were also serviceable items up here in the cheap seats: a few exposed pipes and several old mushroom-shaped cast-iron caps I assumed opened onto the plenum, or the air chamber beneath the balcony floor that provided air circulation—even a theater as big as this one could get stuffy when filled with thousands of patrons.

Daring to go within a few feet of the actual balcony and peeking over the edge to the seats below, I had to fight off the panic and dizziness. I blew out a frustrated breath. The acupuncture treatments were helping—I could climb most stairs now with no problem—but there was no miracle cure for my acrophobia.

But then I was distracted by the sight of Isadora, the head of the squatters, dancing onstage.

Her voluminous, fluid skirts wrapped around her long, graceful legs as she swooped and glided around the stage. It was as if she were truly dancing only for her own joy, and I thought back to the old adage she had recited, "dance as though no one was watching." Isadora's elegant gestures and flowing white garments were ethereal and hypnotic, and after a long moment, I realized I felt moved by the dance the way I'm occasionally moved by an old song: almost to the point of tears.

"Wow, she's really good," I whispered to Gregory.

"What? Who's good?"

"Isadora, dancing onstage," I said. "Surely with her talent she could get a real job somewhere, maybe afford a legal apartment. Right?"

He stared at me, confused. "Isadora? Where?"

"There, in the spotlight. Onstage . . . ?"

"I see the spotlight," said Gregory. "But no one's onstage. What are you talking about?"

I felt a creeping sensation, a tingling at the back of my neck. I was enveloped by the strong aroma of popcorn and cigarette smoke, and heard the crinkling of paper as someone unwrapped a candy bar.

Chapter Five

A murmur, muted at first, grew louder by the second. Gregory had turned as pale as Isadora's scarves. "What in the hell . . . ?" he growled, and squared up as though ready to fight.

I saw something move out of the corner of my eye and whirled around.

The balcony seats were filled with people.

I reached up to stroke the gold ring at my throat, reminding myself to breathe, to remain connected to this earth, to the here and now. Trying, without effect, to slow the pounding of my heart.

"Do you see that?" I whispered.

"I don't *see* anything," said Gregory, his voice strained. "But I *hear* something. Those squatters must be playing a joke . . . or maybe it's an art thing? It's just the acoustics in here. It sounds like it's all around us. And it smells of cigarettes . . . and popcorn."

Interesting. Gregory could hear and smell the spirits, but not see them.

I could see them. And not just in my peripheral vision, but straight on. I looked around the theater: The women were dressed in outfits that would no doubt have pleased Hildy, though most were not as sparkly. Still, they had the 1920s drop waist, the cloche hats, thigh-length belted sweaters. The men wore suits and ties, their hats resting in their laps.

The audience was chatting amongst themselves, smoking, eating popcorn, as though waiting for the performance to begin. The problem was . . . their eyes were wide-open but appeared blind and unfocused, making their expressions seem completely void.

And then, one by one, they fell silent and turned their unsettling blank stares toward Gregory and me.

Hackles rose on my scalp and the back of my neck.

"May I show you to your seat?"

Gregory Thibodeaux screamed.

I whirled around. An usher, dressed in a cap and jacket, stood right behind me.

"May I show you to your seat?" The apparition repeated more forcefully, leaning toward me in a menacing stance. When he spoke, the sound was out of sync with his movements, as though he were an image from an early "talkie" film.

"Shhhhhhh!" said the audience, their blank stares fixed on us.

"I—" My voice shook. My heart pounded and my palms felt sweaty.

Okay, Mel, you're supposed to be the big bad ghost buster. Think of something.

Taking several deep breaths, my mind raced: What would my ghost-busting mentor, Olivier Galopin, have done?

I started to formulate a question for the ghostly usher—"Who are you, and why are you still here? How can I help you?"—when I heard the distinctive *thud* of a body falling.

Gregory lay, appearing unconscious, on the dirty balcony aisle, a smear of blood over one eye.

I looked around, frantic. Had Gregory merely fainted? Had he had a heart attack? Had someone been right here, hiding behind those velvet curtains, and struck him? Or had his injury been caused by something . . . otherworldly?

Trying to keep an eye on the ghostly usher, I squatted down at Gregory's side. "Gregory? Gregory, can you hear me?"

No response. I placed my fingers on his neck; his pulse was fast but steady, and he was breathing. I lifted each eyelid to check his pupils with my flashlight. The beam was dim—*Time to get some new batteries,* I thought vaguely—but sufficient to reveal his pupils were responsive, and equal in size.

I let out a sigh of relief. For a moment I had feared that Gregory Thibodeaux might have become the body I seemed bound to stumble across on every major new jobsite.

"What's going on?" Alyx rushed in. "Mel? Are you all right? What happened to the suit?"

"I think he fainted," I said, reaching for my phone. No luck there. Its battery was drained, though I had charged it just this morning.

"Do you hear the sounds?" said Alyx. "That's what I was talking about. This place . . ." He looked around, not in fear as much as awe. "It's amazing."

"What do you see?" I asked.

"What do you mean?"

"You said you hear noises, but do you *see* anything?"

The ghostly audience around us continued to stare. Most were silent, but a few were smiling, which seemed much, much worse.

Alyx looked puzzled. "Huh?"

"Never mind," I said. "Do you have a phone? We need to call nine-one-one."

"Don't bother. They almost never work in here, especially when the noises start. It drains the battery."

I should have known. This was Ghost Busting 101: Those from the spirit world often ride on the coattails of the energy around them, draining things like cell phones and flashlights and electrical outlets and even the heat from the air.

"Do the noises happen a lot?"

"Often enough to keep us on our toes."

"Could you help me carry Thibodeaux downstairs so we can call for help from the security office? I think he hit his head—he's bleeding."

"I'm down," said Alyx. "But first . . . wait for it."

"Wait for what?"

I heard the muffled sound of a motor, and then the theater was filled with the strains of an organ playing a Bach cantata.

"It's the Mighty Wurlitzer," Alyx whispered in a reverent tone.

In front of the stage below us, a trapdoor opened and a mechanism whirred loudly. Slowly, achingly slowly, the Mighty Wurlitzer rose.

"Who's playing it?" I asked in a low voice.

"No one. It plays itself."

Did that mean it was like a player piano? Or was Alyx suggesting the organ was being played by unseen forces? No pointing in asking; I might well have my answer in another moment, so I waited with bated breath for the instrument to rise high enough to reveal if someone was playing it, Phantom of the Opera style.

Through the trapdoor and up to the foot of the stage, inch by inch . . .

The Mighty Wurlitzer rose.

Chapter Six

The good news was there was no masked phantom at the keyboard.

The bad news was there was a body draped over the back of the instrument.

A body in gauzy white skirts and long scarves.

Isadora.

I could still see her twirling and swaying onstage—dancing like no one was watching—but her body was draped over the Wurlitzer.

No.

I closed my eyes for a moment in shock and sadness.

Jumping up, I pushed past Alyx, raced down the stairs and across the mezzanine, then flew down the rest of the stairs to the lobby and through the double doors into the theater. I felt dizzy with the fear and the running, the crazy pattern of the carpet under my feet.

The seats in the main theater section were also filled with a ghostly audience waiting for the performance to begin. Their heads swiveled as I ran down the aisle toward the stage, their ghastly, expressionless faces following me.

Isadora.

I had been hoping against hope that my eyes had deceived me, or that maybe I had been seeing some kind of ghostly re-creation of some event from a long-ago past. But it wasn't.

It was Isadora, lying unmoving on the Mighty Wurlitzer, her scarves enveloping her like a shroud . . .

I checked for a heartbeat, but there was no pulse. I felt only her unnatural stillness. As a contractor, I was well versed in first aid and CPR, and had dealt with my share of accidents on the jobsite, but I feared Isadora was beyond help. Her bloodshot eyes were open and slightly bulging, seemingly staring at the ornate ceiling. Just in case, I cast my flashlight beam to see if her pupils reacted, as I had with Gregory, but there was no response. I didn't see an obvious cause of death—there were no bloody knife wounds or visible bullet holes— but didn't want to touch her further, afraid to disturb a possible crime scene.

We had been talking with Isadora not long ago. She was a young, vibrant woman with something to offer this world, a creative community to build.

I felt the all-too-familiar sense of grief and shock wash over me. I had hardly known the dancer, but that made no difference. It was difficult even to wrap my mind around what this meant, and what it would mean to her family. The imminent agony of her loved ones. It was beyond tragic to think of her being murdered; who could have done such a thing? And why? Or could this have been a natural death? Some underlying medical condition, or drug related, maybe?

So much for *not* finding a dead body on the scene of my current construction project. I found bodies so often I had SFPD homicide inspector Annette Crawford's cell number memorized.

My gaze shifted to the velvet-draped alcoves and the golden icons with their glowing red eyes. Could a murderer be lurking in the wings even now?

"Isadora!" Alyx ran up to my side and reached for his friend.

"Don't touch her," I said, holding him back. "We have to call the police."

He stared at me, tears in his eyes. "What . . . what happened? What could have *happened*? Who would have done such a thing? *Isadora!*"

"I don't know, Alyx," I said as I tried using my cell phone again. No luck. "It's possible she died of natural causes. But we have to let the police handle this. The less we mess with things, the easier it will be for them to figure out what happened to her."

Alyx wobbled, then sank into the nearest theater seat, whose ghostly occupant squirmed for a moment, then disappeared.

"It's freaking *freezing* in here." Alyx shivered and hiked his shoulders to his ears.

He was right; our breath was clouding before us, the air frigid.

"Does that happen often?" I asked.

"Sometimes. It gets like this when the noises start."

"This happens a lot, then? The Might Wurlitzer rises on its own?"

"Yes, but not with a *body* on it!" Alyx said, a waspish edge to his voice. He added: "You're awfully calm."

"It's . . . I'm sorry to say, this isn't the first time I've encountered something like this."

"But . . . it's *Isadora*," he said, his eyes filled with tears. "She was . . . she *is* our friend. Who could have done this?"

"I was just about to ask you that. Does she have any enemies, do you know? Have you seen anyone suspicious hanging around?" Again my eyes flickered over to the old stage curtain. Was it my imagination, or was it fluttering ever so slightly, as though someone were hiding there, watching us? There were a million places a person could hide in a huge old theater like this.

Alyx shook his head. "*No*. It was just us. And lately Isadora's been so excited, said she'd found something really important with her candy-wrapper project."

"Her what?"

"She found all these old candies."

"In the concession stand?"

"No, they fell through cracks below the seats, I guess, over the years. And she was so excited, said she'd found something that would change things."

His voice broke, and he covered his face with his hands, sobbing.

"I'm so sorry, Alyx. So terribly sorry," I said. "Right now, though, we have to find a functioning phone and call the police."

"Not me." He straightened suddenly, sniffing loudly. "I'm *out of here*."

"No, Alyx—you have to stay and speak with the police. It's important."

He shook his head vehemently. "*No*. The police and I do not get along."

"Alyx, wait, please—"

Alyx ran up the aisle and out the double doors to the lobby, his feathered boa trailing behind him.

The ghostly audience jeered and laughed.

"Shut the hell up," I snapped.

I was *not* in the mood.

There wasn't anything more I could do for Isadora, so I went back upstairs to the balcony to check on today's other casualty, Gregory Thibodeaux. He was moaning but still unconscious. There was no way I could carry him downstairs by myself, so I tried to make him more comfortable by using my coveralls as a pillow, then retraced our steps, passing through the secret door in the lobby and down the utilitarian corridor to the backstage exit.

I banged open the metal door to the alley, and was greeted by wisps of mist. San Francisco's famed summertime fogbank, nicknamed Karl, had rolled in, as if on cue from a ghostly director.

I was surprised to find Skeet in the security trailer. "I thought you were going off duty?"

"Thad didn't show for his shift, so I have to cover it. One of the perks of being in charge. The wife's not pleased, I'll tell you that much. I pull more doubles around here lately than . . ." He noticed my distress. "Mel? What's wrong? Are you okay?"

"I . . ." My voice shook, and I sank down on the top step of the trailer.

"Did something happen? Where's Mr. Thibodeaux? Let me get you some water."

"Thanks," I said, putting my head between my knees. Black spots careened in my field of vision, and I tried to focus on taking slow breaths. In and out. In and out. In and . . .

Skeet handed me a Dixie cup full of cool water. I gulped it down. It helped a little, though juice was more effective at countering the adrenaline shock. This was the sort of thing I had learned over the past few years spent dealing with ghosts and murder.

"We need to call nine-one-one," I said, regaining my breath. "My phone's dead."

"What's going on?"

"I'll explain in a minute. Where's the phone?"

"Come inside."

The security trailer was blessedly warm after the unearthly chill of the theater and the fog-filled alley. The place had the familiar appearance of the trailers Turner Construction sometimes used on really big jobs: a watercooler, a small table with an electric kettle and assorted instant coffees and teas, several folding chairs, and a utilitarian desk. But this desk was tidy, with only one tray of papers, two paperback novels, and a few hardbound books stacked on it. The trailer's faux-wood-paneled walls were decorated with official-looking flyers detailing workers' rights and first aid instructions, as well as a movie poster for the 1941 Humphrey Bogart classic, *The Maltese Falcon*.

Skeet motioned to a molded plastic chair by the desk, and handed me a portable landline. "Cell phones are useless in the theater. The reception is spotty, and the batteries run down superfast for some reason."

"I noticed." I dialed a number I had called too many times: SFPD homicide inspector Annette Crawford's direct line.

Annette picked up immediately. She listened while I explained briefly where I was and what had happened. She asked if I was safe, then told me to stay put—and above all, not to touch anything. She would send uniforms and the paramedics for Gregory Thibodeaux.

"The police and an ambulance are on their way," I told the stunned-looking Skeet as I handed him back the phone. "You heard what I said?"

He nodded solemnly. "I can't believe this. Mr. Thibodeaux is hurt? How did that happen?"

"I'm not sure," I said. "He's unconscious but still breathing."

"And Isadora is . . . *dead*? You're sure?"

"Sadly, yes. And it's definitely Isadora."

I thought of the scarves floating behind her as she leapt and spun gracefully across the stage.

Was Isadora simply dancing one last time on the stage of the theater she loved? Or could her spirit be lingering because she had something she wanted to tell me? Or needed to resolve before she could move on? This was one of my weaknesses as a ghost buster: I'm usually too rattled at the moment of encounter to ask the right questions. Maybe I should start carrying a checklist or a script like the ones telemarketers use. *Good afternoon, ma'am! So sorry you're leaving us today. And just what is it you wish to convey as you pause in your journey to the afterlife?*

"I can't believe this . . ." Skeet trailed off. "I should have stayed with you two. But I thought it was safe . . . Nothing like this has ever happened before."

Maybe once or twice, I thought, recalling the body outline of the poor murdered usher, who was now haunting this place and desperate to show me to my seat.

"It's not your fault, Skeet," I said. "I doubt your being there would have made any difference. I was right there, and I couldn't do anything." At least where Isadora was concerned. Had Skeet been with us, he might have been able to catch Thibodeaux when he fell. "But that's all water under the bridge now. Did you see anyone go in or out of the building?"

He shook his head, quickly noted something in his big journal, and said in a grim voice: "Help yourself to coffee, if you like. I'll go find Mr. Thibodeaux, see if I can do anything for him."

"He's in the balcony. But, Skeet—it's important not to touch anything that could be important to the police investigation. Especially around Is-Isadora." My voice wobbled when I spoke her name.

He nodded curtly. "Lock the door after me and stay inside until the authorities get here."

I watched him go, locked the door, poured myself a cup of coffee, and remained in the claustrophobic but warm guard trailer until I heard the wail of sirens approaching.

Lots and lots of sirens.

For a (usually) law-abiding citizen, I have spent way too much time at crime scenes, so I knew I would be here a while as the official process unfolded. I called home to let Dad know I would be home late, and did the same with Landon. I kept the details vague, saying only that I had run into a snag at work and was running behind.

Soon the alley and the theater were filled with uniformed officers, and the rescue squad had taken a now-conscious but groggy Gregory Thibodeaux to the hospital with a suspected concussion.

I spent a long time talking to a disgruntled Inspector Crawford, taking her step by step through what I had seen in the theater—including what no one else had seen.

The inspector gave me her patented one-eyebrow raise. "You're saying a ghost usher is the perp?"

"I'm telling you, there's some . . . stuff going on in that theater."

When I met Inspector Annette Crawford at the scene of my first murder a few years ago, she thought I was certifiable. But we'd been through a lot together since then, and she'd experienced a few things firsthand herself, so although she remained troubled by the idea of spirits walking amongst the living, she no longer doubted me. Not as much, anyway. And because she was a consummate professional who wanted to solve murders, she would do what she had to, including taking a ghost buster seriously.

"So," Annette said, glancing around to be sure we weren't overheard, "what do you think? Were ghosts involved somehow?"

"I don't think so. But if I learn anything more, I'll let you know."

"You do that." She turned away, then turned back. "Oh and, Mel? If you're smart, you'll walk away from this job. Now. Not worth it."

I nodded. "You're probably right."

"Like you've ever taken my advice in your life. Well, that's all for now. You can go. Call me if you think of anything more or learn anything new."

I nodded again and watched the inspector walk briskly over to a group of officers, who gave her their reports. I lingered on the sidewalk in front of the theater for a few minutes, surrounded by flashing lights and the crackle of police radios, trying to decide what to do next.

I was loath to go straight home. I adore my father, and Landon, and Stan, but at the moment I wasn't up for the barrage of questions the men in my life were sure to ask. I needed to talk this out with someone experienced in my level of crazy.

So I called Luz Cabrera, my best friend. As soon as she picked up, I said "The Pied Piper, stat."

"Be there in twenty," Luz replied.

The Pied Piper bar at the Palace Hotel was old-school fancy and was named after a sixteen-foot Maxwell Parrish mural that had been painted in 1911 to celebrate the reopening of the Palace after the 1906 earthquake and fire. Once upon a time, the Pied Piper had been a "men's" bar, and as one might imagine was lined with wood paneling and filled with comfortable club chairs.

I rarely went there. The once-smoke-filled bar was now smoke-free and welcomed women, but parking in the area was hard to come by, the cocktails cost an arm and a leg, and the hotel bar's well-dressed patrons tended to sneer at my outfits. Luz, who grew up in a hardscrabble working-class family and took crap from no one, insisted I was imagining the snootiness, but I knew better. For me, one of the advantages of San Francisco was being able to walk into just about any establishment, dressed however as I wanted, without raising any eyebrows. The Palace Hotel, though, was an island of stuffiness in a sea of tolerance.

Luz liked it precisely because it was so fancy-schmancy.

I found her sitting at the bar, chatting with the bartender, a dish of maraschino cherries sitting on the bar next to her martini. No matter what she was drinking, Luz ordered a side of maraschino cherries. She considered them a bar snack, and insisted the usual mix of salty nuts and crackers didn't cut it.

Today, Luz wore her long dark hair up in a sleek ponytail, and was dressed in an elegant cream-colored jacket and pants that I would immediately spill something on but that showed off her svelte figure to great advantage. If Luz wasn't my best friend, I might well have held it against her.

"You look like you need a drink, my friend," she said when she spotted me. She patted the barstool next to her. "Have a seat."

"Just a glass of club soda, thanks," I said to the bartender as I set my shoulder bag on the bar.

"Would you like some cherries as well?" the bartender asked, reaching for a tall glass.

"No, thanks," I said.

"Oh, have a martini, Mel. You know you want one," Luz said.

"I'm driving."

"Don't worry. I'll keep you here long enough to metabolize it." At my nod, she turned to the bartender. "A dirty martini for my friend, here. And bring me her cherries."

"Yes, ma'am," the bartender said.

We talked about Luz's summer school classes for a few minutes while the bartender mixed the martini. When he set it in front of me, Luz held up her glass in a toast. "To the perfect way to spend an afternoon."

We clinked glasses and took a healthy swig of our drinks.

"Good?" Luz asked. "The only thing better than salty olives and ice-cold gin is a sweet maraschino chaser. Sure you don't want one?"

I shook my head. Luz munched a bright red cherry, dabbed her lips with a cocktail napkin, and fixed me with a look. "So. What's going on?"

The thing about Luz is that although she teaches social work, she doesn't actually care to hear about other people's problems. Fortunately, she makes an exception for me and always manages to zero in on what ails me.

"It's . . ." I gazed at the colorful Parrish mural above the bar, wondering where to jump in. "Recently, I feel like my life's been getting awfully . . . complicated."

"Welcome to the real world, my friend. This is what my students call 'adulting,' or what my mother would call 'finally growing up.'"

"Yeah, well, it stinks."

"And that is why we drink martinis. Come, now, Mel, don't give me that. You know very well that life is complicated. Need I remind you of some of the highlights of your past year? What's really bothering you?"

"A woman died."

"*Another* murder?" she demanded, her voice carrying across the bar. A couple of corporate types at a nearby table turned to look at us disapprovingly. Luz returned their stares and they looked away.

"And it might not be murder . . ." I trailed off. What "natural causes" would have caused Isadora to be draped over the back of the Mighty Wurlitzer?

Luz continued: "But you're involved?"

"It's not like I've ever been *involved* in a murder," I said, feeling defensive. "I just seem to be nearby when they happen, is all. It's not something I set out to do: 'Today I'll pick up my dry cleaning, check out a new project at the Crockett Theatre, trip over a body, and traumatize myself, again, and then spend the next several hours getting grilled by the SFPD. *Again.*"

Her voice gentled. "Was Inspector Crawford there?"

I nodded, tracing a pattern in the frost on my glass. "You know your life is complicated when you know the homicide inspector's phone number by heart."

"I can think of worse things."

"Yeah? Like what?"

"Knowing a defense attorney's phone number by heart."

"Good point."

Just then, a man approached Luz and said, "Hello, gorgeous. Looking for a friend? I'd like to buy you a drink."

She gave him a scornful look worthy of Bette Davis and said: "I have a friend, here, pal, and it ain't you. Go away and don't come back." As the man slunk off, she continued, without missing a beat. "At least Inspector Crawford knows you. She doesn't think you're involved, does she?"

I shook my head.

"So, who died?" asked Luz, her voice gentle.

"A young woman," I said, choking up. "A, um, woman named Isadora. She was a dancer. She wore long scarves, like her namesake . . ."

"You mean, like Isadora Duncan? Wasn't Duncan strangled by her own scarf?"

I nodded, feeling woozy. I took another sip of my martini.

"What was this Isadora doing at the theater? I thought it closed years ago."

"It did. She's a squatter; in fact she seems like the unofficial leader of the squatters living in the theater. Or she *was*, until a few hours ago."

"When she died."

"Yes."

We both reached for our glasses and drank.

Silence reigned for a long moment.

"You know, Mel," said Luz quietly, "you might consider going back into anthropology. At least then you were dealing with people who got dead long before you showed up."

"It wasn't that kind of anthropology," I responded with a reluctant smile.

This was a standing joke between us: In graduate school I had studied cultural anthropology, which in my case referred to the study of *current* human cultures. Most people thought of anthropology in terms of Indiana Jones–style adventures, but that was actually archaeology. Although all the real archaeology I had witnessed involved crouching in the dirt in the sweltering heat, laying out sticks and strings and screens and grids, and it required a tedious attention to detail. No swashbuckling in sight.

But the old shared joke helped to calm me.

"So, what do you know about squatters?" I asked Luz.

"I don't like them."

"You don't like anyone. Or at least you pretend not to. You're not the curmudgeon you'd like people to believe you are."

"Here I thought you knew me better than anyone in the world, and then you go and say something like that."

"What about those Latino kids you made me ghostbust for? And convinced my dad to let them sleep on his floor?"

"That was different. They were from the old neighborhood."

"The thing is, Luz, these squatters at the Crockett Theatre, they seem like decent folks. In some way it's more an offbeat collective than a homeless encampment; they have rules and chores, and it's very orderly. It's pretty cool, actually; can you imagine being a young artist and living in a baroque Moroccan Renaissance theater, creating your art, a new society . . . ?"

She raised an eyebrow. "Ready to join the commune?"

"I can think of worse ideas."

"I don't doubt that you can. But you're forgetting one wee detail: Somebody was just murdered there."

"Yeah, except for that. Also, there don't appear to be any bathing facilities. But you know what they say, life is full of compromises."

I gazed at the brightly hued mural of the Pied Piper, surely the most famous and romanticized of child snatchers, which put me in mind of the wall paintings at the Crockett Theatre. I made a mental note to start putting out feelers for artists capable of restoring the beautiful artwork, which could be challenging. The highly skilled ones usually had a long waiting list.

"Can you believe the hotel planned to sell this Maxwell Parrish painting during the last 'remodel'?" Luz asked, noting my gaze.

"What I can't believe is that they gave in to public pressure and kept it after all," I said. "Sotheby's estimated it would go for five to seven million. The hotel paid Parrish all of six thousand for it, back in the day."

"How do you know these things?" Luz said, looking impressed.

I shrugged. "My mind works that way."

"Speaking of remodels, how's your own home renovation going?"

"Oh yeah." I had forgotten all about Hildy. "Slight complication there, too."

"I'm afraid to ask. What's wrong? Cracked foundation? Full-copper repipe?"

"A ghost in the attic. Named Hildy."

Luz fixed me with a look and signaled to the bartender. "I'm going to need more cherries."

Chapter Seven

No, no, it's okay," I said. "She doesn't appear to be bent on destruction, or whisper creepily, or anything like that. And no one's been killed in the house, as far as I know."

"As far as you know," Luz repeated slowly, and gave me her patented concerned but vaguely pissed-off look. "Let me offer you a professional's perspective, Mel. It's not normal to have a *ghost* in your *attic*!"

Again, well-coiffed heads whipped around. The fellow who had approached earlier now seemed doubly intrigued. Luz ignored them.

Luz didn't appreciate ghost talk, perhaps in part because she was able to "see" more than most people. After years spent denying her sensitivity to the spirit realm, she was slowly opening up to the idea. Very, *very* slowly.

She continued: "What does Landon think about this?"

"I haven't told him yet. It's been a busy day."

Luz raised an eyebrow. "And . . . ?"

"And . . . renovating the house has caused enough

stress already; I sort of hate to tell him. I'm afraid he'll
blame me somehow or something."

"Why? Did you slay her mortal body and launch her
into the spirit world?"

"Of course not. But these things do seem to follow
me around."

"But Landon knows that already. That's sort of how
you two met, isn't it?"

I nodded. The first time I had seen Landon, he was
kneeling over the dead body of his sister, whose spirit
I had just encountered in the hallway. Not the standard
Hollywood-style "meet cute" story.

"And you say this ghost isn't scary? Was she part of
the déjà vu you felt with the house?"

When I had first walked into the house, I had "visions," not of ghosts but of memories of the house as
my mother had experienced it when she lived there as
a little girl. It was the first time I'd had such an experience, and it freaked me out, but eventually it began to
seem normalized. Rather like seeing ghosts, I suppose.

"I didn't experience any déjà vu with her, no. Just
stumbled upon her when I opened a locked closet in
the attic. She was sweet, actually, and gave me a really
cool dress. I mean, maybe she's masking a psycho killer
personality or something, but so far she just seems like
a flapper from the twenties. She said she was an actress
in early silent movies. She mentioned Charlie Chaplin."

"Huh. Is she connected to the Crockett Theatre
somehow?"

"How do you mean?"

"She's an actress in early films, and you're working
at a theater built during that time . . . ?"

"That occurred to me as well, but how could it be
connected?"

She shrugged and finished her martini. "When it
comes to you and weird supernatural stuff, Mel, all bets
are off."

"Yeah, thanks." In a blatant bid to change the subject, I said, "Oh hey—not to brag or anything, but I climbed up into the attic this morning without panicking, thanks to your boyfriend."

Luz, my way-too-together and always unflappable friend, blushed to the roots of her dark hair.

"He's not my 'boyfriend.' I mean . . . I don't think he is. Not officially anyway." She ate her martini olive and fiddled with the toothpick. "How does a person even know something like that? Frankly, I don't understand how you do it."

"How I do what?"

"Deal with all these men in your life."

"What 'all these' men? There have been all of two boyfriends, which I grant you is one too many, but still. Just Graham, and now Landon."

"You're forgetting Daniel, the man you were married to."

"I didn't forget. I made a conscious choice not to remember."

"He made a good son."

"That he did." I missed that boy something fierce. Caleb had been in Nicaragua for a month, living with a family and working on his Spanish while coaching soccer at a camp for needy kids; in the fall he was slated to start college at the University of California at Santa Cruz. His father and current stepmother had recently had a little girl who was "practically perfect in every way," so Caleb would be spending part of the rest of his summer with his bio parents instead of the Turner Clan, which irked me, even though it was natural and the right thing to do. Being an unofficial ex-stepmother wasn't easy.

"Speaking of whom," I continued, "Caleb is coming over on Sunday. Want to join us for dinner? I was thinking of proposing a Charlie Chaplin film festival. Maybe we could catch a glimpse of Hildy on-screen."

"Her name's really Hildy?"

"Yup. My very own attic ghost, Hildy Hildecott."

"Did you just make that up?"

"No, it's her actual name. She told me."

Luz let out a low chuckle and shook her head. "I'm in, if your dad's cooking."

"As always. Any special requests?"

"He made a beef-and-onion dish once that was out of this world."

"Turner Steak." I nodded. It was a family favorite: slow-braised beef, mushrooms, and onions in a rich brown gravy, made with love and served over a mound of fragrant white rice. Total comfort food.

"Or enchiladas—you know, your Dad's gotten really good at them. Or anything, really."

"You got it."

"Okay, now my turn to ask a favor of you."

I looked at her, surprised. Luz rarely asked favors of anyone. "Name it."

"It sounds silly, but . . . would you and Landon be up for going out with me and Victor?"

"You mean, like a double date?"

"I get so nervous around him. It's really weird. I thought maybe if you and Landon were there, I would be more . . . more myself."

I smiled. First the blushing, now the request of a favor. *Luz must be falling in love,* I thought. "We would love to. Landon likes any excuse to go out—you know how I am."

"You work hard, Mel, and there's nothing wrong with that. Best he know what a homebody you are before you get married."

The antique rock on my hand glittered in the bar's mellow lighting. Landon had given me the ring a few months ago, and I wore it whenever I wasn't working with my hands. The sight of it still tended to surprise me.

The bartender brought the tab and I grabbed it, wincing at the total.

"By the way," I asked the bartender as I signed the credit card slip, "do you know who did the restoration work on your Parrish mural?"

"Local artist, name of Annie Kincaid," he said, handing me a small brochure that explained the history of the mural and its recent restoration. "She's good."

"Thanks."

Luz and I walked down the hallway toward the extravagant marble-lined lobby of the nine-story Palace Hotel. The original structure had been built in 1875, and had survived the 1906 earthquake but succumbed to the subsequent fire. It was rebuilt and reopened in 1909. The hotel stood directly across Market Street from Lotta's Fountain, which had been gifted to the city by actress Lotta Crabtree. In the chaos following the great earthquake and fire, Lotta's Fountain had served as a rendezvous point for separated families and friends.

We paused in front of the hotel's famous "Garden Court," a huge, light-filled space topped with an elaborate multipaned skylight that reminded me of a sumptuous Victorian-style greenhouse. Here, well-appointed patrons enjoyed high tea or champagne brunch or wedding receptions.

"Why do we never come here for champagne brunch?" asked Luz.

"Because we're always working, and don't feel like spending three days' salary on smoked salmon and a glass of bubbly."

"Oh yeah. Still, we should try it one of these days."

"We should." I squirreled away the idea for Luz's upcoming birthday. Everyone should be invited to brunch at the Palace at least once in her life.

As we walked out of the front doors, Luz declined my offer of a ride, since we were heading in opposite directions: She lived in the Excelsior District while I was heading east to the Bay Bridge, which led to Oakland

and home. She called a Lyft, and we waited for it to arrive.

"So, back to the squatters in the theater," I said. "Once the police release the scene, I'll need to go back and deal with them. Any suggestions?"

"My suggestion is that you walk away from this job altogether, Mel. You don't have to solve the mystery of the ghosts, much less the murder of a young woman. Leave it to the SFPD."

I nodded, and then persisted: "But seriously, about the squatters: any suggestions?"

"For how to solve the problem of homelessness in San Francisco? I wish. Maybe call the police to run them out?"

"I can't just toss them out on the street," I said.

She raised an eyebrow.

"And you couldn't either, if you met them. These aren't criminals, Luz, just idealistic artists. Enough with the tough attitude."

Luz let out a sigh. "As you know, this isn't my sort of thing. But one of my colleagues studies homelessness and affordable-housing options. I'll talk to him, see what he suggests."

"Thank you. And now, for the important stuff: Where shall we go on our double date?"

She blushed again and looked adorable, though I refrained from saying so. Luz would have hated the thought. It didn't suit her tough-girl-from-East-LA persona.

"I have no idea," she said. "Where do people go?"

"You're asking *me*?"

"I'll do some research online and get back to you on that," said Luz as her ride pulled up. "We're a couple of live wires, you and I."

We shared a laugh and a hug, and I watched as the car pulled away.

I placed a call to Inspector Crawford, who didn't

answer. I left a message saying I hoped she'd keep me updated as to the status of things—which was entirely unnecessary, since I already knew she would tell me what she thought I should know if and when she thought I should know it. Finally, I called the hospital to check on Gregory Thibodeaux's condition: He was under observation for the concussion, and relatives had been notified. Funny, it was hard to imagine Thibodeaux with relatives; he seemed as though he had walked off the pages of a fashion magazine.

Time to track down my car and tackle the Bay Bridge traffic, not to mention face what awaited me at home. I hated to tell my family what had happened, though it probably wouldn't take them by surprise. Tripping over dead bodies and encountering ghosts on a proposed jobsite, so what else was new?

Just another day in the life of Mel Turner, renovator to the rich and the undead.

Chapter Eight

Forty minutes later, I pulled up to an old farmhouse in the Fruitvale section of Oakland. The neighborhood, true to its name, had once been full of orchards, and my dad's clapboard farmhouse was one of the rare holdouts in an area now populated mostly by modest two-bedroom stucco bungalows. This was the house my parents bought when they had finally saved enough money to purchase a home of their own instead of camping out in the houses they were flipping. It had been a dream come true for my mother, and she had been so excited.

Then, a few years ago, Mom had died suddenly and unexpectedly.

That was when my dad lost it, and his old friend and office manager, Stan Tomassi, stepped in and told me, in no uncertain terms, that if I didn't take over Turner Construction "for a few months" the family business would fold. At the time I was nursing the wounds in-flicted by a painful, though long-overdue divorce from Caleb's father, so running the company gave me some-thing to do instead of just feeling sorry for myself. I moved back in with my dad and Stan, who had lived with our family ever since he had been injured in a fall from a roof. He now used a wheelchair.

I draped the green dress Hildy had given me over my arm, circled around to the back of the house, and opened the kitchen door. A brown ball of fur barreled into me, wagging his tail so hard he smacked himself in the face repeatedly. I had found the abandoned mutt on a jobsite in Pacific Heights. He was starving, so I brought him home for "a day or two" to feed him and find him a new home.

In an attempt not to get too attached, I simply called him Dog. But his temporary stay at Chez Turner had, entirely predictably, morphed into a lifetime commitment, and once it was clear Dog was part of the family, Dad insisted the pup needed a real name. We didn't want to confuse him, so we changed his name to Doug. The pup seemed fine with the name change, but the humans proved more difficult, so now most people began saying "Dog," then changed it halfway into "Doug," resulting in *Daw-ugh*.

I had simply reverted to calling him Dog.

Dog was not the sharpest tool in the shed. He didn't chase balls, he got carsick, and he wouldn't go out in the rain because he hated to get his paws wet. In many ways, he was a bust as a dog. But his soft brown eyes were full of love, his loyalty was unquestioned, and—bonus!—he was the only one in the family besides me who could sense ghosts.

We had fallen for him from day one.

I gave Dog his fair share of pats and coos, then greeted Landon with a kiss, and my dad and Stan with hugs. As I took in the warm smiles of my loved ones, and breathed deeply of the aroma of home-cooked food on the stove, I was once again reminded of how incredibly lucky I was. Not only did I have an extraordinary new house to look forward to with my fiancé, but I had this home, where I was always welcome. I thought of Alyx being thrown out as a teen and wondered what that must have felt like, the betrayal of one's own family.

"New dress?" Landon asked. "I like it. Is that one of Stephen's designs?"

Stephen was an old friend who had grown up with a Vegas showgirl mother, and had a flair for designing sparkly concoctions like the one I was currently wearing. His designs had become a major part of my wardrobe. He was going to *love* this dress from Hildy.

"No, I actually found it in the attic closet, at Landon's End."

"Don't you mean Mel's Haven?" Landon said with a smile.

We had been trying to come up with a name for our new house, since in my business one couldn't just refer to "the house under remodel" and know what one was talking about. Using the street address seemed too pedestrian for such a splendid home. Plus, it was fun.

"But seriously, this dress was in a closet?" Landon continued. "It seems to be in great shape."

"It does," I said, holding it up and out and inspecting it. "Cedar does wonders. There's one bad tear, but that can be mended."

"That'll look great on you, gorgeous," said Stan.

My dad cast a jaundiced eye over it, snorted, and shook his head. He stirred the bubbling stew on the stove, mumbling something under his breath about "fancy-pants duds."

I thought, again, of Alyx. And of poor Isadora.

And of myself. How was I going to tell my family what had happened?

As if on cue, Stan asked: "So, how did the walk-through of the Crockett Theatre go?"

"It went . . . okay," I said.

Everyone—even the dog—turned to stare at me. These guys had been with me through way too many close encounters with ghosts and murder not to recognize the signs.

"What happened?" asked Landon, handing me a glass of Bordeaux.

"It's an amazing old theater. Have you ever been there, Dad? Stan?"

"Long time ago," said Dad. "So, what happened?"

"I remember going there with mom when we were kids. She aided and abetted our escape from a jobsite one summer's day. We watched a matinee and ate Red Vines."

Once again I used the warm memories to ground myself. It was helpful when facing ghosts, or heights, or the worried gazes of my loved ones.

"What happened?" Stan repeated.

"Ghosts?" asked Landon in a low voice.

"Well, you know what they say about old theaters," I said.

"I told you there were rumors about that place," said Stan. "Found a number of stories about it when I was researching its history."

"I'm gonna bet it was worse than ghosts," said Dad, quietly. My Dad and I were different in so many ways, but he had known me from the get-go and could always tell when something was bothering me. "Might as well spill the beans, babe."

I sighed. "Okay, yes, I found a body."

"Already? You work fast. I'll give you that," said Dad, putting the spoon down too quickly and splattering the counter with gravy. His flippant words did nothing to disguise his concern.

"It had nothing to do with *me*," I said.

"It never does, does it?" Dad pointed out.

I let out a long breath. I had begun to wonder, recently, if death was somehow following me around—or if I was somehow following death around, which might be even worse. Either way, though, it was a very unsettling thing to think about.

One thing was certain: I seemed unable to complete a major remodel anymore without coming across something, or someone, sinister.

"Another jobsite, another body," grumbled Dad, as though reading my thoughts. "Right?"

"Well, now, I don't know about that," Stan said. "The Wachowski addition was completed without any bodies being discovered. The Garcia deck was, too. And the Cow Hollow place seems body-free."

"There you go," Landon said. "Yet another example of how correlation does not imply causation. Basic statistics, really."

"Listen to the man of science," Stan said, nodding. "It's a coincidence, that's all."

"Yeah, maybe so," I said. "But something is going on." I took a big gulp of my wine and told them everything that had happened this afternoon at the theater, including my encounter with the phantom usher, the Mighty Wurlitzer rising, and the discovery of poor Isadora's body. "Oh, and the ghosts had these really wide-eyed, vacant stares, and they seemed to be watching us like we were part of the show . . ."

The story was followed by a long silence.

"That's an image that'll fester," Stan muttered.

"Gotta hand it to ya, babe," Dad said. "You do have some interesting experiences."

"A little too interesting," Landon said, frowning. "Mel, I don't want you going back there without me."

"Landon's right. Mel, in all seriousness," said Stan. "We can still walk away from this job. I can't forget what happened in that house in Pacific Heights."

Neither could I. Rolling around on a steep rooftop, fighting off a murderer determined to make me his latest victim, had left its mark.

"Boy, I'm starving," I said in an attempt to change the subject, my tone as upbeat as I could muster. "That stew smells *amazing*, Dad. Oh, by the way, I was thinking that when Caleb comes home on Sunday we should have Luz over for a film festival. She's looking forward to one of your meals. Also, I might suggest she bring her new boyfriend along so you can check him out."

"This the quack in Chinatown?" asked Dad as he started washing lettuce for a salad.

I let out a long sigh. "He's not a 'quack,' Dad. He's a doctor of acupuncture. It's an ancient medical system, thousands of years old."

"And it's helping Mel with the phobia," said Landon. "So I say we give him the benefit of the doubt."

"Thought you were a man of science!" Dad said, because he loved nothing better than a good argument.

"Science requires an open mind," Landon replied. "So far, the weight of the evidence for the benefits of acupuncture is compelling."

"Better be careful there, Landon," Dad said. "Keep your mind too open, you never know what might crawl in."

"So anyway," I said, because when Dad got wound up he could argue for hours, and wasn't above switching sides if necessary to continue the argument, "I told Luz we'd join them for a double date, Landon. Maybe this Saturday?"

"Splendid. Where shall we go?"

"Luz is doing some research into the matter. She'll draw up an itinerary, if I know her."

Dad handed me a knife and said, "Make yourself useful and chop some onions."

I did as I was told.

"Police tell you when they'll release the scene?" asked Dad.

"Soon, I hope. It wasn't . . . I mean, it didn't look like it was terribly violent or anything. With luck they'll find an old boyfriend who flipped out or something along those lines."

"Yes, that would be lucky," said Stan, and I couldn't tell whether he was joking or not.

"Hey," I said to steer the conversation away from murder, "have any of you ever heard of a silent film actress named Hildy Hildecott? From the twenties, I'm guessing."

Stan shook his head. "All I know is . . . dunno, maybe Rudolph Valentino? Or Charlie Chaplin?"

"Same here," said Landon. "And Clara Bow."

"How about a Charlie Chaplin movie night when Caleb's home?" I said.

"Count me in," Stan said.

"I'll make the popcorn," Dad offered.

"And I'll bring the wine," Landon said. "There's a nice little Sancerre I've been meaning to try."

"Wine and popcorn?" Dad said. "Oh so Continental."

Movie night was a cherished tradition at the Turner-Tomassi house. It started in the days of renting VHS tapes, when we had to remember to "Be Kind—Rewind," progressed to renting DVDs and Blu-ray Discs, and now involved downloading films from a streaming service. Over the years, the family television had gotten steadily larger, and a few months ago Dad and Stan had gone in together to purchase a monster eighty-five-inch ultra-high-definition "smart" television with a surround-sound audio system that took up one whole corner of the spacious living room. I liked to tease them about spending so much money on high-tech gizmos, but the truth is, it made movie night pretty special.

It occurred to me that when Landon and I finally did finish renovating our house—Turner Gardens? Demetrius Manor?—spontaneously gathering for dinner or a movie would no longer be possible; instead, we would have to plan our family get-togethers. The idea of once again having my own place was exciting, but there was sadness, too, at the thought of leaving the warmth of this home, this haven. Still, I was no longer the scared, wounded, unemployed woman going through a divorce that I was when I first limped back to my father's house, what seemed like a lifetime ago. It was time.

Also, it was downright embarrassing sleeping with Landon under my dad's roof.

"Recently someone told me that Charlie Chaplin filmed *The Little Tramp* right here," Landon said.

"Right where?" Stan asked. "In Oakland?"

"In Fremont."

"In *Fremont*?" I asked. I knew Fremont as a BART stop, or as a rather nondescript city of suburban developments that scarcely registered as I blew past it on the 80. "What are you talking about?"

"Ever heard of Niles Canyon?" Dad asked. "It was the name of a town that was later incorporated by Fremont. It was an important train stop in its day. Essanay Film Manufacturing Company had a studio and a back lot in Niles Canyon, and Chaplin filmed his iconic *The Little Tramp* there in 1915."

"I had no idea. How did I not know this?" I asked.

Landon flashed me a wink. He knew I prided myself on being a Bay Area Native—there weren't a lot of us—and it galled me not to know something like this.

"You're right. I remember now, hearing about that place," said Stan, already looking it up on his phone. "But I've never been. Says here there's a film museum, and they show movies on the weekends. Maybe we should go check it out."

"I think we should," I said.

"But for now," Dad said, "time to set the table. Let's eat."

"Babe, you got a minute?" Dad asked later that evening as Landon and I were heading into our bedroom.

"Of course."

Landon bid Dad a good night and ducked into our room while I followed Dad into the room he had shared with my mother. I noted several piles of things in one corner: a jewelry box and scarves, stacks of books and papers, a small antique trunk. Alongside these were several bags full of clothes, which my father had asked me to go through last week.

At long last, Dad was cleaning out some of my mother's things. The process filled me with contradictory emotions: Part of me wanted to keep everything exactly as it had been when she was alive, but it also seemed like it was time to make a change. Dad had held Mom's place in his heart for a long time; it would be good for him to open himself up to something new, and maybe even someone new.

"What's up?"

"I thought you might want to take a look at these," Dad said, handing me several old notebooks. They weren't the fancy leather-bound, hand-tooled journals favored by aspiring poets and writers, but simple black-and-white composition books used by students, back in the day.

"Are those my old school papers?"

Mom had held on to *everything* my two sisters and I had created: school papers and graduation certificates, locks of hair and baby teeth, finger paintings and middle-schooler poetry. Like a well-educated serial killer.

"Toss 'em," I said. "At this point I think we can safely say I'm never going to clear up that 'Incomplete' I got in my freshman-year modern-philosophy class."

"No, honey," Dad said, sounding uncharacteristically subdued. "These were your mother's."

"Mom kept a journal?"

I took the stack of notebooks he held out and saw a date written in Mom's familiar cursive. I flipped open the cover to reveal pages and pages of handwritten thoughts, remembrances . . . and talk of spirits.

Our eyes met. Dad nodded, the expression on his face uncertain. "I thought about burning them, but then I thought that was how the Nazis began."

I smiled. "I hardly think it ended at a mother's journals."

He shrugged. "I'm just saying. What your mother, and now you, experienced—you know I don't really go

in for that sort of thing. I think that's why she started
writing her thoughts down . . . She didn't talk to me
about it because I didn't want to hear about her . . .
whadayacallit? Visions?"

"Something like that," I said in a quiet voice.

"So I thought maybe . . . maybe they could tell you
something. Something that might help you." His voice
was husky with emotion. "Since she's not here to do it."

"Thanks, Dad." I gave him a hug. "Love you."

"Love you, babe. Mel?"

"Yeah?"

"Promise me you'll be careful. If anything happened
to you . . ."

I nodded. "I promise. And you, too. Quit smoking
already, will you?"

"Get to bed, babe. You need your rest."

Despite Dad's advice, I stayed up late, perusing my
mother's journals. She wrote in a beautiful old-fashioned
cursive, the writing occasionally wavering as her hand
grew tired.

As Landon snoozed beside me, I read of my mother's
doubts and concerns when she was a young married
woman, juggling the demands of the family business, a
tight budget, and the needs of a husband and three ram-
bunctious children. I smiled at some of her remarks
about me; apparently, I had been a bit of a handful. As
the hours passed, I heard my mother's voice once again,
her phrasing and wry commentary summoning vivid
memories of the woman who had raised me and loved
me, and whom I still missed every day.

I was about to close the journals and turn off the light
when I came across a reference to her first ghost sighting.

*"It dawns on me that my old 'imaginary friend,'
a movie star in a spangly dress, might have been
an actual spirit from another dimension. If only*

I could approach the current owners to ask to visit their attic, see if she would appear to me once more. I wonder why she showed herself to me— what was it she wanted, and needed?"

Could this movie star be Hildy?

I slid out of bed as quietly as I could, trying not to wake Landon. He slept with one arm tossed over his head, looking more like a Scottish Highland rebel than a math professor—or at least any math professor I had ever studied under. Maybe that was why I never did well in the subject.

I studied the dress Hildy had given me. It certainly looked like a genuine dress from that era, not that I knew much about vintage clothing. My mother's journal entry suggested she had seen Hildy's ghost, too, as a child. Was there a connection? Was there some reason Hildy had given me a dress?

I tugged it over my head. It smelled of cedar and cigarettes, was heavy with beads and spangles, and felt scratchy. I imagined a well-bred lady—or a starlet like Hildy—would wear a slip underneath, preferably one made of silk.

In one corner of my bedroom was an old "looking glass" that I had salvaged from a tear-down. I stood before it and gazed at my reflection.

Again, I smelled cigarette smoke. But it wasn't coming from the fabric of the dress.

In the mirror, I held a long cigarette holder between the fingers of my left hand. I watched as a stream of smoke curled and skittered in the air.

Closing my eyes, I drew in a long, slow breath.

I opened my eyes again. This time the image reflected in the mirror was not me at all. It was Hildy.

Hildy, with a bloody knife in her hand.

Chapter Nine

No matter how late I go to bed—whether I'm up half the night thinking about murdered dancers and ghostly actresses, reading my late mother's ghost journals, or seeing visions of bloody knives and wondering what it all might mean—I still rise with the sun.

I blame my father and his chosen profession, which I had inherited. Construction projects start early. We're on the jobsite by six or seven in the morning, which means rolling out of bed by five at the latest.

But this morning, more than most even, I was in desperate need of coffee, stat.

My dad, with many more years of working construction under his belt than I, was already up and bustling around the kitchen. The scents of onions frying and coffee perking, and the clatter of silverware greeted me as I descended the stairs, making me feel nostalgic and homey.

"Morning, Dad," I croaked, walking into a kitchen bathed in early-morning pink-and-orange sunlight. I gave him a kiss on his whiskery cheek.

"You look like something the cat dragged in," Dad said, spatula held aloft.

"Thanks, Dad. One thing I can say for you—you're good for a woman's ego." I yawned while pouring freshly brewed coffee into my favorite travel mug. A very, *very* large travel mug. "I stayed up late, reading Mom's journals."

He turned back to the omelet he was cooking. When he spoke, his voice was subdued. "Learn anything useful?"

"I'm not sure. But I haven't gotten that far in them yet. Did Mom ever mention a ghost she had seen as a girl, in her grandparents' house?"

"You mean the place you and Landon are redoing?"

I nodded.

He inclined his head slightly and blew out a breath. "All I know is she told me that might have been when things started, when she first started seeing things."

"She was just a little kid."

He shrugged.

"What do you know about the history of the house?" I continued.

"Not much. Anything in particular you're lookin' for?"

"For instance, was someone killed in the house? Stabbed to death, perhaps?"

He frowned. "What the hell are you talking about?"

"I don't mean when Mom's grandparents lived there," I said, taking a sip of coffee and savoring the strong French roast. Knowing this coffee was waiting for me was one of the reasons I was able to haul myself out of bed each morning. "I mean, a long time ago, before then."

He shrugged and gave the omelet pan a practiced flick of the wrist, neatly flipping the omelet. "Never heard about any murder from your mother. But in California, any death in a building—homicide or not—has to be disclosed when the building is sold."

"Even if it happened back in the old days?"

He shook his head. "Not sure when that law passed.

I doubt the law applies to every building, though, or no place over seventy-five years old would be without a disclosure. People used to die at home, in their own beds, back in the day. Which is where I want to meet my Maker, by the way."

I hated when Dad talked about dying, which he was doing more frequently now, as he aged. I knew full well that I was likely to lose my father one day, just as I had lost my mother, but I didn't want to think about it. Denial and I had an ongoing and intimate relationship.

"Breakfast?" Dad asked as he did every morning. "I've got sourdough toast."

"Just coffee for now, thanks," I responded with a smile, as I also did every morning.

Dad grunted. My father insisted that breakfast was the most important meal of the day, and that as a woman "in the trades," I especially needed fuel to get through my day. I agreed in theory, but in reality my stomach wanted nothing to do with food first thing in the morning. In fact, the early morning was pretty much the only time I *didn't* feel like eating. This would have paid dividends, had I not more than made up for my lack of appetite in the wee hours by enjoying hearty meals the rest of the day. I was lucky Hildy's beautiful dress fit.

Which reminded me . . . I should probably do something about a wedding gown. Stephen had been asking if I wanted him to design one for me. But the thought of a wedding made my heart flutter, and I tried to tamp down on my nerves.

"So what's on the agenda for today?" Dad asked, sitting down at the kitchen table to enjoy his breakfast.

"I need to do some work in the office this morning," I said. "I got home too late last night to check messages."

"If you change your mind, the offer of an omelet still stands," Dad said.

"I'll keep that in mind. Sourdough toast, too?"

"Toast, too."

I carried my coffee down the hall to our home office and the "worldwide headquarters" of Turner Construction. Here Stan ruled supreme, but he wouldn't be in for a while.

I sorted through my phone and e-mail messages, separating them into piles: urgent, not so urgent, new project queries, and inquiries about my ghost-busting services. After *Haunted Home Quarterly* named me an "up-and-coming ghost buster" a while ago, I started receiving a fair number of requests to relieve homes of unwanted spectral visitors. Usually I referred these to my friend and mentor, Olivier Galopin, because I didn't need the extra business. I encountered more than enough ghosts in the course of my day job.

Case in point: the Crockett Theatre and my own new (old) house.

I took a big gulp of coffee and got to work. First things first: the urgent messages. These were about supplies and permits and had to be dealt with immediately because nothing shut down a jobsite faster than a lack of building materials or a cranky building inspector. I spent half an hour responding to e-mails and making phone calls to the only other people I knew who were at work at this hour: contractors.

Nonurgent messages I set aside. I would deal with them later, when I had time, or later, when they escalated into urgent status. Whichever came first.

What to do with new business queries was more problematic. Checking out potential projects, meeting with clients, working up proposals and budgets, providing references—all the necessary steps to taking on a new client—were enormously time-consuming. I could spend days just drumming up new business. On the other hand, construction schedules were such that if I didn't have new projects in the pipeline we would eventually wind up with nothing to do, which didn't bode well for the future of Turner Construction, Father and Daughter. I set a few aside to see to personally, but earmarked the rest for Stan to follow up on by making preliminary calls. Stan would winnow out the truly interesting possibilities from among the numerous query calls, many of which came from folks who were in the preliminary stages of gathering information, or who were fantasizing about turning their boxy master bedroom into a spalike retreat on a budget of $2,500.

Laying on his thick down-home Oklahoman accent, Stan was a master at letting people know we weren't interested without hurting their feelings—or ruining a possible future relationship.

I then called the hospital to check on Gregory Thibodeaux, partly because I was worried about him, but also because I wanted to ask him what had happened. Had he simply fainted? Or was there something more? Had he heard, or seen, or felt anything prior to falling? Could it be that the theater's ghosts were actively malevolent, to the point of being able to hurt the living? Or had his injury been caused by someone still breathing? And if the ghosts were evil and able to inflict physical harm, then why hadn't they assaulted the squatters?

Unless they had. I needed to talk further with the squatters.

I tried googling the address of my new home— Landon House? Mel's Retreat?—but found no mention of murder. But that didn't mean much; the history of an old and otherwise undistinguished home was unlikely to show up on a website. I should stop by the California Historical Society and see whether they had archived copies of the local paper from the 1910s and 1920s.

Next, I searched for references to Hildy Hildecott. Nothing came up, but then I might have had the spelling wrong. I tried several variations, which yielded phone numbers for people living in Cary, North Carolina, and Binghamton, New York, as well as a few entries in

Germany. A search for "silent movies" yielded thousands of results, but most of the names were the familiar ones: Charlie Chaplin, Rudolph Valentino, and Clara Bow. The list of credits on early movies was far more limited than today; if Hildy had been an extra or a bit player, would her name have even appeared? I tried to remember the names of the movies she mentioned being in, but only Charlie Chaplin came to mind.

I even looked her up on IMDB, a website that included most movies and actors, but it didn't contain much information pertaining to that very early era.

Finally, I picked up the file on the Crockett Theatre and flipped through a variety of documents: architectural drawings, copies of the original blueprints, production schedules for electrical, plumbing, and stucco-plastering repair. We would need to redo the entire HVAC system, of course. When the theater was built, there was no such thing as air-conditioning, but the good news was that the theater had been outfitted with a passive-ventilation system that circulated air through a system of ample plenums and roomy shafts. I could work with that.

Then came the fun stuff: the schedules for painting and gilded finishes, restroom and light fixtures, flooring and carpeting. Which reminded me: I should gather the rest of the salvaged fixtures I saw with Thibodeaux and take them to the Doctor, an impossibly old Czech man who adored antiques and could repair anything. He was a treasure, though he was expensive, and he worked slowly. *Very* slowly. I had to give him as much lead time as possible.

I wondered how long the theater would be considered a crime scene and how quickly I could get back in there, start cleaning up, and work up my renovation timeline. I made a mental note to ask Dad to do a walkthrough with me. Although officially retired from the business, Dad was still the best at estimating costs, and had a nose for problems born of extensive experience.

"Good morning, gorgeous," said Stan as he rolled his chair into the room.

"Morning, Stan. Have you had coffee? I have a few things I need to ask you about."

He held up a mug and took a sip. "I thought as much. Ask away; I'm ready to roll."

We spent some time reviewing the calls that had come in, and the supply orders for a couple of current jobs, including my own home—Turnetrius Hall? Mel-Lan Manor?

Then, naturally, the talk turned to the Crockett.

"Thibodeaux mentioned the Xerxes Group funded a smaller theater in Oregon, as well," I said. "Are these moneymaking ventures? I thought all the money was in high tech these days, not renovations of old buildings."

"Not all investments are driven by profit, Mel. A lot of people love classic theaters. Remember the projects we reviewed when the possibility of the Crockett first came up? The Lerner in Elkhart, Indiana, the Malco in Hot Springs, Arkansas? Those aren't exactly tourist towns, but someone felt their historic theaters were worth the time, money, and effort to restore."

"I'm betting they didn't have anywhere near the labor costs we have here in San Francisco," I said.

"My point is, maybe the Xerxes Group isn't only in it for the money—though the tax funds make it more attractive, of course. But maybe they do it for the same reason you do: the love of all things ancient."

"Is that why I love *you*?" I couldn't resist. Stan was one of my father's oldest friends, and they had worked together until an accident on the jobsite had robbed Stan of the use of his legs. My parents had helped him through rehab and the transition to a new way of life, and when my mother had passed away suddenly, Stan was a steadfast friend to my dad. Now the two men lived together in this old farmhouse that was constantly under construction and quibbled like an old married couple.

Stan was more than a family friend. He was family.

"Yes," Stan said with a smile. "Exactly like me."

"I don't know . . . ," I said, getting back to our discussion. "The whole thing sounds a little fishy to me."

"You're suspicious because they're so wealthy."

True. But I claimed: "That's not true."

"A lot of your clients have money," he noted.

"Exactly. And I'm fine with them."

"To a point. Also, Landon has money."

"Uh-huh.

"Face it, Mel. You have issues."

"I *don't.*" *Don't ask Landon.* "It's just . . . it seems fishy to me."

"So, I expect you heard the rumors about the Crockett Theatre before you ventured in?"

"Not really. I mean, only in general. Why? What have you heard?"

"Supposedly there's an usher who never left—I guess you 'saw' him yesterday?"

May I show you to your seat? I shivered at the memory.

"Probably. What was his background story, do you know?" I asked.

"According to what I read, he was engaged to be married to a young woman, but another man was infatuated with her as well. The rival shot the usher one night when he was showing him to his seat."

"On the mezzanine." I nodded, remembering the outline Alyx had laid down with tape. "When was that?"

"In the forties, I think. I sent a few links to your e-mail."

It was hardly a surprise that the Crockett would be haunted. What *was* it about old theaters? The willingness of actors to inhabit lives and take on personas other than their own? Could "method" acting have an eternal impact?

First ghosts, and now murder.

I glanced at the contract for the Crockett renovation. Stan had specified that the building had to be vacant and ready before the onset of construction, so the investors were officially responsible for relocating the squatters. We still had time to back out of it. I could do as Annette suggested, and as Luz wanted me to do, and as my family would prefer, and walk away. I could turn my back on the majestic lobby and the faded marquee, harden my heart to the gilded dentil molding and the painted panels and huge gold idols and lions marching along the grand stairwell.

I could reconcile myself to the fact that many such historic buildings were torn down and paved over, and life went on. It wasn't the end of the world. After all, everyone liked a nice place to park.

Yeah, right.

Before Isadora's death yesterday, even Dad had thought taking on the renovation of the Crockett Theatre was a good idea.

I downloaded the theater photos from my phone onto my computer, and looked through them quickly: the tapestries, the murals, the chandeliers and niches and terra-cotta carvings.

Though part of me would have loved to simplify my life, it was awfully hard to lay people off. Turner Construction needed the work.

Besides . . . the Crockett Theatre deserved to be saved.

And poor Isadora deserved justice.

And that spooky usher might need a little help to find peace, as well.

And finally . . . could Hildy's fate somehow be connected to all of this?

Chapter Ten

Office work completed, I gathered my things for my workday. I placed Hildy's carefully folded dress into a tote bag; I knew someone in San Francisco who might be able to tell me more about it. In my backpack I packed the ghost-busting equipment I had bought at Olivier's shop: my EMF (electromagnetic field) reader, the EVP (electronic voice phenomenon) recorder, the full spectrum–infrared camera with night vision, the vibration and motion detectors, an extra flashlight, and several sets of batteries. My dusty coveralls still had the cold-water tap from the Crockett in the deep front pocket.

Then I grabbed my toolbox, because after all, besides all this ghost business I'm still "in the trades."

Before joining the bumper-to-bumper traffic queuing up at the tollbooths to cross the Bay Bridge that led from the East Bay to San Francisco, I swung by Berkeley to see the Doctor, on San Pablo Avenue.

I loved this shop. It was jammed full of pedestal sinks and old-fashioned slipper bathtubs. Dozens of antique clocks filled the space with constant ticking, and gongs or cuckoo calls noted the hour. The whole place smelled of dust and old things, adding to the aroma of whatever mystery solvent the Doctor was using on whatever project was the current focus of his skilled ministrations.

The Doctor greeted me with a nod—he was a man of few words—and listened carefully as I gave him the rundown on what I might need for the Crockett job, and sketched several of the items I had seen in the theater's storage room with Gregory.

I placed the cold-water tap on his counter.

"This?" the Doctor said as he picked up and studied the piece. "For what you wish, I will need more than this."

"I realize that," I said. "I just happened to find this piece and thought it might give you an idea of the time period and the style."

He used a pencil to write laboriously on a paper tag: *Crockett Theatre, SF, 1920s, Mel Turner.* Then he tied the tag to the tap with a piece of old string and placed the tap on a dusty shelf next to dozens of other tagged projects awaiting his attention. I could only guess how long it would take him to get to it, which did not bode well, considering the hundreds of items in the Crockett that needed work. But no one in the Bay Area was as talented as the Doctor, so I would just have to wait.

"I will call you," the Doctor said, and returned to his work.

I considered swinging by the new house to chat with Hildy, maybe ask a few direct questions and see if I could get any answers, but in light of last night's unsettling vision, I decided it would be best to find out a little more about my attic ghost before approaching her again. Also, I needed a break. Talking to spirits took focus and energy, and I had been a near-witness to a murder yesterday; I was not at my ghost busting best.

One thing in particular troubled me: Hildy had not seemed the least bit sinister when I met her. So why had

I envisioned her holding a bloody knife? And for that matter, since when did I start having "visions" while looking in mirrors?

So instead, I joined the throng of cars waiting in line for the Bay Bridge tollbooths. As we inched along, I thought about what had happened yesterday at the Crockett. According to Inspector Annette Crawford, most of the squatters were nowhere to be found when the police arrived at the theater.

I thought about the audience with their vacant stares, and the fervent usher, and Isadora's spirit dancing with grace and joy upon the stage. Why had those spirits shown themselves to me? Were they trying to tell me something? Maybe I was the only one who had the necessary insight to solve Isadora's murder. And speaking of which, Luz had a point: If I knew who—or what—had killed Isadora, I might better understand what the spirits wanted. Annette would wave me off, of course, but I felt drawn to the theater. I had my ghost-busting equipment with me . . . Maybe I could talk my way in?

First things first. I made it across the bridge and into the city, where I stopped to check on the progress of a relatively small residential project in Cow Hollow. As I reviewed the final production schedules and went over the punch list with the project foreman, my mind kept going back to Isadora. And Gregory, and the audience made up of ghosts. And the usher. And Hildy with the bloody knife . . .

I spent a few minutes reassuring the home's owners— a nice couple who had saved for nearly twenty years to be able to afford a house in this city—that all was going well, not to worry. Then I drove to the Crockett Theatre, parked, and ducked into a nearby donut shop for coffee and donuts. As I walked around the theater to the alley closed off by the cyclone fence, I glanced at the rear actors' entrance, which was now crisscrossed with yellow crime scene tape.

Another walk-through was probably best done with Homicide Inspector Annette Crawford's permission. And I wasn't likely to get that anytime soon.

Just as I approached the locked gate in the fence, Skeet emerged from the trailer.

"Hey, Skeet, good morning," I said, raising my chin in greeting. "You're here again. Don't you ever sleep?"

"Hey," he said, then shook his head and let out a long sigh. His dark eyes searched me, worried. "You okay?"

I nodded and held up the coffees and a white paper bag. "I brought us coffees and donuts. A nutritious lunch."

"That's nice of you. Thanks," Skeet said as he opened the gate and accepted the cardboard cup of java. "Want to come into the office a minute?"

"Thanks. That'd be great."

We walked down the alley and climbed into the trailer.

"I can't believe what happened yesterday," Skeet said as he took his seat at the desk and added two packets of sugar to his coffee. Stirring thoughtfully, he continued: "I mean, I'm a 'security guard'—I always thought that meant making sure nothing burned down or whatever, not . . ."

Murder. "It's a little hard to take in, yes."

"Mmm," he said as he peeked into the bakery bag. "Old-fashioneds, my favorite. How about you?" He held out the bag, and I chose a maple bar.

We sat in silence for a moment, sipping coffee and relishing our donuts.

"Here's what I really don't get," Skeet said. "Isadora seemed like a real nice person. I mean, I didn't know her well, but—Thing is, I'm no spring chicken, Mel. I've been around the block of few times, and I've met lots of people. Some good, some bad, some *really* bad. Isadora struck me as one of the good ones. Why would someone have wanted her dead?"

"I was wondering that myself. Did she have any enemies that you knew of? Any tension with others in the squatters group?"

"I went over all this with the police yesterday," Skeet said, shaking his head. His eyes were shaded with sadness, and I remember how fondly he had spoken of the squatters yesterday. It had struck me as odd at the time, but sitting by himself in that portable guardhouse all day, every day, he had probably gotten to know some of them and enjoyed their company.

"I know," I said. "I'm just trying to see if I can help."

"How?"

"Just in case I hear or see something, or whatever . . ." I trailed off. Best not to be too specific. *In case the murder has something to do with the ghosts* wasn't a statement most people could handle.

Skeet helped himself to another donut, and so did I, even though I knew I shouldn't. All kidding aside, this wasn't doing me any favors, and I had upcoming wedding photographs to think about.

Still. Donuts.

"I had spoken to Isadora earlier in the day. Right before you and Mr. Thibodeaux arrived, as a matter of fact. She said she had something she wanted to tell me. She seemed kind of excited about it."

"Any idea what it was about?"

He shook his head. "We were both real theater buffs, you know? So I guess she found something in the theater, maybe? Dunno. I guess I'll never know."

Could it have been something valuable enough to kill over?

"Why was the original contractor fired?" I asked. "Do you know?"

"Failure to obtain the objective, I think it was."

"Can you tell me who it was?"

"I'm sorry. I signed a nondisclosure agreement when I was hired. The Xerxes Group requires it."

Did it, now? I hadn't signed one. I made a mental note to ask Stan about that.

"So . . . tell me more about Isadora," I urged.

"I really don't know much about her," Skeet said. "I mean, we chatted a few times, but we weren't what I would call friends. She was a character, though. I can tell you that. Well, you met her. A hard woman to forget."

"She did make an impression. I noticed she seemed to be on good terms with the other squatters, at least from what I could see. Was that your impression, too?"

He nodded. "As far as I knew, she was popular. Maybe too popular—at one point, she had a couple of different boyfriends . . . I couldn't keep up."

"Are the other squatters around? I'd like to talk to them."

"Your guess is as good as mine. All I do during my rounds is walk through the theater and stop at a few checkpoints. Then I come back and log it in this journal, here." He patted a bound book on his desk. "But the inspector asked me not to go on my rounds for the moment. Normally, though, lots of times I don't see anybody at all. They have a way of disappearing, then coming back. Like I said, I don't even know how they get in and out of the building. The police weren't able to speak with most of them about what happened, which was pretty frustrating."

"Were you friendly with any of the other squatters? Or did you see anything else unusual on your rounds?"

He hesitated.

"Skeet?"

"The only thing—I told the police this already. I saw Isadora arguing with her brother. A few times."

"What were they arguing about?"

"The way I heard it, they're part of the Sepety family, from LA."

"What does that mean?"

"You never saw that reality show, *The Sepetys*? You know, with the . . ." He made a curvy sign with his hands, sketching an hourglass figure. "The sexy women buying clothes and all that?"

"I don't watch a lot of TV."

"There's some good shows on these days."

"Oh, I know. I hear about them, but I get up early so I usually fall asleep in front of anything I'm watching."

He smiled. "Anyway, that's Isadora's family. Their dad was already superrich from producing movies and TV shows, and now they're even richer."

"If Isadora was so rich, then why was she squatting in a run-down theater?"

"I think she was disinherited or something. She wasn't involved in the TV show. That much I do know."

"Did she ever talk to you about it?"

"I asked her about the show once, and she rolled her eyes and called it 'pure dreck.' Said she didn't want to be associated with it, or with her family, which was why she always just went by Isadora, didn't mention the Sepety part."

"But she was close to her brother?"

Skeet shifted in his seat and looked away, and I got the impression he didn't much care for Isadora's brother. "That guy. He was always sneaking around. Seemed like a punk, you ask me. Pushy, too. He and Isadora didn't seem to like each other very much."

"I take it he wasn't on the show either?"

He shook his head. "It's just the girls. It's that kind of show, I guess. I think that's probably why the brother proposed his new idea."

"What new idea?"

"The reality show."

I was confused. "What reality show?"

"A reality show based on this place."

"You mean, a show about the squatters and the theater?"

"That's the way I heard it. I told all this to the cops," Skeet said, giving me the side-eye. "But they weren't as interested as you."

Probably because it was just gossip, I thought. On the other hand . . .

"What's the brother's name?"

He snorted. "Get this: Ringo. Like the drummer in the Beatles?"

"Yes, him I've heard of."

"I think he's a friend of Alyx's, too."

Ringo Sepety. If that was his real name, he ought to be easy enough to track down.

"Hey, who was that man you were talking to yesterday when Gregory and I first arrived?" I asked.

"Who?"

"Middle-aged white guy, balding . . . ?"

Skeet shook his head. "Don't recall. Prob'ly someone from the neighborhood asking how long the reno was going to take. That's usually who stops to chat. Though if he had an ax to grind, he might be one of those preservationists."

"I got the sense he knew Gregory Thibodeaux, but they didn't like each other."

Skeet's cell phone rang. He checked the screen and said: "I have to take this. I really gotta get back to work anyway. 'Scuse me."

I was dismissed.

"Of course," I said as I got up and dusted off a few donut crumbs from my lap. "Thank you for your time."

I left the security trailer and walked toward the street, pausing at the temporary cyclone fence to gaze at the decrepit old building and the octagonal old ticket kiosk out front. This place really must have been something, back in the day, bustling with vaudevillian actors, beckoning to all and sundry to come spend their Friday paycheck on an evening of glitz and glamour.

Except what was with those ghosts with their vacant expressions?

Had the appearance of the ghostly audience, followed by the rising of the Wurlitzer organ, been some sort of warning? Or a repeat of the violence that had already happened? Alyx had told me to "wait for it," as though the ghostly sounds of the audience—which he and Gregory Thibodeaux were both able to hear—had occurred before, and usually preceded the appearance of the Wurlitzer.

But Alyx certainly hadn't expected to see Isadora's body draped over the organ.

Duh. I had written down Alyx's cell number, along with those of a few other squatters. I punched in his number, but the call went immediately to voice mail. I tried the others, with the same results. I left a message for each.

"They've gone to ground," said Skeet, startling me.

"I'm sorry?" I said as I turned to face him.

"It's a survival strategy," he said. "These kids, something like this happens, they go to ground. Turn off their phones, disappear. Haven't seen them since this happened."

"Any idea how to get in touch with them?"

Skeet shook his head. "I already told you that, and I told the police, too. Anyway, ma'am, I think it's time you moved along now."

I held his gaze for a moment. His laid-back, friendly demeanor was gone.

"Sure," I said. "But this sidewalk is public property, right?"

"Now you sound like those squatters."

"Just checking. No need to get testy." What was with the attitude? Had the phone call he had received been about me? "See you around."

I returned to the parking spot where I had left my old Scion, climbed in, and sat for a moment behind the wheel. What now?

I checked my messages and found a text from Luz: "Fly-fishing or archery?"

"What?" I texted in reply.

"Fly. Fishing. Or. Archery."

I stared at my phone, then typed, "I'm going to need more info on what you're talking about."

"Double date. Hello?"

Fed up with texting, I called her. "I repeat: What in the world are you talking about?"

"I'm working on the agenda for our double date, of course. What did you think?"

"I thought maybe you'd graded one too many student papers and lost your faculties. Get it? 'Cause you're a faculty member?"

"Very funny. Did you know you could fly-fish in Golden Gate Park? There's even a casting pond, stocked with fish."

"I have questions. First, does Victor like fly-fishing?"

"I don't know. But if not, there's an archery range."

"There are also buffalo in Golden Gate Park. Maybe we should go buffalo riding."

"Is that a thing?"

"Luz, I think simplicity is the key here."

There was a pause. "You're saying I'm trying too hard?"

"Just a tad. How about something wild and crazy like dinner and a movie? Or drinks and then dinner?"

"I want the evening to be memorable."

"Well, somebody getting shot by an arrow *would* make the evening memorable. But maybe something a little more low-key is in order."

"That sounds boring."

"You'll be there, and you're you, which means it is simply not possible for the evening to be boring. Trust me."

"You sound on edge. Did you go back to the theater?"

"I did, but I didn't get past the security guard."

"You must not be trying hard enough."

"Probably."

"That was a joke, my friend. Please promise me you won't go back in there until the authorities say it's safe. What if the murderer is still there, lurking behind the curtain or something?"

"I don't think we have final confirmation on the murder part. Maybe it was natural causes."

"Like maybe she was frightened to death by ghosts?"

That was a disturbing idea. "No. In fact, I'm hoping the ghosts might be able to tell me something about what happened."

"You know that won't stand up in a court of law, don't you? Pretty sure spectral evidence was outlawed after the Salem witch trials. Besides, ghosts are usually clueless about such things. Isn't that what you're always telling me?"

I had to admit she had a point. "Right."

"Did the last contractor see the ghosts? Is that why they left?"

"Good question. I really don't know. Anyway, my vote for our double date is to nix the fly-fishing and archery and focus on dinner."

"Fine." Luz sighed. "Too bad it's not Easter."

Luz is my oldest and dearest friend, and I usually understood her, so I searched my brain for relevant Easter events . . . "You're referring to the Bring Your Own Big Wheel race down Vermont Street?"

"Exactly. Most people think Lombard is the crookedest street in San Francisco, but it's really Vermont Street."

"Victor's a native San Franciscan, though, right? So he probably knows that already." Something occurred to me. "But wait a minute. We're going out this Saturday, right?"

"That was the plan."

"Problem solved: Saturday is the Fourth of July. Drinks, dinner, then fireworks. Fun *and* patriotic."

"You don't think that's lacking in imagination?" Luz said. "Oooh, wait—what about renting Segways and touring Golden Gate Park? You know, those scooter-like things?"

"Sure—that way, the four of us could spend quality time together in the ER after I run into a redwood tree. It'll be great, Luz."

"Just dinner and fireworks, huh?"

"Dinner and fireworks. Pick a restaurant. We'll talk later."

I headed farther down Mission Street to the Office of Permit Services, located on a nondescript city block full of office buildings, where I searched their database for the permits that had been pulled on the Crockett Theatre. But when the files came up, I saw the name of the original contractor had been blacked out. The only name on the forms was Gregory Thibodeaux "for the Xerxes Group."

"Hey, Renata, could I ask you a question?" I said. Renata had worked at the clerk's office for years, and knew me from way back.

"Sure. What's up?"

"Why is this information redacted?"

She spun the computer monitor around, perched a pair of pink-and-black polka-dot reading glasses on her nose, studied the permits, and frowned. "That's odd, for sure. I have no idea."

"You don't remember this project?"

"The old Crockett Theatre? I remember the place, and I remember hearing talk about fixing it up, but that's happened a few times over the years. A while back the city wanted to demolish it for a parking lot, but a community group got involved and shut that idea down, but a place like this is always debated for a long while. Usually nature eventually does the work of making it uninhabitable, and then it's a tear-down anyway. Sometimes owners do it on purpose, let the roof go until the place falls apart and becomes a public nuisance so they can get a demo permit."

"But do you remember any names in conjunction with this latest renovation project at the Crockett? Maybe the contractor associated with these permits?"

She shook her head. "Sorry, Mel. You know better than most how much paperwork comes through these doors. I can't keep track."

"Okay, thanks. Hey, how was your daughter's wedding?" Renata and I were at most acquaintances, but I always asked about her family because my father had taught me long ago that a contractor's relationship with the good people in the city permit department could make or break us. Besides, she was nice, and efficient, and a very proud mama.

"Gorgeous, if I do say so myself." Renata leaned on the counter and scrolled through the photos on her phone, holding out the best ones to show me. "They did a photo shoot at the Japanese Tea Garden. Can you believe how lovely it was?"

"That's beautiful. Congratulations."

"And how about you?" she asked. "Let me see the ring."

I held out my left hand, feeling a bit awkward.

"That's quite a rock you've got there, Mel. Isn't that pretty? So, have you and your British beau set the date yet?"

"Not yet. We're still figuring it out."

In truth, *I* was still figuring it out. Landon was champing at the bit to set a date and find a venue. Sensing my hesitation, he suggested that if I was overwhelmed at the thought of a big event, we could elope to Vegas and find an Elvis impersonator to marry us. But I wanted my family and friends around me: Dad and Stan and Caleb, Luz and Stephen and neighbors, our crew . . . I just wasn't ready to say exactly when and where.

"Don't wait too long, honey," Renata advised, patting my hand and closing the file. "Marriage isn't easy, but a good one is worth the trouble."

I put in a call to Stan and explained about the redacted permits.

"I've never heard of such a thing," he said.

"Neither have I. I really want to talk to the previous contractor, get their take on the theater and the consortium. I'm thinking there are only a handful of companies that could handle a job this size, right?"

"Locally, sure," said Stan. "But the investors are from out of town; they could have brought their own crew with them."

"Maybe. But when I was talking with Thibodeaux, I didn't get the impression it was out of town talent. So if it was someone local, who could it be? Bell Construction, the Miller Brothers, Gemini Construction . . ."

"Don't forget Avery Builders. Josh Avery has really turned the company around over the last year, and he bids on big, showy jobs like this one. They'd be the likeliest candidate for such a large project, I would think."

"Of course. Thanks."

Chapter Eleven

I had met Josh Avery one harrowing night when we were both invited to compete for a contract by surviving a sleepover at a haunted bed-and-breakfast in the Castro.

That went about as well as one might have assumed.

Like me, Josh had taken over running the family business, but unlike me, the world of building things and running crews had been entirely new to him. He also did not have sage advisers like my dad and Stan to help him make good choices. But Josh was no dummy, and Avery Builders was once again on solid footing and even boasted a suite of beautiful offices at the San Francisco Design Center with which to impress clients. I sometimes worried that the comparison with Turner Construction's decidedly down-home office cast us in a bad light, rather like leaving your baby with the unemployed neighbor next door instead of with the professional Irish nanny.

So far, given my father's reputation, our lack of professional offices hadn't been an issue, and Stan had developed and maintained a professional website with photographs of our jobsites and projects.

Still, I thought as I parked in front of the clutch of brick buildings that housed upscale interior designers, builders, and renovators, it would be nice to have a sophisticated office space like these. On the other hand, the lack of such a fancy storefront kept Turner Construction's overhead low. That allowed us to invest our profits in the business and pay our crew more than the going rate, which encouraged loyalty and kept turnover down in an industry famous for its itinerant workforce.

The lobby of the converted brick factory held a café, plenty of verdant potted plants, big multipaned windows, and scads of designer tchotchkes on display for the ladies and gentlemen who lunched.

In penance for eating donuts with Skeet, I skipped the elevator and climbed the three flights of stairs, and was puffing hard by the time I reached the offices of Avery Builders. In the front lobby, subtly lit niches held lovely objets d'art, and behind the reception desk sat an aptly beautiful man named Braden.

His angelic face lit up when he saw me, as though my arrival had given special meaning to his life.

"Oh. My. *Lord.* If it's not the ghost buster to the stars!" Braden exclaimed as he came around the desk to give me a hug. "Mel Turner, as I live and breathe!"

"It's been a while," I said, returning his squeeze. "How are you, Braden? And Josh?"

"Wonderful," Braden said. "Things have been going really well. I mean, you know how this business is—always a bit crazed, right? But still, business is steady, and our crew is much more settled than when we first met you. Tell me." His voice dropped. "Are you still seeing *spirits*?"

His big eyes glanced behind and around me, as though I might be toting a few phantom hitchhikers.

A lot of people have problems believing and understanding that I could see such things. Braden was not one of them—he had been an enthusiastic believer from the start.

"I confess, I am," I said with a wry smile. "As a matter of fact . . . I wanted to ask you and Josh about the Crockett Theatre. Did Avery Builders happen to work on the job there?"

Braden reared back. "We *did*. How did you know?"

"Lucky guess."

"That place," he said, and shook his head. "*Rampant* with ghosts—am I right?"

"Did you experience something there?"

"Oh no, you know me." He let out a sigh. "I'm not a sensitive. Oh, how I wish I were, but I don't have your gift."

"Your talents lie elsewhere. Like this gorgeous decorating job. I should bring you over to Turner Construction, see what you can do with the place." I could just see my father's face upon walking into our den after a Braden makeover.

"I would be honored," he said without hesitation. "Just pick up the phone. But for now you're probably here to see Josh?"

"I am, if he's available."

"Go right on in."

The interior office was even more muted and sophisticated than the reception area, and that was saying a lot. Mozart played softly in the background, and everything, from the artwork to the bookshelf, was subtly lit.

Josh stood up and greeted me with a big smile and a friendly hug, and we spent a few moments catching up and gossiping. Although technically Avery Builders and Turner Construction were rivals, it was rare that we competed head-to-head for a project, and because we both believed in playing fair, we even helped each other out from time to time.

Then I asked him about the Crockett Theatre.

"Don't mention that project to me," he said, frowning.

"That bad?"

"Talk about your headaches. I swear, it was as though the investors were *trying* to make things difficult."

"How do you mean?"

"For one thing, they insisted I work around those squatters. You have any idea what a pain in the ass that was?"

"I thought they were being civic-minded."

"Yeah, not so sure."

"Josh, why wasn't your name on the city permits?"

"What are you talking about?"

"On the permits you pulled for the foundation work, the contractor's name was redacted."

"News to me," said Josh. "I pulled the standard permits, like always. Everything passed inspection."

I nodded and made a note to push Gregory Thibodeaux on that subject, once he was up to chatting. "Did you . . . I know this is an odd question, but did you ever hear or see anything out of the ordinary there in the theater?"

"You mean like the haunted B and B where we met?"

"Yes, just like that."

He gave me a crooked smile and a little shrug. "There were times I could have sworn I smelled popcorn, but I'm pretty sure that was simply the power of suggestion. Some of my workers got a little freaked out . . . but we weren't inside that much."

"Which craftspeople did you bring in for the decorative work? Get any bids?"

"We didn't get that far. Since we were working around the squatters, we focused first on the foundation. In fact . . . I should tell you, there were some discrepancies in the paperwork."

"What kind of discrepancies?"

"There were some no-show jobs listed." He held up

his hands in surrender. "They weren't mine, I swear to all that is holy."

No-show jobs were the sort of corruption common to big projects: charging the client for carpenters or bricklayers or other skilled labor that never actually showed up to work.

"You never figured out who set them up?"

He shook his head.

"How did you get the gig in the first place?" I continued.

"Hey, Turner Construction isn't the only firm with a rep for historical renovation. We did the work on Eamon Castle."

"And here I thought Turner Construction had an exclusive on castle renovations."

"I've heard great things about your work in Marin," Josh said. "Kudos. I'll have to check it out next time I'm in the area."

"You should. But seriously, what's Eamon Castle?"

"It's an old building in Hunters Point, near the old Candlestick Park. It was originally a brewery. The most interesting thing about it, besides the fact that it's built of stone, is that there are caverns underneath with fresh spring water running through them."

"Interesting. Water in the basement is usually a bad thing."

"Not in the land of drought," Josh said. "The brewers used the water to make their beer, and later someone tried to bottle and sell it as spring water. But now it's just an attraction."

"Is it a private home?" I asked.

"No. The owners live on the Peninsula and renovated it for use as an event venue," he continued. "They had a caretaker living there for a while, working on the old piping for the water. A young industrial designer, really colorful character."

"What do you mean by colorful?"

"He's a young man, but he always wore feather boas, that sort of thing."

"Was his name Alyx, by any chance?"

Josh looked surprised. "You know him?"

"We've met. He used to live in Eamon Castle?"

"Yes, but he left before we finished the project. He was the one who mentioned the Crockett Theatre project to me—that's how I got the gig."

"You don't know how I could get in touch with Alyx, do you?"

He shook his head. "You might check with the people who own Eamon Castle, Linda and Alan Peterson. They seemed pretty tight with Alyx."

He gave me the Petersons' phone number. In these parts, "living on the Peninsula" was usually shorthand for "rolling in dough," especially when combined with owning a castle in San Francisco.

"What about the preservationists?" I asked.

"What about them?"

"Did you have any trouble with them? Were they on your case, that sort of thing?"

"Mostly they seemed happy to see us working on the building. They weren't shy about voicing their opinions, but we were working off drawings that were already approved, so mostly I just listened politely."

"Did you hear about a reality TV show to be filmed at the Crockett?"

"You mean Isadora's brother's thing? Last I heard, she was dead set against it. Called reality TV 'dreck,' if I recall. You've met her, I take it? Quite the character. You should ask her about it directly."

I realized Josh hadn't heard about Isadora's fate. This was awkward. "Um, I hate to tell you this, but Isadora . . . Isadora is dead."

He stilled. "She's—? What? When?"

"Yesterday. She was found dead in the theater."

"An accident? Did she fall or get sick?"

"There's no official cause of death yet, but it looks suspicious."

"Suspicious? As in murder?"

I nodded.

"I . . . I don't . . ." He shook his head and let out a long breath. "What a shame. She was so young, and she was . . . a real character."

"What can you tell me about her? Did she give you any problems when you were working on the theater? Mix it up with any of your guys or anything like that?"

"You mean, did one of my men go back to the Crockett and kill her?"

"That's not what I meant. I'm just asking questions, trying to figure it out."

"Like you did at the haunted B and B."

"Something like that."

"You seem to deal with more murders on the job than the norm."

"Tell me about it."

"Don't envy you that," Josh said with a sigh. "Anyway, no, I can't imagine why anyone would want to kill Isadora. She asked a lot of questions, mostly about the ownership of the theater, that sort of thing, but—"

"What, you mean like she wanted to buy the place?"

"Why would you think that? She's homeless."

"She's a Sepety; I've been told the family is quite wealthy."

"Oh right, of course. Still. I had the sense she was asking more about the Xerxes Group—their right to be renovating the place, that sort of thing. Look, Mel, I didn't know any of the squatters well, but I liked them well enough. Other than the fact that they wanted us gone, they weren't difficult to deal with. I've had much worse times with cranky homeowners, if you know what I mean."

"I certainly do."

"Plus, we didn't run into them often." He paused and

looked thoughtful. "There was one fellow, though . . . Mitch? I think? He was a little confrontational, got in our faces a bit. But it was no big deal, mostly name-calling, silly kid stuff."

I nodded. "They seem to have vanished into the ether after Isadora's death. I get the sense they're not fond of the police. I was hoping to talk to at least some of them, ask if anyone saw anything."

"No offense, but isn't that something the police should be doing?"

"I have specialized knowledge the police don't have."

"Yeah? Like what?"

"I found you, didn't I? Bet the police haven't contacted you yet."

Josh inclined his head. "I see your point."

"Don't worry. If I learn anything useful, I'll take it to the police."

"So, do you think one of the other squatters killed Isadora?"

"I have no idea. The security guard mentioned she had more than one boyfriend, so maybe it's simple as jealousy run amok."

"She did have a way about her. Such a shame."

I stood up to leave when Josh said, "Hey, have you tried the tattoo parlor?"

"What tattoo parlor?"

"Down the street from the theater. One of the squatters worked there . . . Can't remember her name. She always wore shoes with a mirrored finish; I think it was her signature."

"It's a place to start. Thank you."

"Good luck. And, Mel? Be careful with the Xerxes Group. Everything was going just fine, we'd hit a few snags but nothing insurmountable, and were even running ahead of schedule. Then out of the blue, I get a call from their flunky, that too smooth Thibodeaux guy, canceling the contract and threatening legal action if I didn't just walk away."

"No reason given?"

He shook his head. "Not really. It took me by surprise."

"How did you respond?"

"I walked. They made it easier by sending me a nice check; wasn't worth the headache to pursue it. There are plenty of juicy renovation jobs in the Bay Area at the moment."

True enough. And his projects probably weren't even haunted.

It was late afternoon by the time I left the offices of Avery Builders. What now? I supposed I should get back to work, but . . .

I looked up Eamon Castle on my phone. Yet another local place of interest I'd never heard of, though in a relatively small city like San Francisco, the number of historical nooks and crannies was impressive. If Eamon Castle had always been in private hands, it made sense I didn't know about it. I thought about driving by and checking it out, but it was on Innes Avenue, not far from the old Candlestick Park. At this time of day, traffic on the freeways leading south was brutal.

Besides, what did I hope to find? Josh had said Alyx no longer worked there. Still, I was interested to see the building and check out Avery Builders' work. If Alyx seemed tight with the Petersons, they might help me to locate him.

I called the Eamon Castle phone listing and asked a very nice woman named Shanice if I could come by to see the place as a possible wedding venue. Even though it was a holiday weekend, she mentioned she was working to set up an event, so we made an appointment for Saturday afternoon. Then I tried the Petersons' home

phone number, but no one answered. I left a message
asking them to call me back about Eamon Castle, at
their convenience.

I checked my phone: None of the squatters had
called me back. No surprise there.

After responding to a few queries from my crews on
our current jobs, I had a long conversation with Mateo
about the windows at Turner Villa. I was committed to
saving the original old wavy glass, but that meant the
wood frames would have to be rebuilt. That would be
no easy feat and would cost a small fortune.

Still, antique wavy window glass? How great was
that?

I fielded another text from Luz, this time suggesting
a hike to the labyrinth created by Eduardo Aguilera at
Land's End, with sweeping views of the Golden Gate
Bridge in the background.

I responded: Dinner. Fireworks. 'Nuff said.

Phone business concluded, I headed to the Haight,
an area famous as San Francisco's former "hippie haven." Long before young people flocked to the neighborhood in search of gentle people with flowers in their
hair, the Haight had been an ethnic enclave, providing
low-cost housing for Irish and Italian working-class
folks. The Haight's once "humble" old Victorians now
sold at a premium. These days there was no such thing
as reasonably priced housing anywhere in the Bay
Area, but especially within the San Francisco city
limits.

Hence the rise in the number of squatters.

I knew someone in the Haight who might be able to
tell me a little something about the dress Hildy had
given me, which had provoked such a disturbing image
when I tried it on. Her name was Lily Ivory, and she
owned a vintage clothing store on the corner of Haight
and Ashbury streets. She was a somewhat odd but very
interesting woman whom I had met one memorable

Halloween while dealing with seemingly possessed dolls found in the attic of an old Victorian named Spooner House.

Lily knew a lot about old clothes, and even more about spirits and magic and things that went bump in the night.

After a few loops around the bustling main shopping drag, I found a tight parking space on a residential side street and made my way down crowded Haight Street, dodging tourists and panhandlers, until I came upon Aunt Cora's Closet.

As I entered, a bell on the door tinkled overhead.

Walking into Aunt Cora's Closet, with its scents of clean laundry and the faint perfume of herbal sachets, was like walking into another world. Taffeta and crinolines, sequins and satins filled the place, reminding me of Hildy's overstuffed closet. Parasols, hats, and gloves graced the shelves, and truly antique dresses and laces adorned the walls. In one corner was an herbal stand touting custom teas and featuring a sign with a quote from the amiable Wiccan Rede: *An it harm none, do what ye will.*

I spend all day, every day, working primarily with men, so it was fun to find myself in such an overtly feminine, woman-focused arena.

"Why, Mel Turner, I do declare!" Lily exclaimed as I came clomping in, my work boots ringing loudly on the bare wood floors. She spoke with the soft drawl of her native West Texas. "It's been too long. What with your wardrobe proclivities, I thought you'd be in here more often."

Lily's pet, a miniature Vietnamese potbellied pig, trotted up to greet me with a snort. I scratched his pink neck.

"I keep planning to drop by," I said. "But life has a way of intervening."

"Don't I know it. What's up with you these days?"

"Oh, you know . . ." I shrugged off her question. Two college-age girls were flipping through a rack of fringed leather jackets, but otherwise we were alone in the store. "How's Maya doing?"

"She's great." Lily's eyes were so dark they were almost black, and had a way of fixing on me as though she were reading my mind. Lily had sworn to me she did not have that ability, and promised that she wouldn't use it without my consent even if she did. But at the moment she didn't need to read my mind as much as my face.

"I'm afraid you find me alone today, with only Oscar for company," Lily said with a tilt of her head. "Are you sure everything's okay, Mel?"

I nodded but let out an admittedly shaky breath. "It's been an eventful couple of days."

"'Eventful' usually means a bit scary in our lives, doesn't it?"

I didn't know Lily well, but we had shared enough to know that we both tripped over bodies much more than was considered normal. She probably had the cell number of an SFPD homicide inspector memorized, as well.

"Do you want to tell me about it?" she continued.

I glanced again at the girls looking at jackets, but they turned and left, the bell ringing over the door. I breathed a sigh of relief. I wasn't sure how this sort of thing went, so if Lily "saw" what I had seen when I put on the dress . . .

"At the moment, I'd like to ask you about something unrelated. Or . . . actually it might be related, but I have no idea how." I pulled the dress Hildy had given me out of my tote bag, and spread it on the horseshoe-shaped glass display case that doubled as a counter.

"Oh!" Lily exclaimed. "Isn't this lovely! I adore this era of clothing."

"Me, too."

"I have too many curves to really pull it off, though."

"Me, too."

Lily chuckled. "Bust and hips. They get you every time. Ruin the line."

I noticed she hadn't touched the dress, but her nostrils flared slightly.

"Cedar and cigarette smoke?"

I nodded. "It was kept in a cedar closet."

"With a smoker?"

"Yes."

Our eyes met.

"What can I help you with, Mel?"

"I tried it on last night and saw something. Like a vision."

Her eyebrows arched. "And that's not typical for you, to see something when you touch a historic item?"

"Not at all." *Please, oh please don't let this be some sort of new psychic ability,* I begged. Seeing ghosts was weird enough. I could just imagine experiencing visions every time I touched something in a historic home. "Is . . . Do you happen to know anything about seeing things in mirrors—things that aren't there?"

"I'm no expert, but many believe mirrors can be portals to the backwards world."

"The backwards world."

"It's another world, one that mirrors ours but is autonomous . . . It's actually pretty complicated to explain."

"What I saw was historical, I think, and attached to this dress. I think."

Lily stuck her chin out as though lost in thought, and then gave a firm nod. "Best not to tell me too much, right off the bat. I don't like to have preconceived notions when I feel for things."

"Okay . . ." The pig came prancing over, butting at my ankles. I leaned over to scratch him behind his pink ears.

When I straightened, Lily was cradling the dress to her chest, her eyes half closed.

She dropped it on the counter.

"*Huh,*" she said.

"Huh? That's all?"

"Well, Mel, you seem to have quite a find here. Where did you say it came from?"

"From an attic closet in a home that Landon and I are renovating in Oakland. It will be our home together." My ring glittered, and its lights caught my attention. I didn't wear it most days, because wearing a ring can be dangerous on a construction site. But on days like today, when I was just meeting people and talking, I enjoyed the audacious sparkle. "Did I mention Landon and I got engaged?"

"*No*, you did *not*. That's wonderful! I was married recently myself. Well, actually, it was a witchy handfasting in the redwoods, so I suppose it isn't legally a wedding per se, but it is to us, and that's all that matters."

I wasn't certain what a "witchy handfasting" might entail, though in my mind's eye, it included a lot of nudity and dancing under a full moon. But perhaps I was too influenced by medieval woodcuts of pagan ceremonies.

"Congratulations, Lily. I hope you will be very happy."

"Thank you. But back to this beauty," she said, laying her hands on the dress again. She looked worried. "Were you planning to wear this for your wedding?"

I coughed. "For what?"

"As your wedding gown?"

"Oh. I don't think . . . I haven't really thought about that yet."

"It can take a while to find just the right dress. I have some options here that I think would suit you, if you're interested."

"Oh thanks. Maybe another time."

"Of course. The thing is, Mel, this dress has seen some trauma."

"I was wondering about that. What kind of trauma?"

"Could you leave it with me for a day or two? I'll be able to feel more when I brew."

"Sure." I didn't really understand Lily's abilities, but I knew I could trust her. "Is there anything you can tell me about it, though?"

"Such as?"

"Was . . . Could the original owner of this dress, for instance, be a murderer?"

She burst out with a surprised laugh. "A *murderer*? Oh, I hadn't thought of that. I really don't think so . . . but the poor soul who last wore this dress departed this life far too soon—that much I know."

"You mean . . . she was killed?"

"I mean she died too young. I just don't know how or why."

Chapter Twelve

There was one more item on my to-do list before diving back into traffic and heading for home. I drove toward the Crockett Theatre, not to further harass Skeet but to check out the tattoo parlor that Josh Avery had mentioned.

A glance in the rearview mirror made me ponder what Lily had told me about the "backwards world." Had I really viewed something through a mystical portal when I put on Hildy's dress? Or had I simply experienced a vision, like when I first walked into that house and thought I was experiencing déjà vu, when I was in fact "seeing" bits and pieces of my mother's memories. Was I developing more extensive psychic abilities? Did I even *want* to? What was I supposed to do with such rarified—and terrifying—abilities? I already had a day job.

None of those questions would be answered anytime soon. I pulled into a parking space not far from the Crockett and headed for the tattoo parlor. I walked in to find a petite, pretty young woman leaning over the beefy biceps of a customer, a lamp shining a harsh bright spotlight on his skin as though he were undergoing surgery. He winced as the woman, peering through a magnifying glass, jabbed him repeatedly with her needle.

The tattoo artist was dressed all in black, but her shoes were as shiny as mirrors. Her name was Tierney, if I recalled our introduction in the Crockett Theatre's ladies' lounge. I remembered how her voice rose at the end of each sentence, as though she were always asking questions.

"Got an appointment?" she asked, not looking up from her work.

"No," I replied. "But I can wait."

"I'll be done in a few? But I have another appointment soon? You can look through those books if you're just trying to figure out, like, your dream?"

Trying to figure out my dream, indeed. I gazed at the art hanging on the wall: The tattoo studio doubled as a gallery. There were scenes of people and nature, landscapes and abstracts. Some were beautiful while others were downright disturbing. All appeared to have been drawn by a different hand.

I took a seat and flipped through the books of tattoo designs. My only experience with tattoos was the transfer kind that came in boxes of children's cereal and washed off with soap and water. Caleb had been mad for them; I put a whole book of temporary tattoos in his stocking one Christmas, and we spent the rest of the day applying them to any and all visible parts of our bodies. His father, Daniel, refused to try a single one, which was one sign among many that we weren't right for each other.

I'd never been to a tattoo parlor, and though many people I knew sported ink, it was never something I'd given much thought to. I was surprised at how varied the designs were. There was page after page of options, from the stereotypical sailor's tats featuring hearts devoted to MOM, to New Agey fairies and elves, to all kinds of sayings in various languages. I couldn't imagine choosing a design to imprint on my skin for a lifetime.

Except in the field of construction, making decisions isn't my strong suit.

As I perused the books, I kept sneaking peeks at Tierney and her client. She seemed to be drawing an intricate portrait of some kind. It was strangely fascinating to watch the process, the application of ink below the skin, dabbing away tiny beads of blood that arose in outraged response to the needle. I thought of what I had learned in anthropology about the traditions of tattooing in different cultures, and how they defined those who were part of a social group. Today, tattoos seemed more a way to define one's individuality.

Tierney finally stood back, tilted her head this way and that, added a few more details, then nodded. "What do you think?" she asked her client.

He looked at his arm in the mirror. The tattooed portrait was red and angry-looking, but I imagined that would settle down in a few days.

"That's awesome. Looks just like him," he said. "Thanks."

"Glad you like it," she said, already busy cleaning and arranging her instruments. She instructed her client to keep the tattoo clean and to apply antibiotic cream twice a day.

They settled the bill, and as Tierney washed her hands, she asked, without looking at me: "See anything you like? I can adapt anything, but maybe the books give you some ideas?"

"These designs are impressive," I said, flipping through a few more pages. "I had no idea there were so many."

"I can also copy anything you bring me, or make one up for you."

"It's a little overwhelming . . ."

"You're a virgin?"

"I'm sorry?"

"A tattoo virgin?"

"Oh yes. I am."

"A blank slate," she said, drying her hands on a paper towel. "I can work with that."

"I like the *idea* of a tattoo," I said. "But when I think about living with something on my skin for the rest of my life . . . I can never decide."

"The secret is to start, like, small? But I'll warn you. It can get addictive." She smiled as she joined me at the table, but the smile froze on her face, replaced by suspicion. "Wait. I know you?"

I nodded. "We met at the Crockett yesterday."

"Isadora's day of transformation."

"What do you mean?"

"Death, the ultimate transformation?" she said, the "duh" implied. "You were there with the suit, talking about the renovation?"

"I was, yes. You're . . . Tierney, right?"

She folded her arms. "What are you doing here?"

"I've been trying to get in touch with all of you. Have you spoken with the police?"

"You think one of *us* is responsible for what happened? We love Isadora. She's, like, family?"

"I'm not saying any of you did it, Tierney. But you were there and might have seen or heard something that could help the police figure out what happened."

"Why? What's the point?"

"To get justice," I said, surprised. "If a friend of mine died suddenly, I'd want to know why and if anyone was responsible."

"There is no justice but karmic justice."

"Um . . ." I was never sure how to respond to this sort of comment. I understand that the legal system might not impose the same justice as the universe, but letting a possible murder go unanswered didn't strike me as acceptable. It wasn't an "oopsie" moment, like failing to return your shopping cart to the cart corral.

"So," I said, changing the subject, because I was *not*

going to chase Tierney down that philosophical rabbit hole. "You work here, full-time?"

"Why do you sound surprised? Squatters have to work for a living, too. We might not pay rent, but survival isn't free, and most of us don't have family money, you know. It's not as though we chose this lifestyle."

Tierney's defenses were on high alert, I thought, and spoke more gently.

"I understand. I got the sense that you all were creating a new society, a creative community, at the Crockett."

She nodded and let out a long, slow breath. When she spoke, her voice sounded wistful. "We were. We are. But when it comes down to it, I think we'd all like to have a hot shower once in a while, maybe a house with a yard. I dunno. Get a cat or a dog, maybe?"

I smiled. "That would be nice, for most of us, I think."

She nodded.

"Where are you from originally?" I asked.

"Small town in southern Utah," she said. "A place nobody's ever heard of, not that you'd want to."

"You like it here, in San Francisco?" *Enough to live illegally in an abandoned theater with no hot water, and ghosts, and murderers?*

She nodded. "It's really, like, open-minded here? I didn't fit in well where I grew up. I saw that movie *The Craft*? And afterward I started reading tarot cards and stuff, and our priest told my mom I was in league with the devil. Practicing witchcraft. You believe that?"

"I just came from visiting a friend who's a witch. She's really cool. Owns a vintage clothing store, Aunt Cora's Closet, in the Haight."

"Oh cool. I should, like, go visit her?"

"I think you'd love her, and her store. Right on the corner of Ashbury. So, do *you* have any tattoos?"

"Only this one." She lifted her hair to show me what

looked like a tribal tattoo on the nape of her neck. "I was in the Philippines and went to see this ancient woman who will tattoo you in the traditional way. You don't choose there, though. She just marks you with whatever she wants. She's way cool."

"I like it. Do you know what it means?"

"She said it referred to strength. I hope it doesn't say something really bad, like 'obnoxious American tourist' or something like that." She let out a low chuckle.

I smiled. "I always wonder about that sort of thing, too. Tierney, I know you don't want to talk about it, but I really want to find out what happened to Isadora. Setting aside the question of justice for Isadora, the murderer might still be around and pose a danger to you and the others."

She shrugged, went over to a tall drafting table, and started adding details to an elaborate sketch of a winged fairy.

"Do we even know it was murder, for sure?"

"Not yet, but it's rare that someone like Isadora—young and in good health—simply drops dead." On top of a Wurlitzer. Also, people around me tended to die a violent death. "It's best to err on the side of caution, don't you think? Skeet the security guard tells me Isadora wanted to show him something, but never got the chance. Do you know what that could have been about?"

She shook her head.

"Did Isadora, or any of you, find items of value in the theater?"

"First you accuse us of murder, and now stealing?"

"I'm not accusing anyone of anything, Tierney. I'm just trying to figure out a possible reason for all of this. Can you think of any sort of motive to kill Isadora?"

She erased a line on her drawing and started sketching anew. Without looking up, she said, "Only thing I can think of is those old candy wrappers?"

"Excuse me?"

"Isadora really got into collecting these vintage candy wrappers? Sometimes they even had candy still in them, which was kind of gross."

"Where did she find them?"

"She said they were in the thingamajig under the balcony."

"What thingamajig?" I asked, trying to picture the balcony.

"If I knew what it was called, I wouldn't call it a thingamajig."

Touché.

"It was, like, the place where things would fall if they were dropped?" she continued. "I guess people lost a lot of things over the years. She found matchbooks, too, and old-fashioned calling cards, bottles, some old lipsticks. A whole bunch of old coins. Whatever people might carry in their pockets. She said they must have fallen through the cracks, or rolled down the floor to the openings and slipped through, or maybe were swept into it by a lazy usher. She said the area was supposed to be cleaned out regularly, but probably wasn't."

Wait a minute—could the opening to the "thingamajig" refer to the mushroom-shaped iron caps over the ventilators that I had seen when I was in the balcony with Gregory yesterday?

"I can't believe this is happening," Tierney said quietly, and her voice caught in her throat. "Isadora was good to everyone. She was such a beautiful soul. I don't know what we'll do without her."

I was hit by another wave of sadness for Isadora's life, cut short. I remembered Alyx glaring at me and asking why I wasn't more affected by the discovery of Isadora's body. I didn't want to tell him: "Because it's not my first corpse." It was human nature to adapt to circumstances, to become accustomed to a new normal, which in my case meant seeing ghosts and finding dead bodies.

But this was a life lost. A young woman forever gone.

Snap out of it, Mel. Focus on what you're good at: remodeling buildings, talking to ghosts, and occasionally tripping over things that help solve murders. Leave the grief to Isadora's friends and family.

Good advice—but easier said than done.

"Is there anything else you can think of? Was anyone acting oddly around Isadora? Was she afraid of anyone? Or has anyone been acting strange since she died?"

"I'm . . . Not in terms of what happened, 'cause he wouldn't hurt a fly, but I'm really worried about Liam."

I searched my memory: Liam was the big, bearlike guy with the wide blue eyes, like an overgrown doll.

"He was sort of like Isadora's shadow?" Tierney continued. "He's been desperate for money, and really tried to talk her into doing that stupid reality show."

"He's desperate for money?"

"Don't judge. I've done some truly wretched things for money myself."

"I'm not judging. Just wondering. Was Liam working with Isadora's brother, Ringo, to convince her to do the reality show?"

She shrugged again. "Maybe."

"How about Mitch?"

"What about him?"

"I just wondered . . . He seemed a little on edge."

"Mitch is always on edge," she said dismissively. "But I mean, he's okay. Anyway, aren't you being a little sexist in your assumption that if Isadora was killed, then a man did it? Maybe *I* killed her. Ever think of that?"

"I'm trying not to assume anything. Just asking questions."

"I already told you: You're looking in the wrong place. We were a community. None of us would have done this."

I decided to try another tack: "Have you ever seen anything odd in the theater? I've heard rumors about ghosts."

She gave a humorless laugh. "You'll have to ask Alyx about that. He was the one who, like, always insisted on it? Every once in a while, the Wurlitzer rose up, but I'm pretty sure Alyx made that happen. He's an engineer, you know? He's always screwing around with the clock-works for the marquee, that sort of thing. Anyway, unless you need help picking a tattoo, I should get back to work."

"Yeah, I should get going. But, Tierney, are you still living in the theater? And the others? Even after what just happened?"

"Where else are we supposed to go?"

Maybe someplace other than a haunted theater where a murder just occurred.

"But—"

"But *what*?" she demanded, her delicate chin raised in defiance.

"I'm just worried about you. Until we know what happened—"

"Don't you worry about me, *Mamacita*. You worry about yourself."

Mamacita? Was I *that* old?

"Okay, one final question: How do you get in and out of the theater? It's considered an active crime scene at the moment, so the doors are sealed."

"Where there's a will, there's a way," she said, glancing at the door. "Anyway, my client is here."

I turned toward the door. Steeped in old movie stereotypes about tattoo parlors, I half expected to see a burly sailor on shore leave.

Instead, in walked a willowy young woman in a sweet floral dress whose smooth skin, I imagined, would soon be imprinted with a drawing of a fairy in a forest glen.

Out on the sidewalk, I surveyed the Crockett Theatre again, zeroing in on the fire escapes. If the squatters were able to break in so easily, then surely I could as well. But the rusting fire escapes looked a little dicey, and a several-story fall to the pavement below would not end well for me.

Not to mention, it made me dizzy, just thinking of it. I still had vertigo to contend with.

But I wanted to get back in that theater, to see if Isadora's spirit would take a break from her dancing to speak to me, tell me something about what had happened.

Not so long ago I would have avoided the murder scene, and its resident ghosts, like the plague. But this wasn't my first rodeo. Ghosts scared the heck out of me, but had never actually hurt me, and as I understood it, their ability to cause harm to the living was largely theoretical. Still . . . the memory of that glassy-eyed ghostly audience made me quail a bit. Not to mention the in-your-face phantom usher. *May I show you to your seat?*

Still, the main reason I didn't try to break in and look around was 100 percent human, and far more formidable than any ghost: Inspector Annette Crawford.

I checked my phone, but she still hadn't called me back.

As I went to find my car, I spied an elegant woman walking a small white dog so fluffy it looked like a plush toy. It was the preservationist Coco—as in Chanel. I admired her apparent comfort with wearing a turban and a flamboyant multicolored wrap and wondered if I would ever be able to pull something like that off.

"Coco!" I called out. She stopped and waved.

I trotted across the street. "I'm Mel Turner. We met yesterday?"

"You'll be working on the theater," Coco said.

"Yes, exactly. I mean, I hope so . . . soon," I said, glancing at the bright yellow crime scene tape that warned us all to stay away.

"What in the *world* happened there? I heard sirens yesterday, and now . . ." She left off with a dramatic sigh.

"Could I buy you a drink, maybe, or a cup of coffee, and we could talk?"

"I'm afraid I must get back home. It's time to feed Martha. My little baby, here." She cooed at the little white fluffball.

I bent down and held out my hand, and Martha's tiny wet nose bumped up against it. "I have a big brown dog. The two of them don't even look like the same species."

She laughed. "I tell you what. I live just around the corner. Why don't you come with me and I'll fix us both a cup of tea?"

"Thank you," I said. "That sounds lovely."

"Here we are," she said just a few minutes later, gesturing to a grand old Victorian that had been divided up into flats.

As we walked into the classic paneled foyer, fragrant from a large floral arrangement on a demilune table, we were joined by a large, bearded man who held the door for us.

"Oh! This is fortuitous!" Coco crooned. "Mel, this is Baldwin. Baldwin just moved into the building, but he and I worked together with the Crockett Caretakers to preserve that beautiful theater. Baldwin, Mel is in charge of the crew that will be *renovating* the Crockett. Isn't that a *scream*?"

I looked at her, not understanding her meaning. She laid a perfumed hand on my arm.

"It's just *marvelous* what women get up to these days," Coco said, pronouncing the word as "MAH-ve-lous."

"It's nice to meet you, Mel," Baldwin said, smiling warmly and shaking my hand. His wrinkled shirt hung loose out of his saggy jeans, and his longish hair was uncombed. Standing beside the sleek Coco, he looked like a humble prop assistant tending to a grand film star.

"What an interesting name," I said. "I haven't met a lot of Baldwins."

"My folks are real movie fans. Guess that's how I got into all this preservation stuff. I—"

"Baldwin," interrupted Coco. "I was about to fix Mel a cup of tea. Would you care to join us? We can talk about the Crockett in a more dignified setting."

I thought the building's paneled entry, with its velvet banquette and chandelier, was itself rather dignified, but Baldwin and I followed her up the stairs.

Coco's second-floor apartment was a San Francisco fantasy fulfilled: bright and spacious, with large windows and high ceilings. One corner of the living room opened onto a round tower room with a built-in circular bench that was topped with soft-looking pillows and wraparound windows that offered a nearly 360-degree view. The walls were lined with bookshelves and posters, and a grand piano held pride of place smack in the middle of the living room.

"I'll feed my little baby, Martha, and put on some water," Coco said, waving a large, graceful hand in my direction. "Please, make yourselves at home. Do feel free to look around."

"This is just beautiful," I said. "So, Baldwin, Coco said you recently moved in? Is your apartment as amazing as this one?"

He smiled and shook his head. "At the moment it's nothing but cardboard boxes and a mattress on the floor. But a man can dream."

From the kitchen came the sounds of Coco cooing to the pup, and the faucet running. Baldwin glanced toward the other room, then back at me.

"Coco's okay, really. I know she can seem a little much . . . but I don't know. I think she's sort of great. I try to look out for her, check in occasionally, make sure she's eating."

"That's nice of you."

"I'm not entirely unselfish," he said. "It's like having a wacky grandma who worked in old Hollywood and knew everyone. She's walking history. I like to think of myself as an amateur filmmaker of sorts; I love old films. Old things in general."

"I'm a fan of old things myself. There are a few of us around, I guess."

"So you're in charge of the renovation now, huh?" Baldwin asked. At my nod, he continued. "Interested in seeing old photographs of the theater?"

"I'd love to." The file supplied by the Xerxes Group had included some old photos, but I would take all I could get. Photographs of a historic building were a boon to renovators. Physical descriptions were better than nothing, but only a photograph could offer the kind of detailed information about the particulars of interior and exterior designs that I needed to do my best work.

Baldwin pulled an iPad from his backpack and started scrolling through photos that, he explained, he had scanned and uploaded. "I run a Facebook group for the Crockett Caretakers. Our page includes historical photos and updates on the theater's progress. You're welcome to join and see what we have there."

"Very impressive," I said. I wondered why Gregory hadn't mentioned it; this could be a resource.

Baldwin flipped past a map, and I stopped him. "Is that a floor plan of the theater?"

"It is, yes. Since you're doing the renovation you probably have the original blueprints, but as I'm sure you know, buildings don't always conform to the original plans. Walls are moved, bathrooms are added, that sort of thing, as needs change."

"What's the date on it?"

"From the 1950s, I think. It's accessible online as well."

"This is really great information, Baldwin."

He beamed. "Thank you. It's a lot of work, but it's

worth it. So, if it's official, I'll post that Turner Construction is taking over the renovation of the Crockett?"

I nodded. "Sure."

"*Bald*-win," Coco called from the kitchen, "would you be a dear and come open this jar for me?"

While Baldwin assisted our hostess, I took advantage of her hospitality and looked around. Even before I was in the trades, I had adored exploring houses, especially elegant historic ones like this. It wasn't just the beauty of the lines or the craftsmanship of the details, the ceiling borders, or the carved lintels. I imagined myself in every home I entered, picturing in my mind the different sort of life I would have lived if this were my home.

My Realtor friend, Brittany, once said I would have been a nightmare client because of that tendency—also because I would have flatly refused to enter any I deemed lacking character.

The walls in Coco's apartments were decorated with numerous framed playbills interspersed with artworks from all over the world.

"These are nice," I said, noting a dented corbel, a small carved cupid, and a chipped finial sitting on a shelf.

"Salvage," Coco said, coming up behind me with two steaming mugs in her hands. "Earl Grey. Mel, do you care for sugar, or honey, or lemon, or cream?"

"No, thank you. This is perfect." I took the tea and blew on it. "So, you salvaged these pieces?"

She nodded. "A couple of decades ago, they started tearing down many of the old buildings in the city. Even plain-looking apartment buildings often had these decorations, little bits and pieces to lift them above the plebeian."

I nodded. "I can see why you became involved with the preservation of the Crockett."

Coco smiled and without warning burst out into a rendition of "Memory," from the musical *Cats*. Her voice wasn't bad, but she had clearly been trained in projecting to the cheap seats, and sang *very* loudly. I wanted to back away but thought that would be rude, so I just stood there, sipping my tea and smiling.

I glanced at Baldwin, who was watching Coco and beaming.

"Let your memory lead you . . . If you find there the meaning of what happiness is, then a new life will begin!"

Coco clasped her hands under her chin. "'I was beautiful then,' so goes the song. And I was."

"You were indeed," I said, looking at a framed glamour photo of Coco taken when she must have been in her twenties. "And you still are."

"I second that opinion," said Baldwin. "Most heartily."

"Oh, *pshaw*," Coco said, waving us off. "I was a dancer, really. Never terribly successful at singing or acting, though I tried."

I pointed to a framed photograph of Isadora Duncan, the renowned dancer from the early 1900s, that was perched on a table next to the sofa. In the photo, Duncan held her head so high she was looking down her nose at the camera.

"Is Isadora Duncan your hero?" I asked.

"I suppose so. Whether people realize it or not, she's probably a hero to any modern dancer. Much like Martha Graham, but so much earlier."

"All I really know about Duncan is her manner of death, I'm sorry to say."

"Ah yes, such a tragedy. Her long scarf got tangled in the wheel of the car she was riding in. She was yanked clear out of the car and her neck broke, just like that." She snapped her fingers. "Very dramatic, very memorable."

The way Coco said this made me wonder if she, too, aspired to an equally dramatic, memorable death.

"But she is worth remembering for much more than her manner of death," Coco continued. "She was a revolutionary artist, a dancer who broke the rules of conventional ballet. She was also proudly bisexual and a communist, at a time when it was scandalous to be either, much less both."

"I didn't know that. Fascinating."

"Isadora Duncan grew up in Oakland, did you know?" added Coco. "Gertrude Stein said of her, after her death: 'Affectations can be dangerous.'"

"Is that right? I saw that phrase in the Crockett Theatre, written on a wall in the ladies' lounge. What does it refer to?"

"I suppose Stein meant that those putting on airs would rue the day, in the end . . . I don't know exactly, to be honest. Perhaps it was simply that we shouldn't wear long scarves, at least not while riding in convertibles."

"Gertrude Stein was also from Oakland," Baldwin mentioned. "The East Bay must have been a happening place back in the day."

"As a matter of fact," I said, "I recently learned that Niles Canyon was the original Hollywood of California, in the days of the early silent films."

"Oh my, yes. Licorice?" Coco held out a plate of candies. "I'll warn you, though, it's black, from Holland. Very strong, and rather salty, actually."

"Oh no, thank you. Don't want to spoil the tea," I said. "I'm more a Red Vines girl myself."

"I'll have one," said Baldwin, taking several.

"So few of us like the classics anymore," Coco said with a sigh. "But speaking of Niles Canyon, the Crockett Theatre was built by one of the partners in the Essanay film company. The Delucci brothers made a fortune producing the early movies."

"Not a lot of overhead in those days," said Baldwin, chewing his candy. "They didn't blow up cars or require digital effects."

"No, indeed." A hard glint came into Coco's eyes. "Things have certainly changed from my era. Back in the day, you needed actual talent to be onstage or -screen. Nowadays it's all reality TV, as though anyone cares."

"Are you referring to the Sepety sisters?" I asked.

"The who?" Coco asked.

"It's a reality show," said Baldwin. "I can't imagine you've seen it, Coco. Not worth your time."

"I don't even own a television set!" she said, as though delighted to share the news. "Anyway, so long as the Space Campus headquarters isn't replacing the theater, I'm happy."

"The what, now?" I asked, looking from Coco to Baldwin.

"It was one of the ideas floated after the parking lot idea was squashed," said Baldwin. "Some stinking-rich guy wants to build himself a rocket, and tried to buy the whole block the Crockett sits on to build his global headquarters. Offered the city a hell of a lot of money for the land and buildings, but refused to disclose what his plans were."

"A rocket, like to go to the moon?" I asked.

"To the moon and back, I suppose. Maybe even to Mars one day. Space tourism, it's a pretty trendy subject."

I had enough trouble reminding myself to remain connected to this Earth, much less taking on other planets. But to each their own—which was especially true when it came to the extremely wealthy.

"A space rocket, can you even imagine?" asked Coco. "Why, it would destroy the entire *feel* of the neighborhood."

Chapter Thirteen

I thanked Coco and Baldwin for the tea and company, and girded my loins to finally join the traffic crowding the Bay Bridge. I headed for Oakland, dinner, dog, and family.

At the home office I received notice from Gregory Thibodeaux that he had been released from the hospital, and that the Xerxes Group was ready to move ahead as soon as the crime scene was released by the police.

Stan had been going through the photographs I had downloaded, comparing them with the former ones the consortium had provided us with for the original bid, starting to work up categories of supplies and specialty items. While we had worked on a lot of highly decorated San Francisco Victorians, Turner Construction had never renovated a theater. We needed to replace stage lighting, for instance, and hire a specialist to assess the Mighty Wurlitzer. I doubted the fabrics could be repaired, which meant finding someone capable of reproducing the massive stage curtain. And of course an enormous movie screen. I started putting out feelers for theater-equipment vendors, and unlike Josh Avery,

I wasn't going to hesitate lining up my favorite decorative painters and craftspeople. The best were in demand, and I wanted to get on their radar.

I noticed orbs in all the photos I had taken. Little shining lights, just about everywhere. It was possible I was just a terrible photographer, but given what I had seen and heard at the Crockett, I thought there was more to the story.

I studied the photo I had taken in the ladies' lounge. It showed the wallpaper hanging down in a strip from the wall, and the phrase "Affectations can be dangerous" written on the plaster, surrounded by paisley designs. Probably it just referred to Isadora's name, and her namesake, Isadora Duncan. Was Duncan Isadora's personal modern-dance hero?

And could it have anything to do with Isadora's untimely death?

In bed that night, I read another few passages from my mother's journal while Landon was brushing his teeth and showering.

She wrote up a list for dealing with spirits:

Always remain calm. Fear agitates and inspires (note to self: work on this)

Many simply enjoy harassing the living and causing mischief; they are like children that way. Don't give in. Let them know you're in charge (is that what was happening at the theater? Childish ghostly antics?)

Just like humans, some are decent, but others should be avoided.

Try, always, to come from a place of empathy. Some want something from you, but not all. Some spirits merely want to be left alone. Much like living people.

I think of it like being underwater: It's strange, and scary, but the calmer you are, the longer your breath lasts. Let the water buoy you.

Landon came to join me, smelling of soap and toothpaste, looking good enough to eat. I didn't want to spoil the moment, but I had to tell him about Hildy.

"So, I've been wanting to talk to you about something," I began as he climbed into bed. "Do you remember when we were at our house yesterday morning?—"

"Turner Arms?"

I smiled. "Demetrius Abbey, maybe? Anyway. Remember how Mateo mentioned a closet in the attic that had been sealed shut?"

"Ah yes. I forgot to ask: What did you find inside?"

"Some great old dresses."

"Like the one you brought home yesterday?"

"Exactly."

"Can't wait to see it on you."

"Yes, I, um . . . About that . . ."

"Are you trying to tell me something?" He scooched down farther on the pillows, leaned on his elbow, and cupped his head in his hand. His voice took on a gentle, lightly teasing tone: "Might that be your proposed wedding dress, Ms. Melanie Turner? Are you ready to set the date?"

"What? *No.* Of course not. I mean, I don't think so. It's not that. It's . . ."

His smile was replaced by a wary look. "What are you trying to say, Mel? Do you think the house is a mistake? I know it was rather impulsive of me, buying the old thing."

"It's nothing like that. I adore the house, Landon. Really I do. I'm so excited about it. It's just that . . . Well, this is hard to put into words."

"Try."

"I found something else in the closet, besides the dresses."

"Something else?"

"Some*one* else."

There was a long pause.

"*Another* ghost?"

I nodded.

"And that same day, you went to the Crockett Theatre and found ghosts there as well? And a dead woman, on top of that?"

"It was something of a banner day."

"My poor Mel," he said softly, reaching out a hand to smooth my hair. "You doing okay?"

I nodded. "So far anyway."

"So, who is our attic ghost?"

"A woman named Hildy Hildecott. I think she may have been an actress in very early films . . ."

"Which is why you were asking about Niles Canyon."

"Exactly."

"How did she die?"

I hesitated. "I don't know. She didn't seem malevolent or anything—quite the opposite, in fact. But . . ."

"But?"

"When I tried on the dress she gave me, I had a vision. As though I were Hildy."

"That's disturbing."

"I haven't even gotten to the really disturbing part."

"Continue."

"In the vision I was holding a big knife. And it was dripping blood."

There was another long pause.

"Come here," Landon said softly, pulling me into his embrace. Then he lifted his head and looked into my eyes. "I thought you were a little on edge. Are you sure you're handling it okay? How can I help? I'd like to go with you next time you're expecting to encounter spirits, and killers, for that matter. I know I can't speak to ghosts, but I want to be your backup."

I smiled, thinking of how lucky I was. "I can't think of anything for you to do at the moment, but do you have any idea how much I appreciate the offer?"

He gave me a squeeze. "I waited a lifetime for you, Mel. For *us*. I'm not about to give that up because of ghosts and murderers and the like. Next time you set foot in any of those haunted structures, I'd like to be at your side."

I kissed him, and he kissed me, and there was no more talk of ghosts. Or murderers, for that matter.

The next morning, what I really wanted to do was to play hooky from work and stop by the new house for a little chat with one Hildy Hildecott. Or go check out the film museum at Niles Canyon, to try to figure out what roles she had played in the early industry, on- and off-screen. Or go back to the Crockett and figure out how to break in to find out what *those* ghosts wanted, if anything, and whether they'd had anything to do with what happened to Isadora. But ghosts and murderers (and possibly ghostly murderers) be damned, I still had a job to do. *Time and tide and construction deadlines wait for no man,* my father always said, though he added *or woman* when I took over the business.

And so, well caffeinated and wielding my coveralls, steel-toed boots, and toolbox, I headed back over the bridge and across much of San Francisco to a gracious neighborhood called St. Francis Wood.

This was a beautiful section of the city, an early planned community from the 1920s with gracefully winding streets and sylvan, clipped gardens.

Here Turner Construction had done a sequential remodel: We started in the kitchen; then the homeowners decided the kids' rooms needed sprucing up, and after that, the dad wanted his shed overhauled, and later the mom wanted the attic transformed into a combined yoga-meditation room. This kind of domino effect was common in my line of work: Once a homeowner likes your work and realizes she can trust you, she remembers all the *other* things on her wish list. And once a relationship was established, and the client proved to be prompt in paying the bill, it was hard to say no—despite whatever other construction commitments we might have.

A few weeks ago, the homeowners watched some kind of home-makeover reality show and decided they had to have a gray-water system, which was environmentally wise but tricky to install in a city like San Francisco, with its stringent building codes. Our elaborate filtering system involved cascading household runoff into a series of ponds with filtering plants and fish, which then would be used to water the garden.

It was a pretty cool design, but a giant pain in my you-know-what.

Turner Construction wasn't officially a "green" builder, but even before it became fashionable, my dad had incorporated recycling and passive-solar techniques into his renovations as much as possible. I shared that commitment, and because of my love for all things ancient, I also saved everything I could from a renovation, from old brass drawer pulls to the drawers themselves.

And ultimately, saving old structures, instead of razing them and starting over, was the greenest building technique there was.

Recently I had also stopped using black plastic bags. The immediate impetus was that Dog had developed a phobia about them; who knew where that came from, but if it bothered Dog, it bothered me. Plus, after an ill-advised late-night viewing of a documentary about the "plastic island" swirling in the ocean, I now insisted on using only compostable bags. They cost three times as much as the cheap plastic ones, but I figured a clear conscience, and a clean ocean, was worth it.

After meeting with the foreman on the St. Francis Wood job and reviewing the final punch list with the clients, I headed to the Ferry Building to have coffee with a possible new client and her architect.

Once that meeting was over, I grabbed a sandwich from Cowgirl Creamery Sidekick Café and sat in the sun at Embarcadero Plaza, gazing at the truly ugly water feature. It was huge, a tangle of industrial-looking squared-off pipes gushing water into the tube below, which always made me think of toxic water pouring into the ocean. As a kid I had gotten in big trouble by accepting a dare from my sister Cookie to scale one of the pipes when I was supposed to be doing my homework while Dad met with a client nearby.

I winced at the memory. My dad was a former marine. He did not tolerate such antics, much less dereliction of duty.

The water feature put me in mind of the nickel tap I had picked up at the Crockett Theatre, not long before everything took a turn. I wondered what the Doctor would make of it, but I imagined it was probably still sitting, tagged, on his dusty shelf.

I checked my phone; he hadn't called me back. Neither had anyone else: not the SFPD, not a single one of the squatters, not Gregory Thibodeaux, not even any of the artisans I had reached out to concerning the specialty finishes at the Crockett Theatre.

The construction business requires a lot of patience. Unfortunately, patience is not my strong suit.

I reminded myself it had only been two days since finding Isadora's lifeless body. It seemed like longer.

In part, this was because I was so anxious to get back into the theater. I wanted to see whether Isadora's spirit, or any other resident ghost, might have something to tell me. I wanted to go through the building at my leisure and continue the list I had started with Gregory. I wanted to see whether I could make sense of the orbs from the photographs. I wanted to wander those halls, haunted or not, and scrape off that hideous pink paint to see what wonders lay beneath.

Even though I had other things I should have been doing, I headed for the Mission, and the Crockett. *Nothing ventured, nothing gained.*

There was a commotion outside the theater. It wasn't cop cars or paramedics, but a handful of reporters and a camera crew, their lenses focused on one man in a suit and two beautiful young women, one blond and one brunette, standing in front of the octagonal ticket kiosk. They were pleading for the public to help find the perpetrator of this heinous crime against their sister.

The Sepety family, I presumed. Holding a press conference.

The women were heavily made-up and crying prettily, dabbing at the tears that trickled down their cheeks, a drop at a time. I'm not a pretty crier—when I cry, I *commit*—and I'm always suspicious of those who are. I couldn't help noticing that the sisters' eyes were neither red nor swollen, and their noses weren't running like mine always did. Were they truly heartbroken at the sudden, violent loss of a family member or just posing for the cameras?

Don't judge, Mel. People grieve in different ways.

As I stood on the sidewalk, listening and wondering whether to try to speak with them or just get the hell out of there, I noticed Coco Stapleton edging over to stand by the family, and to get on camera.

She saw me, smiled, and nodded.

At a lull in the reporters' questions, Coco gestured toward me. "*This* is one of the people working on the theater. In fact, she's the one who found poor, sweet Isadora."

The cameras swung around, and a reporter stuck a microphone in my face.

"What's your name and how are you involved in the death of Isadora Sepety?" she demanded.

"I'm not really involved, per se . . ."

"Who are you?"

"Mel Turner. I'm—"

The blond Sepety sister was already looking me up on her phone, and shrieked, "Omigawd—you're a *ghost buster*?"

"She's a *ghost buster*!" someone else exclaimed, and an excited murmur ran through the small crowd.

"I'm not really—"

But it didn't matter what I said. People started shouting questions at me, and cameras and microphones were shoved in my face.

Apparently this was my fifteen minutes of fame. Problem was, I've never wanted to be famous. Not once, not even as a little kid. So all this attention was not a fantasy come true.

I ducked my head, muttered, "No comment," and tried to leave, but was blocked in. That ticked me off, so I ducked my head and started shouldering my way down the sidewalk.

As I neared a small alley, I felt a hand on my arm, pulling me into a building, and a door clanged shut behind us.

Chapter Fourteen

It was Mitch, the glowering one.

My heart leapt to my throat. *What did he want?* Was I out of the frying pan and into the fire? Had anyone seen Mitch pull me in here?

"Sorry to jerk you around like that," Mitch said. "I thought you could use a hand. So to speak."

We appeared to be in the back room of one of the small shops on the block. Wherever we were, the place smelled heavenly. I noticed some personal items—clothes, a backpack, a pair of shoes—and, in one corner, a neatly made-up army cot.

"That family is too much . . ." He shook his head. "Are you okay?"

I nodded and took a few deep breaths, trying to pull myself together.

"Do you live here?" I asked, looking around. "What smells so good?"

"We're in the back of the donut shop. I work here sometimes."

"And you sleep here?"

"Only when I get thrown out of the theater. Thanks for that, by the way."

"Hey, that wasn't my fault," I said. "But thank you for getting me away from those reporters."

He shrugged. "No problem."

"As a matter of fact, Mitch, I've been trying to get in touch with the folks in the theater. Could I ask you a few questions?"

"Nothing but questions these days, am I right?"

"What's your story, Mitch?" I asked. "How did you end up in the theater?"

"Why would you want to know?" he asked, sounding suspicious.

"Why wouldn't I?"

He paused for a moment, looked around, then gestured toward a wooden chair.

"Have a seat," he said, sitting on the army cot.

I sat, thinking someone had taught him manners.

As if reading my mind, he gave me a quick résumé. "You think I'm sort of a bum, don't you? Well, I'm not. I grew up in a totally bougie household in Princeton, New Jersey—Dad took the train to his fat-cat job in New York City. Mom stayed home and joined the garden club. It was like growing up in the 1950s but, like, a half a century later. It was *surreal*. Frozen in time. Summer camp in the Adirondacks, prep school with uniforms, private college . . ."

"Sounds like a pretty privileged upbringing."

"I know, right? But I never asked for any of it, and I didn't want it. Finished school to keep my parents off my back, then left the day after graduation. Hitchhiked across the country. Met Isadora and a few others, ended up here."

I said nothing, just listened. Mitch's story of disaffected youth was hardly a new one, but it was new to him, and really that was all that mattered.

"You don't understand how important the theater is to us," Mitch continued. "It's ground zero for the resistance."

"Resistance to what, exactly?"

"To the patriarchy—to the military-industrial complex that devalues humans and promotes climate change. We're on a path that leads to destruction, and the clock's ticking. We don't turn this around, we're toast."

I hid a smile at his phrasing. "Oh. That's a lot to resist. Good for you. I recently switched to all-recyclable garbage bags myself."

He gave me an odd look. Hey, it was a start.

"I'll tell you one thing," I said. "I'm impressed by how organized you all are. And you seemed to take care of the place, which I really appreciate."

He waved away my thanks.

"Mitch, can you think of anyone who would want to hurt Isadora?"

"Like, her family?"

"Why would they want to hurt her?"

He shrugged. "They just . . . I guess they didn't understand her. I don't know. I don't like them."

"Do you know the brother, Ringo?"

"He came around every once in a while, always had some scheme for making money. Latest one was to make a reality show out of our situation."

"How would anyone make a show out of your situation?"

"Follow us around with cameras, I guess. Record when we had fights or how we got by. They probably hoped to tape us stealing, or sleeping with each other, or whatever. They really don't understand the resistance at all."

I nodded, trying to think of other possible suspects. I really did need to start carrying around cheat sheets with me.

"What can you tell me about Coco, the preservationist with the Crockett Caretakers?" I asked.

"That old bat? She's never been much of a friend to us. I'll tell you that much. She's rich, so what do you expect? A lot of unexamined privilege there. Thinks the rules don't apply to her. You know, I caught her trying to break into the theater once."

"Coco?" I tried to picture the fastidious Coco, dressed in her fancy pantsuit and scarves, scaling the fire escape or climbing through a window. But I supposed one never knew. "Breaking in how?"

He ignored my question.

"And she's really condescending, told me she had a job for me. Like I wanted to work for someone like that, like I couldn't find my own work if I wanted it."

"What about Baldwin. Did you meet him?"

"As far as I'm concerned, all those preservationists are whack jobs. I save my empathy for folks like Liam."

"Why is that?"

"He used to follow Isadora around everywhere. I think he was in love with her. He used to have a drug problem, but I don't judge."

I recalled Tierney saying something similar. "Do you know where Liam is now? Is he back in the theater? Are you all staying there again?"

I wondered who would be in charge of their creative society now, but hesitated to ask. Isadora hadn't liked to be called "leader"; as she said, the whole hierarchical thing was anathema to their creative vision of the world.

Mitch got up gracefully and peeked out the door. "Looks like it's died down out there—you can probably make it back to your car without being assaulted by the press."

"Thanks again for getting me out of there," I said.

"No problem."

"Mitch, how do you and the others get in and out of the theater?"

"You ever see that movie *Fight Club*?"

"As in 'the first rule of Fight Club' . . . ?"

He nodded. "Don't talk about Fight Club."

After swinging by Beronio Lumber and Discount Building Supplies to check on the status of some current orders, I considered heading to the Bay Bridge and home, but hesitated, thinking of the early Friday traffic. Besides, I was in no rush. I was on my own tonight: Landon had a late meeting with his doctoral students and would grab dinner at the faculty club, and Dad and Stan were meeting a bunch of old construction buddies for pizza and beer at Zachary's.

I wanted to stop by the new house in Oakland to take a stab—pardon the pun—at getting Hildy to tell me why I had "seen" her with a bloody knife. But first things first: I wanted to know more about our resident starlet, and about what happened at the Crockett.

I called Annette Crawford.

"Anything?" the inspector demanded without preamble.

"Not really . . ."

"Then why are you bothering me?"

I liked to refer to Annette Crawford as my "friend in the SFPD," but "friend" is a relative term since we didn't really spend time together except when I had stumbled across another murder. And when she was on a frustrating case, Annette's patience with me tended toward the short.

"I was wondering if I could buy you dinner."

"Dinner?"

"Or a drink, maybe?"

There was a long pause. "Are you asking me out on a date? Not to be too personal, Mel, but you're not really my type, romantically speaking. Besides, aren't you engaged?"

"Um . . ." I was pretty sure, but not entirely certain, she was joking. It was hard to tell with Annette. "The engagement's still on. I have a ring and everything."

"But no date set yet? My mama always said it wasn't a real engagement without a ring and a date."

"I'm working on the second part. Anyway. Do you have time to meet?"

"Let me think about it," she said. "But fair warning: This is an ongoing case, Mel. I can't talk to you about it in detail."

"I know," I said. "Can you at least tell me if the medical examiner has issued a finding on the cause of death? That would be public information, wouldn't it?"

"Homicide. Strangled with her own scarves."

Ugh. I wondered whether this was some sort of homicidal irony or merely a coincidence. After all, if you were planning on killing someone and those long scarves were right there, already wrapped around her slender neck . . . they would come in awfully handy. I shivered at the thought of what Isadora had experienced at the end.

"Your turn, Mel. Remember how I always say you should let me know everything, even if it doesn't seem important? I'm willing to bet there are things you haven't mentioned. Tell me now."

I told her about the Xerxes Group firing the previous contractor, Avery Builders. "Not that I think Josh Avery had anything to do with the murder. He's a good guy. But you might want to speak with him."

"I'll take that under advisement. What else?"

"Well, Skeet the security guard mentioned the Sepety family. Isadora was arguing with her brother about some reality show he wanted to pitch—she wanted nothing to do with it. Also, the family held a press conference in front of the theater a little while ago."

"Yes, my partner showed me some of the footage from that. They identified you as a local ghost buster."

"That wasn't my fault. I was just—"

"What else?"

"I tracked down a couple of the squatters, Tierney and Mitch."

"We've spoken with them already. Did you find anything they said helpful?"

"Not really. They're worried about Liam. He's a former drug user. That's all I can think of, but I'm sure there's more . . ."

She let out a loud sigh. "All right. Meet me at Akiko's on Bush at seven. I could do with some sushi. I'll call and get a table—I know a guy."

"You're so much cooler than I'll ever be."

She chuckled. "I love their *omakase*. Dinner's on you, by the way. I am but a humble public servant."

I had no idea what *omakase* was, but figured I would learn soon enough.

With time to kill before meeting Annette at seven, I checked my phone.

No call from Lily about the dress, but I assumed she would be in touch when she knew something. Before I geared up for another chat with Hildy, I really wanted to know if she might be inclined to kill someone.

Standing with a cigarette in one hand and a bloody knife in the other . . .

If ghost busting had taught me one thing, it was that it could be dangerous to ignore history.

And speaking of which . . . I checked the time. The California Historical Society would be closing soon, but I called one of the head archivists, Trish, who had recently become a friend.

When you're in my line of business, a historian was a very useful friend, indeed.

Chapter Fifteen

By the time I parked the car, the society had officially closed. But Trish unlocked the door to let me in, greeting me with a smile and a big hug.

I loved visiting the archive, especially after hours. Even the smell of the place energized me: a dash of old leather-bound books and newspapers mixed with the energy of inquiring minds.

Trish was in her fifties and had worked here for years. Her dishwater blond hair was streaked with gray, but her eyes were a bright, piercing blue. She wore cardigans and half-glasses on a beaded chain—"My librarian armor," she called it, because it helped to intimidate the occasionally troublesome patron.

"So good to see you, Mel! It's been a while," Trish said as she led the way over to the reading desks. "What are you up to these days?"

"Oh, you know me . . . That can be a complicated question to answer."

She paused. "Another . . . What should we call it? Incident?"

I nodded.

"Well, I'm sorry to hear that. But it always turns out all right, doesn't it? The lighthouse is just lovely. Your friend the innkeeper offered me a complimentary night's stay there. I look forward to taking her up on it."

"Alicia's wonderful. You were so helpful when we were trying to figure out what was going on out on the island."

"I really didn't do anything special. All in a day's work."

"You were a huge help, Trish. You historians are the keepers of precious knowledge, which can be very useful, especially when it comes to spooky old buildings."

She smiled. "And speaking of spooky old buildings, what are you working on lately?"

I gave her a quick rundown of the recent events at the Crockett Theatre.

"I'm so sorry to hear about that young woman's death. What a tragedy."

I nodded. "It really is. So now I'm trying to figure out whether I can help by looking into the history of the place, anything that stands out or seems odd that might offer a clue . . ."

"Hmmm," she said, tilting her head back as she mentally reviewed the society's holdings. Nobody knew them better than Trish. "I don't think we have any corporate records—the early film theater business was pretty wild and woolly, with constant changes and not a lot of record keeping—but I believe we do have a bunch of photos of the Crockett Theatre, if those would be helpful. Last year we got a grant to digitize our photographic collection, so I can e-mail them to you."

"That would be great. Thank you. There's a Facebook page with a lot of photos, as well."

"And there was a man killed at the Crockett a long time ago, if I recall," Trish said. "He worked there. Was it a ticket taker?"

"An usher."

"Let's see . . ." Trish got up and moved to a computer at the counter. "Yes, the crime scene photos."

The black-and-white photos showed a man lying facedown on the mezzanine carpet, just where Alyx had taped the outline. So Alyx knew the poor usher had fallen right there, the victim of a homicide, and yet he decided to make that mezzanine his home? He was gutsier than I.

The usher's arms were splayed out; one knee was cocked. He wore a uniform jacket and a cap, just as I had seen him. A newspaper article identified him as Harold Hancock of San Francisco, age twenty-three. According to the article, his assailant disappeared into a horrified crowd.

"Was the murderer ever found?" I asked.

Trish typed into the computer, skimmed a few follow-up articles, and shook her head. "Apparently he was never apprehended. The *Chronicle* reported: 'The man suspected of the murderous deed was one Carl Jacobs, who vied with Mr. Hancock for the love of a young woman.'"

"What a ridiculous reason to kill someone."

"It doesn't take much," said Trish. "Believe me, the history books are peppered with tragedies caused by utter foolishness."

Other than the fact that the usher Harold Hancock had showed himself to me at the theater, there was no connection I could think of between his death and Isadora's murder. I tried to think of what else to ask.

"I understand a neighborhood association was invaluable in keeping the theater from being torn down," I said.

"That's what I heard, as well." Trish typed more into the computer. "Looks like after the theater was sold to the city, it was slated to be torn down and turned into a parking lot, but the association got involved. Huh, this is fun: The theater used to encourage attendance by holding raffles and giving away free dishes. It was the original 'Depression ware.'"

"Really? I love Depression ware."

I had started collecting bits and pieces of Depression ware when I was a little kid, and it now filled the shelves of my bedroom at my dad's house. When we moved into the new house, Landon kept reminding me, I would have a whole new set of shelves to fill with my beloved artifacts from demolition sites, junkyards, and yard sales. As big as that house was, I wondered whether we'd have room for everything.

"When they say there are tax revenues and fund-raising, how much money are we talking?"

Trish shrugged. "Enough to make it attractive for the group redoing the theater."

Josh Avery had hinted that the Xerxes Group might have had an angle other than a love of old buildings. Was it money? "Who oversees those city funds? Is there an auditor or . . . ?"

"I don't really know, but since they're public monies, there must be some kind of official oversight."

I nodded, wondering why Gregory Thibodeaux hadn't mentioned it—and annoyed with myself for not thinking to ask.

"Seems like the previous owner, Calvin Delucci, really loved the old place," said Trish, who was still reading. "Shame he died before it could be renovated. Officially, he died of a heart attack."

I thought I heard a note in her voice. "What do you mean, 'officially'?"

"There were rumors that his cause of death was more complicated, though that's all they were—rumors. If you're interested, you might try talking to his widow, Lorraine. She lives in the East Bay, in Montclair."

"That's not far from my new house."

"Is that right?"

"How do you know all this stuff?" I asked. "The

rumors and whispers, as well as the documented history?"

"You just have to keep your ears open and know where to look, Mel. People are fascinating. And they *love* to gossip." Trish smiled. "Anyway, Calvin Delucci inherited the theater from his father, William. The building dates from 1923, which was early for film, so they also hosted vaudeville acts and that sort of thing."

"When did movies become a real thing?"

"The first full-length 'talkie' didn't come out until 1927, though filmmakers had been experimenting with ways to coordinate film and sound as early as the turn of the last century. A popular technology was 'sound on disc,' which meant the images were on film and the audio was on a wax record. The idea was to connect the film projector and the record player through a synchronizing mechanism. Didn't always work, though, so it wasn't uncommon for the sound not to match the images being shown on the screen."

Again, I thought of the ghostly usher and the way his words seemed out of sync to his movements.

"Oh, now this is interesting," Trish said, looking up from the city records. "The Crockett Theatre was built on the site of an old fort, which in turn was built on top of a freshwater source. Wasn't that smart?"

"Smart how?" I asked, thinking of the many ways water intrusion could weaken a building. "Why would that be a benefit?"

"In case of siege. With a little planning, it's possible to stockpile enough food to last for months or years. But maintaining a source of freshwater is much, much harder."

"They were preparing for a siege?"

"Military strategists prepare for many contingencies, I suppose. Like the armory, on Mission. Have you seen that place?"

"The porn set?"

"Before it was a porn set, it was the armory, and it has a spring in the basement. Have you taken the tour? It's really interesting."

"I'll bet it is. Especially since it's a porn set." I couldn't resist teasing her. Trish appeared so buttoned-down in her cardigan and glasses, but in her spare time, she loved salsa dancing and was a volunteer organizer of medical supplies for Doctors Without Borders. And toured porn sets.

"That reminds me," I continued. "Have you ever heard of Eamon Castle?"

"The old brewery near Candlestick?"

"So you have heard of it."

"When I was a kid, everyone said it was haunted, but I think that was just because it was old and empty. And built of stone, which is unusual for this area."

"Not a lot of castles in San Francisco, stone or otherwise."

"Nope."

"It's funny . . . There was an underground water source at another one of my other jobs a while ago. Who knew there were so many?"

She blinked. "Isn't that a ghost thing?"

"What do you mean?"

"According to what I've heard, ghosts—death in general, come to think of it—are often associated with water. Then again, you're the expert in that regard."

"Yeah, that's me. The ghost expert." *Not.* "But tell me more."

"My grandmother was from the Balkan Peninsula. There's an old Balkan wives' tale, that when someone dies, you're supposed to put a tub filled with water by the door for Death to wash his scythe."

"Huh. Interesting. Not sure what that has to do with an underground spring at the Crockett, though."

"Again, I'm just spitballing here. My impression is that ghosts are supposed to be able to move along water routes more easily than over land, or something along those lines."

She looked away, as though embarrassed. This was a reaction I often noted when paranormal talk came up amongst educated, scientific-minded souls. It was hard to ignore what we saw and heard, but it was equally hard to forget that there was no scientific proof that ghosts exist.

"Hey," I asked. "Have you heard of a TV show with the Sepetys?"

"Of course. I take it you haven't?"

"I fear I don't have my fingers on the pulse of popular culture."

"You're not missing anything."

"What can you tell me about it? Are they actors or . . . ?"

She tilted her head. "It's a reality TV show that follows young women around while they shop and fight and pursue romance."

"That's it?"

"That's it."

"Why does anyone care?"

"That's one of the great mysteries of our day. Why are you asking about the show?"

"Because the young woman at the theater, the woman who was killed . . ." My voice wavered. "Her name was Isadora Sepety. The rest of the family was at the theater today, holding a press conference. I guess Isadora was the family nonconformist and wanted nothing to do with their show. But according to the security guard at the theater, her brother was trying to convince her to do a reality show set in the theater, about the squatters."

She frowned. "That seems odd."

"It does, doesn't it?"

"And you think that has something to do with her murder?"

"Maybe tempers were running high. They were arguing. Things got out of hand?"

"How was she killed?"

I hesitated. "Does it matter?"

"It might. A fundamental of law enforcement is that to learn about the criminal, analyze the crime. If she was shot, strangled, or died from blunt-force trauma, it may be a crime of passion. If she was poisoned, the murder was most likely premeditated."

"You watch a lot of cop shows on TV?"

"British mysteries," she said with a smile. "Can't get enough of them."

"Isn't poisoning considered a woman's method?"

"That's a traditional assumption," she said. "Poison has the advantage of creating physical distance between the murderer and the victim, which makes it a safer way for a woman to murder a man. However, not only were many of the most famous poisoners in history men, but women are increasingly more comfortable using weapons to kill. Not that that's a step forward in equality, if you ask me."

"Indeed. Oh hey, speaking of murder: Where would I find information about a murder in Oakland in the 1910s or '20s?"

"I would check back issues of the *Oakland Tribune*. It started publication in the 1870s, and by the early twentieth century was a dominant newspaper in the Bay Area and indeed the entire state. If the murder was a crime of passion—as opposed to a simple mugging, for example—it probably would have made the San Francisco papers as well. They were hungry for news."

"This involved an actress in silent films."

"Even more likely, then." Trish glanced at a slim silver watch on her wrist. "But I'm sorry to say I won't have time to look it up now. I was supposed to leave ten minutes ago to meet some friends for dinner. Why don't you write down as much as you know, and I'll see what I can find for you first thing Monday morning?"

Chapter Sixteen

I met Annette Crawford at Akiko's on Bush Street.

"This is my favorite place for *omakase*," she said as we waited to be seated.

"Not to sound like an idiot," I said, "but what is *omakase*, exactly? Normally I'm up for adventures, but I've had a rough couple of days. Not sure I want to accidentally order fish sperm or whale blubber or some such thing."

Annette smiled. "Literally, *omakase* means 'I trust you.' In other words, we leave it up to the chef, who should know which fish is at its peak. Trusting the chef means a lot in a sushi restaurant."

The hostess ushered us to a small table in the corner, and she and Annette had a short exchange—in Japanese.

"You speak Japanese?" I asked Annette as soon as we were alone. "I didn't know that."

"I've been studying a little online and occasionally try it out in sushi bars. I get particularly good *omakase* when I attempt a few words in Japanese."

"And that brings me to my next question: Since when have you started trusting people?"

"I trust people," Annette said, sounding a bit defensive. Then she sat back and shrugged. "Some people anyway. I trust sushi chefs in a restaurant like this one."

"And is good sushi the only reason you're learning Japanese?"

"That's just an added benefit. You know what they say: Learning a language is the key to brain health, and I already know Spanish. So I thought I'd try something completely different."

"Because you have so much free time."

"Mel, if you haven't learned this already, then here's a piece of advice: Sometimes you have to *make* time."

"You're something else," I said with a smile, shaking my head. "Full of surprises."

The server brought us a bowl of edamame and poured mugs of fragrant green tea.

"Also," said Annette as she shelled an edamame and popped the salted beans into her mouth. "It's a nice break from my usual routine. One can only handle so many dead bodies without needing to change gears."

"Ah yes, back to the crux of things."

"You said you have information for me?"

"I wouldn't go that far, exactly," I said, backpedaling a bit. "I mentioned on the phone that I spoke with Tierney—"

"At the tattoo shop." She nodded. "We talked to her earlier today."

"And with Mitch, who is staying in the back of the donut shop."

"Any of the others? We'd already spoken with both of them."

I shook my head.

"The phone numbers you had for them were helpful," Annette said.

"They answered? They don't pick up when I call."

"Of course they didn't answer. Nobody answers my calls either."

"I do."

"And I appreciate it," she said with a smile. "No, we tracked them down through their cell phone records. But let me handle this, Mel—it's my job, not yours. One of them might well be a murderer, lest you forget."

"I'm not actively looking for them, at least not anymore. As a matter of fact, Mitch found me, not the other way around. He sort of rescued me from the Sepetys."

She gave me a questioning look.

"From the cameras, I should say. Oh hey, I also wanted to mention a suspicious man who was talking with the security guard the day of the murder."

"I'm only now hearing about this?" Annette frowned.

"I didn't think of it at the time."

"Description?"

"Let's see . . . average white guy, probably in his fifties, chinos and button-down shirt, balding."

"Well, that's helpful," she said dryly. "What was suspicious about him?"

"He exchanged a strange look with Gregory, as though they didn't like each other. But the security guard—"

"This is Bill Henley?"

"Um . . . I was told he went by Skeet."

"Right, same guy."

"Anyway, when I asked Skeet about it, he claimed he didn't remember who the guy was. Suggested it was probably a neighbor curious about the remodel."

"And you don't believe him?"

"When I saw them talking, they weren't acting as if it was just a casual conversation between strangers."

"That's curious, I'll grant you. But there could be a million reasons."

"Maybe. But there's something else. Skeet writes things down in his journal—it's a log for the security guys. If you haven't looked at it, you should."

"I did check the log. I check everything. In fact, I wanted to ask you about an employee of yours." She flipped to a page in her notebook. "One Mateo Suarez."

"Mateo? He's one of my foremen."

"He has a criminal record."

"He's worked for my dad, and now me, for years. He's a great guy, made some stupid choices when he was younger, paid the price, been straight ever since. Why are you asking about him?"

"Skeet wrote his name down in his journal, about a month ago."

I blinked.

"What's his connection to the Crockett?" Annette continued.

"I have no idea. I didn't . . . He hasn't mentioned anything. Did Skeet write down any details?"

"Just that he stopped by and that he worked for you—his business card is taped next to the notation."

"I don't suppose I could see a copy of the journal?"

"Don't suppose you could."

"I'm just thinking I might recognize something you wouldn't."

"Mel, has anything in our interaction over the years suggested that I would be willing to agree to what you just asked?"

"Not really, no. But I figured it was worth a shot."

"Well, I admire your gumption. The answer is still no."

"Okay, here's something else. Turner Construction wasn't the first company hired to renovate the theater. The previous contractor was fired, and when I asked who it was, I couldn't get a straight answer. So I figured I'd just get the name from the building permits. But when I pulled the file at the city permit office that information—and only that information—had been blacked out."

"Why?"

"I have no idea, and my contact at the permit office

didn't understand it either. I figured out the previous contractor was Avery Builders, and when I spoke with Josh Avery yesterday, he wasn't sure what was going on. According to Josh, his crew was on schedule when all of a sudden he got a check and was told not to bother showing up again. Josh said he got the impression that the Xerxes Group wasn't all that interested in finishing the job."

"Huh." Annette didn't sound especially interested, but she jotted down a few notes in a small notebook she had pulled from her pocket.

"Also, what do you know about the Delucci death?" I asked.

"Who are you talking about now?"

"Calvin Delucci was the former owner of the Crockett Theatre. He conveniently died of a heart attack that rumors suggest may not have been a heart attack."

"'Rumors suggest,' huh? And what would that have to do with my body?"

"I don't know. Maybe nothing. Maybe more."

"I swear, Mel," she said, jotting "Calvin Delucci" in her notebook, then fixing me with a look as we sipped our miso soup. "I can't tell if you're a crime-busting savant or just paranoid."

"Maybe a bit of both?"

"I thought you brought me here to talk about ghosts."

"Why would I do that?"

She shrugged.

"So, when can I get back into the theater to start work?" I asked. "I don't have to tell you that this will be a pretty big job."

"I plan on releasing the scene by Monday, provided the medical examiner doesn't find anything more."

Trays of sushi and sashimi were set in front of us, and the server explained each piece of *omakase*. Annette thanked her but studied the food silently, her expression troubled.

"Annette? You okay? There's no whale blubber, is there? 'Cause there's a burger place around the corner. We could slip out the back."

"It's not that," Annette said quietly. "In the movies and television, it looks easy."

"What does?"

"Strangling someone to death. In reality, it requires a lot of strength and takes much longer than most people realize. Standing right up close to the victim, watching them struggle for breath, seeing their panic and pain . . . that takes a pretty cold heart, if you ask me."

I played with mixing wasabi into my little dish of soy sauce, sobered by her words. "So we're looking for someone strong enough, and ruthless enough, to have strangled Isadora."

"No, 'we' are not looking for anyone," insisted Annette as she skillfully manipulated the chopsticks to pick up a piece of sushi, the orange of the fish contrasting beautifully with the white of the rice, all wrapped up like a little present with seaweed for the ribbon. "Remember? *You* are working on a remodel, whereas I, the trained police professional, am looking for a killer."

"But maybe I can help," I said as I struggled to work my chopsticks. I could manipulate one at a time, but not both together, and wondered how embarrassing it would be to ask for a fork. "Sometimes the spirits have something to say to me, some kind of clue."

"I thought you told me that the murder victims can't remember what happened to them, and therefore can't tell you who killed them."

"That's true. They can't. At least, I haven't yet met a spirit that could. But they often do remember parts of their lives before the murder, so if someone had been threatening her, or something like that, Isadora might be able to put me on the right track."

"You really think she could tell you . . . ?" Annette

trailed off and shook her head, as though warding off a spell. "Wait a minute. We're talking about a ghost here. How would I begin to explain to my lieutenant that my confidential informant was not of this world?"

"You don't have to explain it, once you find the killer. You can work backwards, say you had a hunch. Or I could be your informant. They get paid, right?"

Annette laughed out loud. "Yeah, that's not gonna happen."

Another tray of beautifully prepared and artfully arranged food arrived. I had sort of gotten the hang of the chopsticks, and we dug in for real, savoring the salty soy sauce, the spicy wasabi horseradish, the buttery fish. Annette asked about my father, whom she had met at the scene of another homicide that now seemed like a very long time ago. We chatted about my new house— MelLand House? Landon's Walk?—and my reluctance to set a date for the wedding, and she told me a little about having been engaged once herself. But, she said, they had parted ways. Last she heard he worked security as a special agent with the US Secret Service, which was probably also not as cool as it sounds.

"Speaking of security, what's Skeet's story?" I asked.

"He passed a standard background check. Why?"

"He seemed so friendly and easygoing at first, but then he seemed to change. Asked me to leave the premises, didn't even want me standing on the sidewalk in front of the theater."

She raised one eyebrow.

"I know, I know," I said. "Not everyone finds me as charming as you do. But he was perfectly friendly yesterday until he got a phone call, and then all of a sudden he wanted me gone ASAP."

"You think the phone call was about you?"

"Could be. In any event, my presence was no longer welcome."

"Didn't you tell me Skeet mentioned Isadora had something she wanted to tell him or show him? Ever find out what that was?"

I shook my head. The server refilled our teacups, whisked our trays away, and asked if we wanted anything else. Stuffed with fish and rice, we asked for the check.

Annette leaned back in her chair and let out a long breath.

"Here's something that's been bothering me," she said, flipping through her notebook and reading an entry. "You said you 'saw' Isadora dancing onstage *before* finding her body."

"Yes."

"And the spotlight was following her around on the stage."

"That's right."

"So who was directing the spotlight?"

I hadn't thought about that. "Good question."

"Is that something spirits could manipulate?" Annette looked uncomfortable asking me this, but soldiered on. "Is it possible that her energy somehow conjured it? Or are we talking human intervention of some kind? What do you think?"

"I think I have no idea how to answer those really quite excellent questions."

"You know, when it comes to ghosts you're not as helpful as one might hope."

"I could have told you that," I said, smiling. "I have an idea. Let's go check out the theater."

"You and I?"

I nodded.

"Now?"

I nodded again.

"Why do I feel I have allowed myself to be lured into a trap? Is this what this dinner is all about?"

"You really think I'm that Machiavellian? Annette, I know investigating a murder is a job for the SFPD.

But I met Isadora shortly before she was killed. I was in the theater when she died. I feel like I'm part of this, somehow, that I need to help figure it out, if I can. At least with the ghost aspect."

She nodded slowly. "I get it."

"So I was thinking . . . it's usually easier for spirits to materialize at night. There's less energy for them to fight or something like that. Olivier Galopin could explain it better. Anyway, I just happen to have my ghost-busting equipment in the car. What do you say we go chat up some ghosts?"

Landon had wanted to come with me the next time I entered the ghostly halls of the Crockett Theatre, but having a homicide inspector as backup should appease him. She carried a gun, after all. It wouldn't be any use against a ghost, but it would stop a murderer.

"That idea makes me nervous," said Annette.

"I don't have to tell you that we're dealing with the untimely, violent death of a young woman."

"No, you don't have to remind me of that." She took a swig of her green tea. I wondered if she wished it were sake.

"Maybe Isadora herself will appear and tell us something."

"Tell *you* something. Personally, I'll be watching your back."

"Is that a yes?"

Her lips pursed together as though she were highly displeased. But she gave a firm nod.

"Dinner's on you, right?" she asked, handing me the bill.

"Right."

"Then pay the tab, and let's get going before I come to my senses and change my mind."

Chapter Seventeen

It was only eight thirty in the evening, but the neighborhood looked like a ghost town.

The businesses that shared the block with the Crockett Theatre—the jewelry store, the tattoo parlor, the donut shop, the *taquerías*—were shut up tight for the night. Even the trendy diner across the street had long since closed its doors to customers. San Francisco wasn't a twenty-four-hour city like New York, and many restaurants didn't serve past nine.

Annette and I stood in front of the theater and gazed up at its majestic façade. The building loomed huge and ominous before us, shadowy against the city-lit sky.

The colorful marquee lights flickered on for a moment, then went dark again.

Our eyes locked.

"Maybe it's saying hello?" I said.

Annette grunted. She was not enjoying this.

We went around to the side. The gate in the cyclone fence was locked, so Annette pressed a button to summon the security guard. The thin, pale young man who emerged from the trailer could well have passed for one of the squatters. His hair was tousled, and I wouldn't have been surprised if we had caught him napping. The name on his badge read THAD.

"Dude, this is a closed—" Thad began, squinting at us nearsightedly.

"Police," Annette said, flashing her gold badge. "Open up."

"Yes, ma'am," he said as he hurried over to unlock the gate. "Sorry, Inspector. I didn't expect to see anyone tonight."

"No problem, Thad. Thanks for letting us in. Long hours for you today, huh?"

He smiled and scratched at a nonexistent beard. "Skeet worked a double yesterday, so I volunteered to take his shift tonight. Have to study for a midterm anyway."

"Good luck with that," said Annette as we passed through the gate to the alley behind the theater. "By the way, did you turn on the electricity a few moments ago?"

He looked confused and shook his head. "What? No. I turn it on when I'm doing my rounds, but you told us to stay out of the building, so I'm just sitting out here in the trailer. Studying."

She nodded and consulted her notebook. "I have reports of a 'balding, middle-aged white guy' who stopped by here the day of the murder. What can you tell me about that?"

"Um . . . nothing? I mean, there are a lot of balding, middle-aged white guys. Can you be more specific? I haven't been threatened by anyone, if that's what you mean."

"Let me see the security logs," Annette said.

"That's Skeet's thing. We just check in using an app on our phone; he's the one with the journal. I think it's, like, private."

"Okay. Thad, this is Mel Turner. She's with me. We're going to do a quick walk-through of the place."

"You can't." He gulped and his Adam's apple bobbed in his long neck. "I mean, there's crime scene tape up."

"And it just so happens that I have the special weapon to defeat the crime scene tape." Annette held up a small jackknife.

"But . . . I thought no one was supposed to go in there. Not even me."

"That's right. You're not," Annette said as she walked over to the nondescript door and cut the tape. "But I was the one who gave that order, remember? We won't be a moment."

I thought we might be more than a moment, but kept my mouth shut.

"Yes, ma'am," Thad said, and returned to the trailer.

"Give me just a second," I said as Annette started to open the theater door. I stroked the ring at my neck and tried not to feel awkward because Annette was watching. I did my body scan to prepare, reminding myself that I was in the land of the living. My feet were connected to the concrete, which was laid upon the soil, which connected to bedrock, all the way to the core of the Earth. After a moment I let out a long breath.

"Are you quite finished?" Annette said. "Make me wait much longer and I'm going to change my mind."

"Okay, ready," I said.

Annette shone her flashlight beam on the electrical panel and flipped the main switch, and we walked in. The dim, unadorned lights of the pink corridor gleamed their anemic Pepto-Bismol glow. I followed her down the hallway toward the door to the lobby.

She opened it, and we stepped into the spectacular but tattered lobby of the haunted Crockett Theatre.

Entering a building after I had seen ghosts and found a body was always disconcerting, even with a homicide inspector as backup. So I tried to do as my mentor Olivier always coached me: not to anticipate what I might see, hear, and feel, but to be open to anything. The Zen approach to ghost busting.

And, rather like Zen meditation, communing with ghosts was a lot easier said than done.

The lobby was as breathtaking as ever, despite the cobwebs and grime, or perhaps in part because of them. There was something eerie yet romantic about an abandoned building. Although this one wasn't exactly abandoned, I reminded myself. I wondered whether the squatters were still here, and whether we would run across any during our after-hours visit.

"Why did I let you talk me into this?" Annette whispered. "This place gives me the heebie-jeebies. What are you writing down?"

"Just a note to myself to check on the wiring of those chandeliers. Notice how they keep dimming? Not good."

"I thought we were here to look for ghosts," Annette said with a raised eyebrow. "Not to make to-do lists."

"Professional weakness," I said, feeling a bit sheepish as I slipped my notebook back in my pocket. "Sorry."

We walked around the big lobby, checking out nooks and crannies, the concession stand, and the alcoves.

"This place is as spooky as you-know-what," Annette whispered.

"The whispering isn't helping," I said, snapping photos with the special night-vision thermal camera. I fiddled with the EVP recorder and made sure it was on, in case it might pick up the sound of voices from beyond the veil. I hadn't had much luck with this ghost-busting equipment so far, but one could never tell. Besides, it gave me something to do other than wander around, hoping something or someone would materialize.

"Can't help it," Annette whispered. "It's like a cross between a mortuary and a church in here. So what are we looking for?"

"Ghosts. And a murderer."

"Is that all?"

"I like to cast a wide net."

"Great."

"Actually, what I'd really like to do is see if I can contact Isadora's spirit directly. I'm hoping she might remember something that could provide us with a clue, like if someone had been threatening her or what she wanted to show Skeet."

"Too bad she can't just tell you who murdered her."

"Would that it were so easy. In my experience, the ghosts don't remember the pain and trauma of their deaths, which is good. But at the same time, they don't always realize they're dead. Which can be . . . awkward."

"And I thought informing a murder victim's next of kin was difficult," Annette said. "I can't imagine informing the murder victim that they died."

"Welcome to my world."

I mounted the first flight of stairs to the landing at the mezzanine level, still taking pictures and checking my equipment. Alyx's things were no longer here, and I wondered if he had moved out.

The building carried the mingled scents of dust and mildew, the aroma of abandonment. I realized I didn't smell popcorn or hear anything from a jeering audience. Despite trying not to anticipate what I might see, I couldn't help but steel myself against Harold the phantom usher, who had kept demanding my ticket stub and trying to shoo me into a seat.

"Hello?" I asked in a loud, clear voice. "Anybody here to help me to my seat?"

Annette looked around at the empty theater. "Are you seeing something right now?"

"No, nothing, as a matter of fact." Still, the needle on my electromagnetic field reader was stuck in the red zone. "But the EMF gizmo is registering energy off the charts."

"Which means what, exactly?" Skepticism and uneasiness were sketched on Annette's strong face.

"I hate to have to tell you this, Annette, but I don't actually know what I'm doing. Usually I stumble around for a while until things start to fall into place or someone tries to kill me to shut me up."

"How very reassuring," Annette muttered. "So glad I let you talk me into this."

"Hey, I'm still alive, aren't I? My method works. It's just not something I can predict." The EMF reader was still registering an overload of otherworldly vibrations. I studied the heavy velvet drapes that hung over the niches in the mezzanine, looking for someone lurking, and searched the corners of my eyes for signs of spectral movement.

Nothing.

I glared at the EMF machine, remembering why I'd never been overly impressed with the gadget. The EMF reader sometimes picked up problems with wiring, or energy bouncing off pipes and other metal objects in the "energy box" common in places such as basements. Speaking of basements . . . I thought about the watery caverns Trish had said were underneath this theater. Could the water really serve as a sort of ghostly superhighway? Should I check it out?

"Where to next?" Annette asked.

I jumped at the sound of her loud whisper.

"It would be a lot more comforting if you weren't so damned jumpy," Annette commented. "Just a suggestion."

"I'll work on that. Let's go."

"Hold on," Annette said, following me down the stairs to the lobby. "I thought you saw Isadora onstage? Shouldn't we check out the main theater? Since we're here, I mean."

"I'd rather keep that for later."

"Why?"

"Just in case."

"Just in case of what?"

In case we're scared and run, screaming, out into the night.

In case there's another body draped over the Mighty Wurlitzer.

In case that creepy ghostly audience does more than jeer.

"Just . . . in case. The SFPD searched everywhere, right?"

"Yes, of course. We searched the entire theater. Nothing particularly pertinent was discovered."

I led the way down the side corridor. "I can't get over this pink paint. Can't you just imagine what must be underneath?"

"Yeah, sure. Dying to know." Annette did not sound sincere. She turned her head this way and that, constantly scanning the surroundings.

There wasn't much to see in this hallway, though: Everything, from the baseboard, to the walls, to the ceiling, was painted that same shade of icky pink. Only the worn, decaying carpet on the floor broke the chromatic monotony. "Anyway, where are we going now?"

"The ladies' lounge. That's where Isadora was living. She told Skeet she had something to show him, and later that same day she was murdered."

"Post hoc, ergo propter hoc?"

"I'm sorry?" Was Annette speaking in tongues now?

"It's Latin. 'After, therefore because of.' It's an assumption that because something came after something else it was caused by that something else. It's a logical fallacy."

"First Japanese and now Latin?"

"What can I say? I went to a rigorous high school. In other words, just because Isadora told Skeet before she died that she had something to show him doesn't mean it was connected to her death, much less causally connected."

"Can't argue with that, in English *or* Latin. Anyway, we're here."

We stood in the mirrored vestibule that led to the ladies' lounge.

There were the handprints in red paint on the mirror that I remembered seeing the last time I was here. But now there were others, the kind of heat imprints from hands that had just been there. As I watched, more appeared, then faded away, almost as though there were someone on the other side of the mirror, trying to get through. I felt a shiver on the back of my neck. The backwards world?

I turned to Annette. She was watching them as well.

"Art installation?" she suggested in a whisper.

"So you can see them, too?"

She nodded. "Art installation referencing the temporary nature of human life on Earth, perhaps?"

I swallowed hard. "Yeah. That's probably what it is."

The needle on the EMF reader hadn't budged out of the red zone. I snapped more photos with the thermal camera, and checked the EVP recorder. It still hummed— recording something, I hoped.

I opened the door to the outer room of the ladies' lounge, and we walked into chaos.

Isadora's desk had been flipped on its side and ransacked, the drawers removed and flung on the floor. Papers, pens, paper clips, staplers, and vintage candy wrappers were strewn all across the threadbare carpet. The ancient divans and chaises longues had been sliced open with a knife and their stuffing ripped out. A ventilation grate had been pulled out of the floor and lay on its side.

"This is new," Annette said. "It wasn't like this when we searched the place. Somebody's been busy."

"Maybe a poltergeist?"

"More likely someone looking for something. What's with all the old candy wrappers?"

"Tierney mentioned those. They're not old. They're vintage. Apparently, Isadora found them under the balcony seats."

Annette stepped into the inner washroom, and I followed. Inside, I noted that the original marble toilet partitions were still intact, but most of the sinks had been pulled out. That would be why the taps were collected in the storage room I saw when here with Gregory, I supposed. Less clear was *why* they would have been pulled out.

Suddenly we heard the loud whir of a motor running and the strains of an organ playing. It sounded as if it were in the lounge with us, rather than all the way in the main theater.

"That's not good," I said.

"What the hell is that?" Annette whispered.

"The Mighty Wurlitzer."

"*Damn it.* No one's supposed to be in here." She stopped and fixed me with a look. "Or are you saying the ghosts are doing this?"

"I'm not saying anything, at the moment." I was fiddling with the EVP, which didn't seem to be working anymore; then I realized the camera was also dead. I set the backpack on the ruined divan, took out some fresh batteries, and replaced the ones in the camera and recorder.

"What's with you and that equipment?"

"The camera can sometimes capture things too fast for the human eye," I said, "and the recorder—"

"Captures things too fast for the human ear?" Annette guessed.

"That's what they say. Or on frequencies the naked ear can't hear, I guess."

"You believe that?" Annette raised one eyebrow,

which always intimidated me. Luz could do it, as well. I was very jealous of this skill.

I shrugged. "We'll check the results later, see if they show any—"

The overhead lights went off.

Annette switched on her flashlight, but it was dead, too. I was reaching for more batteries when a movie started to project onto the screen on the lounge's far wall. It was in black and white and starred Isadora. It was a "silent" movie, and her lips moved without any sound.

"What the hell is going on?" asked Annette.

"There is a series of mirrors that projects the films in here so women wouldn't miss anything while they were in the lounge."

On-screen, Isadora began to dance. Her legs and arms moved to the music from the Wurlitzer, her long scarves fluttering gracefully behind her.

"So someone's in the projection room right now? And why the hell is nothing working?" Annette was checking her phone and police radio, but in this energy hotbox, nothing worked.

"Batteries drain quickly in here," I said, handing her fresh batteries for her flashlight. "I blame the ghosts."

"Yeah, well, I'm in the mood to kick some spectral butt," Annette said. "Let's go see who we're dealing with."

"*Wait*. Look." I gestured to the screen. Isadora had stopped dancing, and was laughing and speaking to the person behind the camera. The camera pulled in for a close-up, and the look on Isadora's face turned from joy to anger, and then fear.

Gloved hands reached out, grabbed the ends of her long scarf, and pulled it tightly around her neck.

Chapter Eighteen

Isadora's hands reached up, clawing at the scarf to loosen it, but the gloved hands kept pulling. Her head fell back, her mouth gaped open, her eyes bulged . . .

I couldn't watch any more.

Annette ran out of the lounge, leaving me in the flickering light of the horrifying silent movie.

I scrounged in my backpack for my own flashlight and chased after Annette. The beam of my flashlight bounced as I ran down the pink hallway toward the main lobby, up the stairs past the mezzanine and balcony, then up the final flight of stairs to the small projection booth.

I found Annette there, panting. She was alone.

Whoever—or whatever—had started the film projector was long gone. The movie was still playing, projecting on the raggedy curtain in the main theater below.

I glanced down. The image was distorted by the folds of the drapery, yet horrifyingly clear. Isadora was still dying, still being strangled. I looked away.

"Why does it smell like popcorn in here?" Annette said softly. "Is that just the power of suggestion?"

"I'm afraid not." Above the strains of the Mighty Wurlitzer, I could now hear the audience. "Do you hear anything?"

"I hear the organ. It's like a player piano, I presume? Or wait a minute—do you 'see' someone playing? Also . . . how is it that there's power for the projector, but not for the overhead lights?"

I peered out the small project room window. The Wurlitzer did seem to be playing itself, but the balcony was now full of ghosts.

One man turned his vacant-looking face toward me. Then the woman beside him, and then another and another. They began to yell and jeer as the film came to an end, leaving only the bright white light projected onto the curtain.

I blew out a breath and remembered to ground myself.

What did they want? What did they need? Who was this phantom audience, and could they tell me anything?

"Mel?" Annette asked. "You still with me?"

I nodded. "I'm going to check out the balcony."

"I don't think so. Time for us to go, Mel. My radio and phone aren't working, and I need to call in some uniforms to go over this place, inch by inch."

"I get it, Annette. But I promise you, we're dealing with ghosts here."

"It was a flesh-and-blood person who put this film on. Someone who likes Good and Plenty." She pointed at a movie-theater-sized box of candy on the floor. "Likely the same someone who made this grotesque film in the first place."

She pulled on a pair of gloves, removed the film reel from the projector, and put it into an evidence bag, along with the box of Good & Plenty. "Put these in your backpack, will you? Let's go."

We headed out of the projection room and made our way down the steep stairs, the pitch-blackness interrupted only by the increasingly dim beams of our flashlights.

I switched mine off to preserve what was left of the battery and followed Annette closely, holding tight to the railing.

We reached the balcony landing and started down to the mezzanine, where we saw light peeking out from below the double doors to the main theater and heard the organ and the sounds of laughter.

"This is *bizarre*," Annette said. She sounded angry.

"I have to agree with you there," I said. The trip down the stairs seemed to take forever.

At the mezzanine level, we came face-to-face with the ghostly usher.

"May I help you to your seats?"

As before, his voice was out of sync with the movement of his mouth.

I ignored him.

By now we had reached the small seating area of the mezzanine. One more flight to the lobby. The fire doors were closed; they had been open when we went up.

Annette pushed on one of the doors. "This isn't good."

"What?" I asked. "I don't like the sound of that."

"You're going to like this even less. The fire door is locked."

"*What?* How is that possible? There aren't supposed to be locks on fire doors."

"Beats me. Where's the emergency exit?"

"This way."

But the emergency exit door was also locked. Considering the rusty condition of the bolts on the fire escape outside that might have been just as well.

"Now what?" I asked Annette.

She was looking around and sniffing. "Do you smell smoke?"

My heart raced for a moment; then I sniffed and relaxed.

"That's cigarette smoke. Back in the day, people were allowed to smoke in the theater."

"But who's smoking those cigarettes?" Annette demanded. The idea that what we were hearing and smelling had a ghostly origin was not in any way comforting to her.

"Let's keep looking," I said. "Surely there's another way out."

Wait a minute. I thought back to the original floor plans Baldwin had shown me earlier in the day. There should have been a door to the service stairs somewhere.

"Check the paneling," I said.

"Okay. What are we looking for?"

"A raised panel of some kind. There should be a door to the stairs used by the staff during performances."

Annette and I began feeling around, the flashlight growing dimmer every moment.

"Found it!" Annette said, and a panel opened to a narrow passageway with stairs leading down. "Follow me."

At the bottom of the stairs, there was a door that led onto an alcove in the main theater. Annette pushed it open.

The phantom usher stood there, right in front of us.

"Ma'am, I must insist you show your ticket stub."

Annette slammed the door in his face and leaned back against it.

"I don't think he can actually do anything to us," I said.

"He? He who?"

"The usher. You didn't see him?"

"I didn't see a damned thing, but I smell that smoke and hear people laughing. That's not another art installation, is it?"

"Let's put a pin in that for the moment and see if this leads to an exit."

We continued down the corridor, which led backstage. I was reminded that the Crockett had not only been a movie theater, but had had vaudeville shows requiring makeup rooms and changing rooms for the actors.

In one room a woman in silk pants and a teddy was sitting in front of a mirror. Her spectral head swiveled toward us as we passed.

In another, a man in short pants and suspenders waggled his eyebrows and leered.

"Just keep walking," I said, not sure how much Annette could see or hear, but knowing now was not the time to discuss it.

The flashlight was growing dimmer, but our way was lit by the light from the makeup tables.

We kept going, checking anything that looked like an exit, but they were all locked.

"Can't you find another secret door?" Annette said, pushing all the panels she could find, just in case.

"I'm working on it," I said.

Finally, one opened, and we peered inside. A set of metal stairs led down into a dank, dark space. The basement, I presumed.

Annette directed the fading flashlight beam down the stairs. "Do you see anything—"

"Ahhhh!" I screamed.

Annette pulled out her gun in one swift move, shoved me behind her, and crouched into a shooter's stance, scanning for an attacker.

"Police!" she called out. *"Freeze!"*

"Sorry," I said, chagrined, as I frantically wiped at my cheeks and forehead. "Spiderweb, right in the face. Don't you just hate that?"

Annette glared. "If I drop dead of a heart attack, you're going to be here all alone. You know that, right?"

"I'll get a grip."

"See that you do." Annette started down the stairs.

I took a moment to repeat my mantra, held tight to the handrail, and followed. Vertigo began to set in, and I tried to turn back, but the door banged shut behind me. I tried the handle. It was locked. I swore under my breath, and I heard Annette do the same.

"I don't think this is a good idea," I said, but I slowly progressed down farther into the belly of the beast.

"Of course it isn't. It's a *terrible* idea. But what other options do we have? We were locked in up there, and personally I don't fancy the idea of spending the night in this hellhole."

We paused near the bottom of the stairs.

"Do you hear that?" I asked.

"Now what?" Annette said. "Another ghostly usher?"

"Water."

There was a dripping sound and a trickling.

"We must be in the caverns," I said.

"Is that bad or good?"

"It depends. If there's a siege, we're all good."

"This is spooky as hell," Annette whispered, her voice reverberating off the rock walls. "And my flashlight's going out *again*."

Just then it went from dim to dead. I tried mine, but it was the same story.

We both stood stock-still. It was pitch-black, uninterrupted by the slightest light. We were, indeed, in the belly of the beast.

"Wait. My camera has an infrared lens," I said, feeling for it in the backpack.

"Give it here," said Annette.

I couldn't see a damned thing, but I assumed she was looking through it. I heard her gasp.

And at the top of the stairs, the door flew open.

A man loomed there, backlit by light. I blinked, blinded by the sudden brightness after the black of the underground caverns.

Before I had time to react, Annette had her gun out and was holding it in front of her.

Unfortunately, the man at the top of the stairs had a gun pointed at us, as well.

Chapter Nineteen

Y‌ou scared the living *bejesus* out of me!" said Skeet
the security guard, holstering his weapon and illu-
minating the steps with a large flashlight. "Pardon my
language, ladies. Are you all right? What's going on?"

Annette and I hurried up the stairs to join him, our
footsteps clanging on the metal steps, ringing out in the
underground cavern. I hardly felt any vertigo this time,
anxious as I was to leave this sepulchre.

"We're fine," I said with a nod. "But glad to see you.
We seemed to be locked in."

"You're fine, good," he said, then glanced at Annette. "Inspector, are *you* okay?"

Annette appeared ashen but nodded. "Show us the
way out of here, please, Mr. Henley."

"Call me Skeet. Everybody does," Skeet said, waving
us through the open door. "It's a real rabbit warren in
here. Doors lock automatically to keep people out."

"Yeah, well, you need a better system," said Annette.
"Because not only do the locked doors not keep people
out—they trap people *in*. That's a serious fire code vi-
olation. Mel, make a note."

"Yes, Inspector," I said.

"I don't understand it. Everything should have been locked up properly," Skeet said. "How'd you two even get down here?"

"We're intrepid," I said. "Can't keep a good woman down."

I heard Annette muttering. We traipsed through a twisting and turning corridor, up another set of steps, and finally found ourselves back in the once-resplendent lobby. The lights were back on, and the ghosts were gone. No more otherworldly moans, no jeering audience, no Isadora dancing onstage.

Outside in the fresh night air at last, we joined Skeet in the security pod. He made us mugs of coffee from freshly ground beans, in his personal drip coffeemaker. I approved. We coffee people have to stick together.

"Where's Thad?" Annette asked.

"Dropped by and found the boy napping. Don't blame him, used to do that myself from time to time. Late-night shift can get pretty quiet. But he's not much good asleep at the wheel, so I sent him home. Good thing I did, huh?"

Skeet noticed me staring at the movie poster on the wall of the trailer. He held up his hands in surrender.

"Yup, I took that one. I mean, I don't like to think of it as stealing, as much as taking care of it for its rightful owner, whoever that turns out to be. There are a lot of those posters in the theater, just rolled up and left on the floor. Most are falling apart, but this one was in decent shape, so I figured if I framed it, it would help to keep it nice. I also rescued those things." He gestured to a shelf in the corner on which sat a grimy roll of paper movie tickets and a broken saucer in a jade green that looked like Depression ware.

"Again, I hope you don't think I was looting. I mentioned it to Mr. Thibodeaux, who said I could hang on to them for the interim. I planned on giving them over to the owner of the place, whenever I figured out who that was."

"I understand the love of old things," I said with a nod. "You should see my place."

"Always been a big fan of the movies," Skeet said. "Used to come here, back in the day. My mom used to take me. She loved movies, too."

"Don't we all?"

"Some more than others, I guess."

"Mel said you told her that Isadora had something she wanted to tell you the night she died," Annette asked.

"That's what Isadora said," Skeet agreed. "Don't know what it was, though."

"Did she give you any indication about what she intended to discuss?"

Skeet shook his head. "After she—well, afterward, I asked a couple of the squatters about it, but no one seemed to know what she was up to. I noticed, though, that someone has gone through her stuff in the ladies' lounge."

I shivered. It had been one heck of a night.

"You're a local boy, are you, Skeet?" asked Annette, sipping her coffee and acting as though she had all the time in the world to chat. I knew her well enough now to recognize that Inspector Crawford was back and asking questions.

"San Francisco, born and raised."

"You don't meet many natives in the city anymore."

"True that."

"Your folks from here, too?"

"My mom was orphaned young. From the Town." Around these parts, San Francisco was the City, and Oakland was the Town. "She came from nothing, worked hard her whole life. It was a tough childhood, so she wanted us to have the best. We weren't rich, but we got by, even had a little house over near Hunters Point for a while, but we lost it to back taxes."

"You mentioned you loved the stage. Did you do any acting?" I asked. If Annette's gambit was to get him talking, I could play along.

"In high school, sure. Dancing, singing. Wasn't half bad either. Spent a little time doing community theater, that sort of thing. But soon enough I had to go to work."

"What kind of work did you do?" I asked.

"Picked apples for a while, then decided to see the world." He gave a chagrined smile. "Got as far as Washington and Oregon before running out of money. Came back and landed a warehouse job driving a forklift. Worked my way up to warehouse manager, got married, raised a family. The wife and I get over to Reno every once in a while, see a show and do a little gambling, but that's about all for the travel."

"And now you're working security?"

"You know how it is," he said, shrugging. "I got old, but I guess I forgot to save enough for retirement. Also, I've got grandkids in college, and I'm trying to help them out. Want them to outshine their grandpa, have all the opportunities I never had. My granddaughter shows a real talent in the arts. So here I am most days, and a few nights."

Annette placed her empty mug on the desk. "Mel here said you were speaking with a fellow when she arrived with Thibodeaux the day Isadora died. What can you tell me about him?"

His eyes got wary. "She asked me about that already. I don't remember him."

"Don't remember the incident at all?"

"You know how it is. Memory fades. Didn't write anything down in the book, so it must not have been important. But if Thibodeaux saw him, you might ask him."

"I will. Thanks," said Annette, standing. "By the way, why did you come looking for us in the theater? You aren't supposed to be doing rounds until we release the scene."

"I saw the tape had been cut, and Thad told me you'd gone in. I waited a while, but it seemed like you were in there too long."

She nodded. "Well, I'm awfully glad you came looking. Appreciate your help and the coffee. We should let you get back to work."

"I'm just sitting here until my shift ends."

"You should get a TV."

"Management doesn't approve," he said, patting the book on the desk. "But I've got stuff to read. I'm all set."

"Thanks for the coffee," I said, standing and setting my mug down next to Annette's.

I glanced once more at the poster and the little assemblage of items Skeet had collected from the theater. Could there be something valuable in the theater, something worth killing for?

Back at our cars, I handed Annette the reel of film and box of candy she had collected in the projection booth.

"Well, this should keep me busy tomorrow," she said. "I can't wait to see how I write up that field report. Remind me to scratch 'encountering ghosts' off my bucket list."

"Was encountering ghosts ever *on* your bucket list?"

"Not really, no." She let out a wry chuckle, then took a deep breath and sighed. "I see a lot of awful things in my line of work. But nothing as shocking as what I saw tonight. I honest to God don't know how you do it, Mel. For what it's worth, I don't think you're so crazy now."

"Did you think I was before?"

"Crazy-ish. Not so much as some, a lot more than others."

"I don't blame you. It's one of those things that's impossible to imagine until it happens to you."

"Speaking of which . . . tell me something straight."

"Shoot."

"Could the ghosts, or whatever those things were, have had anything to do with Isadora's murder?" A worried frown marred Annette's forehead.

I paused a moment before replying. "I don't think they could be responsible for Isadora's death, if that's what you're asking. Ghosts are immaterial. They can't strangle someone, even if they wanted to. But often violence and sudden death seem to stir things up. Especially when . . ." I trailed off, wanting to get the words right.

"Especially when what?"

"When there are parallels between past and present. From what I understand, the ghostly usher was killed by a romantic rival. Maybe Isadora was murdered for similar reasons?"

"We've spoken to the two men she was rumored to be intimate with, but they have alibis. I don't like them for this crime."

"Okay," I said. "What about her brother, Ringo Sepety? There was bad blood there."

"He also has an alibi and seemed genuinely broken up by her death. I've been fooled before, of course, but Ringo wanted Isadora's help with his project. Killing her wouldn't make a lot of sense."

"Since when does murder have to make sense?"

"Hmm, seems *somebody's* been listening to her favorite homicide inspector," Annette said. "True enough. You can drive yourself crazy trying to find a rational reason for a murder because in most cases there is none."

"I hear you," I said. "Rational reasons don't explain ghosts either, yet there they are."

She nodded. "Anyway, thanks for dinner. I'm going to limp home and try not to think about what I just experienced, then get up in a few hours and try to catch a killer. You?"

"Me, too. I mean, the getting-up-in-a-few-hours part, not the catching-a-killer part. Because that's a job for the professionals in the SFPD homicide department."

"Very funny," Annette said with a reluctant smile. "But seriously, Mel, be careful."

"You, too, Inspector. You, too."

Chapter Twenty

There were more cars on the Bay Bridge than one would expect at eleven o'clock at night. Not so very long ago, a person could commute into San Francisco without too much trouble and even find parking. All that had changed, and now there was almost no time of day or night that one could be sure the traffic would be light.

I realized my conscious mind was ruminating about traffic while my subconscious processed everything that had just happened in the theater. I wished it good luck.

Poor Annette, I thought as I drove across the bridge, the lights from Oakland's busy shipping terminal far below reflecting off the dark water. This sort of thing messed with a rational person's worldview.

I plugged in my dead cell phone and saw several messages, including one from Lily Ivory. "I'm not big for talking on the phone. Any chance you could stop by to chat about your dress?" That put me in mind, again, of going by the new house—Land-Mel's Manor?—and talking to Hildy directly. After all, she had been easy enough to communicate with the first time. But the image of her holding that bloody knife gave me serious pause. After what had happened with Annette at the Crockett, I felt like one of my flashlights: I didn't have a lot of battery left, and my beam was dimming fast.

Going straight home was the right decision. Dog rushed to greet me at the door, and I spent a few moments hugging him. It always helped to hug a dog. The house was quiet; a few bowls and spoons in the sink suggested a round of ice-cream sundaes before bed. My father's keys sat beside a small stack of mail, right where he always put them. A mess of photos—my sisters and me as kids, my mom in later years—and notes and novelty magnets were stuck in a hodgepodge on the fridge.

Everything was blessedly normal.

Stan had already turned in for the night, as had Landon. Dad had fallen asleep in his comfy chair in front of the television. I crept through the room and up the stairs, trying not to wake him.

Landon was in bed reading, but put the book down as soon as I walked in.

"Hello, my love! At long last. I wondered when you'd—Are you all right?"

"Yes. Why?"

"You look . . ."—he seemed to search for the word—". . . tired. Long day?"

I nodded. "I just got back from the theater."

"You went back to the Crockett?"

"Annette was with me—Homicide Inspector Annette Crawford. She carries a gun."

He did not look mollified. "What did you see?"

"We saw a number of things. I'm pretty sure Annette's traumatized for life."

"And you?"

"I was already pretraumatized," I said with a smile. "Unfortunately, nothing we encountered was any help in solving poor Isadora's murder."

"So it was definitely a murder, then?"

I sighed. "No doubt about it." My mind flashed on

the black-and-white images of Isadora, the scarves tightening around her neck . . .

"I'm going to take a shower," I said. "I'll join you in a minute. I'm beat."

When I emerged from the bathroom, Landon was still reading. My mother's journals sat on the night-stand, calling to me. I started reading one—I was hop-ing they might point me in a helpful direction—but managed only a few lines before I gave up and laid my head on Landon's shoulder, listening to the reassuring beat of his steady heart.

"Tomorrow's Saturday," Landon said softly. "You should sleep in late, if you can. Remember, in the eve-ning we're meeting with Luz and Victor."

"Ugh," I said. "Totally forgot."

He laid his book on the nightstand, turned out the light, and wrapped his arms around me.

"Sleep, Mel. Sleep."

"What the hell were you doing on the TV last night?" Dad asked as I walked into the kitchen the next morn-ing. Stan was sitting at the little pine table, reading the local paper, while my dad stood before the stove, cooking eggs and bacon. "Saw you on the six o'clock news."

"It wasn't my fault," I said, leaning over to greet Dog, who met me with a wild wagging of his plume of a tail.

"You were on the news?" asked Stan. The newspaper crackled as he lowered it to fix me with a questioning look. "Everything okay?"

"There was a press conference in front of the Crock-ett yesterday," explained Dad. "And they labeled this one here a 'local ghost buster.'"

"Better than being a ghost buster from out of town, I suppose," I mumbled, yawning as I poured coffee into my mug.

"That explains all the calls we got last night," said

Stan. "It seems there's plenty of work in the ghost business, Mel, in case you ever want to branch out."

My father rolled his eyes and grumbled.

"I think I'm good with running Turner Construction for the moment," I said.

"Breakfast, babe?" Dad asked me as I cradled my coffee.

"No, thanks."

"What did you eat last night?"

"Dad, I love you, but you are inordinately concerned with my eating habits."

"Grabbed some tacos from a truck, as per usual, I'll bet," said Dad.

"As a matter of fact, I had a lovely meal with Annette Crawford at Akiko's on Bush," I said. "It's a sushi place."

"Raw fish?" Dad said, shaking his head. I wasn't fooled; I knew for a fact that my dad was a more adventurous eater than he let on. He had done two tours in Vietnam and raved about the food. But he loved playing the curmudgeon. "Should have brought it home for the grill."

Landon joined us then, freshly showered and shaved but wearing a pair of old jeans and a stained T-shirt. These were his "chore clothes," and it was one of my favorite outfits on him. I did like the look of a well-built man in construction gear. Today he and Dad were planning on reglazing the dining room windows.

After wishing everyone a good morning, Landon poured a cup of coffee, leaned against the counter, and said, "Did you tell them about going back in the theater, Mel?"

"Last night?" Stan asked.

"You went back in the theater?" Dad asked, pausing in flipping the hashed browns. "At night? By yourself?"

"No, Inspector Crawford went with me."

"Crawford seems like a sensible woman," Dad said. "What'd you do, get her liquored up on sake?"

"Of course not. I suggested the ghosts might be able to tell us something, and that they usually manifested more at night. She carries a gun, you know," I added to appease the concern on all their faces.

"Did you see anything?" Stan asked.

"We saw a lot," I said, thinking back on the horror of the murder film, of Isadora's face at the end. "But we're no closer to figuring out what's going on. Can anyone think of anything in that theater that would be valuable enough to murder someone over?"

"Vintage film equipment—or a print of an old film?" suggested Stan. "Or posters, maybe? Lots of people collect old film memorabilia, though I have no idea how much that stuff might fetch on the open market."

"That reminds me," I said. "Want to go to Niles Canyon tomorrow? I'd love to check out the Essanay film museum and see if they can tell us anything. Caleb's coming home; we could make it a family outing."

We were all eager to see him. Caleb might have no longer been my official stepson, but in the Turner house, he was one of us. Forever.

"I'd love to go," said Stan, already looking it up on his smartphone. "I'll check their hours on Sundays, and see if the museum's wheelchair accessible."

Stan had to go through life checking to see whether or not he could go places. Not for the first time, I was grateful for my two working legs.

"Will you be enjoying the fireworks tonight?" Landon asked Stan and Dad. As Oakland residents, we had been treated to more than a week of illegal fireworks leading up to the Fourth of July. Fortunately, Dog didn't seem to be bothered by them. I wasn't sure he even noticed.

"We might step outside and take a look," said Dad. "But they're predicting fog in San Francisco."

"No surprise there," I said, and made a mental note to call Luz in case she was panicking about tonight's big date.

Stan and I headed down the hall to the office to catch up on business. I showed him the Facebook page set up by the Crockett Caretakers, and he showed me a stack of phone messages inquiring about how to deal with "unwelcome visitors" and asking about my ghost-busting services.

"Already referred those to Olivier Galopin," Stan said. "He should pay you a finder's fee."

"I'll suggest that to him," I said. "Stan, let me ask you something: Have you ever had any doubts about Mateo?"

"*Our* Mateo?"

I nodded.

"No, why? Did something happen?"

"Nothing really. It's just that his name came up last night with Inspector Crawford."

"Mel, I know he has a past, but I would no more suspect him of homicide than I would suspect you. You know him as well as I do."

"You're right. I agree. Just wanted to check."

I called Mateo, but he didn't pick up. I left him a message to call me back.

"They've been awfully patient," I said, riffling through my other phone messages.

"Who?" asked Stan.

"The Xerxes Group. Nobody's called to see where the project stands. I figured after Thibodeaux was hurt, someone would get in touch."

"It's only been a few days."

"I get that, but they lost their first contractor, finally signed a second contractor—us. Then their guy on the scene, Thibodeaux, gets hurt and is out of commission— and nobody from the consortium that is investing millions of dollars in the project reaches out for a status update? Doesn't that seem odd to you?"

"Like I said, it hasn't been that long."

"How long is it before we normally hear from clients during construction delays?"

"That's a good point."

"Here's another question," I said. "Who's the city liaison for the Crockett Theatre?"

"No one's listed," said Stan. "I asked Gregory Thibodeaux about that when we were going over the initial proposal. He said there had been turnover in the city office and he'd get back to me with the name. Never did."

"That's odd."

"There are a number of odd things about this job."

"You can say that again. But, Stan, you should see the place."

"These photos are pretty impressive—that's for sure," he said as he flipped through the pictures posted on the Facebook page. "There are a lot more here than what Thibodeaux sent."

"It's an amazing theater. It's going to be a masterpiece when we're done. It's not particularly wheelchair accessible at the moment, but that's something we'll be amending."

"I have no doubt," said Stan.

"Gregory mentioned the consortium renovated a small theater in Oregon; do you have the name there?"

"Let's see . . ." Stan selected a folder from his meticulously kept files, and scanned a few papers. "The Strand, in Roseburg."

I looked it up on the computer. The photos were charming: The Strand was a much smaller theater than the Crockett, but featured a lovely neon marquee and a sweet façade with an octagonal ticket kiosk of its own.

But then I found a newspaper article stating that the entire city block had been sold to a developer, and the theater torn down. I felt a chill run over me.

"What a shame," said Stan, reading the article over my shoulder. "Not to mention a waste of time and resources. Why tear down a building that's just been renovated?"

"Let's find out," I said, calling Gregory Thibodeaux.

This time he picked up. He said he was feeling much better, and should be back to work on Monday, adding, "I saw you on the news yesterday."

"Yeah . . . my fifteen minutes of fame are up, or so I hope. Anyway, it wasn't intentional. I sort of got ambushed by the Sepety family."

"I think that's their specialty."

"Still, they're grieving a profound loss, so I suppose we should cut them some slack."

"Of course. I still can't believe what happened to poor Isadora. And we had just been talking to her, not two hours before."

I nodded, then realized I was on the phone. "Yes, it's hard to accept."

"Anyway, I'm glad you called. I wanted to let you know the latest from the police is that the scene should be released by Monday, but there's no immediate rush. Another week or two won't matter in the long run, and it's critical that the police have everything they need."

"Of course. Thanks." No way was I waiting a week or two—I was itching to get started at the Crockett, now more than ever. "Gregory, do you remember seeing anyone before you fell?"

"I'm embarrassed to say I don't remember anything after going up to the balcony. It's really strange, as though I had blacked out, like a drunk, which is odd because I don't drink. The doctors say with head injuries it's normal not to be able to remember what happened, but it's an odd sensation."

"I'll bet. One more thing: I wanted to ask you about the city liaison."

"What about him?"

"Who is it?"

"The name must be in the paperwork. You probably overlooked it."

"Don't think so." I might have overlooked such a thing, but Stan was a details guy. "I just checked."

"Let me see." I heard papers rustling. "Here it is: Alan Peterson. I'll send you his contact info."

"Alan Peterson . . . Why do I know that name?"

"I have no idea. Head injury, remember?" He chuckled. "I can milk that excuse for a while, don't you think?"

"Lemonade out of lemons," I said absentmindedly, quoting my mother. "Oh, before I let you go—you said the Xerxes Group funded the renovation of a theater in Roseburg, Oregon. Did you know it was recently torn down?"

There was a long pause. "What? Are you sure?"

"According to an article in the local newspaper, complete with before and after pictures."

"I'll look into it."

I stashed my backup EVP recorder, EMF reader, and thermal camera in my backpack, grabbed Dog's leash, bid good-bye to Stan and Dad, and made plans with Landon to meet up this evening in San Francisco for the big double date.

The pup was ecstatic to be invited along on a car ride, even though he had a tendency toward motion sickness. We had been working on it, and he was better than he used to be, but the struggle was real.

We headed to our new house—MelStone, maybe?

I exited the freeway at Grand Avenue and, as I waited for the light to change, studied the Grand Lake Theatre on the corner. It, too, was a grand old movie palace—not nearly as over-the-top as the Crockett, but still built in the florid style of the early movie palaces.

I had gone to many movies at the Grand Lake over the years; it was my favorite theater in Oakland, hands down. In the lobby, the owner had put historic camera equipment on exhibit, and a panel of antique Tiffany stained glass was behind bulletproof glass. I remembered wondering if anyone had ever tried to steal those precious items, though it would have been tough to get them out of the lobby unnoticed. A large glass panel was not something that could be snuck out under a sweatshirt.

Could there be something similarly precious hidden amongst the junk and ephemera in the Crockett? Something that had been ignored through the years of abandonment and neglect? Maybe the Crockett's ghosts had protected their home by keeping scavengers and looters at bay. But the squatters lived there—had Isadora found something? And if she had, why would she want to confide in Skeet, of all people?

I pulled up to our "new" old house. All was quiet this morning. When we're behind schedule, we work on Saturdays, but this job was on schedule so far, and whenever possible I liked to give my crew a full weekend off to spend time with their families.

And at the moment, I was happy to have the place to myself. I wanted to check on the progress of the renovation, but also maybe have a little chat with a ghost named Hildy.

In the yard there were a stack of slate intended for the backyard patio, a pile of two-by-fours, a dumpster, and a bright blue Porta Potti that we had tried, with only partial success, to camouflage with lattice.

Inside the house, evidence of the ongoing renovation was everywhere. Power tools, air compressors, lumber of various sizes and quality, and above all the scent of freshly sawn wood. I took a deep breath. To me, this was the beloved aroma of childhood. The old lathe-and-plaster walls were peppered with exploratory holes, and in one corner the 1950s-era grass wallpaper had been pulled off to reveal a penciled message underneath. I hurried over, hoping to read some amusing old graffiti, or maybe even a secret message, but saw instead: "Splice to center of batten piece."

Oh well. Even old construction notes like this one were a fun connection to the past.

This was my favorite moment in the construction process: When the historic bones of a home were laid bare, but the possibilities were still limitless. Would this wall be better moved or taken out altogether? Should we replace the French doors that used to be here, or leave as is for more wall space? How would that stained glass window look once it was cleaned and releaded? I loved creating peace of mind by installing new electrical wiring and copper piping, playing with the paint colors and wallpapers. The woodwork on this home, miracle of miracles, had never been painted, which was rare for a home that had been around for nearly a hundred years. I thought of the back hallways of the Crockett Theatre, painted a putrid pink. I would have to make that right.

Despite all the frustrations, despite the difficult clients and the cost overruns and the surprises behind every wall, I was clearly in the right business.

Dog sniffed around, seemingly unperturbed. I had brought him with me partly to give him a walk in the woods after we were done, and partly because he was the only one of my family, besides myself, who could sense ghosts.

Ostensibly I was here today to start going through all that junk/fabulous stuff in the attic. But I imagined I might well also run into one Hildy Hildecott.

I didn't know much more about Hildy than I had yesterday, but I trusted Lily's assessment of the dress, which was that Hildy didn't "feel" like a murderer. And I wanted to ask Hildy if she had indeed spoken with my mom. If that went well, maybe I'd also ask if she had any idea about how she died, why she was still hanging around this house, and what I might do for her.

As I mounted the stairs, I heard something.

Music. Very old music, as from the 1920s.

Then something—or someone—bumping around in the attic.

Those of us who have contact with the spirit dimen-

sions, who are able to access the portals through the
veil that separates our worlds, are few. My mother was
one. I am another. As Lily Ivory had pointed out, it was
a "privilege."

"It's a privilege," I said to Dog as we climbed the
stairs. "I can't chicken out." Dog indicated that he
agreed with me completely.

But when we reached the upstairs landing, Dog
started doing the strange crouching, mewling thing that
he did when he sensed ghosts. He wouldn't be able to
go up into the attic anyway; he wasn't about to scale
those ladder steps, and he was too big for me to carry.

"You wait here," I said. "I'll be back soon."

I held the EMF reader in one hand and had the EVP
recorder strapped to me. I took a moment to ground
myself, stroked the ring on my necklace, then pulled
down the hatch, folded out the ladder, and climbed the
steps up to the attic space.

Hildy was out of her closet, making me wonder: Did
she have access to the entire house, then? Or just the attic?

She was dancing to a scratchy old song playing on
an ancient radio. A radio that wasn't plugged in.

"Have you ever heard such a thing?" she asked, panting, the look on her face delighted. "I finally figured
out how to work this piece of machinery!"

The radio was probably from the 1940s. I had never
given much thought to how ghosts from different eras
might interact with items from the current world, but I
supposed it made sense that if she was trapped up in the
attic space for eternity, she had time to figure it out. Where
the music was coming from, exactly, was another question.

"Do you know how to do the Charleston?" Hildy
asked, exhilarated.

"I'm not big on dancing," I said.

The singer on the radio held a last long note, and the
song came to an end. A slower song came on.

Hildy stood, breathing hard, and tilted her head.

"You don't go to the movies. You don't go dancing . . . What *do* you do, honey?"

"I work a lot."

"But ya gotta spend *some* time havin' fun, too, right?" A troubled look came into her eyes, and I was sorry to see her frown. "Life's too short, doll. Take it from me."

"That's good advice," I said.

"At least you're dressed up real nice," Hildy said in a perkier tone, her bright blue eyes taking in today's outfit. It was one of Stephen's recent creations, a fiery red shift—it seemed appropriate for the Fourth of July—striped with fringe. I had topped it with my dad's old leather flight jacket to ward off the early-morning chill. "Is that your boyfriend's jacket? He a soldier? I just love a man in uniform."

"It's my dad's jacket, actually."

Another wave of sadness seemed to pass over her. "I had a fella in the army once. Real nice fella."

"What happened to him?"

"He went to fight the Germans. Died in France, they say."

"I'm so sorry."

"It happens. Anyway, he sent me a postcard from Paris. Can you beat that? Prettiest place he ever saw, he said. Later, my Jimmy said he'd take me to Paris one day, but he never did."

"I've always wanted to go to Paris, too."

"Good for you! You keep your dreams, honey. They're the only thing a girl has sometimes." As Hildy spoke she roamed the attic, looking at things: an old lamp, a rocking chair, a stack of books, a bunch of old playbills. As she trailed her fingers over them, I wondered if she was able to open boxes, manipulate them the way she had the radio. I felt I should be more of a scientist, try to figure out some of the details of how this ghost thing worked.

But as I was formulating a question in my head, she said: "Gotta watch out for yourself, ya know, 'cause when it comes to girls like us, no one else will."

"That's good advice," I said, wondering what experiences had led her to this conclusion.

"Only one I really miss—only one I'll never stop missing—is my sweet Darlene. Jimmy promised he'd take care of her, that he'd take care of us both. And I believed him. I really did. That last night, we was at the picture palace in the city. He said he had something to show me. But I never seen it . . . He dropped it. You believe that? And then after, his brother showed up, and that's when . . ."

"What happened?"

She shrugged.

"Can you tell me about that last night?"

No response.

"Who is Darlene?" I asked.

"Right here," she said, pausing in front of a sepia-toned photograph of a young girl dressed in lace, holding a bouquet of flowers that trailed from her lap. Hildy sighed. "Isn't she just the prettiest thing you ever did see?"

"She's beautiful. Her name's Darlene?"

She nodded. "My daughter."

"And who is Jimmy?"

The song on the radio sped up until the words turned to jibberish. From the hall below, I heard Dog let out a high-pitched howl.

Hildy froze. She hesitated so long I thought she wouldn't answer. But finally, in a voice somehow more menacing for its calm quiet, she turned to me and said: "Why, ain't you read the papers? Jimmy's the man I stabbed to death, dontcha know?"

Hildy rushed toward me, her face twisted in anger, reaching out, as though she wanted to kill me.

Chapter Twenty-One

Ever the professional ghost buster, I screamed and fell back onto my butt. The EVP reader flew out of my hands and crashed, and I felt the recorder in my pocket crunch under me as I fell.

My heart pounded and I felt nauseated, but Hildy was gone and the radio had fallen silent.

Dog was barking like crazy.

Still shaking, I gathered up the detritus of the ghost-busted equipment and deposited it into the ample pockets of the leather jacket, then carefully climbed down the ladder and sank onto the dusty floor of the upstairs landing. Dog climbed into my lap, all seventy pounds of him, and began frantically licking me.

I sat there, hugging him and murmuring reassuring words until my heart stopped pounding.

Well, that was interesting. Hildy had apparently murdered her lover, the father of her child. One Jimmy Delucci, I presumed. What had happened to little Darlene? How old had she been when Hildy died? And why was there a photo of her in this house? For that matter, why was *Hildy* in this house?

Also, I hadn't had a chance to ask Hildy about my mom. "Much less go through any of the boxes. Those are both going back on the to-do list," I said to Dog, who supported my decision.

What now?

Trish had mentioned that Lorraine Delucci, Calvin Delucci's widow, lived in Montclair. It was a beautiful part of the Oakland hills overlooking the Town and the bay, with San Francisco in the background. It wasn't far, and I had planned on taking Dog for a hike in the woods near there anyway.

I dialed information and found a listing for Lorraine Delucci in Montclair. That was easy.

Feeling like quite the supersleuth, I dialed the number and explained that I was working on the renovation of the Crockett Theatre. Lorraine Delucci was pleasant enough but hesitated when I asked if I could come by and speak with her about the history of the building, claiming she didn't know much. When I explained that I was going to be in her neighborhood walking my dog anyway, she said she would love to meet my dog and invited me to stop by for a chat.

"And that, my friend," I said to Dog, "is the power of dog lovers."

I grabbed a quick bagel sandwich for lunch in Montclair's shopping district, then drove slowly along the twisty roads that snaked through the hills. There were no bike lanes here, not that this stopped ambitious bicyclists who wanted to train on the challenging hills while imagining themselves competing in the Tour de France. In fact, there were also no sidewalks, and very little parking other than the dirt shoulder on the side of the road, which dropped off steeply to the hillside below. I spotted Lorraine's address on a wooden sign tacked to a redwood tree, and squeaked into a spot behind a car in the driveway.

An American flag and a stars-and-stripes wind sock

blew in the soft breeze. Bunting decorated the front of the house, which was deceptively simple. Built in the 1970s, it was the sort of place that would have sold to a middle-class family in other parts of the country. But in the Bay Area, given the view of San Francisco beyond the bay, this home was probably valued in the millions.

I was surprised when Lorraine Delucci opened the door. For some reason I'd expected a little old lady, white haired and frail. In reality, Lorraine was of medium height and heavyset, with a rather garish shock of obviously dyed red hair framing a pleasant seventy-something face. When she saw Dog in the car, she urged me to bring him in.

"I have a Chihuahua named Lulu. I'm sure they'll get along!"

I brought Dog in, and after greeting Lorraine enthusiastically, he and Lulu sniffed each other, tails wagging. Tiny Lulu seemed unimpressed by his size, and Dog appeared thrilled to find a canine playmate.

"There you go!" Lorraine said, ushering me in and offering me coffee. "Dogs are so genuine, aren't they? They either like someone or they don't."

"Indeed. I appreciate your speaking with me," I said as I took a seat in a comfortable sunken living room with a multimillion-dollar view shining through large plate-glass windows. "What a gorgeous view. Perfect for watching the fireworks, I'll bet."

"They're predicting fog, as usual," she said with a smile as she handed me a mug of weak but fragrant coffee. She let out a sigh. "Frankly, I never really cared about the view. That was all my husband, Cal. He liked that sort of thing. I would have preferred to be able to walk somewhere myself. But now that I don't get around as well, I suppose it's nice to have the view. I was never one for watching television, so I enjoy watching life unfold out there, in the world beyond."

The remoteness of these residences in the Oakland hills always gave me pause. The views were indeed stunning, but the more central location of our new house—LandonHenge?—would allow us to walk to the lake, to the grocery store, to the venerable Grand Lake Theatre, even to an old-fashioned neighborhood hardware store. I spent a good portion of my day in my car as it was, driving from one job to another, fighting traffic, so I was happy not to have to get into a car in my free time.

Framed movie posters crowded the walls, and more Fourth of July stars-and-stripes paraphernalia decorated the bookshelves and tabletops.

"I was sorry to learn about the loss of your husband," I said. The whole way here, I tried to figure out a nice way to ask if his death had been suspicious. I decided there wasn't one, so I hoped she might volunteer that information. "A heart attack, was it?"

She nodded. "He ate a lot of red meat; we both did back then."

"I understand he owned a couple of local theaters. As I mentioned on the phone, I'm working on the renovation of the Crockett."

"That's such a spectacular place. It was my Cal's dream to bring it back to its former glory, but we never managed."

"What kinds of problems did you face?"

"Simple lack of funds. My husband, rest his soul, was raised quite wealthy and was never all that good with money. As I'm sure you know, a project like the Crockett will take *millions*, not to mention a lot of time." She shook her head and sipped her coffee. "In the end, I suppose he—*we*—simply ran out of time."

We sat silently for a few moments. Cal Delucci had died several years ago, but as I knew only too well with the loss of my mother, time might alter the grief, but did not make it less intense.

"This might seem like an odd question," I said, "but

have you ever heard rumors about the theater being haunted?"

She chuckled. "Oh yes, that's what they say. Never saw anything myself. I believe buildings have different feelings about them, but what some people call 'ghosts' are probably just our picking up on those historical sensations, don't you think? Or do you think there are really spirits floating around?"

"I, uh . . ." One of my many failings as a ghost buster is that I didn't know how to tell people I was able to communicate with ghosts, if only because it wasn't something that can be dropped into a conversation without a lot of follow-up discussion. *I see ghosts* is a conversation starter, not a conversation killer. I wondered if I should tell Lorraine about my experiences at the Crockett or just wimp out.

I wimped out. "I think there's a lot more out there than we understand."

She nodded.

"So," I said, "your husband inherited the theater from his father?"

She nodded. "Yes, he did. His father, William Delucci, was a very wealthy man. He made a lot of money investing in the early film industry, and a fortune off of those theaters as well. Back in the day, the theaters were real cash cows. Of course, he lost a lot of it in the Depression, but managed to hold on to the theaters."

Lorraine got up and brought over an old-fashioned scrapbook full of old photos and newspaper clippings touting the Niles Canyon Essanay film studios.

"I'm embarrassed to say that I've never been to Niles Canyon," I said. "I'm planning on going with my family tomorrow."

"It's well worth a trip. They have a lovely little museum there. We donated several items before Cal passed away."

"What can you tell me about Cal's father?"

She hesitated. "I never met my father-in-law; he was sixty years old when Cal was born, and passed away long before I met Cal. But by all accounts, he was not a very nice man, and was ruthless when it came to business. From bits and pieces of family lore that I've put together, it was something like the Wild West in the film industry back then. William's brother, Jimmy, was the one who was most involved in producing the films; he was a very early investor—most prescient of him really."

"His name was Jimmy Delucci?"

She nodded and sipped her coffee. "They say Jimmy had a 'thing' for starlets, if you know what I mean."

"Did he . . . Do you happen to know if Jimmy ever had a child by one of those starlets?"

"Oh, I really don't know, though I wouldn't be shocked to hear that he had. Bad behavior is hardly limited to current generations, now, is it? I do know that Jimmy and his wife never had children, so when Jimmy died, William inherited the theaters, which were later passed down to my Cal."

"Jimmy died early?" I asked.

"Yes. I'm sorry to say that Jimmy did not come to a good end: He was killed by one of the starlets he toyed with. Stabbed to death, as a matter of fact; she killed herself after."

I shivered at the memory of Hildy telling me about killing Jimmy and rushing me in the attic.

Lorraine flipped the scrapbook to a newspaper clipping that described the crime in salacious detail: The married producer, the ambitious starlet, the murder-suicide when the "murderess" turned the knife on herself. I was happy to note, at the very least, that the murder did not occur on the grounds of my new house, but in a "gentleman's club" near Lake Merritt. Lorraine read the article over my shoulder and pointed out the passage that read: *"Miss Hildecott was an out-of-wedlock mother to a young child."*

"You may be right," said Lorraine. "It says here Jimmy's killer had a child; I suppose it might have been Jimmy's. But there's no way to know, is there? Well, what's done is done."

"It was a long time ago," I said, though to Hildy it was still very relevant, indeed.

"Cal received many offers to buy the theater over the years," said Lorraine, putting away the scrapbook. "He was involved in a court battle and had to sell the Grand Lake Theatre, and the new owners did a splendid job sprucing it up. But Cal never gave up on his dream of bringing the Crockett back to life."

"Why did you finally decide to sell?" I asked.

"When Cal passed, the dream died with him," she said. "I held on to it for a while, then decided it was time to pass the torch to a new generation, as they say."

I nodded. "That makes sense."

"Plus, I got a heck of a lot of money for that old rat trap," she said with a cat-and-the-canary smile, sipping her coffee and gazing out at her multimillion-dollar view.

I collected Dog, said good-bye to Lorraine, and headed to Skyline Drive to take a long walk in one of my favorite local spots, Redwood Regional Park. And then I did something I almost never do: I turned off my phone.

As Dog darted about, marking trees and getting cussed out by squirrels, I thought about what Lorraine Delucci had told me.

I was sure that Hildy's daughter, Darlene, was also Jimmy Delucci's daughter. I wondered what had become of her; nearly a century had passed, so it was highly unlikely she was still living. But maybe Hildy simply wanted to know that her daughter was all right.

I knew the yearning for one's child did not cease upon death: The last ghost I had dealt with, at a lighthouse, had been searching endlessly for her lost son.

I breathed deeply of the evergreen-scented air, gazing up at the July sunshine as it filtered through the branches of the tall redwoods. Isadora would never again smell this scent, never be able to look up into the trees and feel the breeze. I took a moment to appreciate all that I had.

As always when I took the time to hike, I vowed I would come more often. It felt good to get away, if only for a little while, from work and home and ghosts and murder, to simply stroll amongst the trees with my dog.

Victor, my acupuncturist (and Luz's "boyfriend"), called this "forest bathing," which seemed like a pretty highfalutin name for a walk in the woods. Still, he urged me to take a moment while on my walk to close my eyes and stand still, and I did so now, noting what I heard: the distant sound of roadwork, birds singing and flitting, a plane high overhead, kids at a summer camp yelling and laughing, the wind in the leaves, the water trickling in a small creek.

I stayed that way for a moment, concentrating. What else could I hear? The whisper of my own breath.

And Dog, whining, wondering why I was just standing there interrupting his good time.

"Sorry, bud," I said as I finally opened my eyes. I leaned down to scratch his neck and pull a foxtail, the bane of Bay Area dogs, from his thick fur. "Let's go sniff some more redwoods, shall we?"

Chapter Twenty-Two

Whenever I turn off my phone for any length of time, I usually end up paying for it, and today was no exception. While I was communing with nature, I received three calls: two from artisans declining my invitation to bid on the Crockett, and one from Mateo, returning my call, hoping everything was all right, and informing me he was spending the holiday weekend in Tahoe, where he had spotty cell reception.

I dropped Dog off at home, happy and ready for his midafternoon nap, then drove across the bay to San Francisco. I had an appointment to see Eamon Castle.

It wasn't what I was expecting. For one thing, it wasn't really a castle, though I supposed buildings made of stone with six-story towers are rare enough in these parts that the "castle" moniker was appropriate. It was very pretty, though: Tall and slender, with narrow windows, it was surrounded by manicured grounds and elaborate topiary.

I was met at the door by a young woman who introduced herself as Shanice and insisted she was "so very glad!" I had come.

Inside, there was a lot of chunky woodwork, beamed ceilings, and lofts, and the castle had been decorated throughout in a muted palette of beige and taupe that set off the white stucco and stone walls. A massive gray stone hearth was topped with a pounded-copper mantel that gleamed in the occasional ray of sunlight.

"So do tell," urged Shanice. "What's the date of your wedding? And will the lucky man—or woman—be having a say in the venue, too?"

"I haven't set the date yet."

Her eyes dropped to my left hand, and she cocked her head. "But that's a *beautiful* ring. Somebody loves you," she said in a teasing, singsongy voice. "Lucky girl!"

I smiled, unsure how to respond. By far the most awkward thing about being engaged was how public it was, how many people now felt free to comment upon my love life without knowing either Landon or me. I didn't take it personally, because I assumed they meant well, but I felt a bit like a pregnant woman who has strangers laying hands upon her belly on the subway.

We toured the venue, which didn't take long. Despite its impressive façade, Eamon Castle was not a large building. Still, it was historic and it was definitely beautiful.

"Oooh, I forgot your wedding-planning kit!"

"I really don't need—"

"Nonsense! I love putting them together." Shanice leaned in as if sharing a confidence. "It's really just a folder with a brochure and a few informative items and photos of previous events, but with luck it will help to fire your imagination! At Eamon Castle, your wedding can be everything you wish it to be—and then some!"

"That sounds nice," I said. Shanice was sweet, so I didn't want to be rude and confess that I was in the running for the title "Least Inspired Bride in the World."

"It's in the office," Shanice said. "Feel free to look around while I run and get it."

I'd used the wedding-venue idea as a ploy to get in, but as I looked around, I had to admit Eamon Castle would have been a really nice place to celebrate a special occasion. I tried to envision myself here, surrounded by my family and my friends, holding hands with Landon, drinking champagne and sharing a tiered wedding cake . . .

I turned around slowly as I imagined it in my mind's eye.

When I opened my eyes, I found myself face-to-face with the balding, middle-aged white guy I had seen speaking with Skeet outside the Crockett Theatre a few days ago.

It's possible I let out a little screech and flailed a bit. I'm nothing if not cool under pressure.

"You startled me," I pointed out, unnecessarily.

"Sorry." He didn't sound sorry. "What are you doing in here? Did you have an appointment?"

"Yes, I did. Shanice just ran back to the office for a moment. I'm . . . I'm looking at the castle as a possible wedding-reception venue."

His gaze shifted to my hand, as though looking for an engagement ring. Landon had insisted on a big rock, so big it sort of embarrassed me. But I had to admit I liked the way it sparkled.

The man stared at me another moment. "Have we met?"

"No, I don't think so." I told the truth: we hadn't been introduced. I waited for him to introduce himself now, but he didn't, so neither did I. After all, I *was* the bride.

His mien changed abruptly. "I think you'll find this is the perfect venue for any occasion, but especially for fairy-tale weddings. Follow me and I'll show you the courtyard, and the cisterns if you're interested. What do you think of the place? Isn't it amazing? I grew up in this neighborhood, and whenever my parents took us out to eat at the old Dago Mary's restaurant across the street, I would gaze at this old place and wonder."

"'Dago Mary's'?" I asked. "That was a restaurant's name?"

"It was a different time," he said. "People said what they meant, none of this political correctness nonsense."

"*Mmm.*" I wondered how someone in the hospitality industry could have been so insensitive. He had no way of knowing if I, or my fiancé, was Italian. "This building is really something, all right."

Shanice returned and handed me a folder made of heavy card stock, with WEDDING-PLANNING KIT—FOR YOUR SPECIAL DAY embossed in a curlicue script.

"I see you've met the boss!" she said, and assured me that I could get in touch with her anytime, and that she could not *wait* to meet again to discuss my special day and make my dreams come true.

"I'll just hand you off now! You're in good hands! It was lovely to meet you!" Shanice hurried out of the room. I watched her go, wondering at the odd interaction.

"This way, please, ma'am," he said, and I followed him down the hall and out into a medieval-looking courtyard made of the same stone as the building. A rough-hewn handmade ladder led up to an outdoor terrace.

"Back then the whole place was overgrown and encircled by a cyclone fence. The kids in the neighborhood said it was haunted." He chuckled and shook his head. "I haven't seen anything. Still, fun to think about. Am I right? Maybe your guests will have an 'encounter'! That would perk up any reception, don't you think?"

"I should think it would." Again, I wondered about this man's business sense. A haunted venue seemed more likely to repel wedding celebrants than attract them. After all, it was supposed to be the bride's special day.

"Tell you what, though. Those old haunting stories helped protect this place. Don't get a lot of people willing to poke around in the dead of night, if you know what I mean. By the way, it's also available for short-term rentals on Airbnb."

"I'm surprised you don't live here."

"The wife and I have a place on the Peninsula. This is just a hobby, or so says the wife. An expensive hobby, though. Want to pour your money down the drain, might as well get a boat. Am I right?"

"Wait—you and your wife own this place?" *That's* where I'd heard the name before. "You're Alan Peterson?"

"I am, yes. Excuse me! I should have introduced myself. Alan Peterson, at your service. And you are . . . ?"

"Mel Turner, of Turner Construction. You know, it occurs to me why we might look familiar to each other: I was at the Crockett Theatre the other day. I'm doing the renovation there."

A hard look came over Peterson's features. "That's the one they took away from Avery."

"I had nothing to do with that—just ask Josh Avery. He's a friend."

"My apologies. I jumped to a conclusion. Please, have a seat." He pulled out a redwood chair from a patio set, and we sat down.

"No worries. I do that all the time. Tell me, are you the Alan Peterson who is the city liaison for that renovation project?"

"In theory. Someone has to oversee the money, and I don't trust that Xerxes Group as far as I can throw them."

"Why not?"

"They . . . It's hard to explain." He crossed his legs and clasped his hands over his knee. "They just don't feel right. I realize that's vague, but it's true. I've worked on a number of preservation and renovation projects, including this one, and after a while, you get a nose for these sorts of things."

"Do you know the squatters there?"

"Are you asking about the young woman who was killed? Such a tragedy. Have you talked to her brother yet?"

"You mean Ringo Sepety? I haven't spoken to him—do you happen to know how I could get in touch with him?"

He shook his head. "I know his idea of a reality show set in the theater sounds nuts, but I was actually in favor of it. If done right, it could have produced a lot of revenue for the project, and promoted public awareness of the importance of renovating instead of destroying old buildings."

'Why didn't it happen?"

"In a word: Isadora. Without her support and cooperation, the rest of the squatters wouldn't sign on, and without them, there was no show. It could have been great, showing them working on their art, falling in love, fighting, all that kind of thing, with the backdrop of that great old place." He shook his head. "I couldn't believe what I read in the paper about what happened to her . . ."

"What did the Xerxes Group think about the idea?"

"You got me," Peterson said bluntly. "I never was able to get past that flunky, Thibodeaux. Usually investment groups are more accommodating and will at least meet with me to hear a proposal. Not this one. I've never dealt with such a secretive group. So all I know is that Gregory Thibodeaux was dead set against it, and that was that. I don't even know if he brought the idea to the consortium itself."

"And what about the audit of the city funds? Does anything seem strange about how the money is being handled? Josh Avery said something about no-show positions?"

An uncomfortable look came over Peterson's face. "I really don't know what was going on there. I'm not even sure I was right. It's just that I couldn't figure out who was drawing the money . . . I trust Avery. He did a great job here and no problems at all. So I'm inclined to believe him when he says he was innocent. These jobs are so big, and there are so many people involved, that those no-shows could have been set up by anyone, really. We weren't able to track the money, so we finally had to take the hit and write it off."

"That sounds frustrating."

He nodded. "They've gone through a lot of the city money already, but these projects are expensive, as you know. But we haven't had a full audit yet. I've been pushing for one, but Thibodeaux, or Xerxes, or *some*-one, must have a lot of clout with the city."

"How do you mean?"

"The audit never gets approved. The paperwork always gets lost." Peterson stood up and began pacing, his hands shoved deep into his pockets. His voice dropped, and he looked at me with suspicion. "So were you actually here looking for a wedding venue, or did you just want to talk with me about the Crockett? You could have called me, if so."

"I left a message on your home phone, as a matter of fact."

"Sorry. I should check it more often." His eyes dropped to my ring finger again. "I thought that rock looked fake."

"It is *not*," I said, rather indignant. "I am engaged, to a Berkeley college professor in fact, and I'm looking at possible venues. Ask Josh Avery. He'll vouch for me."

"My apologies. As you can tell, I'm a little on edge these days."

"Understandably. I've enjoyed seeing what you've done with Eamon Castle. It really is quite special."

"Thank you. But you really shouldn't leave without

seeing the caverns. It's the whole reason this place was originally built."

I hesitated, but followed him around to a wooden door in one wall of the terraced courtyard. He unlocked it, stood back, and waved me through. Narrow stone stairs led down into a deep, cool cave.

"The original builders were beer brewers who saw the potential for a brewery built on top of a natural spring. They dug out and deepened these cisterns; but as you can see, it's beautifully clear water."

It was a clear, soft aqua color, enticing on this warm day.

"It's gorgeous," I said.

"After the brewery shut down, Eamon Castle was owned by an artist, and then by a spring water company. But now I'm the only one who drinks the water. We put in a whole filtration system; it's really good. Would you like to try it?"

"I'm okay for now, but thank you. Did you do all this yourself?"

"I oversaw everything, but a young man who worked here did most of it. Nice kid, had a knack for industrial design."

Overhead, pipes moaned and water gurgled. It sounded vaguely menacing, like a basilisk moving through deep, wet tunnels.

"The system makes that sound when someone turns the water on upstairs," Peterson said softly.

"Thank you so much for showing me everything, but I really should be going. My fiancé's expecting me." I had had about enough of the moody Alan Peterson. There wasn't anything overtly menacing about him, but I didn't feel comfortable being alone in these cisterns with him. The water was beautiful, but the place didn't need ghosts to feel spooky.

"Do you know how I could get in touch with your industrial designer?" I asked as we climbed the steep stone steps back up to the surface. "His name's Alyx, right? He moved on to the Crockett?"

"Alyx is at the Crockett?" he asked, sounding surprised.

"I take it that's news to you?" I hoped I hadn't outed Alyx in some fashion.

He gave a curt nod.

"Do you have any contact information for him?" I asked.

"I haven't heard from him. But you just said he was at the Crockett, so you'd probably know better than I."

I was very glad to walk back out into the sunny courtyard.

"Well, I've got my wedding-planning kit for my special day right here," I said, patting the fancy folder. "So I guess I'm all set. Just have to figure out the date, and we're golden. I'll give Shanice a call."

Peterson escorted me to the front foyer, gave me another curt nod, and closed the door.

What had set him off? I wondered.

I hurried to my car, locked the door, and thought about what Peterson had said about the city audit—or lack of same. *Who do I know who works for the city?*

It was a Saturday—and the Fourth of July—so I couldn't check in with my contacts in the permit department, but I doubted they would know anything anyway. They were low-level bureaucrats who handled specialized construction paperwork. Who could Xerxes Group have working for the city, in a position to make requests for financial audits disappear?

Dealing with city hall was beyond my ken, so I texted Annette Crawford to tell her I had found the "balding, middle-aged white guy" at Eamon Castle, and that he was in charge of oversight for the Crockett Theatre project. She could probably shake things up, learn more from him—or figure out what was up with the city.

I tried Mateo again, but it went straight to voice mail. Then I checked in with Luz.

"It's getting late," she said. "I'm a nervous wreck."

"I thought we were meeting at six. It's not even three thirty."

"Yeah, but I have to get ready. Don't you?"

"Um . . ." I glanced down at my getup. "I have some shoes in the car, so I can change out of my boots, but otherwise I'm pretty much dressed."

"Could you come over and get me so we can ride together?"

I couldn't help but chuckle. "Sure, Luz. I'm running some errands, but I'll call you when I'm done. *Relax*, as my acupuncturist would say—Oh wait. He's your *boyfriend*!"

"You're not nearly as funny as you think you are. You should know that. I'm a woman in pain here, Mel."

"You're not in pain, Luz. You're just a little wound up. Take ten deep breaths. See you later."

Just as I was hanging up, I got a call from the Doctor.

"It was an unusual tap," he said, dispensing with hellos. "Special ordered from a manufacturer in Cleveland, Ohio."

"Are they still being made?"

"No, of course not. Factory's long gone. But I noticed there are several for sale on eBay."

"On eBay?"

"Yes, it is an online auction site."

"I've heard of it." Funny to have the very old Czech man explaining technology to me. "Where did the taps come from, and who's selling them?"

"Someone local, I believe. I will forward to you the link. See if you are interested—it would be less expensive than having them reproduced."

The idea appealed to me. How great would it be to have genuine vintage fixtures adorning the restroom sinks? I made a note to review the taps on the website when I got home and could look at them in detail on Stan's large computer monitor.

I stashed my phone and headed to Haight Street. As usual, it took me a while to find parking on a residential side street. Just as I reached the corner of Haight and Ashbury streets, I saw Lily slipping out the door and hailed her.

"Mel! So nice to see you. I was just running for coffee. Walk with me?"

"I'd love to. I could use a caffeine boost myself about now."

"You'll like this place. It's Coffee to the People. Ever been there?"

"I don't spend much time in the Haight," I said with a shake of my head. "But I like the name."

We walked for a moment without speaking. I noticed Lily paused to collect a few velvety wisteria pods that had fallen to the sidewalk and slipped them into the deep pockets of her early-1960s-style dress. I wondered whether she was going to use them to brew something, and then realized that I was now friends with a witch who brewed potions—and it all seemed perfectly normal. My life had changed a lot over the past few years.

"What can you tell me about the dress?" I asked Lily as we made our way to the café.

"Did you notice there's a tear in it?"

"I did. It looks reparable, though, right? And it's sort of hidden by the folds, so it seems worth trying to fix."

"Oh yes, I agree. But you should know, it's not a tear. It's a knife slash."

"A what?"

"It was caused by the blade of a knife." We reached the café, and Lily held the door open for me. "I'll show you when we get back to Aunt Cora's Closet."

Coffee to the People was a funky café that harkened back to the Haight's hippie heyday. The walls were studded with protest posters that reminded me of the

Crockett Theatre's rolled-up vintage movie posters, and I wondered if any of them were worth money. Collectors would pay exorbitant amounts for the objects of their desire.

We both ordered double lattes, and Lily ordered a chai latte as well, and waited while the tattooed and pierced barista worked his magic on a large espresso machine.

"There's something more, Mel," said Lily. She seemed to be searching for words.

"It's okay. You can tell me," I urged.

"Oh, I know that!" she said with a chuckle. "It's more that it's hard to put my finger on. Sort of like when you have a vivid dream, but the more you try to remember, the farther away it goes? The visions and sensations are a bit like that."

The barista handed us our drinks, Lily thanked him warmly and tipped him well, and we left the café and headed back up Haight Street.

"Anyway," Lily said, "there's violence. That's obvious. I mean, land sakes, we're talking about a hole made by a *knife*. But there's something else there . . . some sort of confusion or misunderstanding."

"You mean the reason Hildy stabbed her lover, and then killed herself, was over a misunderstanding of some kind?"

Lily stopped in the middle of the sidewalk and fixed me with a look. "She stabbed her lover and then herself?"

I nodded.

"You're sure?"

"That's what the newspapers said."

"Huh," she said, walking again. "That would explain things, I suppose, except that . . . it doesn't quite fit."

"How so?"

"Again, it's hard to explain, but I don't feel murderous rage from that dress."

"Oh well, that's good, then." I thought back to the fierce look on Hildy's face when she flew toward me in the attic, scaring the you-know-what out of me. That looked like it could have been murderous rage, as far as I could tell.

"I really don't feel that," Lily continued. This was obviously bothering her. "Nor do I feel suicidal tendencies—those are usually terribly bleak or, oddly enough, profoundly self-contained and peaceful. They're quite specific, is my point."

"Okay. Are you sure, really sure?"

She smiled at me. "Mel, what do you say when someone asks if you're sure, really sure, that you see a ghost?"

"I say, you bet your ass I am."

"Well, there you go, then."

I laughed. Point taken. "So if what you sense from the dress isn't homicidal or suicidal, then what *is* it?"

"Fear. Betrayal. A sense of profound misunderstanding, or perhaps a feeling of being misunderstood. Mel, I think that is what your ghost is trying to tell you. I think that is what she needs to rest: to be understood."

Back at Aunt Cora's Closet, Maya was tending the store. We greeted each other with a warm hug. I'd met Maya on a volunteer renovation project at a house museum, and she had introduced me to Lily when it turned out there was more to the Spooner House than I could handle by myself.

"Chai latte for you," said Lily, handing Maya the cardboard cup.

"Mmm, thank you!" said Maya. "I'll see to our patrons—I know you have business to discuss. Cool dress, though, Mel."

"It is, isn't it?" I said as I followed Lily through a curtain into the store's workroom, where the green dress was laid out on the table, arranged to expose the tear. As I looked at it closely, I noticed faint stains around the torn fabric.

I touched the slash mark with my fingertips.

"And that would be very old blood," Lily said quietly. "Someone cleaned it as best they could."

"I wonder why anyone bothered to keep the dress at all."

"You say you found it in a closet?"

I nodded.

"Were there other dresses in similarly good condition?" she asked, a gleam in her eye. "I love this era, and I like your ghost's vibrations. If you're ever looking to unload the rest of them, give me a call."

"A vintage-clothing merchant to the core, eh?"

"I suppose I am," Lily said with a smile.

"One more question." I chose my words carefully. "I spoke with Hildy, my ghost, this morning. When I asked about her death and the murder, she became agitated, and flew toward me in a rage. But you're sure you don't feel anger from the dress?"

She shook her head and sipped her latte. "I mean, you probably know this much better than I, communicating with spirits as you do. But I imagine it must be very frustrating to be a spirit and not understand where you are, and what happened to you. Perhaps once the ghost realizes they've reached someone in this world who can communicate with them, and possibly help them, they have a slim glimmer of hope. So if you don't understand what they are trying to convey, maybe they get agitated?"

"Like a preverbal toddler?"

"Maybe so." She chuckled again. "I visited your friend's shop, the ghost-busting place in Jackson Square? So much fun. I'll bet he'd be able to offer some thoughts on ghost psychology!"

"I'll bet he would." I needed to pay Olivier Galopin a visit anyway, to replace my ghost-busting equipment.

"So, the bottom line is that we still don't know what happened in Hildy's last moments."

She shook her head. "I'm sorry I couldn't be more help."

"Were you able to read anything from what remains of the blood?"

"There's a definite shimmer there . . . Mel, I know she scared you, and I could be wrong, but everything is telling me that Hildy was a good person. Ambitious and not especially well educated, but based on what I can feel, she does not have the soul of a killer."

Since it looked like I would wind up living in a house Hildy was haunting, those were encouraging words.

Lily folded the dress carefully and placed it in a bag. From the shop floor came the sounds of women chatting and the bell tinkling as people went in and out.

I stood to go and let Lily get back to work, but one more thought occurred to me. Could Jimmy Delucci have threatened Darlene, Hildy's daughter? I would kill anyone who threatened Caleb . . . In fact, it was always my go-to example when trying to understand being pushed far enough to take a human life. If anyone tried to harm my stepson, I doubted I'd hold back.

"Could it have been self-defense?" I asked. "Or maybe she was protecting her child when she struck out with the knife?"

"That would make more sense to me than premeditated murder," said Lily.

"But if Hildy had been protecting her child . . . why would she have turned the knife on herself?"

"I suppose that's the question. Maybe that is part of the misunderstanding."

Chapter Twenty-Three

Olivier Galopin's "Ghost-busting Shoppe" was on the other side of town, not far from City Lights Bookstore in North Beach, which Luz had—finally—decided to set as our rendezvous point for our double date.

I called Luz to let her know I would meet her at City Lights, but she insisted I pick her up early and come with me.

"Are you sure?" I asked. "You're not fond of the whole ghost-busting angle, last time I checked."

"It's either that or let me wait here. I'm so nervous that if left to my own devices, I'll start drinking till I'm too drunk to go anywhere."

"Luz, there's a reason you like Victor. He's a very gentle, decent man. What are you so nervous about?"

"Just never you mind. Come get me, will you, please?"

When I pulled up to her apartment building, she was waiting at the curb, resplendent in a pearl gray silk wrap dress with a peekaboo camisole, matching high heels, and artsy silver jewelry. Her sleek black hair was done up in a "sloppy" knot on the top of her head, which I'm sure took at least twenty minutes to accomplish, and she had a white swing coat draped over one arm and a white designer clutch tucked under the other.

I glanced down at my bright red shift dress and leather bomber jacket—interesting, yes; classy, not really—and wondered how we managed to remain friends.

"You look *wonderful*, Mel," Luz said. "I love that dress on you."

And *that*, I thought, was why we remained friends.

"Thank you," I replied. "And you are simply drop-dead gorgeous."

"Not too uptight?"

"Perfect."

"Distract me," Luz demanded as we headed across town to Jackson Square, so I gave her the update on what had been going on, including my trip to the theater with Annette.

"I thought Inspector Crawford had more sense than that," she said.

"Dad said the same thing. By the way, we're on for tomorrow: Niles Canyon and then dinner and movie night, yes? Caleb's joining us."

"Count me in," she said, and seemed to relax a bit.

We reached Jackson Square and spent fifteen minutes looking for a parking space. Even though it was early, this area was full of restaurants, nightclubs, and tourists, and filled up fast on a Saturday evening.

Originally from France, Olivier Galopin was a ghost enthusiast who made money selling ghost-hunting equipment and occult paraphernalia, and by exploiting his natural tendency toward showmanship. He led popular ghost tours through the city and even taught ghost-busting classes in the haunted hall above his store. I had taken a few sessions and learned a thing or two.

I wasn't sure, though, that I agreed with a lot of what Olivier said. Ghosts and ghost busting were complicated stuff.

Olivier's assistant, Dingo, was a grizzled old fellow with a lot of opinions. We found him at his usual post behind the counter.

As I was introducing Luz to Dingo, Olivier joined us.

"Mel! I saw you on television yesterday. 'Up-and-coming ghost buster,' it said below your picture. Congratulations!"

"I had no idea so many people watched the local news anymore," I said. "Believe me when I say it wasn't on purpose."

"You are too modest," Olivier said. "I wish you had mentioned my shop, though. I couldn't buy that kind of publicity."

"I bet you could if you wanted to," Luz said, looking around the large and well-appointed shop. Jackson Square was not a cheap address. "Nice place you got here."

"I told all the folks who called me after the broadcast to get in touch with you," I said. "And I'm not even asking for a finder's fee. So that should keep you plenty busy."

"I am very grateful," Olivier said, smiling.

"Also, I'm pretty sure having to replace this extremely expensive and often quite useless ghost-busting equipment you talked me into buying, which broke yesterday by the way, will help keep you in the black," I said, placing a bag with the many parts of my former EMF readers and EVP recorders on the countertop.

"You bought two sets of everything just a little while ago," said Dingo, peeking into the bag. "What happened?"

"Long story," I said with a shrug.

"Were ghosts involved?" Dingo asked.

"When are they not?" I replied.

Olivier beamed at me.

"Are you that happy to see me?" I asked. "Or are you just seeing dollar signs?"

"Both, I assure you," said Olivier, his smile broadening. "What can I help you with today, *ma chérie*? I am here for you. Ask me what you will."

"First off, I wanted to clarify something: Ghosts don't have to haunt the place where they died, right? They can go other places sometimes?"

He nodded. "Sometimes they attach themselves to an object, such as a painting or piece of furniture, or even to the land itself and linger after a building is destroyed."

"Could they attach to clothing?"

"They could, yes. It seems feasible."

Of course, what Olivier deemed "feasible" could fill a book. I wondered why Hildy would have been so attached to my house. Was it just the dresses or something more?

"Okay, next question. Let's go over why spirits linger at all," I said, and gave him the CliffsNotes version of what I had seen, heard, and felt at the Crockett Theatre.

"Most often seen and felt are the tortured souls, deaths by suicide and murder, unfinished business . . . ," Olivier began.

"Why would theaters have a reputation for being haunted, then?" asked Luz. "I mean, they don't see more tortured souls than other places, do they?"

"They might, as a matter of fact," said Olivier. "Artists in general tend to be more open-minded and nonconformist, and seek something beyond the here and now. Sometimes that leads to a sense of tortured souls. Some buildings are more attractive to spirits than others—obviously anyplace old, but especially insane asylums, prisons, theaters, caves, or any kind of underground labyrinth—"

"Why are caves or underground areas prone to ghosts?" I interrupted.

"Some say it has to do with the electromagnetic fields that can be felt there," said Olivier. "But I've always believed that it is because the areas under the earth are sheltered from light and noise, from the outside world in general. A cocoon, in a way."

"A ghostly cocoon?" Luz said. "That must result in one hell of a moth."

Olivier looked unsure how to respond.

"Continue," I said.

"Also, subterranean spaces are primordial, closer to the core of the Earth."

"And creepy crawlies," Luz muttered, then wandered off to check out the display of crystals.

"What about waterways?" I asked. "I've heard that water is an attraction to spirits."

"Yes, certainly. There has been a lot of writing about this. Some think it is because of the ionic changes of the air near water; some think that, like a mirror, water offers a passageway to the backwards world."

I thought of the hands Annette and I had seen on the mirror in the ladies' lounge vestibule at the Crockett Theatre. Could those be trapped souls, trying to reach out . . . ?

Luz rejoined us and said, "Wait just a darned minute, here. You're saying the mirror in my bedroom is a door to the *backwards* world? What is *that*?"

She glared at Olivier, who simply smiled. Dingo shrugged and scratched his ear.

"Just don't say Bloody Mary three times, and you'll be fine," I suggested.

She looked horrified.

"Seriously, Luz," I said with a chuckle. "Millions of people look in the mirror every morning but don't get sucked into the backwards world."

"A few of them do," Dingo piped up.

"That's not helping, Dingo," I said.

"Mel is right, Luz," Olivier said, his accent turning "Luz" into a long, soft sibilant that was lovely to hear. I saw Luz relaxing. "I promise you, this is not something you need to worry about. Although Mel is correct: It is best not to tempt fate with the Bloody Mary dare. Let us return to Mel's experiences at the Crockett Theatre. What are you doing there, Mel? They hired you to rid the building of ghosts? That would be a huge job and probably not possible."

"No, I was hired to renovate the theater, which is a huge job in itself," I said. "Have you heard anything about spirits in the building?"

"Isn't that the place with the usher?" asked Dingo. He started flipping through a massive journal into which he jotted down ideas and stories of hauntings. It was a wealth of information but was recorded in his illegible chicken scratch, and there appeared to be no organizational system for the information.

"There is an usher there," I responded. "I've encountered him several times."

"Excellent!" said Olivier. "Did you get him on camera?"

"I don't think so . . . but I can't really tell." I held up the broken camera.

"That is not a problem," Olivier said, plucking the SIM card out of its little chamber. "The images are on here."

He popped the SIM card into a slot on his computer. The images displayed reflected what I had seen and experienced, but at the same time was nothing like it. It looked like some kind of indie film project, shaky and the lighting was off. Then he did the same with the EVP recorder. There was a lot of static and unidentifiable noise.

And then a ghostly sound, muffled and distorted.
"May I . . . ?"

"What was that?" Luz asked, looking ill.

"Mel, is that one of you speaking," Olivier asked. "Or is it a spirit?"

"I think that's the usher," I said. "He kept wanting to show me to my seat. He was pretty pushy."

Olivier stared at me. "Do you realize what you have captured here?"

"An incomplete recording?"

"The voice of a person who has passed on! And the words are so clear, too. Such a thing is very rare. Did you remember to ask questions and note the time, as we have discussed, time and time again?"

"Um, not exactly," I said. There was a whole science— some would say pseudoscience—connected with how a professional ghost buster was supposed to go about collecting data. Since I wasn't a professional ghost buster so much as someone who stumbled her way through these things, I wasn't overly concerned with being consistent in my evidence gathering. Olivier, on the other hand, truly wanted to document information in a rigorous and scientific manner that could be used to prove to the world that ghosts existed.

Olivier pursed his lips in irritation. I was simultaneously his best student and his worst student.

"What does this mean, Olivier?" Luz asked, curious now.

"As I was saying," said Olivier, "certain buildings are more prone to hauntings than others. But some of these apparitions are merely energy imprinted onto the physical locale. These we call residual hauntings. They are not interactive but keep repeating, rather like a film on a constant loop."

"So they're not looking to move on?" Luz asked.

"Not if they're merely repeating themselves. Other spirits demonstrate a clear personality and are interactive to some degree. These we call intelligent hauntings."

I thought of Isadora. Would she be forever dancing upon the stage? And if so, was that okay, merely a residue of her personality lending itself to the character of the historic theater?

"Is there something you feel called to do for these ghosts?" Olivier asked me.

"I'm trying to figure out whether they have anything to do with the tragic death of a young woman."

"That does not seem likely," he said. "Spirits may incite feelings in people, and sometimes people act on those feelings. But most often they are simply stirred up by the energy of a tragedy. May I ask . . . who died?"

"A young woman, a dancer, who had been squatting in the building."

"That the Crockett?" Dingo asked in his raspy voice. I nodded. "I'm surprised. Heard tell was it was gonna be torn down."

"It was, but a preservationist group got involved, and an out-of-town investor consortium has combined funds with the city to save it."

"What about the Space Campus?" asked Dingo.

"What's a Space Campus?" asked Luz.

"Some billionaire wants to build his own rocket, send people into space, maybe even back again," Dingo said. "Which might be all kinds of exciting. Thought there was a lot of money riding on it . . ."

"It looks like the city decided to do the right thing and preserve the place," I said. I pulled up the Crockett Caretakers' site on Facebook on my phone and passed the device to Olivier, who scrolled through the photos, Dingo peering over his shoulder.

"Who maintains this site?" asked Olivier. "I've been trying to get Dingo here to create one for the shop, but he's even less tech savvy than I am."

"It's Facebook," I said. "Even *I* can handle Facebook. A member of the neighborhood preservation group created it."

"Nice digs," said Luz. She was looking at the "about" section, featuring a large photo of the elegant Coco posing in front of her apartment building. Coco was identified as the "founder and chair" of the Crockett Caretakers.

"It's a great old apartment building," I said. "She even has a turret seat. I wish *I* had a turret."

"Don't be greedy," said Luz. "You have a fantastic new house."

"Still wouldn't mind a turret," I said. "But you are right. There are too many people with no home at all."

"You mean the squatters?" asked Dingo.

"What does this word mean, 'squatters'?" Olivier asked. "As in the squats we do at the gym?"

"Squatters are people who move into a building, though they have no legal right to be there," I said. "They're often homeless."

Olivier looked troubled. "You are going to run them out of the theater, then?"

"No. I mean, yes. But no worries. Luz will find a place for them. She's a social worker. That's her job."

"That's right," Luz said with a touch of sarcasm. "Mel and I are solving the problem of homelessness in San Francisco. Any day now. Don't know why the city didn't approach us sooner."

"This is very good," said Olivier in all seriousness. "Because it is a real problem that must be solved."

"Speaking of problems that must be solved," I said, "every time I'm in the Crockett Theatre, my batteries die. Don't you have some sort of spirit-energy-resistant batteries?"

"Nope," Dingo said. "But if you ever figure that out, better patent it. That'd be real useful."

"Well, in the meantime, why don't you set me up with two more EMF readers and EVP recorders, just in case?" I said, handing him my credit card and wondering if Stan would let me write them off as a business expense.

"Mel," said Olivier, "may I keep the SIM cards and study them, see if I can see or hear anything more?"

"Knock yourself out," I said.

"Okay, so give me the rundown of tonight's events," I said as Luz and I walked along Gold Street toward

North Beach, where the Financial District meets Italian meets Chinatown meets sex shops. A little farther down Columbus and we would be at the Cannery, Ghirardelli Square, and the wharf.

"I suggested we meet at City Lights so whoever gets there first can browse the bookstore," said Luz.

"Great bookstore," I said.

"Yes, it is, which is why I suggested it."

"You get me in there, though, and it's at least an hour." She looked at me in alarm. "Kidding! I'll refrain from book shopping even though it's one of my favorite things in the world. What's next?"

"Drinks next door at Vesuvio's—I know it's a stereotype, but I love that place. Then dinner at Tosca. It's rated very highly on Yelp. Had to pull a few strings to get a table tonight, but a colleague went to grad school with the maître d'. And then after we can go to the Saloon for music, if we feel like it."

"There are also fireworks tonight, don't forget," I said.

"It's supposed to be foggy."

"It's always foggy in San Francisco on the Fourth of July. But it's still fun," I said, turning onto Pacific, toward Columbus. "At the very least, the clouds light up in different colors. In any case, it sounds like a lovely evening. And dare I say, so much more fun than fly-fishing."

"Have you ever *been* fly-fishing?"

"Can't say that I have."

"Then how would you know?"

I smiled. "Besides, fly-fishing would have required a wardrobe change. Definite no-no for a first date."

"It's not our *first* date, exactly," Luz hedged. "I've tried a couple of times. Just hoping this might go better tonight."

I stopped and looked at her. "Wait—have you and Victor been out on a date before? If so, then why are you so wound up?"

"We tried. I had to cancel. Not my fault."

"You sure about that?"

"I don't want to talk about it. The important thing is, we're here tonight."

We continued walking to the bookstore, Luz staring at her cell phone.

"Just out of curiosity," I said, "did you write up an actual agenda for the evening, maybe store it on your phone?"

"Don't be ridiculous," Luz said, slipping her phone into her shoulder bag.

I laughed and nudged her with my elbow. "This is great, Luz. Thank you for suggesting it and for making the plans. Did you know that Tosca has been around since Prohibition? They say the cappuccino machine used to hide booze back in the day."

"I don't know how you know these things, my friend," Luz said, smiling and looping her arm through mine. "But I like it."

Chapter Twenty-Four

M uch later the four of us—me, Luz, Victor, and Landon—sat in a booth at Tosca, chatting over luscious bowls of olives, halibut crudo, Caesar salads, meatballs, bucatini and lumaconi pastas, and grilled salmon and polenta. We started out with separate orders but quickly devolved into "family style," sharing and tasting the various dishes. The ever-polite waiters didn't seem to mind.

Tosca was thronged with people and very loud, what with the open kitchen on one side and the hopping bar on the other. Nonetheless, I managed to give Victor a brief rundown on what had happened to Isadora, and to update everyone on my visit to Eamon Castle and the nice Alan Peterson, who gave me the creeps.

I thought I'd hold back on telling Hildy's story until I was able to piece it all together. I had a hunch Hildy and I might be housemates for a while, and I didn't want to weird anyone out about visiting a home where the ghost of a "murderous starlet" dwelled.

"I keep thinking there must be something valuable at the Crockett," I said.

"Something worth killing over," said Landon with a thoughtful nod.

"I think we all know it doesn't take much," said Luz as she sipped her Chianti. "Most murders are pretty stupid—somebody gets drunk in a bar and starts a brawl, that sort of thing."

"True," I said. "But this was no bar brawl. I think there was a reason for it, however despicable or selfish."

"I read about some coins from the time of Imperial Rome that were found under a theater in Italy," said Victor. "There were hundreds of them in a soapstone jar, apparently very valuable. Would that sort of thing provide enough of a motive?"

"This isn't that kind of theater," said Luz.

I had never told Victor about my ability to see spirits. It was something I just didn't feel comfortable talking about, but since the television broadcast yesterday had effectively outed me, I figured I might as well come clean.

"In our acupuncture treatments for my vertigo and fear of heights," I said, "I may have left out the part where I see ghosts. Not all the time. But sometimes."

I was curious to see how Victor would respond, and saw Luz and Landon watching him closely as well. Dr. Victor Weng was a considerate, contemplative man, a third-generation American who had been raised in San Francisco's Chinatown. But he had traveled a great deal, gone to school back East as well as in China, spent time in Britain and South Africa, and returned to San Francisco to take over his uncle's acupuncture practice. He was very successful and had *amazing* hands.

Victor took a sip of his wine, sat back, nodded. "Fascinating."

"Is it, though? I find it less interesting than . . ." I left off with a shrug. "Dunno. Seems more traumatic than fascinating."

Victor grinned. "That might be a cultural thing."

"Ghosts are a cultural thing?" Luz asked.

He shook his head. "No, the trauma associated with seeing ghosts. I grant you that it can be unsettling, but in traditional Chinese culture, for instance, it is assumed that we live side by side with all kinds of spirits and apparitions. We have whole categories of ghosts."

"Categories of ghosts?" I asked, reaching for the plate of briny, earthy olives. I was stuffed with pasta, polenta, and fish, but one could always fit in another olive or two. "For instance?"

"Well, let's see. The *E gui* are called the 'hungry ghosts,' those suffering from the sins of greed and condemned to perpetual hunger after death. On the other hand, a *Gui po* is usually a kindly ghost who helps with children and housekeeping."

Luz raised her hand. "I'll take that one. I like any ghost that helps with housecleaning. Hey, Mel, remember that kitchen-cleaning ghost you banished?"

"Why would you banish a ghost who liked to do the dishes?" Landon asked.

"It also terrorized the people living there," I explained. "So it was a bit of a wash."

"I want to hear about more ghost categories," Luz said.

"One of my favorites," continued Victor, "is the *jiangshi*, which is sort of like a cross between a zombie and a vampire. It hops around and eats bugs to absorb their energy."

"Also not a bad trait in a ghost," said Luz. "Not a bug fan."

"I fear I am now fixated on the idea of Dracula hopping like a bunny," Landon said. "Mel, I may need your assistance in banishing that thought."

"My favorite part of that story is the way to keep a *jiangshi* from coming into the house," said Victor.

"Garlic?" I said.

"Silver?" Landon suggested.

"Place a bag of rice at the door," Victor explained. "The *jiangshi* are compelled to sit and count the grains of rice, which gives you plenty of time to make a getaway."

"The power of rice compels you!" said Luz.

We all laughed. Landon refilled our wineglasses.

"Why would it feel compelled to count the grains of rice?" Luz asked, still chuckling at her own joke.

Victor shrugged and speared another meatball. "It's just the way it is. Every spirit has a weakness, I suppose. Good thing, too, or we'd all be in trouble."

I sipped my wine and thought about that. I had no trouble believing every spirit had a weakness; in fact, most of the spirits I encountered were in torment or in need. Many were angry, yes, but that was understandable, given the circumstances.

"Tell us more," urged Luz.

He gave her a crooked smile. "I'm no expert on Chinese ghosts—there are a lot of them. But another that comes to mind is the *yuan gui*, or the restless spirits who died a wrongful death and are seeking redress."

Landon and Luz both looked at me.

"Yeah, I suppose those last are my specialty," I said with a nod. "There's a lot of that going around, I'm sorry to say. I wouldn't mind checking out the hopping zombie fellow, though. Keeping a bag of rice by the door sounds easy enough, and it would be pretty entertaining to find him on the doorstep counting grains of rice. Funny how you never see a zombie movie about *that*."

"Indeed," said Landon. "I can't think of a single zombie movie involving rice at all, much less the counting of grains."

"But enough about my ghosts," Victor said. "Mel, Luz mentioned you've become interested in early film history."

"I have," I said. "We're going tomorrow to Niles

Canyon to check out the film museum there. I'm hoping the curators might be able to point me in the right direction."

"Which direction is that?" asked Landon.

"To something of value in the theater. Victor, would you like to join us?" Surviving a Turner family outing was a litmus test every potential partner had to pass. Landon had passed with flying colors, and I was willing to bet Victor would, too.

"I wish I could, but I have plans with my grandmother tomorrow. Promised to take her to church. Another time, I hope?"

"That can be arranged," I said.

"*I* have a question about the Crockett," announced Luz. "A very important question."

"And what might that be, madam?" I asked.

"Why does the Crockett Theatre spell the end of 'theater' 'r-e' instead of 'e-r,' like a normal person?"

"We're discussing ghosts and squatters and a murderer and hopping zombie vampires, and *that* is what you fixate on?"

"I'm just saying, it's a theater, right? And we're in America, right? Why spell it like the Brits?"

"I have no idea," I said. "But more importantly, I don't care."

Victor laughed.

"I blame *you*." Luz gestured toward Landon with her wineglass. "As a Brit, I mean."

"I'm not sure you can blame Landon for the quirks of the English language," said Victor.

"No, no, I'll take that one," said Landon. "Actually, as I understand it, Noah Webster was responsible for this sort of thing. He wanted to make American English phonetically simpler and more predictable than British English, so when he published his dictionary in the early nineteenth century he began by taking the 'u' out of the words 'colour' and 'favour,' for instance."

This was one of the things I loved most about Landon: He had a quirky mind that forgot the names of people he had just met, but remembered linguistic history and other useless tidbits of arcane knowledge.

Rather like me, I supposed.

The four of us chatted about linguistic flukes and how difficult English was to spell, Luz described the general consistency of phonetic Spanish, and Victor spoke of the differences between the Mandarin and Cantonese versions of Chinese.

Over my weak protests that I was too full, Luz waved to the server and ordered plates of cannoli and tiramisu with four forks.

I like to think of myself as a team player. I did my best.

Chapter Twenty-Five

After dinner we headed down Columbus toward the Saloon, on the corner of Grant and Fresno. As we crossed Broadway I gazed at the big neon signs advertising the Condor, Big Al's, and the Roaring 20s, all of which I assumed were seedy strip clubs and/or sex shops, though I'd never actually taken the time to find out. They had adorned this part of Broadway for as long as I could remember and then some, and I felt strangely nostalgic about them. I still missed the old Condor sign that featured the buxom stripper from the 1970s, Carol Doda, complete with light-up neon nipples. I hoped the encroaching gentrification of San Francisco never led to their demise.

Strange to feel nostalgic for strip clubs and sex shops, especially since I'd never even been to one, but there it was.

"We can get an after-dinner drink, and then see the fireworks," said Luz. "The Saloon is one of San Francisco's oldest bars, established in 1861. Mel's not happy unless she's in the oldest, dive-iest bar possible."

"Hey, I *love* the Saloon," I said in protest to her implied criticism.

"Proves my point," said Luz.

"I love it, too," said Victor with a smile, hugging Luz to his side.

"I've never been," said Landon. It was a safe bet that Landon had never been anywhere, since he had arrived from England not all that long ago. He had settled in the East Bay, was quickly absorbed by his work commitments, then became associated with the likes of me, who almost never went anywhere. "But I look forward to discovering its many charms."

A little farther down Broadway, we passed yet another strip club and a burlesque show. The poster for the burlesque show featured none other than Alyx, the elusive cross-dressing squatter, as the star performer.

"Hey," I said, checking my phone for the time. "I've been looking for this guy! He's one of the Crockett squatters. Anyone want to check out the burlesque show? Starts in fifteen minutes."

"A burlesque show? And you were the one who was weirded out by fly-fishing," said Luz. Victor flashed her a questioning look. "Long story."

"What about the fireworks?" asked Landon.

"You mean the commemoration of when we colonists kicked your imperial British butt?" asked Luz.

Landon smiled, unperturbed. "As a true hybrid, I play both sides on this one."

"Usually the fireworks are obscured by the fog anyway," said Victor. "All you see is are the clouds changing colors, which is pretty, but not a must-see. Luz, what would you prefer?"

"Burlesque, baby," Luz said, and I was pleased to see that she was back to being her usual self. Victor appeared thoroughly smitten.

"Well, in that case, the burlesque show it shall be," said Landon.

We paid the substantial ticket price and descended a staircase, making our way through a crowded bar to a group of small tables in front of the stage. The place was jammed with people; all the laughter and chatting made me wonder how the performers would get their attention. Would Alyx have to fight with the bar noise, Vegas-cocktail-bar style?

There were no empty tables, so Landon and I went to the bar to order drinks while Luz and Victor stationed themselves at a small ledge that had been affixed to the wall to hold drinks, and waited for a table to free up. A large, bearded man was busing tables with gusto, clearing them of dirty glasses.

"Do you think I could go backstage to talk with Alyx?" I asked the bartender after we gave our drink orders. "He's an old friend."

"He's the headliner," said the young mixologist as she smoothly made several cocktails at once for the thirsty throng. "He's on in a few minutes, but maybe after. Talk to the producer, see if he'll take you backstage."

"Where would I find him or her?" I asked.

"Ringo!" she called out.

The man busing tables looked up. "Yeah?"

"Visitors," the bartender said.

Ringo came over and set his tray full of dirty dishes on the bar. "Help you?"

"You're Ringo?" I asked. "As in Ringo Sepety?"

"The one and only," he said with a smile.

I try not to judge people on their looks, because that's one test I wouldn't always pass, but Ringo was an aggressively unattractive man. He had a heavy, almost Neanderthal brow ridge, a nose that appeared to have been broken more than once, and teeth the color of tobacco. It was hard to believe he was related to the famous reality show beauties, the Sepety sisters.

Now that I thought about it, Isadora hadn't been particularly beautiful herself. She had been strong and vital, but did not have the modelish features of her famous sisters. I wondered whether that was part of the reason she wasn't involved in the show, or whether she just had high standards when it came to her art. Perhaps the reality show really was "dreck." The one time I had spoken with Isadora, she certainly seemed intent on creating an authentic, creative life. No doubt that was hard to find on a reality show.

"I'm Mel Turner," I said, "And this is Landon Demetrius. I'm doing the renovation of the Crockett Theatre, and—"

"Wait! I knew you looked familiar—you're the ghost buster. Am I right?" He seemed as excited as a kid on Christmas morning. "I saw you on TV!"

"I, um, yes . . . that was your family's press conference, right?" I asked.

"I gotta tell you. I was pretty miffed that they didn't ask me to join them," he said, shaking his big head. "I mean, I get that I'm not pretty enough to be on their show, but still . . ."

"Ringo, I'm so very sorry about your sister."

"Yeah." He hung his head for a moment. When he looked up, he appeared to have dealt with his momentary grief. "That was a shock. I mean, Isadora and I have had some arguments over the years, but she was still my sister. We were there for each other, from the gecko."

I almost corrected his word choice, but held my tongue. "I heard you were trying to put together a reality show starring your sister and the other squatters in the theater?"

He nodded his head. "Could you imagine how epic that would be? That weird architecture and the crappy carpets and everything? Totally awesome, right? Surefire appeal these days. Can't fail, something like that."

Luz and Victor, apparently tired of waiting, joined us at the bar.

"What a great idea!" Luz said with false enthusiasm. "You could have contests, see who can jump off the balcony railing without dying, or how long could a person could live on the stale popcorn they find under the seats!"

I glared at Luz.

"Yeah . . . I think that might not work so well, though," said Ringo, sounding thoughtful. "That popcorn's, like, fifty years old or something? Dunno if it's even still, like, legible. But anyway, what are you folks doing here? Oh! Do you know Alyx from the Crockett?"

"I do, as a matter of fact. Any chance you could take us backstage after the show?"

The music ratcheted up, and the crowd quieted down to a murmur.

"Sure thing," Ringo said in a loud stage whisper. "Catch me after the show."

The view from the bar was decent, so we remained where we were while the emcee came out, cracked a few jokes, and introduced Alyx.

Alyx emerged in full makeup, with an elaborate headdress and a long feather boa, fishnet stockings, and very high heels. He strutted onto the stage to the classic "You Can Leave Your Hat On"; then the music stopped abruptly and Alyx made a joke. He looked fabulous, and before long the audience was eating out of his hand. He told a few more jokes, told a funny story about the first time he tried on his sister's clothes, and then sang a seductive, slow version of "Big Spender." Alyx popped the cork off a bottle of champagne, and poured its contents over himself. He danced and twirled and began peeling off bits of clothing, not stripping completely but enough to reveal a fantastic body that was decidedly male, despite the clothes and makeup. A few in the audience gasped, then applauded, so I guessed it was supposed to be a surprise.

Alyx bowed and left the stage, and three young

women came on and began a coordinated pole dance while singing "Let Me Entertain You" more or less on key as they shimmied and pranced and did acrobatics on the poles. The audience hooted and cheered. The performers, the staff, and the audience all seemed to be having a raucous good time.

"I can take you to see him now," said Ringo in that very loud stage whisper. "The only flying ointment is that you'll miss this act, which is really good."

"That's okay," I said. "I'd like to catch Alyx, if I can."

"Follow me."

Ringo led the way through the packed seating area, through a curtain at one side of the stage. I followed, Luz trailing behind, and Landon and Victor on her heels.

"So," I said as we hustled past piles of props and the performers milling about backstage, waiting for their turn in the spotlight. The walls were decorated with framed photographs of Mae West, Isadora Duncan, Josephine Baker, Martha Graham, Gypsy Rose Lee, Bettie Page, and a number of other dancers I didn't know.

As always these days, my eyes went to Isadora Duncan.

"So, Ringo, you produce the show?" I asked.

He let out a laugh. "Producer, prop manager, barback and bottle washer, ticket taker, busboy—I do whatever needs to be done. But, yeah, I help Alyx produce his show."

"He's really good," I said.

"Isn't he, though? Burlesque is one of those things, in my view, where you either got it or you don't. And he's got it."

We found Alyx sitting in front of a large makeup mirror ringed by warmly lit lightbulbs. It made me think of the dusty old backstage changing rooms at the Crockett, and what Annette and I—or at least I—had witnessed there.

"Hi, Alyx!" I said. "Remember me?"

Alyx started to stand, as though to flee, then spotted Landon, Victor, and Luz and settled back onto the stool.

"Um. Hi," he said, a wary look in his eyes.

"You're a hard man to pin down," I said.

"I told you, cops and I do *not* get along."

"You're not in trouble," I began, then realized that maybe he was. He was a squatter, after all, so at the very least he was guilty of trespassing. How did I know he wasn't the killer?

As I gazed at Alyx now, though, with his tousled locks and heavy makeup, he didn't seem like a murderer but like any starlet of old trying to make good. I just didn't get a homicidal vibe from him. Also, would he even have had time to kill Isadora, set her up on the Mighty Wurlitzer, then race up several flights of stairs to join me and Thibodeaux in the balcony?

"I mean," I amended my statement, "assuming you didn't hurt anyone."

He gave a wry chuckle and turned back to the mirror, using a broad-headed brush to put a thick layer of powder over an already thick layer of makeup. I had to admit, he looked good. *Really* good. I could have taken a few makeup lessons from this young man.

"I think if you knew me a little better," said Alyx, "you wouldn't even consider such a thing for a second."

"I liked your show," I said. "I've never seen a burlesque dancer in real life."

"Me neither," said Luz. "It's really fun. You're *gorgeous*, by the way."

"Thank you, doll," said Alyx. "You know the difference between a burlesque dancer and a stripper?"

"What?" I asked.

"The stripper makes money."

I smiled. "So you don't make money here?"

Alyx glanced at Ringo, who shrugged and said,

"Hey, I'm doing my best. No need to make a molehill out of it."

"We're working on it, I guess," said Alyx. "The thing is, burlesque has historical roots in satire. It's just plain fun. I like the adrenaline rush of dancing before a crowd, the energy in teasingly taking off my clothes. Burlesque isn't mainly about showing one's body, but an onstage performance piece. Plus, in burlesque you get to wear all this."

His arm made a wide arc toward the rack of outfits, all of which featured feathers, crystals, glitter, and spangles. I made a note to tell my friend Stephen, the frustrated dress designer, about this place. His designs would be appreciated here.

"Also, since I'm not binary, people watching me dance don't know at first if I'm a man or a woman. Screws with their heads, but in a good way."

"Alyx, do you know what Isadora wanted to talk to Skeet about?" I asked. "Had she discovered something valuable in the theater?"

"Valuable enough to kill over?" Alyx shook his head, and tears came to his eyes. "I've been thinking about that a lot. Isadora was like our housemother, you know? And she had a strict rule against stripping the theater of valuable things. It might seem hard to believe, but we all really love that place, want the best for it. We just want to live there, soak up the vibes."

"I was there last night," I said. "It looked like you had moved out."

"Not officially, but with the police poking around, and then you said you were starting construction . . ." He shrugged. "I'm hoping for a reprieve, like maybe the construction will stop again like it did before. In the meantime, I'm on a friend's couch."

Alyx was so talented—in costuming, singing and dancing, *and* industrial design. Surely he could find decent employment somewhere. Maybe if he had a steady place to live . . . I thought of my big new house (Demetrius Manse?). Should I . . . ?

Luz caught my eye and shook her head. "No," she mouthed.

"You worked at Eamon Castle, right?" I asked Alyx. "I was there today. It's quite something."

"It is, isn't it?" Alyx said, his face lighting up. "Did you see the cisterns? I set up a piping system there. It was sick. I did the same thing at the Crockett. That's how we had some toilets we could use. It's probably not potable, but it's good for washing and the toilets."

"Very clever. But, hey, I hope I didn't say anything out of turn, but I might have mentioned to Alan Peterson that you were living at the Crockett Theatre."

Alyx grimaced.

"Has he . . . threatened you?" I asked.

"Oh no, nothing like that. I just had a thing going there for a while, with him and his wife and . . . I can see I've now horrified you all. Bad choice on my part, I know. It's really not worth going into, but suffice it to say, I didn't leave a forwarding address."

I was going to let that one go.

"I noticed a lot of the plumbing fixtures had been taken out at the Crockett," I said. "Did you guys do that?"

"No way. Isadora would never have allowed that. You know Coco the Crockett Crackpot?"

"Um . . . I know Coco Stapleton, yes."

"She was obsessed with those fixtures. Not sure why. Freaked out when she saw they were gone."

"You don't think Coco could have had anything to do with Isadora's death, do you?" I asked. I couldn't imagine how; Coco wouldn't have been able to overwhelm Isadora through sheer brute strength, though I supposed she could have hired someone to do her bidding. Mitch had mentioned Coco had tried to hire him once, though he didn't say for what.

"I'm not saying anything like that. It's just that she's pretty wealthy, one of those 'actors' who always had family money. So she doesn't really get the struggle the rest of us face. And she felt really proprietary about the Crockett; I always got the feeling she would have bought it for her own private fun house, if she had the chance."

"Suppose there's still time for fireworks?" Landon asked as we exited the burlesque theater.

"The fireworks started at nine thirty, at the foot of the Municipal Pier and off barges north of Pier 39 at Fisherman's Wharf," Luz rattled off, apparently having memorized the schedule. She glanced at her watch. "It's not even ten."

"Well, then, let's go check it out," Victor said.

Pier 7 was jammed, and it was, in fact, pretty foggy but the kaleidoscopic grandeur of the lower fireworks was on full display, and the tallest ones did, indeed, light up the clouds in reds, greens, blues, and oranges.

Music was piped in, and then a man's deep, resonant voice came over the loudspeakers, reading the Declaration of Independence.

"We hold these truths to be self-evident, that all men are created equal, that they are endowed by their Creator with certain unalienable rights, that among these are life, liberty, and the pursuit of happiness."

I always got a little choked up at that part. We were all created equal, and yet . . . I thought of how some people—many of my clients, for example—had more than enough, while others, like Alyx and Tierney, had no real home at all.

On the other hand, many of my wealthiest clients seemed to be miserable, whereas someone like Skeet, who had to work past retirement age, had a family he loved and a good attitude in general.

Had Isadora been killed over money? Was it that easy?

"It's probably ridiculous to say, but I'm hungry," announced Victor. "And cold."

"Ditto that," said Landon.

"The pasta didn't hold you?" I asked, amused. I was still more than full.

A look of panic entered Luz's eyes. This was not on her agenda.

"Remember to breathe, Luz," I murmured. "Hey, you know what would be fun? A *taquería*. Or maybe a food truck—it's Saturday, they serve late."

"Or El Farolito in the Mission," Luz said. "That's the best place to go when everything's closed. They have great burritos and agua fresca."

"Are you a fan of burritos?" Victor asked Landon.

"Sounds like just the thing," said Landon. "I'll call for a Lyft."

So we ended our night in the heart of the Mission neighborhood, mere blocks from the Crockett Theatre.

As we passed it on our way to El Farolito, I leaned out the window: The theater loomed huge and dark against the bright night sky, the clouds still painted with fireworks like an echo of the lights that had illuminated the old marquee, once upon a time.

Chapter Twenty-Six

The next day, Luz, Stan, and I piled into the back of the wheelchair-friendly van, while Dad drove and Landon rode shotgun.

We stopped at the Fruitvale BART station for a joyous reunion with Caleb, who had come in from the city. His olive skin was a shade darker from the time spent in the Nicaraguan sun, his dark hair was shaggy, and my once-smooth-cheeked stepson now sported a five o'clock shadow that threatened to form one of those scraggly goatees sported by a lot of the area's baristas. Caleb looked hale and hearty and was such a sight for sore eyes that I had to fight back an embarrassing attack of "mom tears."

"I'm so happy you're home," I whispered as I embraced him.

"Me, too, Mel," he said, and hugged me hard.

"So, what's the deal?" Caleb asked after answering the questions we peppered him with about his trip to Nicaragua as we drove south on 80. "Am I being kidnapped? Where are we headed?"

"We're going to a museum in Fremont."

"A museum. In Fremont. *Yaaay*," he said in a dying voice. Sarcasm was Caleb's fallback position. I couldn't imagine where he had picked that up. "Just what I wanted to do on my vacation."

"Watch the attitude, son," Dad said, glancing at Caleb in the rearview mirror.

"Yessir, Pops," Caleb said with exaggerated meekness, and we all laughed.

"Have you ever heard of Niles Canyon?" I asked. "Back in the day it was an important train stop and the home of some of the earliest films made in this country. Charlie Chaplin filmed there."

"Oh cool. All I know about Niles Canyon is there's a ghost story about a lady in white on Niles Canyon Road," said Caleb. "A friend of mine told me."

"Ugh, no more ghosts," I said quickly.

"Why are ghosts always dressed in white?" asked Luz at the same time.

"Now, that's an interesting question," Stan said. "Mel? Any thoughts on that?"

"Don't look at me. Like I said, I've got plenty of spirits in my life at the moment; Fremont is on its own. I wonder if the city allocates any tax money for that."

Caleb looked at me. "Why do I get the feeling I'm missing something? What's going on?"

"Mel's dealing with murder and mayhem," said Dad over his shoulder. "As usual."

"Are you okay?" Caleb asked, dropping his sometimes smart-alecky teenage mask.

"I'm okay. Of course I am," I said, glaring at my dad.

"Does this have to do with the Crockett Theatre you said you were going to work on?" Caleb asked. "I looked it up; it's haunted by the ghost of an usher."

Among others, I thought to myself.

"Yeah, maybe, maybe not," I equivocated.

"But there are squatters, for sure," said Luz. "And a murderer."

"What happened?" Caleb asked.

"A woman was killed there a few days ago," I said. "It had absolutely nothing to do with me."

"It never does," said Caleb. "Except that you're always the one who finds them."

"What can I say?" I replied, trying to keep my tone light. "Everybody has to have a hobby."

Dad pulled off the freeway, and we drove through the city of Fremont, passing strip malls and housing developments. My phone kept ringing and beeping, annoying everyone, so I turned off the volume. I had received messages from two more of the artisans I had contacted but each claimed to be too busy to bid on the Crockett Theatre project.

That seemed strange. Skilled craftspeople were in great demand and often needed long lead times, but the opportunity to work on a gem like a 1920s theater would normally bring them out of the woodwork. So to speak.

The Crockett was scheduled to be released as a crime scene tomorrow. Part of me was itching to get back, to put together a real list and poke some holes in the walls. Another part of me wasn't quite ready.

"A lot of Afghani restaurants in Fremont," I said to change the subject.

"Largest concentration of Afghan Americans in the US," said Stan.

"Really?" I asked. "I had no idea."

"They settled here after the Soviet invasion of Afghanistan."

"The Soviets?" asked Caleb. "Wait. I thought *we* were the ones in Afghanistan."

"Different time periods," I said. "Different invasion."

"History," Caleb said with a shake of his head. "I don't get it."

"It's wasted on the young," Dad said.

"Theirs is a tragic history," said Stan. "But one result is that Fremont now has some very good Afghani restaurants and a diverse community."

At long last we arrived at a charming, five-block-long commercial district lined with historic brick buildings and old-timey wooden storefronts boasting antiques shops, restaurants. Several had clever names, such as the Devil's Workshop and Mercantile, and Thyme for Tea. The Niles Canyon Railway station had a vintage steam train out front, and the town was bedecked in American flags and stars-and-stripes bunting. A city worker was sweeping up burned sparkler wires and spent fireworks.

"This area was considered 'America's First Hollywood,'" said Stan, consulting his phone. "Charlie Chaplin was here in 1914 and shot a handful of films, including *The Little Tramp*. Says here they filmed part of that on a path you can still walk today, though now it's paved."

"Looks to me like the kind of town where one might find an ice-cream parlor," I said. "Who's up for ice cream before we hit the museum?"

Dad grumbled about our ruining our appetites for dinner, which was still hours away, but he was outvoted. We found frosty root beer floats at the Remember When Deli, where a pint-sized Charlie Chaplin doll sat behind the counter.

Then we walked past antiques stores sporting old glass bottles of Coca-Cola and model trains from the 1950s, to arrive at the Niles Essanay Silent Film Museum and Edison Theater.

"More Charlie Chaplin," said Caleb as we passed another image of the actor's iconic Little Tramp. "Why do I get the feeling I'll be watching some old movies tonight?"

"How'd you guess?" asked Dad. "Maybe Broncho Billy Anderson, too. Love me an old Western."

"Yay," said Caleb. More sarcasm. "Why'd they set up shop way out here, though?"

"Glad you asked, young man," said the jolly man who took our tickets. He wore a name tag that said MR. RAYMOND, had a walrus mustache and a large belly, and seemed thrilled to be part of the museum. I half expected him to have a gold watch on a chain in his pocket. "The transcontinental railroad snaked through the Niles Canyon and connected the San Francisco Bay Area to the rest of the nation. The critical railroad link between the gold mining town of Sacramento and San Francisco was completed right here in Niles in 1869."

"Oh. Thanks," said Caleb. "Interesting."

Movie posters from decades past adorned the walls, and there were film equipment and wooden theater seats, costumes, and other movie-related paraphernalia.

"Very sorry to tell you this, folks," said Mr. Raymond, "But our projector's on the fritz. Normally we'd be screening films shot here in Niles, many of which star leading A-listers who made brief pit stops in Northern California's own version of Hollywood."

"Oh, that's too bad," I said. "I wonder if we could find some of them to stream at home?"

"No doubt," Mr. Raymond said to me in a quiet aside, as though sharing a secret. "But we also have DVDs for sale in the gift shop. Charlie Chaplin and Broncho Billy, a history of Niles, all sorts of great things."

"We'll check that out," I said.

"Don't miss the tin-lined projection booth, young man," he called out after Caleb.

"'Kay, thanks," said Caleb as he wandered off.

"Are you the historian here?" I asked. "I was hoping to ask someone a few questions."

"Happy to help, if I can," said Mr. Raymond as he took tickets from an older couple and directed them to the restroom.

I explained to him that I was involved in the renovation of the Crockett Theatre, and he spent a few minutes explaining the connection to Essanay. Most of what he said I already knew: Jimmy Delucci, the original owner of the Crockett, had also invested in films shot in Niles.

"I'm wondering if there might be something in the theater valuable enough to incite violence."

"I guess that depends on how badly someone wants something. Am I right?"

"Of course. Can you think of anything offhand . . . ?"

He pushed his chin out, as though pondering the possibilities, while taking tickets from a young couple with a toddler in a stroller. "There are collectors of all kinds of old paraphernalia, of course, but their value probably wouldn't amount to much. Though I suppose you never really know, do you? Every once in a while, someone poking around old movie theaters or sets hits pay dirt."

"For example?"

"Well, the 'Holy Grail' of movie paraphernalia was a stash of letterpress blocks for movie ads from a publishing house in Omaha—back in the day, that place made the posters for just about every movie released in the States. Usually the blocks are destroyed after being used, but the owner of this shop kept each block and plate they created."

"And they're worth a lot?"

"Eventually they were sold to an antiques shop, and years later two women found them on a shelf of miscellaneous junk, bought them for a song, cleaned out the gunk and the white powder left over from the ink that had collected in all the crevices." He rubbed the back of his neck and chuckled. "I guess everyone thought those women were crazy. But they got the last laugh when they sold those blocks and plates for fifteen million."

"Fifteen million *dollars*?"

"Cash money." He nodded. "But like I say, that treasure trove is considered the Holy Grail. Most movie collectibles aren't worth near that much. Still, some movie posters from the 1930s were auctioned off recently for half a million each, and one was traded privately for more than a million."

I thought of the rolled-up old posters lying around the Crockett Theatre. There was also one hanging in the security trailer, and Coco had several in her apartment as well—could those be from the Crockett? Even if so, how would that explain Isadora's murder? She urged the squatters not to loot the theater, but it wouldn't be hard for someone to take a poster or two.

"Those posters were in pristine condition, of course," said Mr. Raymond. "One small museum in Ontario, Canada, recently found a bunch of silent-movie-era posters lining the walls of a little garage out back. There were several layers of them, and they had been covered over with cardboard."

"Why in the world?" asked Landon, who had joined us.

"Insulation?" I guessed.

The museum curator nodded. "Exactly right, young lady."

"I find old newspapers stuffed behind walls all the time," I told Landon. "People didn't waste things back then, and tended to find uses for most of what they had. Old posters, considered worthless, would have helped to keep out the wind and the cold."

"This little lady knows her business." Mr. Raymond gave a wink to Landon. "You'd best keep her."

"Thanks," said Landon, putting his arm around me. "I'm trying my best."

"Of course, those posters were falling apart," said Mr. Raymond. "Only value was historical."

"This might sound odd," I said. "But would vintage candy wrappers have any value?"

"Candy wrappers?"

"Some still have the candy," I said, realizing as I said the words aloud that they sounded pretty far-fetched.

The look on Mr. Raymond's face said it all. His walrus mustache twitched.

"I didn't think so," I said hastily. "Just a thought. One last question: Have you heard of an actress named Hildy Hildecott?"

"Doesn't ring a bell . . ."

"Okay, I've taken enough of your time. I'll let you get to other people's questions," I said, though the other patrons seemed absorbed in the museum's various displays. "Thanks so much."

Landon and I went to join Dad and Stan, who were checking out an antique camera. Caleb and Luz were looking at an exhibit of Chaplin on location in Niles.

"The murderess?" Mr. Raymond asked loudly from across the room. Several heads swiveled first to look at him, then at me.

"Um . . . ," I said.

"You said 'Hildy Hildecott,' right? The one who murdered her lover, Jimmy Delucci?"

I cleared my throat. "That's what they say, yes."

"You are *such* an interesting woman," Landon whispered in my ear as we returned to speak with Mr. Raymond. I stifled a giggle, which seemed inappropriate when talking about murder.

"I don't know much," Mr. Raymond said. "In fact, if you know enough to ask about her, you probably know more than I do. I just don't like it when I can't remember a name, and of course, Delucci's death was quite the scandal back then. He was married, and there was talk of an illegitimate child as well."

"Do you know any of the movies Hildy Hildecott was in?"

"The Heiress is the only one that comes to mind."

"Oh right, she mentioned that one to me the first time we met," I said without thinking. Landon smiled, and Mr. Raymond looked confused. "I mean—the friend who *told* me about Hildy mentioned that one to me."

"I repeat," murmured Landon, "so very interesting."

We went through the rest of the museum, learning about everything from Broncho Billy Anderson to the inspiration for the stunt double to the fire risks posed by early nitrate film, which was why projection booths were built as separate rooms with only a small porthole window and were often lined with tin.

I checked my phone and found Mateo had called again, and there were two more text messages. I swore under my breath.

"What's up?" asked Luz.

"I missed a call I've been waiting for. Also, I've been trying to line up artisans to look at the Crockett, but none of them are interested."

"They're getting back to you on a Sunday?" asked Luz. "I call my building super after five on a Friday and I don't hear from him until Monday, earliest."

"Professional courtesy," I said. "Contractor to contractor, the communication is usually pretty fast, even on weekends. Also, that's when a lot of us catch up on our messages. What's weird, though, is that they're saying no without even seeing the place."

"Maybe they're just busy?" suggested Luz.

"Wouldn't matter," said Dad. "Not many subcontractors would refuse the chance to check out an old theater like that, and most would be racing to submit a bid. Must be something else going on."

"That's what I thought, too," I said.

"Maybe they're scared of ghosts?" said Caleb.

"The boy's got a point," said Stan.

At long last we made it through the gift shop—one of my favorite parts of any museum—and headed home with several DVDs of early films issued from the Essanay studios, including a short shot in downtown

San Francisco in 1906, just days before the great earth-quake.

We piled back into the van, Dad grumbling the whole time about it being too late now for him to pre-pare a proper dinner. Dad was committed to eating at six, and it would take a while to get home.

"Let's just stop somewhere, Dad," I suggested.

He looked appalled. "You've eaten out the last two nights, Mel. I guess someone's getting pretty big for her britches."

"I've been big for my britches for a while now," I said. "But that has more to do with your delicious cook-ing than anything else. How about Afghani food, since we're here in Little Afghanistan?"

"Good idea," said Caleb. "Stan says it's the bomb."

"I said that?" asked Stan, but he was already looking up reviews of nearby Afghani restaurants on his phone.

"You seriously want to eat at a restaurant that'll cost an arm and a leg, instead of my home cooking?" Dad grumbled.

"I can't wait for your cooking, Bill," said Caleb, showing a keen ability to stay in my dad's good graces. "Thought about it every day in Nicaragua, and when I'm with my dad, well, you know, he's not much of a cook, and neither is the baby's mother." Caleb wasn't close to his new stepmother. "But we don't want you to have to cook so late tonight. Or for us to have to do dishes, for that matter."

"He's right, old man," said Luz. "Give in. You know you want to. Where to, Stan?"

We wound up at a simple, intimate restaurant. The place was only about half full on this Sunday evening, and the owner cheerfully pushed some tables together to accommodate our large party.

Not being familiar with the culinary traditions of Afghanistan—and inspired by Annette's example of *omakase*—we threw ourselves on the mercy of the owner, who doubled as our server. He brought us several fragrant dishes: Kabuli palaw, a rice dish cooked with pistachios and fried raisins and slivered carrots; Qormah e Alou-Bokhara wa Dalnakhod with chicken; several different kinds of kebabs; and a stack of steaming naan.

"How hard do you think it would be to make this at home?" Dad asked. "I saw an Afghani grocer down the street here. We could get whatever spices we need."

Dad rarely ate out, but when he did, he picked up recipes and ideas to try at home. Once again I felt the bittersweet emotion of knowing I would be leaving his home soon and would no longer come home after a long day to his home cooking. I might even have to start cooking myself—or rely on Landon to do the cooking. We should probably discuss that at some point.

Of course we would visit Dad and Stan often, but it wouldn't be the same. But that was okay, I mused. Time passed and things changed.

"*This* is my favorite part of history," said Caleb, grabbing his third mantu, a dumpling filled with ground lamb. "The kind you can sink your teeth into."

"Good man," Dad mumbled, tearing apart a fragrant piece of naan.

"I have a question for you, Caleb," I said. "As the sole representative of the under-thirty crowd at this table, can you explain why the Sepety sisters are so famous?"

He shrugged. "Big booties, maybe?"

"So they don't actually do anything?"

"How do you mean?"

"Do they dance, or act, or do something along those lines?"

He chewed on a mouthful of rice, a thoughtful look in his dark eyes. "I think they mainly don't wear many clothes and marry famous guys—one of 'em's married to a rap star and another to an NBA player."

"It's almost as if feminism had never happened," Luz murmured.

"Have you ever heard of the brother, Ringo?" I asked.

"They mention him on social media sometimes, but not much. Listen, I'm no expert, though. I don't, like, watch the show regularly or anything."

"I get it. Thanks."

"Why are you asking?"

"The woman who was killed at the Crockett Theatre was a Sepety."

"Whoa—was she the sister who didn't want any part of things?" Caleb asked. "They mention her sometimes on social media. In fact, once they joked that someone should kill her, and I think one of their crazy fans tried."

"They joked about *killing* her?" I asked, horrified. "What happened?"

Caleb shrugged. "Not really sure. They didn't, though. Or . . . you think they did, after all?"

"No, of course not," I said. Worth mentioning to Annette, though.

Landon slipped off to use the restroom and smoothly arranged to pay for the dinner, demonstrating his own keen ability to get on my dad's good side.

As we drove back home, I tried calling Mateo once more, but again got voice mail. I left a message that I would be at the Crockett Theatre tomorrow morning at seven, in case he was back in town and able to join us.

That reminded me: I called Annette to double-check that the crime scene would be released so I could do a walk-through in the morning.

"As promised," Annette said. "Anything else?"

"Apparently Isadora had gotten death threats from the Sepety sisters' fans."

"We checked that out already. There wasn't anything there."

"Well, okay, then. Just doing my civic duty, informing the SFPD of everything I know."

She gave a wry chuckle. "Say hi to your dad for me."

The moment we got back home, Dad started popping popcorn. Huge dinner be damned, fresh buttered popcorn was de rigueur on movie night. Landon uncorked the Sancerre he'd been wanting to try, which he and Luz agreed was the perfect pairing for popcorn.

We gathered in the living room and Caleb loaded the DVD of *The Heiress* into the player.

About ten minutes into the tale of a young heiress who had been mistaken for a commoner, there she was, up on-screen: Hildy Hildecott, in black and white. She was playing a bit part as a maid, but she was lovely and funny, with a flair for physical comedy. It was fun to see her in all her celluloid glory.

I couldn't stop thinking about her stabbing Jimmy Delucci and turning the knife on herself.

Oh, Hildy, I thought, blowing out a long sigh. *What did you do?*

Chapter Twenty-Seven

All was quiet the next morning when Landon and I pulled up to the Crockett Theatre. Dad arrived right behind us in a separate car.

Even though Dad was "retired," he always helped to estimate materials and costs at the beginning of large projects. Landon came along to "make sure I didn't die before the wedding," which I appreciated. I wasn't entirely sure he was kidding.

I noticed a sign in the tattoo shop window stating it was closed on Mondays, which was too bad—I wanted to ask Tierney for help in getting in touch with the others. I had decided to hire any squatters interested in doing some basic cleanup and other unskilled jobs for the theater renovation. I might have been kicking them out of the only home they knew, but at the very least I could employ them temporarily.

Gregory Thibodeaux was waiting for us at the theater, sporting a small bandage over his eye. He assured me he felt "fit as a fiddle." As I was introducing him to Dad and Landon, Mateo emerged from the security trailer, a cup of coffee in hand, followed by Skeet.

"Good morning!" Mateo said. "Mel, is everything okay? I was so frustrated I couldn't get through to you this weekend. Did something happen at your house? I stopped by there this morning, looked things over, but didn't see anything wrong."

"No, everything's fine there," I said, pushing away the memory of Hildy rushing at me. "I hope I didn't spoil your weekend. I just wanted to ask you a question."

I introduced Skeet and Gregory to my father and Landon, then asked Mateo if we could speak privately. We moved over near the cyclone fence.

"Mateo, did you come by here a few weeks ago?"

"I did, yes. In fact, I think that might be how Turner Construction got the job. I spoke with Skeet here and left your name and my card."

"Why?"

"Skeet mentioned they were looking for a new contractor to take over the job."

"I meant, why did you stop by in the first place?"

"It's . . ." He looked away.

"Mateo?" I asked, worried now.

He smiled sheepishly. "It seems silly, but you'll probably understand. You know that armoire in the attic at your place?"

"The one blocking the closet door."

He nodded. "I found a playbill peeking out from under that armoire. It was for a show that was playing here at the Crockett Theatre, way back when it first opened. There's a whole stack of old playbills in a box in the attic, but this one was sitting right there against the armoire, almost like it was put there on purpose." He shrugged as though embarrassed. "So next time I was in the city, I swung by to take a look at the place, and that's how I met Skeet."

Had Hildy managed to put the playbill there, wanting me—or anyone, really—to make the connection?

"Did you have a good time in Tahoe?" I belatedly thought to ask.

"We sure did. It's beautiful there. A friend of mine has a place near the lake and invited us. My wife is staying a few extra nights with the baby."

"I hope I didn't ruin your weekend," I said again.

"It was no problem. I was just worried about your house. Glad everything's okay."

"And you already went by there this morning? You must get up even earlier than I do."

He shrugged. "You know how this business is. And I'm excited to see inside this beautiful old place."

"You won't be disappointed."

Mateo was a good friend and a hard worker, and we were lucky to have him. I felt ashamed for having doubted him, even for a second. I wondered if, on top of dealing with dead bodies and murderers on a daily basis, Annette Crawford went through life having to doubt everyone. No wonder she made time to focus on something entirely unconnected, like learning a new language.

Skeet unlocked the actors' entrance door, and we proceeded down that utilitarian hallway to the spectacular lobby, where Mateo, Dad, and Landon stood stock-still, gazing in wonder at the ornate columns and baroque carvings, the curtain-covered niches, and the intricate moldings.

It was that kind of place.

"So," said Gregory, "what's first on the agenda?"

"A thorough cleaning, left to right and top to bottom," I said. "It sounds awfully basic, but on a job like this one, we can't really tell what needs what until the place is cleaned and we can inspect the state of the decorative finishes. They're really what make this old theater a palace."

"I'm surprised Avery didn't already attend to that," said Dad.

"Me, too." To Gregory, I said: "Luckily, cleaning's not expensive. I mean, this is a huge space, so it will add up, but I'll get a good crew in here and it won't take long."

"Doesn't look too bad to me," Gregory said. "A little sweeping, maybe."

"I wish it were that simple. See the top of the column, there?" I asked, pointing to the acanthus leafing out of the Ionic fluted column. Streaks of black had settled in the crevices of the carving, and rust-colored drips ran down the flutes. "That means water damage. Once we get up there and clean, we'll be able to see if there's a problem with dry rot or insects, and if so whether the column will need to be replaced or can be repaired with putty and infill. At this height we might be able to fudge it. But of course we also need to address the source of the water intrusion in the first place . . ."

I realized Gregory was no longer listening. He checked his phone, asked if we were all good here, and said he'd be on his way and "leave it to the professionals to handle."

Worked for me. In my line of work, clients frequently ask questions but aren't actually interested in the minutiae of construction.

"Oh, Gregory, before you go," I said. "Did you look into that theater in Oregon? The one that was torn down after being renovated?"

"I don't have the whole story, but from what I've pieced together, it seems that after the remodel the theater was sold to new owners. They could do whatever they wanted with the land and the buildings, as I'm sure you know only too well. We live in a tear-it-down society, more's the pity."

"Also, I ran into Alan Peterson the other day, the city liaison? He's supposed to oversee an audit of the financials but said he hasn't been able to get the paperwork through the city."

"As far as I know, there have been several audits done, but I'll check into that, as well." He tilted his head and gave me a charming smile. "I wish you wouldn't worry so much, Mel. Leave that up to me, and you concentrate on bringing this grande old dame back to her beautiful heyday. You've got your work cut out for you, but I feel confident she couldn't be in better hands."

I watched him walk away. I was unconvinced. Also, there was nothing quite like telling me not to worry to make me worry.

After Gregory left, I gave Dad, Landon, and Mateo a brief tour of the whole theater, minus the basement, where I had been trapped with Annette. I added a note to check on those locking mechanisms to my already massive and ever-growing Crockett to-do list.

Today the theater seemed almost creepily quiet: There was no ghostly usher trying to shoo me into a seat, no jeering audience, not even a graceful Isadora leaping and twirling onstage. Presently the Crockett Theatre was just what most passersby assumed: a gorgeous old building in desperate need of love and attention and money. Lots and lots of money.

There were still signs of squatters, but it was impossible to know whether they had left and abandoned their "things"—candle stubs and old pillows and blankets— or were simply hiding somewhere or were out for the day.

Dad was already adding up numbers in his head, making notes, and taking measurements with the new-fangled Leica DISTO X3 laser distance meter I had given him for his birthday. He had groused about his good old-fashioned tape measure being perfectly good enough, until he realize just how much easier it was to use the laser on a jobsite.

Dad and Mateo conferred about supplies and methods and timelines, while Landon trailed me, poking behind curtains and exclaiming about the artwork and the decorative details. He wasn't content until he tried turning on every faucet he found, intrigued by Alyx piping water in from the basement.

I brought a step stool over to a nearby pink hallway and scraped lightly at some of the pink paint on the woodwork just below the ceiling, in an attempt to see what lay underneath. A historic building like the Crockett might well have five or six layers of paint and paper slapped over the original finishes. Ultimately it would be up to the decorative painters to discover the original color scheme, but I was too anxious to wait.

Landon helped me take measurements for the stub outs for fire sprinklers throughout, two-inch pipes for each room off of the main. It didn't fit in with the beauty of the theater, but sprinklers saved lives. Air-conditioning and updated heating also needed to go in early.

I could already see in my mind's eye the complex web of scaffolding that could reach the hundred feet to the ceilings above. And then we needed skilled workers who would not blink at the thought of climbing those structures and working up there all day long.

Until developing my fear of heights, I had been one of those scaffolding monkeys. As a kid I had loved to climb them on my dad's jobsites, like bars at a playground.

I felt sure I'd get back up there one of these days, with continued therapy and practice. But today was not that day.

At the moment I was feeling pretty darned fancy for navigating the four-foot stepladder.

It was easy to lose track of time in a place like the Crockett Theatre; the scale of the job was breathtaking. Bigger than anything Turner Construction had taken on before, but I felt confident we could handle it. The trick was to break the job down into parts, like any small residential job: structure repair, electrical, plumbing, roof, rot and other wood issues, walls, windows, drywall/plaster, paint and decorative finishes, floor coverings . . . and of course all the specialty items unique to a theater space. Another trick to successful construction jobs was getting materials on order in a timely manner; nothing like bringing a job to a standstill while waiting for items to be delivered.

After several hours, Dad went home to crunch the numbers and confer with Stan. Landon, not mollified by the apparent lack of ghosts and murderers in the theater, continued to follow me around uncomplainingly, making notes of his own—they probably consisted of trying to figure out a mathematical problem he was working on. At home, I often found little equations of numbers and figures—including an intimidating number of x's and y's—near the toothpaste tube, on the grocery list, scrawled in the margins of newspapers. The man's mind seemed never to stop working.

I was tinkering with the vintage-popcorn popper behind the concession stand, wondering whether it was worth trying to fix, when I remembered what Tierney had said about Isadora finding candy wrappers and other small items in the "thingamajig" under the balcony floor.

I asked Mateo and Landon to accompany me up to the balcony level.

The theater remained eerily quiet. I was jumpy with anticipation, wondering if and when the spirits would show themselves—and whether I would have to try to explain it all to Landon and Mateo.

Up in the balcony, the men used their combined strength to unscrew the cast-iron "mushroom caps" that covered the access to the plenum. It was a tight fit—too tight for either of the men—but I turned my headlamp on and managed to crawl through the access hatch.

The crawl space was less than three feet high, and

the floor was full of trash, as though it had collected for many decades, perhaps as much as a century. Apparently no one had cleaned it out—or even actively swept things in. In older buildings trash in the ventilation shafts like this one is no big deal, but in modern buildings, plenums are often treated as soffits to run cables for communications and high tech, and since the shafts pull in fresh air and oxygen, they can become a fire hazard.

And any anthropologist knows that trash heaps are gold mines when it comes to understanding the past. In former gold mining towns people now dug under old outhouses, looking for treasures, just as the shell mounds of ancient peoples gave insight into their lives.

This plenum was a time capsule of refuse.

I scooted through old hot dog wrappers, twine and tools, and cigarette packs. I found vintage soda bottles, old coins, and even two hip flasks. There were newspapers dating from the period before the theater opened, meaning they must have been tossed aside by the builders almost a century ago, the paper yellowed and brittle and full of fascinating old ads and articles.

And there were candy wrappers. Baby Ruths, Dots, Milk Duds, Red Hots, Good & Plenty, alongside a number of vintage brands I didn't recognize. They were all there. Apparently the packaging for a Butterfinger has barely changed in all this time.

From outside, I heard a mechanism whirring, and then the strains of the Mighty Wurlitzer. From within the crawl space, I heard a rustling and feared a rat.

But when I looked up, I squeaked in surprise.

The usher was right there in the plenum with me, on his hands and knees; his cap would have bumped the ceiling if he weren't a ghost.

"Ma'am, you shouldn't be in this restricted area."

My heart pounded; my breath caught. Again, I tried to formulate my thoughts to ask him something, anything that might be helpful. I racked my brain for his name from the article Trish had shown me.

"Y- . . . you're Harold, right?" I stammered. "Harold Hancock?"

"Could I see your ticket stub, please?"

"Harold, was there something down here? Did Isadora find something valuable?"

"The show will commence when everyone has taken their seat."

Olivier had said residual ghosts repeated themselves over and over. Was it possible Harold the usher could only speak in sentences he'd said repeatedly through the years? But unlike what Olivier had told us about residual energy, Harold appeared to be plenty interactive. What could he be trying to tell me?

"Harold," I said, crawling closer to him, crunching a small compact that lay open, its mirror broken but intact. "I—"

But he was gone.

I twisted around to see if he was behind me, but nothing remained, save the detritus of a century of theater patrons.

When I turned back, a bunch of papers flew past me as though tossed by a gust of wind. I squeezed my eyes shut against the dust. When I opened them, I saw a handwritten note: "Balcony reserved September 26 for Mr. Delucci and guest."

I picked it up, caught a glance of my face in the cracked mirror of the little compact, and suddenly . . .

I was there.

I was wearing Hildy's green dress.

In front of me, two men were arguing. One had a mustache; both were clad in fine suits. The mustachioed man punched the other in the face, knocking him down, and then he pulled out a knife.

Without hesitation, the mustachioed man stood over

the other and stabbed him once in the gut. The injured man knocked the knife out of his assailant's hand. It skittered along the floor toward me.

"Jimmy!" I cried out, picking up the bloody knife.

"Kill him, Hildy," said the stabbed man, his voice raspy and desperate as he pressed a hand over his bloody belly. "Kill him or he'll never let you have it. He'll never let you . . ."

The other man stomped him in the gut, and he spoke no more.

"Jimmy!" I cried out.

The other man turned his attention to me.

I backed up, the knife held in front of me defensively.

"You don't have to do this, Mr. Delucci. I swear . . ."

"Where's the will?" he asked.

"I don't know what you're talking about! Jimmy said he had something to show me, but he dropped it somewheres right on the floor, easy as that, and it rolled away. He said he was gonna have to rewrite it, make a new one."

"Sure," he sneered, still coming toward me, excruciatingly slowly. "He dropped it 'somewheres.' You two had your fancy date at the Crockett tonight. Am I right? It's there somewhere, isn't it?"

"I dunno . . . I dunno what you're talking ab-bout," I said, stammering as I continued to back up, coming up against the wall behind me. "Mr. Delucci, please, we gotta get Jimmy to the doctor! He's gonna bleed to death!"

"Tell me!"

"It's in the ladies' lounge!" I said, but I was lying. I could feel it. I started to weep. "Right there, in the ladies' lounge at the Crockett. I'll go there and get it for you. You can destroy it. I won't tell anybody, Mr. Delucci. I promise. You pay off the lawyer who wrote it, and he won't say nothin' either."

He snorted, his face twisted in rage, coming so close

to me I could smell the whiskey and cigar smoke on his breath.

"Why does your precious Jimmy have all the luck, huh? He's got the Midas touch. I'll tell you that much. Who knew there was so much money to be made in motion pictures?"

I was crying, tears running down my face, dripping onto the hand that still held the bloody knife. He was close enough now, I could plunge it into his big gut. I *should* plunge it in. I pulled in a shaky breath, trying to steel myself.

It was as though he could read my mind.

"Go ahead, girlie. Go ahead and kill me, and get your Jimmy to the doctor, and you and he and your little girl can live happily ever after, right? Maybe you'll have to slip a little arsenic into his wifey's tea, though, just to make room."

I was shaking my head. *Go ahead, Hildy, go ahead. You have to.*

"Hildy . . . ," I heard Jimmy moan. "Do it!"

I looked over to where he was lying on the floor, and in that moment, Mr. Delucci grabbed my hands, still holding the knife, turned the blade toward me, and plunged it into my own belly.

Chapter Twenty-Eight

"Mel!" I heard someone calling my name. "Mel! Are you all right?"

Landon.

"*Mel?*" came another voice. "What's going on? Can you speak to us?"

Mateo.

"There's got to be another way in there," I heard Landon saying from afar.

"There are probably access panels down in the ceiling of the mezzanine," said Mateo. "But we'd have to locate a ladder."

"I don't want to wait. She's not responding; something's wrong. What about ripping up these floorboards?"

"Good idea. I'll get the crowbar," said Mateo. "We'll have this floor up in a hot minute."

"*No!*" I called out, finally rousing from my fugue state. "No, I'm okay, guys. Sorry. I'm coming out."

"What happened?" Landon demanded as I squeezed back through the access port. He enveloped me in a hug, paying no heed to the grimy state of my coveralls. "Are you okay?"

"I'm fine," I said. It didn't seem the time and place to mention that I had just experienced being stabbed in the abdomen. "I . . . uh . . . I'm sorry. I didn't mean to check out like that. I got kind of far in there. It needs cleaning out in the worst way."

"Sure," said Mateo. "We'll get on that right away, no big deal. Right away."

"Thanks, Mateo," I said. "But I just wanted you here today for your thoughts. I'd appreciate it if you could stay on our house in Oakland until it's done. I'll be in charge here."

"Of course, whatever you say, *jefa*," Mateo said with a nod, using the Spanish word for "boss."

Landon was looking at me with a worried expression. "Maybe we could wrap up for the day? It's getting late."

"Sure," I said, though part of me felt like one of the squatters, wanting to move in. It was hard to leave this theater. Maybe that was why so many spirits remained lurking within the structure.

As Landon drove us over the Bay Bridge, the rhythmic *thump* of the wheels over the seams of the bridge sections lulled me. I couldn't keep my eyes open, even though it wasn't late. If I thought the ghost-busting thing was exhausting, this psychic-time-traveling deal was even worse.

I couldn't stop thinking about what I saw, much less what I had experienced. I was going to have to ask Olivier and Lily if they had any insights as to why I was experiencing visions while looking into mirrors. Not *every* mirror, thank goodness, but enough to put me on edge. What was I seeing and why? And most important, what did I do about it?

For now I was certain of one thing: There was a last will and testament, a document Mr. William Delucci was willing to kill to get his hands on.

But William had inherited his brother's fortune, and the theaters had then passed down to William's son,

Cal, so I had to assume William had found and destroyed the will or it had never been found at all.

I—as Hildy—had been lying when I said the will was hidden in the ladies' lounge at the Crockett. But I—she?—was telling the truth when she said it had rolled away "somewheres."

Could it have fallen into the plenum opening or been swept in there by a lazy usher? But in all the trash I had looked through, I certainly hadn't found a last will and testament.

Time for a little excavation, anthropology-style.

As we pulled off the freeway in Oakland, I roused myself and turned to Landon.

"Please don't mention that last incident to my dad. He'll worry."

"*I'm* worried, Mel. You haven't even told *me* what happened, so how could I mention it to your father?"

"It's a little hard to explain. I thought I saw something when I was down there in the plenum."

"A ghost? Mateo and I saw the Wurlitzer organ come up, but I figured that could have been an electrical glitch, perhaps. Do you think it was supernatural?"

"Yes, but believe it or not, ghosts weren't the scary part."

"But something scared you."

I nodded. "Something . . . something happened. I had a kind of vision. I thought I saw something that had to do with how Hildy died."

"Hildy, our attic ghost? What does she have to do with the Crockett Theatre?"

"From what I've pieced together, she was having an affair with Jimmy Delucci, the original owner of the theater. He was married, but Hildy had a child by him. I think he tried to leave something to her, maybe part of his fortune or the theater itself. She said he promised to take care of her and her child."

"But she died?"

"According to the papers, she killed Jimmy during an argument, and then turned the knife on herself. But in the vision I just had, it was Jimmy's brother, William, who murdered them both when he found out about the will."

Landon pondered for a moment. "Poor thing. What happened to the child?"

"I don't have any idea. This all happened nearly a century ago, so even if she had lived a long life I doubt she'd be able to tell us anything, even assuming I could track her down. All I have is the name Darlene."

We pulled up in front of my dad's house. The garden was in full bloom, a little wild and overgrown but welcoming, with lemon, peach, and nectarine trees laden with fruit, showy blue lilies of the Nile, and bushes of Mexican marigolds, rosemary, and lavender lining the walkway.

And then we walked into a kitchen smelling of roasting chicken and potatoes. I was so lucky.

"Here's the deal," Dad said as we all sat down to eat, after Landon and I had showered off the dust from the Crockett. "Stan and I went over the numbers, and some things aren't making sense."

Our eyes met, and I knew what he was thinking.

It didn't *look* like there had been millions already poured into the Crockett. Avery Builders was pricier than Turner Construction, but still . . . People unfamiliar with building sites often didn't understand where the money went, but Dad and I sure did—permits, architectural drawings, invisible things like foundation work, electrical, and plumbing.

But at the Crockett Theatre, other than the foundation work and some basic plumbing, it didn't appear that enough had been done to justify the time and money spent so far.

"Could Josh Avery somehow have been milking this project for his own gain?" I wondered aloud.

"I thought you liked him," said Dad.

"I do. But when it comes down to it, I don't know him all that well, and like you say, the project seems overrun with costs. He did mention some mysterious no-show positions . . . The other obvious culprit would be the consortium itself."

"I checked out their financials before giving the whole thing my go-ahead," said Stan. "But that was based on the information and documents they gave me. It would have been easy enough for Xerxes to make things look good on paper."

"But why would they want to spend a lot of money on the project in the first place?" asked Landon.

"So far most of the project has used city funds, or at least matching funds, so they haven't put all that much into it," said Stan. "And they bought the place for only ten dollars from the city."

"Ten *dollars*?" said Caleb. "*I* wanna buy a cool old theater for ten dollars."

"It was with the agreement that they would take on the multimillion-dollar renovation, however," said Stan.

"There's always a catch," said Caleb.

"Were there any outs to that agreement?" I asked Stan.

"Only if there are 'unreasonable delays and/or cost incursions,' or if the building was found to be 'beyond reasonable repair.'"

"What constitutes 'reasonable' and 'unreasonable'?" Landon asked.

Stan shook his head. "That's not spelled out."

I thought back to my discussion with Renata at the permit department. Sometimes the city wouldn't allow a property owner to destroy a historic building, so the owner would allow the roof to rot—or actively sabotage it—until the building was ruined beyond repair. After which, the building was considered a hazard and the owners were granted permission to demolish it.

"So if they wanted to delay things sufficiently, and to run up the cost . . . what's the ultimate goal?" I asked. "To tear it down?"

"Or cash in on the land, like in *Who Framed Roger Rabbit*," said Caleb around a mouthful of chicken.

"I haven't seen that one for a long time," I said. "Remind me."

"In the movie aren't they, like, buying up land that becomes valuable so they can sell it for the freeways or whatever? It's like sitting on oil, or gold, or whatever. Same deal in that movie *Chinatown*—about water, I think?"

"You're becoming quite the film buff, Caleb," said Dad. "How about going to class or studying every now and then?"

We all laughed and the conversation moved on to Caleb starting college at UC Santa Cruz in the fall, but I couldn't stop thinking about the Crockett.

What was more valuable than oil or gold in these parts? *Land.* San Francisco was a thriving city located on a relatively tiny thumb of land, with no room to expand. City lots had become unbelievably precious, even in formerly run-down parts of town.

After dinner I sat at my computer to check into the "space guy" who had wanted to buy the entire city block. How much had he been willing to pay? I found a few references to a billionaire who had made a bid, but none mentioned a dollar amount. Still, the fellow had enough money to try to build his own personal rocket to the moon, so I imagined it was a tidy sum.

While online I checked the link to the eBay ad the Doctor had sent. The seller's handle was Cocoapuffs24987. The parts were still for sale and without many bids—who wanted old plumbing fixtures?—so I bid on them and sent a personal message, asking whether the seller knew where the items came from.

Also in my e-mail was a message from Trish with

links to articles from the *Oakland Tribune*'s searchable archives, with the same article that Lorraine Delucci had shown me, plus a few variations. But the upshot was the same: One Hildy Hildecott, her profession listed as "starlet," age twenty-nine, had stabbed to death her married lover and then turned the knife on herself, at a gentleman's club near Lake Merritt "following a night on the town in San Francisco," on one bloody September night in 1924. One article stated that the "lovers'" bodies were found by none other than William Delucci, brother of the deceased, who was said to have stopped by the club to share a late-night brandy with Jimmy Delucci.

Brother, and murderer, of the deceased.

Their deaths had not occurred in my new house, and yet Hildy was lingering in the attic, haunting me. Was she simply attached to her dresses, or was there something more?

Chapter Twenty-Nine

Days passed, and it was a joy to really get to know the nooks and crannies of the Crockett Theatre, cleaning up and getting our hands dirty.

I called all the squatters for whom I had numbers; none picked up, but I left messages that there was temporary work for them if they were interested in helping with the cleanup.

I found Tierney at the tattoo parlor and once again begged off of getting a tattoo, even a little one, but asked her to spread the word to the others in case they wanted jobs. Most seemed to have moved out of the theater once my crew and I showed up with equipment— the racket of compressors has a way of clearing the area—but I worried about where they might have gone.

Meanwhile, Luz's colleague who dealt with homelessness and affordable housing also agreed to meet with them to discuss options, and came to the theater laden down with brochures and application forms.

I never heard back from most of the squatters, but Alyx, Liam, Mitch, and Tierney showed up, along with a few others. Tierney was especially helpful because she was so petite and thus able to get into the plenum and move around much more easily than I could. We set up a bucket brigade. Tierney filled buckets with trash and handed them up through the cast-iron openings, and they were then passed hand to hand to a staging area on the ample balcony landing. There the buckets were dumped and the contents sorted into piles of like items: candy and food wrappers; smoking-related items such as cigarette packs, matchbooks, cigarette holders, an old pipe, and tobacco pouches; twine and nails and tools and building-related items; newspapers, playbills, and magazines; other miscellaneous papers.

It was this last category that most interested me, but there was no last will and testament to be found.

When Tierney declared the crawl space to be "trash-free," I climbed in to take a look. She had done an excellent job. It was indeed completely trash-free.

Maybe I was wrong. Maybe Jimmy Delucci and Hildy Hildecott hadn't passed their last night together here in the balcony. Maybe Jimmy hadn't named Hildy his heir and dropped the darned will and then was unable to find it. After all, it sounded a bit incredible when I put it out there like that.

Once we finished with the plenum clean out, I ordered pizzas for all my squatter employees, and we gathered on the balcony landing to eat together.

"Don't give up altogether, Liam," I heard Tierney say as I set the pizzas down in the middle of the circle. With Isadora gone, Tierney seemed to have stepped into the "house mom" position, even though this house had dispersed. She was young and soft-spoken, but nonetheless the others tended to fall quiet and listen when she addressed them. "Remember that one Crockett Caretaker guy? He found a place right around the corner?"

"That's true," said Alyx as he helped himself to a

second slice of mushroom-and-pepperoni pizza. "Who knew the city paid so much?"

"Is he getting assistance from the city to pay for the apartment?" I asked.

"What?" said Alyx. "No, like, he works for the city."

"The city of San Francisco?" I asked.

Alyx exchanged looks with Liam, as if to say, "She's a dim one, this one."

Tierney leaned forward and spoke gently. "Yes, Mel? He works for the city of San Francisco? He's, like, in their records department?"

"Are you talking about Baldwin?" I asked.

They nodded.

"You're right, then." I thought back to Coco's classic Victorian apartment building, with its paneled entry decorated with a chandelier and a flower arrangement. Baldwin had mentioned he had just moved in. "That's an awfully nice place for someone on a city salary."

"Maybe he has family money," said Mitch. "In fact . . . I wanted to tell you guys that my family has suggested maybe buying a place in Oakland or someplace a little cheaper, and maybe we could live together there and see if we could make it work."

They spoke excitedly about the possibilities. It seemed the new situation would include paying some rent, but Mitch's family sounded willing to subsidize them at least in part. That would be a nice solution, at least for some of the squatters.

"Okay, guys," I said as we finished up. "This pizza is actually a bribe: Will you finally tell me? How did you slip in and out of the theater all this time?"

They exchanged looks, and Alyx shrugged.

"The tunnels down below, with the cisterns."

"They lead somewhere?" I asked.

"They're connected to the tattoo shop," said Tierney. "First time I wandered through and wound up in this theater, I seriously thought I was hallucinating."

"There's also a connection to the donut shop," said Mitch.

"They both have access? That's . . . interesting." And it was something that should be addressed. As fun as secret entrances and tunnels could be, they could also pose a significant public-health risk.

"But you locked everything up, right?" asked Liam.

"How do you mean?" I asked.

"Somebody put locks on all the doors down there?" said Tierney. "We assumed it was you?"

"It wasn't me, as a matter of fact. I'll check it out. But one other thing I wanted to mention before you all leave for the day," I continued. "I was thinking, now that the main theater is pretty well cleaned up, would you like to use it for a memorial service for Isadora? You could invite any other friends and family."

"That would be awesome," said Tierney. "I think Isadora would really like something like that. Probably not her whole family, but I'm sure Ringo would like to join us."

"I'd like to come, as well, if it's appropriate," I said. "I know I barely met her, but I feel I know Isadora in some important ways. And I am so sorry for her loss."

In fact, I still saw Isadora dancing onstage, especially toward the end of the day when there were fewer people left in the building. Often I stopped to watch, and several times I tried communicating with her, but she would not pause in her dance of joy.

Speaking now of Isadora, it dawned on me: If Isadora had found a will in the plenum and realized what it was, of course it wouldn't still be in the plenum.

Also . . . why had she been so committed to showing it to Skeet?

It was late. I closed up the theater behind everyone and locked the back door. Then I went to the open door of the security trailer. Skeet was on duty tonight.

"Skeet?" I called out as I approached.

"Well, hello there, Mel. How are things going?"

"The cleanup has gone well so far. We don't have any of the big equipment here yet, but the scaffolding is scheduled to be delivered and set up tomorrow, so we ought to start kicking up a real racket. I apologize in advance."

He smiled. "There's an old saying about breaking a few eggs to make an omelet that comes to mind."

"True."

"Coffee?" he asked. "Would you like to come in?"

"No coffee, thanks. But I wanted to ask you something."

"Shoot."

"The other day when I stopped by . . . why did you change your tone suddenly and ask me to leave? It seemed like you had received a phone call that put you on edge."

He shrugged. "Sorry about that. It was that Alan Peterson guy, asking questions, trying to get to the Xerxes group, and refusing to believe that I have to respect the nondisclosure agreement I signed. That man treads on my last nerve."

"He does have a way about him, I agree."

"Anyway, I apologize. I think I was just tired; I shouldn't have taken it out on you."

"No worries. Hey, you mentioned that your mother was an orphan, from Oakland. Did she ever mention her own mother?"

Skeet shook his head. "She was too young when her mom died, didn't remember anything. She got taken in by a family over there, in Oakland, the family in the house where her mother had rented a room. She used to talk about that house, said it was special, that she always felt drawn to it."

"Do you know the address?"

He shook his head. "Can't say that I do. She took me over there one time when I was a kid, though."

"Do you remember anything about it? What did it look like?"

"It was a big old house, with a redwood in front, old garage out back. Not far from the Grand Lake Theatre, as a matter of fact." He smiled. "I remember after, we went to a matinee. It was a real nice day. That's why I still like to take my grandkids out, spend time with them; childhood goes by too fast, and those are the memories we treasure."

"So true. Skeet, what was your mother's name?"

"Darlene. Darlene Henley was her married name."

"And her maiden name?"

"Hildecott."

I didn't tell Skeet about what I had put together, about his grandmother Hildy, and the possibility that he should, in fact, be the owner of the Crockett Theatre, over which he had been standing guard for so many months. I wasn't entirely sure I was right yet. Even if I could find the will, it would have to be authenticated, and even then there would probably be lawyers and judges involved.

Landon had taken Dog for a walk in the Presidio and was supposed to pick me up at five, but texted to say he was stuck in traffic and running a little late. So I went back into the theater and proceeded to the ladies' lounge.

Isadora must have found that last will and testament in the plenum along with her candy-wrapper collection. I wondered if there was any way she had uncovered Skeet's family connection to the Crockett, or if she simply trusted him to know what to do about her discovery of an old will. For all I knew she simply thought it was a fun piece of historical data to be displayed alongside her candy-wrapper collection or on the shelf with his Depression ware shards.

Unless I could get her to talk to me, I doubted we'd ever know for sure.

I made my way through the spectacular lobby, down the ugly pink hallway, to the mirrored vestibule that led to the ladies' lounge.

It looked rather sad and empty.

We had cleaned up the mess that had been made by someone searching, I now believed, for the will, just as I was. The chaise longues and benches had been removed to be restored and reupholstered, and the old desk now sat out in the alley in a giveaway pile.

I stared at the place where the wallpaper hung down, and the slogan "Affectations can be dangerous" had been painted directly onto the stained plaster and surrounded with paisley designs.

As I ran my hands along the peeling wallpaper, I felt something not visible to the eye. I felt it with my fingertips, a very slight edge to something.

I grabbed the wallpaper and gently but firmly pulled it back, realizing I was onto something—this was new glue, the kind you could unpeel without ruining the plaster underneath. The old adhesives weren't nearly so forgiving.

I spied the corner of plastic and carefully pulled it out. Within a sealed plastic Baggie was an official-looking document: a last will and testament, signed with a flourish by James Anthony Delucci, leaving the Crockett Theatre of San Francisco to one "Hildegaard Marie Hildecott, of Oakland, California, and her issue."

Hildy's "issue" was Darlene Hildecott Henley, mother of one Bill "Skeet" Henley. A man too old to be forced to work nights, in my opinion.

A man who, if we could authenticate this last will and testament, was about to become the owner of one venerable Crockett Theatre and the valuable land on which it stood.

Chapter Thirty

'll take that. Thanks," came a man's voice from behind me.

I turned to find myself face-to-face with Baldwin, who was holding a gun on me. A 9mm Glock, unless I missed my guess. My dad's favorite firearm.

I didn't have much choice, so I handed the will to him, and he shoved it roughly into the pocket of his oversized sweatshirt.

"Cell phone, too, please," he said, holding out his hand.

"The battery doesn't hold a charge in here anyway," I said, but did as I was told.

"C'mon." He gestured with his head.

"Where are we headed?" I asked.

"Basement. *Move.*"

As I walked through the labyrinthine back hallways of the theater and down to the dressing room area, I tried to think. It wasn't easy: My heart was pounding, and my nose was running, and I felt sick to my stomach.

I *hated* having guns pointed at me.

Baldwin was a lot bigger than me, and he held a very deadly weapon. Skeet was outside in the trailer, but he'd never hear me, no matter how loud I might scream. There were no security cameras or anything else that would give anyone a clue as to what was going on inside this building. Landon would show up pretty soon, but he'd probably chat for a few minutes with Skeet before coming to look for me, and even when he did, how long would it take him to search the entire theater?

"Why the basement?" I asked as we neared the door Annette and I had passed through, the one that opened onto the creaky metal steps.

"I've got everything all set up."

I didn't dare ask what, exactly, was all set up. When I paused at the top of the stairs, Baldwin said: "I won't hesitate, you know. One tiny squeeze of the trigger and bye-bye, Mel Turner."

"I just get a little vertigo with heights," I said.

"Want me to push you down? It'd be quicker."

I couldn't tell if he was kidding, and even if he was, it was in poor taste. I took a deep breath, held tight to the handrail, and started down.

When we finally got to the bottom, I saw he had set up a bunch of antique camera equipment and standing lamps.

"What's all this for?"

"Told you, I'm a film buff. Did you like my short of Isadora dying?"

"It was horrifying."

"Right? All for the love of art, I always say."

"Why did you put the film of killing Isadora on when I was here? Did you want me to see it for some reason?"

"Didn't even know you were there until after I put the film on. Just wanted to see it on the big screen. And then I heard you two in here and figured a little time down here in the basement might give you a new perspective on things. Go stand over there—I put your mark on the floor. See it? I need to take some readings on the light."

I moved over to a chalk mark on the ground. "So, I have a choice? Death by gun, or by drowning?"

"You're a tad deluded there, Mel. You're not the big contractor now. You're just a bit player. Your death is not your choice. It's mine. I'm the director here."

He started playing with the lights and fiddling with the camera.

"You ever see the tunnels at the armory?" I asked.

He snorted. "I don't watch those kinds of movies. Do you?"

"This is just an evocative space for making a movie, is what I was thinking." What I was really thinking was that if I could get him chatting, maybe Landon would show up. Or Skeet would get curious. Or someone would show up from the donut shop or the tattoo studio. Or some other miracle would occur.

"You're a fan of Good and Plenty?" I asked.

"Why do you ask that?"

"I noticed you liked black licorice when we were at Coco's. Also, you left a box by the film of Isadora dying." He nodded but kept working on the camera, looking through the lens, checking a device that measured the light. As though he really did care about the outcome of his little film. Was this the birth of a serial killer who kept taped "souvenirs" of his kills? "I like Red Vines myself. But I only eat them when I'm at the movies, interestingly enough. It's not like I ever buy them elsewhere, even though I'm sure they're available."

He finally looked up. "Why are you talking to me about candy?"

To keep you distracted while I try to figure out how to escape, I thought to myself. Like every bad movie I had ever seen.

"You were trying to sell parts out of the theater?" I asked. "Cocoapuffs on eBay, that's you?"

"Yeah, that eBay ad's been up there for a while, I guess. Didn't produce as much money as I thought it would. Thibodeaux caught me, though, trespassing. All these squatters in here, but they found *me* stealing stuff, so I had to put most of it back. Still, they gave me a job, so who's complaining?"

"So, you were on Xerxes' payroll? Were you the one who doctored the city documents?"

"Or 'lost' them, like the request for the audit. Always useful to have friends in the city—don't doubt it."

"Did Xerxes hire you to murder Isadora?"

"Not in so many words. I overheard her talking about the last will and testament, and told Xerxes. They instructed me to get my hands on it, if it actually existed, but Isadora wouldn't tell me where it was."

"Why kill her before she gave it to you, then?"

"They asked me to do whatever was necessary to slow down the process of renovation on this big place. They didn't specify how."

"I guess a homicide investigation bought you a few days, but at the cost of a life."

"It wasn't intended to stop it for a few *days*. I thought—I dunno. I thought it would put an end to things, maybe. People already think the place is haunted. Let them think it's cursed, too, and maybe that would bring everything to a standstill."

"Why did Xerxes want to slow things down?"

"They absorbed the city money but didn't want to put a lot of their own into it. If we delay it long enough, they'll be able to turn around and sell it to that space billionaire guy. That way they'll make pure profit. They're cutting me in on a percentage."

"Clever. So you're saying all of this was over money. That's why you turned yourself into a killer?"

"That's a little harsh, isn't it?" he asked. "I mean, I wouldn't say I'm a 'killer.' I just happened to have killed one person."

"And now aren't you planning on killing another?"
I winced as soon as I said it. *Way to remind him why
we're here, Mel.*

"Yes, as a matter of fact, I am. And we should get to
it. After all, you know what they say: Time is money in
the movie business."

I heard scratching at the door, and a faint sound of
dripping grew louder.

"What's that?" he asked, whirling around.

"The ghosts are back," I whispered.

"Get out of here," he said, turning back to me before
I could reach for anything to hit him with. "There's no
such thing as ghosts."

"You don't think so? Then what's that sound?"

Someone had turned on a faucet upstairs, and Alyx's
system had kicked in, siphoning water into a pipe that
gurgled and moaned overhead as the water passed. I
didn't blame Baldwin for finding it strange; just as it
had in the caverns below Eamon Castle, it sounded a
bit like a basilisk moving through the pipes.

A look of confusion passed over his face. "Are you
doing that? *How* are you doing that?"

"It's not me, Baldwin. I'm telling you, believe in
them or not, but this place is haunted as all get-out. For
instance, were you the one who knocked Gregory over
the head?"

He shook his head. "I made myself scarce after . . .
you know. In fact I didn't even realize you guys were
up there. Isadora and I had something of a stand-off
down under the stage, and I gave her one more chance
to tell me where the will was. She declined my offer, so
I made good on my promise."

"Your promise to kill her."

He nodded.

"And why put her on the Wurlitzer?"

"I had my film equipment all set up down there 'cause
I was planning to make a movie of the Wurlitzer rising,

but I couldn't figure out how to get it to move, much less play. After the thing with Isadora, it started up all by itself, so I placed her on it. I'm only sorry I didn't have a second camera up on the main floor so I could have filmed her rising on the Wurlitzer, all the way. *You* got to see it, though. It must have looked *awesome*."

More scratching at the door, now with added whining and whimpering; more gurgling and dripping from the direction of the cistern.

"That's what I figured," I said. "I think the ghosts made Gregory faint, and they probably started the Wurlitzer, too."

The scratching and whining at the door intensified.

"And there they are now," I said.

"That's no *ghost*," he sneered. "What, you bring your dog to work?"

"One of the perks of construction. But the thing is, Dog can see ghosts, too."

Baldwin snorted. "Yeah, right."

"And he's not a small pup. He might well claw his way through that door."

"Like I care."

"I thought you were Mr. Conservation. That's an original door, you know. His claws can do quite a number on it. Plus, he'll start on the moldings next, if he hasn't already."

"All the more reason to get on with it," Baldwin said, though I thought I saw a glimmer of doubt in his eye.

"So, you were the one who locked Inspector Crawford and me down here?" I tried to keep the desperation out of my voice. I had to keep him talking until Dog made it through the door, or Landon or Skeet caught up with him.

"You're lucky I didn't do more," said Baldwin. "I thought about it until that security guy showed up, but I didn't even have my filming equipment set up. But I mean, really, what does it take to get *rid* of you people?"

"You really don't want to do this, do you, Baldwin? I mean, one murder could be explained away as manslaughter, a crime of passion. Maybe even get a suspended sentence if the story's convincing and you squeeze out a few tears. But there's no way you can talk yourself out of *two* murders. This one would be premeditated, plain and simple."

"No kidding, genius. I'm *filming* this. That's pretty clearly premeditated."

I was hoping he wouldn't think of that.

And then, of all things, a ghost came to my rescue.

May I show you to your seat? Harold the usher hissed from behind Baldwin.

"What?" Baldwin whirled around to see who had snuck up on him.

Then *bam!* Dog—or was it Landon or Skeet?—threw himself against the door, and Baldwin spun around the other way. This time I didn't hesitate. I grabbed the antique camera and swung as hard as I could, smashing him on the head.

He stumbled and dropped to his knees, losing his grip on the gun. We both dove after it, but it skittered away and fell into the water with a splash.

"Oh great," Baldwin said, standing up slowly and glaring at me. "Now neither of us can use it! So I guess that answers your question: death by drowning."

He leapt at me, taking me with him into the water. I can swim, but I'd never had to fight off an attacker underwater. Operating purely on instinct, I grabbed his beard and yanked; he grabbed my hair and pulled. I tried to go for the vulnerable points, as I'd learned in self-defense class: the eyes, the groin. But each time the water prevented my blows from striking him with any significant force, whereas he easily succeeded in holding me under. I was losing strength and starved for air.

He was much stronger than I—and cold-blooded

enough to have strangled Isadora for no reason other than to delay a construction project.

I struggled to keep away from him, but I was running out of time—and air.

I thought, then, of what my mother had written in her journal: *I think of it like being underwater: It's strange, and scary, but the calmer you are, the longer your breath lasts. Let the water buoy you.*

I went limp, pretending I'd drowned, and let the water buoy me.

Perhaps because he needed air as much as I, Baldwin believed my ploy, and swam toward the surface. I was practically convulsing with the need for oxygen, but I knew I had one last chance. I reached for the gun lying at the bottom of the cistern. Would a waterlogged gun still fire?

A 9mm Glock would.

Baldwin reached the surface of the water. In the bright lights that Baldwin had set up for the camerawork, I could see Dog's face at the water's edge, and though it was muffled, I could hear his loud snarling and snapping.

Baldwin reared back.

I retrieved the gun and, feeling oddly calm, with the last of my breath, I pushed off the bottom and surged up, aimed, and fired before even breaking through the surface of the water.

"Lucky shot?" Annette Crawford asked a while later.

Baldwin had been taken away in an ambulance, bleeding profusely, escorted by several patrol cars. Dog and I were wrapped in blankets and sipping hot coffee. Well, I was anyway. Dog was alternating between wanting to lick my face and sleep in my lap.

Landon was similarly devoted, except rather than trying to sleep in my lap, he refused to take his arm from around my shoulders. He had followed Dog to the door that led to the basement, and heard the shot. He burst in to find me holding the gun on the injured Baldwin, both of us panting and soaking wet, but neither of us dead.

"I thought about going for the groin," I said, "but went for the knee instead."

"Good aim."

"It's nothing. I grew up with my dad."

"He the one who taught you that pistols can fire underwater?" asked Landon.

I nodded.

"Good idea," said Annette. "That knee will give him trouble the rest of his natural life."

"And his *un*natural one, as well," I said. My fear had given way to rage. I was sick and tired of low-life scum trying to murder me.

"That's the spirit," Annette said, approvingly. "By the way, you'll be glad to hear that the Delucci last will and testament survived, thanks to the sealed Baggie."

This was one use of plastic bags I wasn't going to quibble with.

"So the will spells out that Hildy was supposed to inherit the theaters," Landon said, "and that upon her demise the properties would pass to her daughter, Darlene?"

I nodded. "After Hildy's death, little Darlene was taken in by the Jeffress family, who lived in the house—our house now—where Hildy rented a room. They never knew that Darlene was actually an heiress."

"And Darlene went on to have one son, named Skeet."

"Skeet, otherwise known as Bill Henley," said Annette, "who is now likely to become a very wealthy man."

"Not to be hokey," I said, "but he already was wealthy in love and family. But now he no longer has to work a security job, or nights, if he doesn't want to. More time with the grandkids."

"So poor Hildy was set up for her lover's murder," said Landon. "Was that why she's hanging around in the attic? Or was she trying to get justice for her child and grandchild?"

"I'll talk to her about it—I think she helped push us toward this crazy renovation job in the first place. But it's possible we'll never know for sure," I said with a yawn. Adrenaline crash. "As I like to point out to people, it's not as though I know what I'm doing with these ghosties. But I guess I'll keep trying."

Epilogue

In the majestic lobby of the newly renovated Crockett Theatre, the aroma of freshly popped popcorn had replaced the scent of mildew and abandonment. Tonight, the concession stand had an "open bar" policy, serving popcorn and candy—and as a treat, tonight only, wine and champagne.

It was a special evening.

Overhead, the massive crystal chandeliers sparkled and gold-gilt moldings gleamed. The domed ceiling, painted with clouds and flitting birds, was illuminated by soft uplighting hidden behind the moldings, and all signs of water leaks had been carefully touched up. The walls were a riot of original colors, with reds, ochers, teals, and greens painted throughout. Lions marched up the stairwells, and velvet benches in the mezzanine had replaced Alyx's temporary "home," but three of his industrial designs were on display in subtly lit niches. Inside the main theater, the curtain had been reproduced, the chairs reupholstered, and even the waterfall had been made to work again.

I asked the bartender serving at the concession stand for a glass of Napa Cabernet.

"Is that the proper pairing for Red Vines?" Luz asked.

"Absolutely. Says so in *Wine Spectator*. You know me. I'm a wine snob."

"This is really amazing, Mel. I've known you a long time, and I've seen your work through the years, but this tops them all. You're really good."

"You didn't know that already?" I teased.

Caleb was home from UC Santa Cruz, where he had started his college career. Even though the school was right over the mountains from Oakland, I still missed that kid like crazy. But tonight he had joined us, and I watched as he stood there looking like a grown-up, standing tall, complete with whiskers, his neck thickening and shoulders broadening in that way of boys becoming men.

We weren't actually finished with our renovation—I still had a punch list longer than my arm of items to attend to, so it would be several more months before the general public was allowed into the theater, but tonight we were enjoying a special evening to thank all of those who had helped us get to where we were.

I tinked my glass to get everyone's attention.

"A toast to the Crockett Theatre, and to everyone who has poured their heart and soul into keeping the demolition crews at bay, to redoing all the finishes, and draperies, and upholstery—"

"And the ladies' lounge," said Tierney.

"And to the ladies' lounge," I said, "though the gentlemen's room is nothing to sneeze at."

"Hear, hear!" called out the crowd.

Stipulated in the negotiated settlement with the Xerxes group was that they would forfeit the theater to Skeet's estate, repay the city funds, and pay a hefty fine on top of it. Skeet turned around and sold the Crockett for a tidy but not exorbitant sum to the city, with the stipulation that the remodel continue. With the tax funds, the Xerxes fine, and continued fund-raising—Coco Stapleton had kicked her efforts into high gear and was working with Alyx and Ringo to produce a burlesque show to raise money for the Crockett—we were able to make it work. Turner Construction didn't see as much profit as we had originally been promised by Xerxes, of course, but everyone involved volunteered part of their time, and the results were gorgeous.

Gregory Thibodeaux had turned out to be something of a dupe himself, not realizing the full extent to which the Xerxes Group had been misleading investors, appropriating funds, and allowing buildings to be demolished. Or so he claimed. He never did regain his memory from the night he hit his head, and my best guess was that he had, indeed, seen a ghost that night and fainted at the sight. I noticed he remained wary of going back into the theater, not venturing beyond the main lobby. He had declined the invitation to join us tonight, to everyone's satisfaction.

Several of the old movie posters were framed, and they now decorated the walls of the back hallways. A few others had been auctioned off, with the proceeds benefitting the theater. There were several art installations throughout the building, from local artists and also the squatters who had chosen to work with us: Tierney and Mitch and Liam and Alyx. Isadora's candy-wrapper collection—sans original candy—had been arranged in a nice display and hung by the concession stand, along with a photograph of Isadora dancing.

In fact, Isadora still occasionally danced upon the stage at the Crockett Theatre. I saw her there from time to time, after hours, when I was locking up after the crew had gone home. One night I took a seat in the front row and watched for nearly an hour. As she danced her graceful swoops and dips, I thought of the young woman who had turned her back on easy wealth and fortune to follow her creative dreams.

She was going to turn me into a modern-dance fan.

One night I found Harold Hancock, the ghostly usher, sitting next to me. He turned to me with the saddest eyes in the world and said: *One shouldn't play with guns.*

I nodded. He still gave me chills down my spine, but he wasn't a bad guy.

"Very true, my friend," I said. "One should never play with guns."

And then he and I lingered, watching Isadora dance together. Her dancing was full of sorrow and joy both.

"Congratulations, Mel," said Dad. "Keep up this sort of thing, and you'll charity us all the way into the poor house."

"You've been threatening me with the poor house since I was a child, Dad," I said with a smile. "When am I going to actually see it? I'll bet it needs a little sprucing up. Maybe I'll volunteer a little renovation work."

"Yeah, yeah," he grumbled, but granted me a smile.

"Anyway, the Crockett is now a nonprofit theater, remember?"

As I looked out onto the assembled workers and their families gathered around the food and seated at the little tables we put out—Mateo with his wife and baby, Jeremy, Waquisha and Jaime and Tyrone and Paul and Dave and Steve with their partners and families—I knew we were doing the right thing. We made payroll every two weeks, and the partners in Turner Construction—Dad, me, and Stan—made a respectable living. We would not be buying powerboats or grand old movie palaces of our own anytime soon, but we did okay, even when we devoted some of our time to charity work.

Also invited tonight were Josh and Braden from

Avery Builders, along with some of our other construction friends, as well as Ellis Elrich and Alicia, Annette, Olivier and Dingo, Stephen and Trish and Victor, and of course Skeet and his entire extended family. People from the neighborhood, and the Crockett Caretakers—sans Baldwin, of course—were also enjoying the evening, as well as Renata and a few others from the city-permit department, and even the mayor herself.

Last I saw her, Luz and Victor had cornered madam mayor to discuss ideas to address the issue of homelessness in San Francisco.

The extraordinarily wealthy Ellis Elrich in fact offered to fund a community theater in an area of Detroit that needed help, along with some seed money so the squatters could create their own creative community. Some of the former squatters had taken him up on the offer. Others turned it down, but at least they had an opportunity to form their own special society, if they were willing to relocate from the wildly expensive Bay Area. It wasn't an easy choice, but at least they had options.

A muted pinging invited us all to take our seats in the theater.

"Shall we grab a seat?" asked Landon. "Better to be safe than sorry."

I smiled, handed Landon a tub of lavishly buttered popcorn close to the size of a beer keg, and grabbed my Red Vines and wine, and we proceeded into the main theater. Happily, the ghostly audience members were not occupying the seats this evening—as far as I knew I was still the only person who had "seen" them, but their occasional frigid presence played havoc with our heating bill. Coco once told me her worst fear of being onstage was that the audience would simply give her vacant stares or even jeer. Olivier, who was still studying the SIM card I had given him for tangible proof of a haunting, suggested the spirits might be manifestations of the stage fright attached to so many actors that had set foot on the Crockett's historic stage for over a century.

But at the moment, the only ones occupying the theater were entirely human and alive. Flanking the stage, the red eyes of the golden icons gleamed, and overhead hundreds of "stars" lit up the deep blue ceiling, while gilded lions crept along the moldings. I thought about coming here with my mother and my sisters that one time, so many years ago, and wondered if my mother had somehow reached out from beyond the veil to help Hildy.

When I went back to the attic to explain to Hildy what had happened with her daughter, she replied: "Yeah, I seen her here, tried to watch over her. The Jeffress family was real nice folks; they even kept all my dresses, even the one I had on that night! Anyways, they took care of my little Darlene. That's one reason I was hanging around . . . but then she left, and a time later there was another little girl."

"I think that was my mother."

"She was a real sweet little girl. We used to sit and talk, and she liked trying on my dresses."

I explained to Hildy that Darlene had had a son, named Skeet, who had a big, close-knit family and grandchildren. And that he'd finally inherited the Crockett Theatre, after all this time, and been able to retire in style.

Hildy seemed pleased at the news, but remained in our attic. I still heard her bumping around overhead occasionally, and when I was alone in the house, I often heard the radio play and the sound of Hildy's heels tapping loudly on the wooden floors while she danced.

"I do believe I've come up with a name for our new home," said Landon, looping one arm lightly around my shoulders as we settled into the plush red velvet seats. An old cartoon came on the new big screen: *Roadrunner.* Afterward, we would watch several vintage short films, including *The Little Tramp* and *The Heiress*. "Don't know why I didn't think of it before."

"Really?" I whispered, reaching for a fistful of popcorn. "What is it?"

"Hildy's Haven."

"Of course! That's perfect."

Landon had never "seen" Hildy, but he heard her from time to time, and he remained remarkably sanguine about her presence. Unfortunately, the construction project had hit a few snags with a prickly City of Oakland building inspector, so the renovation had been delayed. It was frustrating, but I really didn't mind spending a few more weeks in my dad's house; I cherished the day to day with him and Stan, knowing it would soon come to an end.

Also, Landon and I had managed to maintain, and even deepen, our relationship—and our senses of humor—despite the extended remodel. An excellent litmus test.

"And I've been thinking, too . . . ," I said. "Maybe it's time we set a date. Why don't we get married at Hildy's Haven, as soon as we finish with the renovation?"

"That sounds perfect, indeed."

Landon and I, at long last, had gone through the boxes in the attic and found some treasures to keep in the house: old books and photographs, a few decorative tchotchkes. I offered Skeet the childhood portrait of his mother, Darlene, but he suggested it stay in the house. I left it out on a table in the attic, by the old radio, so Hildy could see it whenever she wanted.

We left the closet, with all of its dresses, intact. Maybe Hildy would move on; maybe she would stay. Perhaps she would find a way to move back and forth, between this world and the beyond on the other side of the veil.

But I found myself hoping she might remain.

After all, every great old home needs a ghost or two in the attic, right?

Don't miss

BEWITCHED AND BETROTHED

Available now! Keep reading for a preview.

A salty, heavy shroud of fog obscures the night.

Frigid waters close over my head. Sparks of silvery moonlight dance on the surface of the bay, calling to me. I flail and kick, struggling to lift myself, to breathe sweet air, my arms and legs numb with cold and exhaustion. The cheerful lights of San Francisco peek through the fog, tantalizingly far away; the island behind me is closer, but gleams and pulsates in the light of the full moon like a living, malevolent thing. The Golden Gate is the third point on the triangle, and I am in the center.

A foghorn sounds in a mournful cry.

Strong currents wrap around my legs, tugging at my feet, pulling me toward the Golden Gate and out to the vast Pacific Ocean. Lost at sea. Lost forever.

I can't go on.

I fear drowning, but remind myself: *Witches don't sink.*

At least *I* don't. I had been in the bay once before and popped up like a cork. But . . . what about now?

Icy fingers grip my ankles, drawing me down. The water closes over my head again, and I try to scream.

"Mistress!"

I struggle toward the surface. Fighting, flailing. I have to.

I *have* to.

"Mistress!" a gravelly voice called again. "Are you all right? Why are you all wet?"

I opened my eyes. I was in my own home, in my own bed. Safe.

Oscar, my ersatz witch's familiar—a shape-shifting cross between a gargoyle and a goblin—perched on my brass bedstead, leaning over to peer at me. His fearsome face was upside down and his breath smelled vaguely of cheese.

Soaked and shivering, I let out a shaky sigh. I wasn't sweaty from fear, but *dripping* wet—and smelling of brine—as though I had, indeed, just emerged from the San Francisco Bay.

"I had a nightmare," I said.

"Yeah, no kiddin'. That's one heck of a nightmare if you're manifesting in your sleep. Were you swimming or something?" Oscar waved a handful of travel brochures under my nose. "Hey, check these out. I think we should go to Barcelona first, maybe."

"Oscar, I *cannot* discuss my honeymoon plans with you at the moment." My brain felt fuzzy. I sat up and glanced at my antique clock on the bedside table. Its hands glowed a mellow, comforting green that cut through the darkness. City lights sifted through my lace curtains, but even raucous Haight Street was hushed at three o'clock in the morning.

"But it's the witching hour," Oscar whined.

"Ideal for spellcasting, not for making travel plans."

Oscar cocked his head. "What better time is there?"

"In the morning. After coffee. When normal people are awake."

"But we're not 'normal people'—like we'd even *want*

to be, *heh*!" He chuckled, a raspy sound reminiscent of a rusty saw.

I'm Lily Ivory, a natural-born witch from West Texas who wandered the globe for years, searching for a safe place to settle down. On the advice of a parrot named Barnabas, whom I had met in a bar in Hong Kong, I had come to San Francisco—specifically, to Haight Street—where a witch like me could fit in.

I love it here. For the first time in my life I have friends, a community, a *home*.

If only the beautiful City by the Bay weren't so chock-full of murder and mayhem.

Oscar was right, I thought, plucking the soggy nightgown away from my skin. It was unusual to manifest during a dream, to bring a physical object—in this case, water from the bay—from the realm of slumber into the waking world.

I shivered again.

"Just saying, we're both awake right now," Oscar continued. "And not for nothing, but you might want to dry off and maybe put a towel down before you ruin your mattress."

Throwing back the covers, I hopped out of bed and headed to the bathroom to take a shower. Washing away the waters of the bay with lemon verbena soap, I lingered under the hot spray until warmth settled down deep in my core.

I emerged from the bathroom to find that Oscar had gone. He had left the travel brochures fanned out in a semicircle atop my comforter, and on the nightstand was a steaming mug of chamomile tea. He had also managed to dry the bed, somehow, and to make it up with fresh sheets.

Oscar might not be a typical (read: obedient) witch's familiar, but he definitely had his moments. Not to mention he had saved my life on more than one occasion.

I sat on the side of the bed, sipped the tea, and picked up a brochure with a glossy photo of Barcelona's famous Sagrada Família. The next brochure featured the Eiffel Tower, and the last the Voto Nacional de Quito, in Ecuador.

I had promised Oscar he could tag along on my honeymoon so that we could search for his mother, a creature suffering under a curse that transformed her into a gargoyle. The problem was he had no idea where she might be, only that "gargoyles live a *long* time." I reminded myself to discuss this with my fiancé, Sailor, so that we could come up with a targeted approach before Oscar whipped up an entire world tour for us. Recently it had been difficult for Sailor and me to find the time—and the peace of mind—to talk about much of anything, much less gargoyle-guided tours.

I yawned. Speaking of honeymoons, I had a bucketload of decisions to make before the wedding, and more than a few wrinkles to iron out. My grandmother's eccentric coven had recently arrived in town; I was about to be married to a beautiful but secretive man—an attachment to whom, I had been warned, might weaken my powers. Oscar kept disappearing to search for his mother even though he was supposed to be helping secure the perfect venue for my upcoming wedding, and recently I had come to realize that instead of one guiding spirit, I had *two*, and they weren't getting along, which was messing with my magic. And finally, my beloved adopted city of San Francisco was facing a frustratingly nonspecific existential threat that primarily involved a cupcake lady named Renee.

I took another sip of tea. I also still needed to find just the right vintage bridesmaid dresses for my friends Bronwyn and Maya. Under any other circumstance I would have said "Wear what you like!" but the style editor for the *San Francisco Chronicle* was planning to do a feature on our antique bridal wardrobe, which would be great publicity for my vintage clothing store, Aunt Cora's Closet.

I may be a witch and a soon-to-be bride, but I'm also a small-business owner vying for customers on increasingly competitive Haight Street. I needed the exposure.

I also needed some rest.

Grabbing an *in fidem venire praesidii* amulet off the dresser mirror, I held it in my right hand and walked the perimeter of the bedroom in a clockwise direction, chanting:

I have done my day's work,
I am entitled to sweet sleep.
I am drawing a line on this carpet,
over which you cannot pass.
Powers of protection, powers who clear,
remove all those who don't belong here.

As I lay back down and switched off the light, waiting for sleep to take me, I couldn't shake the sensation of the waters closing over my head.

It wasn't like me to have a nightmare. Much less a *manifesting* nightmare.

It was enough to worry a weary witch like me.

Ready to find
your next great read?

Let us help.

Visit prh.com/nextread

Penguin
Random
House